JACK SHEPPARD;

OR,

LONDON IN THE LAST CENTURY.

A ROMANCE OF REALITY.

ARRANGED FROM SOME RARE AND ORIGINAL DOCUMENTS,
IN CONNECTION WITH THE REMARKABLE HISTORY
OF THE ABOVE NOTORIOUS INDIVIDUAL,
ONLY RECENTLY DISCOVERED.

BY A
BARRISTER OF THE MIDDLE TEMPLE.

LONDON:
G. MANSELL, 115, FLEET STREET.

1847.

TABLE OF CONTENTS AND LIST OF ILLUSTRATIONS.

JACK SHEPPARD,

OR,

LONDON IN THE LAST CENTURY.

PROLOGUE.

TOWARDS the close of a fine day in the autumn of 1845, when those who had the means or inclination, were enjoying the light of a gorgeous sunset far away from the smoky canopy that concealed the brightest portion of its beams from the dwellers of the Great City, there was seated beside a window, looking down upon one of the most populous thoroughfares of the metropolis, a young but studious-looking individual, whose avocations, betokened by a number of carelessly-arranged legal documents on a table at his side, evidently were connected with the higher branches of the legal profession. It might have been the natural manifestation of a contemplative mind that now induced him to lean his arm pensively on the casement, and watch the ever-flowing current of humanity that hurried on below, or it might have been the contrast of his own position that required, in unremitting study, his hours to be spent in the confined atmosphere of that region, rather than where that glorious orb was now sinking in unclouded effulgence, lighting up the summits of distant mountains with its brilliant rays, and scattering genial light on glistening lake, and tawny hide, and feathered wing. Whatever immediate cause, however, had induced him to occupy that position, it was apparent mere idleness or vacuity of mind had not influenced his choice. His thoughts were evidently bent upon some subject of importance, and in the rapid, and occasionally uneasy changes of his countenance, a physiognomist, skilled in his art, might easily have traced the working of some hidden passion.

A loud knock at the door of his chambers startled Vincent from his meditations. The summons was eagerly responded to, the door opened, and Sidney Hamilton, a senior barrister of Gray's Inn, and intimate friend of Vincent's entèred.

"I have not more than a few minutes to spare for our interview," exclaimed Hamilton, after the first warm greetings had been interchanged, "for to-night I quit England for Germany, in accordance with the terms of the will that entitles me to property in that country. Here, however, are the papers and documents I promised."

Vincent eagerly took the packet that was proffered.

"The pictures," continued his friend, "will be forwarded here immediately. You, who are alone acquainted with the strange history of my relationship to that unfortunate family, will prize these portraits for my sake. The detailed recital of circumstances that first led one of that family into crime, I would wish given to the world from your hands alone. I have arranged the papers that fell so singularly into my possession, and therein you will find, for the first time, a true account of the exploits that have handed down *his* name to posterity. If they cause one to retrace his erring footsteps, and return to the paths of rectitude, or convince the world of the danger of punishing too severely the *first* falsé step, the end I have in view in wishing their publication will be fully answered."

* * * *

It is unnecessary to communicate further particulars of their conversation, which terminated in a promise on the part of Vincent, to fulfil the wishes of his friend. Sidney Hamilton left soon after to embark in the steamer that was to bear him to the Rhine, and Vincent, in the sombre solitude of his chamber, was soon absorbed in a perusal of the exciting incidents recounted in the manuscript with which he had been furnished.

* * * *

There is one mystery which the readers may feel anxious to have at once unravelled. The following paragraph that, as the phrase goes, "went the round of the papers," about two years back, may perhaps tend to throw some light upon the subject.

"JACK SHEPPARD.

"A portrait of this notorious highwayman and one of his mother, were recently sold by a tavern-keeper, near Clare Market, *to a barrister of Grays Inn* for ninety seven guineas. On removing the portrait of Jack's progenitor from its frame, there were found, below the moulding, seven guineas, together with a number of copper coins of the period. Put thus accidentally upon the scent of some of Jack's secrets, it was an easy inference that it might be worth while to make a careful examination of the other frame, which, besides, was of a suspicious thickness; and it yielded up its treasures accordingly. Between the moulding and lining were found a number of papers and documents relating to his life,—some extremely curious, and all bearing the post-mark of the time; besides furniture more characteristic, and which should have been left as appropriate frame-work to the portraiture of Jack. There was also the portion of a note for £10, and a check for £17."

The intelligent reader may at once surmise that the barrister of Gray's Inn was Sidney Hamilton, and that his great anxiety to obtain at any price possession of these relics, arose from the knowledge of one of his ancestors having been the father of the most notorious robber England ever produced.

CHAPTER I.

THE COUNTRY VILLAGE.—THE MYSTERIOUS STRANGER.—THE NIGHT ATTACK.

"——'Tis the sixth hour,
The village clock strikes from the distant tower,
The Ploughman leaves the field; the traveller hears;
And to the inn spurs onward. Nature wears
Her sweetest smile—the day star in the west,
Yet hovering and the thistle down at rest."

It was the eighteenth of September 1704. The time was evening, and the setting sun had nearly reached the western rim of the horizon, when a solitary wayfaring stranger, clad in the costume of the period, and apparently from his garb one who had held no unimportant position in society, stopped at the turning of a little footpath, which wound down the sloping side of the hill overlooking the picturesque little village of Caversham, in Berkshire.

Since the early hours of the morning, he had been steadily progressing onward, and had not yet reached the place of which he was in search.

As he gazed down on the village that occupied the valley, he saw scattered in careless groups about the pleasant green, a number of its inhabitants enjoying the rustic sports that then were characteristic of the peasantry of "Merrie England." Some to the minstrelsy of an itinerant musician were dancing beneath a venerable grove of elms; others were rivaling each other in such athletic and sportive exercises as quoits and bowls. The rest were either intent upon the busy pastimes going on around them, or discussing the latest politics that agitated the court of Queen Anne.

The stranger seemed, however, but little interested in the hilarity that prevailed, and though the scene appeared to awaken some half-forgotten remembrance, he scarcely paused to notice its chief features, but turned quietly away down a gentle declivity, that led by a circuitous route past the spot where all wore an aspect of joy and happiness.

Passing over the old bridge which crossed the clear and shallow stream, he now entered a lane, the banks of which were overgrown with wild flowers and straggling bushes of birch, sufficiently thick and high to meet over head and form a perfect bower of rural growth.

A poor woman was returning home through the lane with her children, an infant sleeping soundly on her bosom, and a laughing curly-headed urchin at her side, distending his cheeks in an attempt to inflate a small painted wooden trumpet, one of those Dutch toys that had then both the advantages of novelty and noise.

Inquiring the road to a cottage that lay in the vicinity of the place where they stood, the traveller was directed to take a winding pathway that turned out of the lane through a small copse immediately above.

Following the direction, the stranger, wrapped in his own melancholy thoughts, pursued the pathway indicated until it emerged on the open road. The cool fresh air, thegurgling flow of the river, the tinkling of the sheep-bell and all those dreamy and distant sounds which on a fair calm evening in the quiet fields, fall so sweetly indistinct upon the ear, seemed to tranquillize and soothe his spirits. So influenced was he by the stillness of the landscape, that the sun had set before he was recalled to a consciousness of the immediate object that had brought him thither.

He gazed eagerly around. There were green and sloping hills, the same calm river winding gently below, and at last where the leafy shade was deepest, he discovered a pile of old and quaintly shaped chimneys looming out against the glowing sky. He had not proceeded far in the direction of the farm house, which was now plainly apparent among the trees, when a measured heavy footstep that fell at sudden intervals behind him, impressed the stranger with a belief that some one was following in his path. On endeavouring to penetrate the misty gloom that was now gradually deepening over the autumnal landscape, there was however no step audible nor figure to be seen. Attributing therefore the sound to the creation of his own excited fancy, the stranger proceeded without further delay.

Arriving at the threshold he was startled by the gloomy air of desolation that appeared to pervade the building, and its precints. All was hushed and still as if the place had been for some time at least deserted and untenanted.

"And yet," muttered Sir Hugh Trevanion to himself—for there is no occasion longer to conceal the true rank and position of the traveller—"and yet I cannot have erred in the right reading of the missive. This must be the place, and this the house where—"

The sudden appearance of an aged crone, who hobbled forth from behind one of the outbuildings arrested the train of his meditations.

"May I ask your business at Holtsead Farm? inquired the Dame, casting a suspicious glance at the knight.

"I would speak with one who lives here," answered the other, slipping a silver coin into the hands of the questioner to expedite the reply.

"Her name, good sir!" respondent the old woman, marvellously softened in her manner and tone by the courteous present of the inquirer."

"Mrs. Sheppard."

"Alack! you have spent both breath and time in vain. She dwells no longer at the Farm."

"How mean you? Surely no sad event."

"No, no! She has removed to London.—A year ago she set out from here to seek, she said, her husband who resides there."

"And her child," faltered the Knight,—"is it with her—well and living?"

"Aye! for aught I know—'twas a strapping boy—and healthfully it thrived. Though none of us e'er knew who Mrs. Sheppard was, nor where she came from,—she was a kind and gentle lady—heaven bless her!"

"Know you not where in London she may be heard of?"—emphatically urged Sir Hugh. I have that of importance to communicate to her which concerns her interests nearly."

"I think I heard her say some hostel in the Savoy."

"The Lollard's Crest?"

"Aye! 'Twas sure enough some name that sounded like it!"

"And you can give no further information about the one I seek!"

"None! since she left, the place has gone to ruin."

Sir Hugh, finding that his interrogatories failed to elicit further intelligence from the old dame, doubled his previous gift as a reward for what she had communicated and slowly retraced his steps toward Caversham. His thoughts were strangely disturbed by the interview that had just been concluded. "Was it for this," he exclaimed half-audibly as he proceeded, "that alone and on foot I have traversed a weary length of road to make Constantia that fair recompense I promised. That the better to conceal my name and rank, I have resigned the companionship even of one follower, that the mother might not know the father of her child was—"

"One whom she must *never* know!" suddenly ejaculated a voice at his side, as Sir Hugh entered the thicket that skirted the bridle-road. "Upon him lads—to the death."

Before Sir Hugh had time to stand upon his guard, four men with their faces severally concealed in vizors, and each having a drawn rapier in hand, sprang over the stunted bush of furze that had concealed them, and seized the knight with one hand, whilst with the other they pointed their weapons at his throat.

The first impulse of Trevanion was to draw his own sword in self-defence, but by an anticipated movement on the part of one of the assailants, it was wrested from his grasp before he had time to employ it effectually, and thus he became at once defenceless.

"If money be your object," cried Sir Hugh, "there is my purse in the left pocket of my vest. Take it and begone."

"Nay," exclaimed one who only now ventured on the scene. "We war not now with petty game, we strike higher than the vest and must reach the head, before our craving is satisfied. Our instructions are to secure possession of your person—show no resistance, and your safety—at least with us is secured."

"Too well I guess the object then. Is not my brother's hate already satiated?"

"Nay," continued the other, "we have no time to parley now. Hearing of your return to England he has kept us here on the watch for your arrival at least a month, and I for one have business to execute in other quarters. I have no fancy for this game at 'hide and find,' in villages, and had he not paid as well as he did for the affair, Sampson Kirby would have seen all the Trevanions at Jericho, before he would have stirred limb or finger to kick his heels about in this dreary hole. Once safely lodged in the Mint and there my part of the bargain ends. So up lads and away back to the old quarters." Finding resistance useless, Sir Hugh suffered himself to be conducted to the coach that was awaiting their return at the end of the lane and though firm in a resolve to seize the earliest opportunity of escape, offered no opposition to those who forced him to take a seat in the vehicle.

The darkness of the night and the few travellers that at this period ventured to take the road after dusk militated, indeed, against the probability of a rescue, but as Kirby and two of his companions also occupied places in the interior, and with loaded pistols in their hands, were fully prepared on the first alarm to silence effectually their prisoner, the chance of evading their vigilance became doubly problematical.

. Wrapped in his own reflections, which as may be imagined were not of the most agreeable kind, Trevanion did not exchange a word with his forced fellow-passengers, who did not however suffer his silence to interfere with the enjoyment of their own conversation. The constant topic was some recent violation of the laws of their country, and though conveyed in a language chiefly unintelligible to more refined ears, Sir Hugh heard enough to convince him that the ruffians his brother had employed to effect the capture, formed a portion of the lawless and unscrupulous gang whose head-quarters were in the Borough, and who occasionally sallied forth to commit those depredations for which the Mint served as their sanctuary. Notwithstanding the comparatively rapid rate at which they travelled and the due precautions taken previously by Kirby to secure a relay of horses on the road, the grey light of an autumnal dawn was breaking in the east, when the rumbling wheels of the old chariot rolled over the ill-paved streets that led to the Alsatian region, which was to be their destination. Having crossed the river at the old wooden bridge that then spanned the Thames below Hampton, they had avoided the more frequented outlets of the metropolis, and now entered Southwark at the outer barrier of the Mint which at that time extended westward, as far as what is now the Southwark Bridge Road.

Having transferred his prize to the custody of Master Roland Digby, the then "Sovereign of the Mint," as he was styled, Kirby saw Sir Hugh Trevanion secured in the "Mouse Tower," one of their most important strongholds; and here leaving him, at present to the mercy of the reckless crew among whom he had been so suddenly and strangely brought, we deem it advisable to acquaint the reader with some particulars of the region which allowed such deeds to be practised with such impunity.

CHAPTER II.

THE MINT.

"I will example you with thievery."
—— SHAKSPEARE.

AT the period of which we write, this quarter of the Borough of Southwark was the receptacle for all the vice and iniquity that the metropolis generated. The houses, with tottering chimneys, broken roofs, and walls bulging outwards, from age and decay, were inhabited by the very lowest order of thieves, burglars, beggars, and insolvents, who either fled thither to avoid the penalties due to their various crimes, or to evade the payment of their debts. Though an edict of Parliament, then recently enacted, had restricted the inmates from enjoying some of its more dangerous privileges, there was quite enough of viciousness and immorality within its walls to render the asylum it afforded for the dissolute a den of frightful depravity to the more staid portion of the community. Indeed it was not considered safe to traverse its limits even in daylight, and at night the danger of so doing was considerably increased by the utter absence of all control, the watch never daring to penetrate those narrow alleys where the faint glimmer of an uncertain oil lamp only served the purpose of guiding fugitives to a place of temporary safety, and misleading their pursuers.

The Mouse Tower, where Trevanion was imprisoned, formed the only remaining portion of the Palace of the noble Duke of Suffolk, whose royal brother-in-law, the uxorious Henry VIII., converted it for a short period into a mint, until the source of coinage in the next reign was transferred to the Tower.

As some care was necessary on the part of the minters to preserve their territory inviolate from the incursions of those gentry of the law, who tempted by a weighty bribe occasionally ventured into the interior with a view to seize the person of a debtor, or malefactor, every precaution that could be imagined was taken to secure its perfect invulnerability, and only stratagem could effect a seizure. That all accidents or surprises might be duly guarded against, watchmen in their pay were stationed as scouts at the three main outlets of the sanctuary, ready by concerted signals to alarm the neighbourhood at the first intimation of an invasion from the official authorities. Barriers were erected, which on emergency could be thrown immediately across the thoroughfares. Every alley had its gate, and every gate its appendage of locks and bolts, which were never withdrawn until the applicant had been duly reconnoitred from within through the sliding wicket. Every window, particularly those that were placed at the back of the houses, had a barricade of iron, and were kept invariably closed, whilst in those places where the defence of the sanctuary was considered weakest, mounds of earth had been thrown up, and ditches cut which totally precluded any entrance or exit from those quarters. To increase the chances of escape there was also a maze, formed of narrow winding walls, and the name of which is still retained in the district where it was erected. Into this intricate labyrinth the debtor could enter at any time, but the unfortunate official who attempted to follow without having a clue, found himself speedily bewildered by its windings, and was rarely suffered to depart without some personal punishment, which served as a convincing proof of the tenacity with which these *desperadoes* guarded their privileges. As Salisbury Court and the Savoy were no longer to be relied upon as places of refuge for the debtor, and Whitefriars had lost the greater portion of its privileges, the "Island of Bermuda," as the mint was then styled, formed the only spot where a successful resistance to authority could be made; and was trebly strengthened in consequence. Even now if the seekers after lingering relics of Old London chose to penetrate the tottering lanes and alleys that lie between Union Street and Stoney Street, at the back of the Borough Market, he would see enough to convince him that the landmarks of the region just described, are not altogether extinct, and though the immunities of the place may have been thrust aside by the increase of civilization and the strengthened hand of justice, years will yet elapse before the crumbling dens of vice and iniquity, and the wretched squalor of their miserable inhabitants, will yield to the spirit of improvement so apparent elsewhere.

It was late in the afternoon of the day after that, when the adventures recorded in the previous chapter took place, that the door of a humble and obscure tenement situated in the better part of the neighbourhood above described, was carefully opened by one who was evidently a stranger to that locality, and unqualified to claim the protective privileges of its precincts. His age was apparently that which children regard as somewhat venerable, and which those who had numbered the same years would probably characterise the "prime of life;" in other words the testimony of his baptismal register would have shown he trembled on the verge of forty, but the hand of time had passed so lightly over his brow, and had left such few wrinkles on his good-humoured physiognomy, that he might fairly have claimed a less lengthy sojourn on the earth.

His dress was a little in keeping with this assumption of juvenility, and forming a fair specimen of the costume of the period as displayed by those whose position in society was similar to his own, manifested the tradesman who was, as the phrase then went, "well-to-do" in the world. A substantial woollen coat with ample skirts reaching below the knees, a coloured drugget vest beneath, almost shrouding the knee-breeches from sight, and square-toed shoes, glistening at the instep with smart steel buckles, completed the attire of his person, and on his head was poised a small three-cornered hat, which allowed a profusion of brown straggling hair to escape over the thick netted comforter that was wrapped in full folds round his throat.

Finding no one appeared to intercept his progress, he slowly groped his way in the murky twilight through a long passage, that led to a flight of stairs at the extremity, and ascending these he came at last to the threshhold of a small and scantily furnished room, the door of which being open revealed the circumstance of its being also at that moment untenanted.

There were, still, however, signs of recent occupancy; a few embers were glimmering in the cheerless grate, and on a heap of blankets carelessly thrown into a corner which seemed to be the place allotted to a bed, was a child, pale and emaciated, from insufficient food, dreamily reposing. Stepping softly, so as not to disturb the slumbers of the infant, the visitor glanced mournfully round the apartment, noting with a commisserating expression of his countenance the numerous evidences of poverty and discomfort that presented themselves. There was but one article of furniture visible, a crazy deal table that seemed to betray such alarming symptoms of insecurity, on an attempt made by the new comer to convert it into a seat, that resigning all hope of a resting-place, he spread his skirts open under his arms and stood before the dingy casement in the hope of beguiling the time by looking out upon the slanting roofs and pointed gables of the wretched buildings opposite.

The increasing dusk of the evening that threw the further part of the room into strong shadow, prevented his noticing, soon after the entrance of another person. He had just turned to rake together with his stick the few cinders that were still smouldering underneath, in the vain expectation of obtaining by their means a little extra light and warmth, when he was startled by suddenly encountering a female figure at his side.

"Dear me, Mrs. Sheppard, is it you?" exclaimed the individual, after a pause, during which he regained his equanimity; "You positively alarmed me. I have stopped so long in this dismal place that I have become quite nervous."

"Why, Mr. Wood," returned the other, recognizing the voice, "this is, indeed, kind of you to pay me a visit so promptly. I had but stepped out a few minutes to sell a few trifles by which I trusted to procure some food for myself and child, and scarcely anticipated finding you here on my return, else—" she added wtih a faint smile, "I would have endeavoured to have come better provided."

"Say no more, my dear madam," responded the other. "It is my belief a good deed has double value when it comes quickly. Here is a little sum for immediate use, and now let me beg of you to leave this dreary abode as soon as possible. The very air seems to choke me as I breathe in it;" and as he said this, the good-natured carpenter slipped a couple of guineas into her hand.

"I know not how I shall ever be able to repay your kindness, Mr. Wood," faltered the poor woman in broken accents. "I have indeed, lately suffered much—*very* much;" and the speaker burst into tears.

"Well! there—don't talk about it," rejoined Wood, lighting a horn lanthorn to enliven the conversation and conceal his emotions;" it's all over now, never to return, I hope; and now listen to a little proposal that I am going to make to you."

The flickering light thus emitted from the lanthorn which Wood placed upon the table, revealed a change in the features of the woman with whom he spoke, for which he had been scarcely prepared. Her figure though still retaining some of its former symmetry and beauty, was thin and attenuated; and the once lovely face betrayed in every lineament the ravages that poverty and illness had made. Her apparel was of the slightest kind, and only served to show more clearly the slenderness of the form which it covered; whilst though not more than three-and-twenty her wan and pallied complexion seemed to belong to one who was getting prematurely old.

"I must confess," remarked Wood, diverted for a moment from his immediate object, by observing the marked alterations that had taken place in the woman he was accosting. "I must confess you have not improved much in appearance since I saw you last. Time works sad changes as well as wonders, Mrs. Sheppard; I should have hardly recognized in you the daughter of my poor brother. Heaven rest his soul!"

"Ah! Sir. I was left an orphan at too early an age to much remember him, but all the country round still speaks of his kind heart, and forgive me, if I say you take after him in that respect."

"Poor John, he was more for gift than thrift, as the proverb says, and though I never saw him much after his marriage with your poor mother, when he took the old farm down at Caversham, many's the jovial hour we spent together. But mercy on us, he has been dead these fifteen years, come next Martinmas, and your mother died soon after—rest her soul!"

"Mine has indeed been a sad fate!" murmured the young mother, looking, as it were for consolation on the form of her sleeping child.

"Aye! and to make it worse—you must needs marry a handsome scapegrace whom nobody knows anything about, except that he called himself Sheppard, and be abandoned by him a few months afterwards with this child to support," said Mr. Wood with some bitterness of tone.

CHAPTER III.

JONATHAN WILD.

"If thou be'st a man show thyself in thy likeness; if thou be'st a devil, take it as thou list."
TEMPEST, Act III. sc. II.

THE low attic into which Orford, Kirby and the rest had penetrated, had no apparent outlet, nor had they in their progress thither met with the object of their pursuit. Baffled in their hopes of discovery, a council was now being held to determine their future proceedings.

"I would give a hundred pounds this moment to be put on the scent of their trail," exclaimed Orford, as he rested breathless from unwonted exertion on his sword.

"I beg to accept the offer, and will clench your Lordship's bargain at once," responded one who had just entered.

"Aye, if any here can find him, Jonathan is the man," cried Kirby, extending a nod of recognition to the new arrival, "he would ferret out a fox from its lurking hole before the hounds had given tongue."

As this singularly-gifted personage will hereafter have to play an important part in our history, a rapid sketch of his personal appearance and previous pursuits will serve to explain better in this place the causes that led to the various events that follow.

He was a stout, brawny, bull-headed looking fellow of about three and twenty, with coarse large features, and a remarkably shrewd, but extremely vicious expression of countenance. His grey eyes, peculiarly small, and shaded by thick shaggy eyebrows of a sandy colour, seemed to glance *through* the objects at which they were directed. His hair was of a deep reddish hue and grew low down the forehead, imparting a craftiness to his ill-favored visage that was not belied by his general character, and the gleam of savage triumph that played about his mouth, heightened in ferocity by the protruding canine teeth that were displayed on every occasion of its being opened, showed that he was rather a dangerous person to encounter as an enemy. The birth-place of Jonathan Wild, was Wolverhampton, in Staffordshire, where his family had long resided, but in such a state of poverty, that to eke out a miserable existence, they had occasionally employed him in his younger days to sell fruit and vegetables to the chance stragglers that came to the market. Having obtained such a smattering of the arts of reading and writing, as his quick comprehension enabled him to gain from a few week's tuition at the parish school, he was bound apprentice at the age of fourteen to one Bright, a buckle-maker, of Birmingham. During his servitude he contrived to appropriate whatever trifling valuables came in his way, and the other apprentices being kept in awe and subjection by his domineering, and threats, they bore the blame of these petty larcenies and were expelled, whilst Jonathan escaped, and managed to retain his situation unsuspected. At the expiration of his indentures, finding that neither his father nor his relatives were able to set him up in business, he relinquished his intended trade and took the situation of livery-servant to a barrister, with whom he came to London in the summer of 1703. Having robbed his master, the hue and cry that was raised in consequence, rendered a temporary seclusion in the Mint a matter of necessity, and whilst here sharing its privileges, he gained a sufficient knowledge of the complex machinery of villany that was at work around him, and of the habits and practices of its inhabitants, to turn them to a sufficiently profitable account, as we shall find hereafter.

It was this remarkable individual, destined in future years to acquire such unenviable notoriety, that now proffered his services.

Finding them accepted, he disclosed the existence of a trap-door in the roof, which had previously escaped their notice, and raising himself up until his nimble form had forced itself through the aperture, he found by the light of the dark lanthorn he had slung in his belt, some tiles removed from the roof as if dislodged by a recent blow.

"As I suspected," muttered Jonathan, "the fox has flown to cover hereabouts, but he must have been a wary churl to have broken bounds at the Mouse Tower." Bidding the rest await his return in the street, he masked his lanthorn once more, and crept slowly and cautiously along the tiles that formed a narrow sloping roof to the house from which he had just emerged. Confident that he was in the right track, he kept on his way with great perseverance, but extreme caution, only pausing at intervals to peer into recesses that were found along the pointed gables that he passed.

Carefully threading his way along the roof of the adjoining houses, Jonathan at last found his progress stopped by a narrow parapet, that on one side looked over at a dizzy height into the street below, where lights were glancing in every direction, and on the other terminated by a junction with a lofty wall that showed the next building to be higher, by another story at least, than the rest of the structures that surrounded it.

"Confusion! baffled!" muttered Wild to himself as he eagerly looked for some place of egress, "this height is too great even for a reckless man to risk the dropping down on the gables below, and my head, proof as it is against trifles, feels dizzy as I gaze. I cannot have passed him surely; no, there must be an outlet somewhere," and as he spoke, his knee struck against some impediment that protruded from the wall. It was a ladder.

An exclamation of delight escaped from his lips, and the smile of triumph that lit up his features as he unmasked the lanthorn to confirm his first supposition, showed that he was fully aware he had now entered upon the right track.

Rapidly ascending the ladder he found himself, when at the summit, before a trap-door that evidently communicated with the roof or interior of the building to which it was attached. Aware that some resistance might be offered, Wild, before unclosing his lanthorn, drew a pistol from his belt, and then burst through the trap-door into a small attic, at the further extremity of which stood the discovered fugitive with the full light of Wild's bull's-eye flashing full upon his person.

"Aha! my crafty friend," exclaimed Jonathan, by way of salutation as he entered, "I have found you out at last, have I?"

"Who, and what are you, sir?" sternly responded the other, prepared to struggle with his expected assailant, the moment an opportunity offered."

"No enemy of yours at least," was Jonathan's reply, coolly clicking the lock of the pistol, and replacing it in his pocket, as he spoke, "else had I not ventured alone on such an infernal break-neck expedition."

"Your object then in thus so impertinently seeking out the place of my concealment?"

"It would occupy too much time," answered Wild, to tell you that now, and you have none of that commodity at present to spare. Let it suffice to say, money is part of it."

"My purse is but scantily lined now, but

once safe from my pursuers, I can better show my gratitude."

"Pshaw. Feed fools with promises, I want something more substantial. Give me all you have about you, however, and I'll take that as an instalment of the rest."

"You speak somewhat imperatively however," said Hugh Trevanion, as he detached a purse from his girdle, and placed it in the eager hands of Wild—"Here is what you require."

"There is no time now for wasting moments in needless civilities," cried the other, rattling the contents of the purse in his ear; "The jingle is not very promising, but I suppose I must e'en be content. It is after all, though, not the recompence I expected in aiding you to make your escape."

"Hark you sir," added Trevanion, "though your manner and voice would hardly induce me to trust you, I am driven by circumstances to those extremities in which it does not behove a man to be over particular. Let me find that I may place faith in you, and a valuable signet ring that I now wear on my finger shall be yours the instant you have secured my escape."

"Ah! that's something more like business," rejoined Jonathan, chuckling over his anticipated prize. "I need scarcely tell you to mind where you place your feet, for that you must have had some practice in, as you came hither, but follow me with a wary and cautious step, and we shall soon be out of harm's way."

"Hold, sir," interrupted the other, still hesitating to quit the spot, "I have mentioned to you the reward that awaits you on my safe deliverance from this danger, but it is only fair that I should warn you any attempt to play me false, or any movement on your part to betray me on the road, will be visited by immediate retribution from my hand."

Wild suddenly turned round and glared contemptuously on the speaker, but only replied to his threat audibly with a kind of grunt that might have been understood either as an assurance of intimidation or indifference. Leading the way without further remark, Wild followed by Trevanion, slowly and with some difficulty retraced his steps down the ladder and secured a safe passage along by the parapet.

Leaning cautiously over the side they discerned amidst the gloom a party of minters returning with their torches from the various places where they had been to seek the escaped prisoner. The noise and tumult that prevailed amongst the rioters below, was a proof that their disappointment had resulted in a disturbance among themselves.

"You see the nature of the men with whom you would have had to deal," said Wild, pointing to the angry excitement of the mob beneath. "It is fortunate for you that I am the only one amongst them acquainted with the road you took, else had your life not been worth a minute's purchase."

An impatient gesture from Trevanion, who still feared discovery, hastened Jonathan from the spot, and they pursued their course onward in silence, until the slanting roof that belonged to the house which Mrs. Sheppard had made her dwelling intercepted their further progress.

"If you would not mind risking a fall of some twenty feet," observed Jonathan in an undertone to his companion, "our safest plan would be to clamber over the roof here on to the lower leads beyond; there is another way by the window below on the second floor, but I question if the coast is as clear as the other, for I hear voices still in consultation."

After a momentary pause during which the buz of earnest converse in the apartment beneath was distinctly heard, Trevanion adopted Wild's suggestion and the roof was scaled with a recklessness of danger that nothing but the imminent peril of the occasion would have provoked. The nimble form of Jonathan seemed however fitted to encounter and overcome every difficulty, and he was the first to hazard the descent from the coping. Trevanion followed, and clambering over the wooden railing at the side, Jonathan opened a small window that looked out upon the back portion of the premises.

"We must get through here," cried he, "whilst the occupants of the room are busy in the riot going on outside. This is the most perilous part of our enterprise—if they return before we are safe out of this place I cannot answer for the consequences."

They had just succeeded in entering the room, and descending the short flight of stairs that led from it to the yard at the back, when the hurried sound of footsteps, and the approach of lights from the front showed they had only evaded discovery by a few minutes.

"Quick," exclaimed Jonathan, unlatching a small wicket at the further end of the yard, "you must now trust to your own speed, for this is as far as my aid can go. Six stone steps will bring you to a court leading directly into Noah's Ark Alley, thence it is a straight line to the waterside."

"The very place I desire," returned the other. "I must take a boat at St. Saviour's stairs."

"And now, having effected your escape, have I kept that faith with you that you doubted a short time since?" demanded Wild.

"You have, and here is your guerdon—my signet-ring, which I value at fifty guineas, but which in happier times I would be willing to ransom at double the amount."

Wild instantly fixed the proffered treasure on his finger.

"One word more," continued the fugitive.

"I would for the purpose I have already mentioned, learn the name of its present possessor."

"That need be of no consequence," returned Wild, "*if* you ever want it again apply to Giles Shalders, the landlord of "the Fox-in-the-Mint," and he will procure its restoration on those conditions. And now away, or the bull-dogs will be on the scent."

"Which direction did you say for St. Saviour's, after I leave the alley;" asked Trevanion, as he reached the last step.

"Bear to the left, and then straight on," answered his guide.

"Good night!" and the speaker was lost in in the darkness of the place he had dashed into at full speed.

"A good night indeed for me!" exclaimed Jonathan, as he fixed the ring tighter on his finger, and drew a coarse gauntlet over it. I have made a pretty fair business of this doubling, and now having started the roebuck, to put the hounds on the right scent."

With this heroic design he crossed the yard, and re-entered the house which he had passed through on his way thither.

Making his exit by the door that led into the main thoroughfare of the Mint, he found Orford, Kirby, and the rest in close consultation. At his approach they all involuntarily made way for his coming amongst them, and eagerly inquired if he had been successful in his pursuit.

Jonathan merely pursed his lips, and remarked that any information the nobleman required must be purchased.

"Here is fifty pounds then to obtain it," said Lord Orford, placing a canvas bag containing that amount in the hands of Wild. "The very instant I find you have enabled us to make our capture certain, the sum shall be doubled."

"Enough. I am satisfied," rejoined Wild; "I found him, as I suspected, among the roofs of the houses here at the back, but before I could come up with him he gave me the slip. However I have learned enough to know that he takes water at St. Saviour's stairs, so hasten thither and you will be sure of your prize."

At that moment a violent gust of wind shook the houses to the foundation, and extinguished several of the torches carried by the minters. "It will be a rough night on the Thames," observed Jonathan, "he will scarcely be able to make good the passage, even if the men at the Ferry are bold enough to venture. There is a squall now brewing, which will make old London Bridge strain its hardest."

"No matter what the weather is, he must be secured at all risks and hazards," exclaimed Orford, "To the Ferry—quick!" and taking with him two of his attendants, Orford departed on his expedition.

Leaving him to continue the pursuit, whilst Wild elated with the success of his night's adventures, proposed an adjournment to the "Fox," which formed a kind of house of call for the Borough Thieves, and was the only tavern in the Mint for good brandy. We must now return for a few moments to the unfortunate woman whom we left under the benevolent protection of Mr. Wood, and, who was now still receiving from him what little attention he had it in his power to bestow.

"There Mrs. Sheppard," cried Wood, as he saw her slowly regaining her senses, "you'll do now I warrant you, a little rest and quiet will be better nurses for you than an old carpenter. I fear it waxes late and the good folks in Wych-street, will be wondering at my delay."

"Where is my child?" faltered Mrs. Sheppard, not heeding the averted look with which the question was received.

Mr. Wood scarcely knew how to reply, but believing that in her present excited state it would be better to veil the peculiar circumstances under which it disappeared, quieted her fears by stating that for better security he had left it in charge of a woman who belonged to the sanctuary.

"I must at once assure myself of his safety," continued the bereaved mother. "So many strange events have passed before my vision this night, that my brain is well nigh distraught, but I feel I cannot rest until I place him beyond the reach of danger."

"Well, Mrs. Sheppard," said Wood in reply, "I am sure if you make enquiries, you will learn all is quite right, but you must excuse me from volunteering my assistance in the search, I have a little girl myself at home and a wife besides, who will scarcely take my word for the cause of this prolonged visit, and so—"

"Say no more my generous benefactor," interrupted the other, "I have already—how unwillingly Heaven knows—been the cause of to much unhappiness; you will still believe me grateful for the kindness you have rendered but the impulses of a mother's heart, will not let me think of aught, until I have recovered my son; doubly dear to me, since to night I believe that I have encountered the phantom of his father."

Finding all remonstrances useless, and believing besides that such a step might possibly lead to his recovery, Wood desisted from advising her not to run the risk of going alone into the street, and contented himself with the assurance that accident, and not design, had been the cause of its detention. Bidding her wrap herself well up, and setting himself the example, by twisting the huge woollen comforter comfortably round his throat, the carpenter therefore bade her good night, and set off on his way to the Ferry, whilst Mrs.

Sheppard turned in the opposite direction, to endeavour from inquiries of her neighbours, to elicit some paticulars of her child's fate, and where she at that moment might find him.

CHAPTER. IV.

THE CHRISTENING OF JACK SHEPPARD.

"I have great comfort from this fellow; methinks he hath no drowning mark upon him; his complexion is perfect gallows."—The Tempest.

In the very heart of the district just disturbed by the events related, was situated a low slanting public-house, which from the ill-painted sign that swung on the creaking crazy hinges above the door, went by the name of "The Fox-in-the-Mint." In the daylight the aspect of the place was wretched in the extreme. Crowds of both sexes, mostly bare-legged and bare-footed, with many who seemed to have surmounted the prejudice of nakedness, sat upon the threshold, or filled up the street. A coarse garment, half-gown, half-sack, was the usual amount of the feminine accoutrements, and dirty children in all the innocence of infantine nudity were to be seen playing sportively about the doors, or in the gutter. As night came on, these characteristics changed to others of a less repulsive but equally squalid description. Men, brutalised by drink, and rendered desperate by crime, lounged round the bar of the tavern and gave vent to their passions uncurbed by the stringent laws which elsewhere held them in subjection, and acts of violence even among themselves were affairs of such ordinary occurrence, as to be invariably passed over unnoticed.

It was to the drinking room of this "retreat," as the place was colloquially styled among themselves, that the Minters, thirsty, and excited by the fray in which they had been called upon to participate, now retired. Their principal accomplice, a young man whose swarthy visage and creole origin had got him the appellation of "Blueskin," was elected chairman, and the rest drew round the tables and gave orders for beverages of various degrees of strength in such formidable profusion, that it was apparent their determination to spend a festive night, was not to be diverted by any trifling interruption.

"Vy Captin' Blueskin," enquired one of the party as soon as they had got duly settled in their places, "vot on airth have ye got screwed up in that parcel there?"

"Its a kinchin my darlin'," responded that individual, "a blessed babby vot I picked up behind a door ven the row begun. I mean to let him out by the hour for the blessed twin-dodge now, and arterwards to eddicate him for a respectable prig."

"Let's have a look at the jigging cove!" roared a dozen voices.

"Vell, easy does it—there," answered Blueskin, unravelling the short cloak he had wrapped round the child, which it is needless to say was the offspring of Mrs. Sheppard—"take a look at his nob, and say vether that ain't a werry respectable model for a lully-prig anyhow."

"Dat lad vill never die in his bed," said an old grey-bearded man, who with profound attention was gazing on the child.

"Vell, and vy not?" exclaimed Blueskin, striving to imitate the guttural voice of the greybeard.

"Hush! let Von Broendenbrak cast the child's fate," whispered a minter at his side.

"It ish not necessary for me to look vader" continued the Dutch astrologer—"there ish a black mole, of a shape like a coffin, under de childsh's right ear, which bodes no good, and a line on itsh neck, which meets in de form of a nooshe. Ja! Ja! he will have de Hempen Fever before he ish in his two and twentieth year;" and contenting himself with this prediction the Dutchman rose from his seat and strode out at the door.

"Never has Von Broendenbrak been known to augur falsely—the youngster's fate is as certain as my name is Giles Shalders," said the landlord who had entered during the Hollander's speech—"if I live, however, to see it, he shan't mount the horse that's foaled by an acorn without my being one of his last witnesses."

"Vell, never mind, the kinchin's mine—I makes him my protegy, as the great folks calls it—and come vot vill I'll bring him up like a honor to the gang. Let's have a glass of gin, landlord." The desired liquor was brought.

Blueskin having tested by the application of his own lips, tho excellence of the spirit, cried "Now my dolly pals ve'll christen the infant von of us, and vhatever he may grow up into, Blueskin vill stick to him like vax."

So saying he dashed a portion of the liquor into the child's face, and forced the remainder down his throat, which called forth sundry screams and struggles from the boy, that seemed to testify an attempt at opposition. Having wiped away with his cloth cap the few superfluous drops that descended from the child's brow. Blueskin appeared highly satisfied with the ceremony, and now to enliven the company, volunteered a song, which as one eminently characteristic of the singer, and the period in which it was sung, we give to the reader in its original form at the risk of his finding some of the expressions employed in its construction unintelligible without the aid of a glossary.

Having waited until the clamour of the vibrating pipes and drinking-vessels had in some degree subsided, he thus began.

SONG OF BLUESKIN.

As from ken to ken I was going
  Doing a bit on the prigging lay;
Who should I meet but a buxom blowen
  Tol lol, lol lol tolderol ay.
Who should I meet but a jolly blowen
  Who was fly to the time o'day.

I pattered in flash like a covey knowin'
  Bubby or grubbery, Miss, I say?
"Lots of gatter" says she are flowing,
  Lend me a lift in a civil way.

"You may have a crib to stow in,
  Welcome my pal as the flowers in May,"
To her ken at once I go in,
  Where in a corner out of the way—

To her ken at once I go in,
  Where in a corner out of the way;
With his smeller a trumpet blowing,
  A reglar swell-cove lushy lay.

With his smeller a trumpet blowing,
  This reglar swell-cove lushy lay;
To his clies my hooks I throw in,
  And cellar his mopusses clear away.

Then his ticker I set agoing,
  With his onions, chain, and key;
Next slipt off his bottom clo'ing
  And his gingerbread topper gay.

Then his other toggery stowing,
  All with the swag I sneak away;
"Tramp it, tramp it, my jolly blowen,
  Or be grabbed by the beaks we may."

"Tramp it, tramp it, my jolly blowen
  Or be grabbed by the beaks we may;
And we shall caper a-heel-and-toeing,
  A Tyburn Hornpipe some fine day."

"And we shall caper a-heel-and-toeing
  A Tyburn Hornpipe some fine day;
While fogle-hunters are a doing
  Their morning fake on the prigging lay."

The uproarious applause that followed this elegant lyric had not ceased when Jonathan Wild and Sampson Kirby entered the room together.

"I'faith! my lads," said Kirby, taking the seat at the head of the table, which Blueskin instantly vacated, "we have had a busy night of it certainly, and you seem bent upon making the few hours remaining a merry one, eh? Well, Jonathan here, has volunteered to stand a glass of max round as his share of the plunder."

"Hurrah, for Jonathan Wild," chorussed the whole company, already somewhat inebriated by their potations.

"Ay, Hurrah for Jonathan, my little gallows-skin," exclamed Blueskin, to the child, as he endeavoured, in the excess of his hilarity, to pour another dose of Geneva down its throat. "Hurrah! for cunning Jonathan, you and he will work many a prigging day together yet, if Mynheer's words come true."

"Whose brat have you got there?" asked Jonathan, as he observed Blueskin, handling the infant with rather more energy than gentleness in his touch; "Do you want to poison or strangle it; which?"

"Why neither," answered the creole, "I'm only a saving of it up till old mother Hawkins comes home, who'll dandle it properly. I means to make it the heir to all my property, and so I is a qualifying of it with a precious drop of blue-ruin."

"What woman have you been robbing now," demanded Jonathan, "Whose is it?"

"Nay, I don't know nor care," was the reply; "I found it hid behind a door-post, and so I picked it up, and took a fancy to it."

"Give it me," cried Jonathan, fiercely, rising from his seat as he spoke.

"No thankee," drily responded the other, "go and find a baby for yourself, if you want one. This is mine? If there's a reward offered for it, well and good; and if there isn't, why I'll stick to it like a father."

"Will you hand the urchin to me?

"Not at no price votsumdever," returned the creole.

"The darkey's right," observed Kirby, he found the kid, let him have it. Keep your seat, Wild, and your temper, too, if you can. Come, drink; the fellows will have an ugly night on the water, for the winds' getting up enough, to tear the very words out of one's throat."

And as if to confirm the assertion, a sudden gust swept over the roof at the same instant, and dislodging a pile of chimneys, sent them toppling over into the streets below where they dashed into a thousand fragments.

Jonathan, unused to have his commands disregarded, growled out some expression of discontent, and internally vowed to have revenge, for the slight cast upon him.

"I'm much mistaken," he continued, finding a pause had ensusd in the conversation, "if I don't know the dam that kid belongs to. I had a purpose to serve by it, which would have been of some service, to us all here. No matter, the time *will* come when he who thwarts Jonathan Wild, will have no child's game to answer for." And he sullenly tossed off a bumper of the hot liquor the host then brought in.

From the savage glances of both parties, as they glared upon each other, it is probable the quarrel would have been brought to a speedy termination, by the test of physical strength, had not an interruption occurred, by the entrance of one, who seemed, even to that hardened assemblage as appalling as a spectre. It was Mrs. Sheppard, who, struck by one of the bricks that had been cast down by the storm, now staggered in, pale and bleeding. As she tottered towards the table, where each had been previously so riotous, a dead silence ensued.

"Give, oh give me my child," she faltered in trembling accents,—"I will for ever bless you, if you restore him to me unharmed."

"Vhy, there's more fuss about the kid than if he vas a Lord Mayor in petticoats," exclaimed Blueskin, hazarding an attempt at pleasantry which the others did not appear to appreciate as he anticipated; "he need grow up somebody I think, if he makes all this fuss vhen he's a cove in long clothes."

"Oh, restore to me my poor child," repeated Mrs. Sheppard, "and a mother's blessings—"

"There is an article, marm, ve don't care to deal in here," answered Blueskin, "but if so be you like to tip us a trifle for the care ve has taken of him, vhy there's the blessed cherubim and velcome."

As the two guineas given her by Wood, occurred to her at the moment, though it was the entire sum she possessed in the world, Mrs. Sheppard did not hesitate for one instant in their disposal. Giving them to Blueskin, she gladly received in exchange the boy.

"Vell, there he is, marm, none the vorse for my being his nurse for a few hours I assure you. He has had a reglar christening for his perfession, and I'll be bail he takes to it like sack and sugar."

Having succeeded in the object for which she had ventured thither, Mrs. Sheppard retreated in unconcealed disgust from the group, before Blueskin had concluded his speech; glad to regain her child even at the cost of a ransom which was to her the sacrifice of the means of living for some time at least.

"Vell!" cried Blueskin, "some people has no more purliteness in 'em than you could get out of a scraped parsnip! Howsomdever, I bears nobody ill-vill, and as my reglars, there's half the rowdy to go for punch all round, to make us all out-an-out pals vonce more. But what the deuce has come of Jonathan; he hasn't been a comin' the soft cove over the voman surely."

At this observation of the creole, each turned round in amazement, and became for the first time conscious that Wild had left the room. A few shook their heads significantly.

"The worst of that fellow is," remarked the chairman, filling a capacious Dutch pipe with a plentiful supply of the the fragrant weed, "the worst of that fellow is, you never know how he get's away, or where he's likely to turn up. Its my belief he has been eddicated for a ghost, and didn't take to the business."

"Oh, let him bide!" added a burly ruffian, who was bestowing undivided attention on the liquors before him," he has only got rusty through Blueskin putting a wet blanket on him, and so he's gone out a bit to polish himself up for 'spectable society."

As this sally was received with general laughter, the appearance of Giles Shalders with a reeking bowl of hot punch, provided at Blueskin's expense, only contributed to increase their mirth; and in the boisterous revel that succeeded, all anxiety respecting their late companion was absorbed.

Here leaving them to continue their orgies, which as tending rather to disgust than divert the reader, we shall not attempt further to describe; we must now follow the footsteps of Jonathan, who had passed behind Mrs. Sheppard as she entered, and awaited her return at the porch.

Scarcely had her light footsteps crossed the threshold, than seizing her by the arm Wild compelled her to recognize his features. The poor woman enfeebled by her accident, and weakened by the privations she had recently undergone could scarcely testify by a scream, the alarm she experienced by this encounter, but if it had been more shrill and loud than it was, the violence of the wind would have borne away the sound.

"It's no use crying for help, woman," said Wild, "no one could hear you, and if they could, there would be no occasion for them to come. I mean you no harm, now, at all events; it isn't part of my purpose."

"Oh, let me go," cried the unfortunate mother, tightening her thin shawl closely around her—"I am ill—very ill—and if not to me, show some compassion towards the child I now bear in my arms."

"You know who I am, I suppose?"

"Too well, alas!" shuddered Mrs. Sheppard.

"And did you ever hear that compassion was one of Jonathan Wild's failings? No, you thwarted me when I would have had your aid, rejected me when I would have had your hand. I swore to you I would be avenged, and I will keep my word."

"Jonathan Wild, are you a monster or a man?" exclaimed the woman, raising herself up with firmness as she spoke, and recalling the lustre to her eyes that had long been absent.

"Call me what you will now, one title I will establish a claim to—that of *your persecutor*," growled Wild between his clenched teeth, "and if that sickly brat of yours lives to become a man, I'll haunt him until I drive him to the gallows."

Unable to move, Mrs. Sheppard leaned over the infant and burst into tears.

"I will ring his destiny daily in his ears and instead of being the comfort of your age, as you expect, he shall drive you to distraction and an early grave. All the torments I can heap upon his head shall be redoubled by your beholding them without the power of seeing them averted, and thus will I keep my oath and gratify my revenge."

The loud roar of the wind at this moment suspended Wild's denunciation, and before he could resume it, the upper portion of the house beneath which they stood was hurled down with a terrific crash, and buried them in its ruins.

CHAPTER. V.

THE GREAT STORM.

MESSENGER.—"Who's there besides foul weather?"
KENT.—One minded like the weather most unquietly.—KING LEAR, Act III. sc. 1.

WHEN the carpenter found himtelf fairly out of the reach of the minters, from whose hands he dreaded in the event of detection some personal indignities might be conferred, he slackened the quick pace at which he had been proceeding, and impelled thereto by the descent of a few huge rain-drops, cast his eyes upwards to ascertain the probable state of the weather which would accompany his return home. The appearance of the sky was remarkably wild and ominous of evil. Dark patches of black clouds flitted rapidly across the heavens, and a very startling and unusual light appeared in the eastern horizon which shed a lurid and unearthly glare over the dense masses of vapour that went drifting along. Hollow gusts of wind swirled mournfully through the deserted streets, and during each pause in the gale a smart pelting shower drove furiously into the face of the pedestrian who was making head against it. From the lateness of the hour there were few persons traversing the thoroughfare, and a faint light illuminating the higher apartments of the houses, formed the only indication of the place being inhabited. The lamps were at this early period of metropolitan extension, not only few and far apart, but deriving their illuminative power from a very scanty supply of oil, rarely replenished, the uncertain glimmer only served to bewilder rather than guide, and where they jutted out from some projecting corner or signboard, most of them had been early extinguished in the evening by either the wind or rain. From this outline of the impediments offered to a Borough pedestrian, it may be easily imagined progression was a matter requiring skill, as well as patience, to maintain.

Impressed with no very agreeable sensations from the scenes he had witnessed, and the present aspect of the night, Mr. Wood pursued his way through the intricate mass of buildings that skirted the waterside, and reached by the Clink an old hostel, called the "Waterman's Arms," which presented in its overhanging portico, and quaint old fashioned windows, a very fair specimen of the architecture of the period. Finding that he stood in need of some cordial to restore the equanimity of his frame, the carpenter, late as it was, determined to avail himself of the invitation suggested by the faint red light that still glimmered behind the curtains of the lower apartments, and lustily knocking at the door, demanded admittance.

A heavy shuffling of shoes, and a corresponding murmuring of voices confirmed his belief that the inmates had not yet retired to rest, but no friendly latch was uplifted in answer to his summons.

Mr. Wood repeated the knocking, accompanied by an earnest entreaty for the admission he found so sternly withheld. His clamour at last brought the footsteps closer to the threshold.

"You are too late" exclaimed a voice at length from within, "we are closed for the night!"

"What David Gwillym," urged the applicant changing his tone, "are you churlish enough to refuse a moment's shelter to your old friend and countryman, Owen Wood, of Wych Street?"

"Bless my heart," cried the host, at once withdrawing bar and bolt, and giving free egress to the bar to which the door immediately conducted—"Bless my heart, Mr. Wood, why who would ever have expected to have found you penetrating the lawless regions of such a place as this, at this hour too.

"Ifaith, David" jocosely returned Wood, "I have as much astonished myself as you, but in the name of all that's friendly and hospitable, let me have a dram of your best brandy to cheer my heart with, for what with the night and what with the neighbourhood, I have neither a spark of warmth nor courage about me."

"Ah! there have been wild doings up at the mint yonder, but they have not harmed you, I hope?"

"Not I! but the brandy good, David!"

The landlord looked askance, as though he had suspicions of the carpenter's visit to that quarter, but contenting himself with the concentration of them into an expressive wink, he opened a small cupboard, formed out of the wainscot behind him, and proceeded to detach therefrom a curious shaped bottle, which, with the ruby liquid it contained, was placed before the belated passenger.

"There!" said Gwillym, filling a horn cup with the spirit, "drink that off, and I'll warrant it leaves no care nor head-ache behind it. It's right, Nantz, that I keep for mine own especial service."

"I, faith," gasped the other after his draught, "that's excellent stuff, David, and does thy house credit. It throws one into a

perfect glow of bravery," and the carpenter smacked his lips approvingly.

You had better stop here until the storm has abated," added the host, finding his guest was making preparations to depart.

"Inclination and duty seldom travel the same road, David," returned Wood; "I don't much fancy venturing across the river, when 's blowing great guns like this, but needs must when—you know the old proverb."

"I question if you'll find a waterman at the ferry, who'll take you, sir," chimed in an old mariner, who had been indulging himself with a pipe in the chimney corner, and who now endeavoured to join in the conversation which he had listened to with great interest before. "I know, I, for one, would'nt hazard a boat out, if I was to have its weight in gold for my fare, when I got to the other side."

"Ah! Sam Harris is no bad judge of the weather, I assure you," remarked Gwillym—"you had better take my advice and stop where you are. Hark! how the gale rattles the windows even now!"

"Gale, or no gale, I must venture," answered Wood—"I have more faith in its doing no damage than I have in its abating."

The old sailor shook his head doubtingly.

"It will be no easy matter to keep a boat to its course," cried he, re-kindling his pipe, and deliberately discharging a few copious puffs of smoke, before he applied his lips to the grog before him—"I know what the signs of a storm look like, and take my word for it, sir, we shall have one to-night that'll send many a poor seaman down to old Davy Jones's locker. The sky looks just for all the world as it did, when the Marlborough and I were wrecked off Cape Horn."

"And how did the storm come up then?" inquired the landlord, not unwilling to draw the mariner into a repetition of his adventures, for the sake of detaining Wood, although he had heard the narrative duly delivered every Saturday night, in his parlour, to the attentive ears of all the wharfingers, who there held their weekly meeting."

"Why you see," continued Harris, eagerly seizing the opportunity to relate a story of his favorite element, "we were bound for the Cape, and an uncommon tidy run of it we had for about twenty days, when just as we had got to the westward of the banks, we fell in with unaccountable foul weather, rain, and hail, and wind, and fog, and more on all of them than we much cared for. Howsumever, we kept on making west'ard, in hopes of getting a southerly blow, till at last, with just such a sky as this, down it comes, all of a lump, tails up, a reglar roarer about nor'-nor'-east. The first thing as happened partic'lar was just as we had clewed up top-gallant sails, away went our main-topsail yard in the slings. "Oh! dear!" squeals our skipper, shooting up the companion way, and clappin' his two fins fast together, "what's that?" no sooner said than, puff, away flies the foresail and foretopsail yard—jam goes the two skipper's fins again, chock—block: snap, snap, flies cross-jack-yard and mizen topmast, and with that out bolts——"

What the seaman's story was going to introduce at this moment will probably ever remain a mystery, for at this crisis the door which Mr. Wood had been holding impatiently ajar, was thrust suddenly back, and a man of powerful build and strongly-marked physiognomy entered.

"Anybody here for the ferry to-night?" inquired the new comer, looking round with a glance of friendly recognition at the seaman and his host, "I'm just going to haul up the boat."

Wood gladly hailed the opportunity to depart, and a bargain for the passage having been concluded, he discharged his reckoning, and bade adieu to his companions.

"Beg your pardon, sir—one moment," cried the sailor, "I want to speak half-a-word with Jack Sanders, your sculler. You ain't agoin' to risk it, Jack, to-night, surely;" he continued in an undertone to the waterman.

"There's no help for it, Sam," responded the other. "One musn't give in to a capfull of wind, with the lives of wife and children hanging on your hands at home. No boat, no bread, comrade," and so saying, he shook his old messmate heartily by the hand, and followed Mr. Wood, who had gone on a little in advance.

"It's my opinion he'll never live to give them bread again," muttered the old sailor, returning to the house. "There's a lull in the gale now, but it will make up for lost time presently."

The dead calm which had succeeded, and to the foreboding nature of which the mariner had just referred, raised hopes both in the minds of the waterman and his passenger that they might get across without much difficulty, though as they neared the flight of steps descending to the ferry it was easy to perceive streaming through the darkness, long lines of spray churned into white foam, by the action of the tide which was running down through the arches of old London Bridge, then the only one that spanned the river. Seizing the sculls and bidding his fare remain seated as firmly as the constant oscillation of the sides would allow, the waterman cast the boat adrift and made for "Arundel Stairs," as Mr. Wood had directed, that being the nearest point to Wych Street.

They had hardly got into the middle of the stream, however, before another boat was observed to be thrust off in the same direction, and from the rapid plashing of the oars, as they followed each other in vigorous strokes upon the water, it was apparent that haste as well as necessity had been considered in their departure.

Hardly had they become aware of this, when by the light of torches, gleaming on the Surrey side, it was evident that another boat had been likewise put off from St. Saviour's stairs, apparently in pursuing of the one that had gone before.

"The watermen seem in luck's way to-night master!" observed Sanders. "One would think all Southwark wanted to cross the Thames, not that it's such a pleasant time for a jaunt either—I can hardly see from stem to stern."

Wood returned a short answer, and then continued to watch with interest the turn that affairs had taken; partly guessing from what he had seen in the Mint the nature of the pursuit then pending, and partly conjecturing that some political schemes in connexion with the Jacobite interest might have something to do with this sudden influx of passengers on the Thames at midnight.

The dead lull of the wind which had allowed the hoarse voices in the last boat to be distinctly heard, directing the exertions of the scullers, was now succeeded by a sudden and violent hurricane, which drove the water up in sheets of spray, and hurled the boats back towards the bridge with a power against which it was useless contending. The torches carried by the scullers in the boat that had last been pushed off were utterly extinguished, and the roar of the wind as it swept impetuously over the river, drowned the sound of the voices.

"Sam Harris was right," ejaculated the waterman, looking with terror on the scene around him, "We shall have a fearful night of it. There's a fall of twelve feet at the bridge to-night, and we're drifting rapidly towards it. Heaven help us!" The other two boats were similarly situated, though the distance between them was evidently quickly diminishing.

"He will be caught," thought Wood, as he saw the proximity of the two boats only rendered distinguishable by the screen of white foam behind them, and as much engrossed in their movements as in his own peril. The flash of a pistol kindled up the gloom for an instant, and during its momentary glare the carpenter saw the figure of a man fall with a heavy reverberating plunge into the river.

"There's one poor soul gone to his last account," cried the waterman.

The next minute the two boats were in contact, the pursuer and the pursued, and borne swiftly on towards the centre arch of the bridge. The same force of wind and current had turned the boat in which Wood was seated, in the same direction, and he was now enabled to see the contest that was going on.

The fugitive, in his anxiety to elude the vigilance of the others, had thrown the head of the boat directly towards the stream, and the man who rowed him having received the shot intended for himself, he had been compelled to undertake its entire control. In the other boat were three persons, one of whom had leaped over the side, and was now grappling with his opponent.

The hurricane at this time raged with greater violence than ever, carrying away everything before it in its wild impetuosity, and so powerful was its force, that finding it impossible to resist yielding, the carpenter flung himself down in the boat, and the waterman abandoned all further attempts to keep it back from the swirl of the arch.

"Save yourself, sir—quickly, or we are lost;" shouted the waterman to Wood, as a violent concussion caused him to start uprightly and discovered to him the perilous position in which they were placed. The boat had struck against one of the wooden piles of the bridge, and when Wood, who had clung to the masonry above, turned round to look after his companion, he found that the boat had been gulfed in the eddy, and that the waterman in attempting to reach the framework of the arch had missed his aim, and staggered back into the dark surge of the waters below. Clinging with the frantic grasp of one who finds himself hovering between life and death, Wood passed his hands over the slippery shelf of stone on which he had gained a precarious footing, and found from it receding slightly at one point there was a recess where he might screen himself from the action of the wind. Working his way gradually into this niche, where the slightest variance from the path would have consigned him to the same fate as that of the poor fellow who had shared with him the perils of the storm, he found that it sloped back into a place where he might remain with comparative safety. Exhausted by his efforts to reach it, he was leaning against the damp corner-stone, when a loud plunge under the arch next to that which sheltered him, announced that accident or design had thrown one of the persons he had left struggling into the water.

Straining all his powers of vision to penetrate through the darkness, he saw the fugitive battling with the current, and making towards the place where he stood. The dark, cold water closed over his head, and roared and bubbled in his ears, as he saw the swimmer borne through the arch, wildly extending his arms in all the agony of a drowning man. Shouting to him to make for the place on which he stood, the carpenter had the satisfaction to find that his voice had reached the ears of the fugitive, but as he struggled to climb the buttress where Wood was hoarsely endeavouring to direct his footsteps, the wind bore the friendly sounds away, and misunderstanding, or not hearing them, he saw the drowning man fall from the treacherous stone on which he had poised himself, and carried away by the torrent, sink down the fall.

Dizzied and distracted by the tumult of the storm, Wood scarcely retained possession of his senses, and he sank in a state of torpor on the cold wet surface of the masonry.

The next morning, when he came to himself, he awoke, in a small but cheerful room, through the windows of which the sun was shining brightly, and casting its most genial rays on the features of a tall and elderly man, whose sombre garb bespoke the physician.

From him the carpenter learned that the inmates of the house, where he then was, and which formed one of the narrow tenements that stretched like a street across the bridge, hearing cries for help from the arch beneath, had lowered ropes and rescued two watermen from the fate that seemed to await them. From the testimony of one of them, who stated he had seen, in his ascent, the form of a man, reclining on the stonework of the buttress, and who, he believed, to be the party that hired them; further search was made, and the storm fortunately abating, the exertions of the adventurous owner of the dwelling, were rewarded by the discovery and rescue of Wood, who otherwise would have perished from cold, or the violence of the waves. It appeared that they had, however, mistaken the carpenter for Lord Orford, who was the passenger that engaged them, in pursuit, as he alleged, of a Jacobite spy, and merely adding, that, unable to preserve the boat, they had been compelled to cling for safety to the frame-work of the arch, and that, from their observation, those who had attempted to cross the water, must have suffered the same fate as their own fare—they went away early in the morning, and thus Wood was led to believe he and the two watermen were the only survivors of the perilous night upon the Thames.

By this storm, London alone, sustained a loss of two millions. Steeples and stacks of chimneys strewed the ground in every direction. The leaden roofs of churches were stripped off, and rolled up like a scrool. The Eddystone lighthouse was utterly destroyed and all its inmates perished. Thousands of trees were torn up by the roots, and uplifted to considerable height; immense numbers of cattle were killed; ships were blown from their anchors, and never again heard of; rivers overflowed their banks; the public buildings were all so severely damaged, as to be closed for a considerable time afterwards, and it is conjectured that upwards of 10,000 persons perished on that memorable night.

END OF EPOCH THE FIRST.

EPOCH THE SECOND.

1714.

CHAPTER I.

THE CARPENTER'S SHOP IN WYCH STREET.

"Ten years ago, ten years ago,
Life was to us a fairy scene,
And the keen blasts of worldly woe,
Had seared not then its pathway green.
Youth and its thousand dreams were ours,
Feelings we ne'er can know again,
Unwither'd hopes, unwasted powers,
And frames unworn by mortal pain,
Such was the bright and genial flow,
Of life with us ten years ago."—ANON.

TIME that never slackens speed, that wings his flight with unflagging wing, season after season, and day after day, had entombed ten years in the sepulchre of the past, since the incidents recorded in the previous pages had occurred. It was now the commencement of the year 1714.

The month was April, that pleasant harbinger of the blue skies of summer, and fosterer of the rich green verdure of the fields. The drowsy humming of murmuring bees lost amidst the busy brawling of the brook; the soaring skylark, piercing the floating shadows of the clouds until the sky rained melody; the pallid primrose, thrusting aside the leafy covering of the woodland path, were each and all characteristic of the season, but with these our present scene hath little affinity, for to the very centre of London's busy traffic must we now direct the attention of the reader, and bid him select from the crowded mass of habitations of which that narrow thoroughfare is composed, the dwelling of Mr. Wood in Wych Street, Drury Lane.

It was, then, one Thursday afternoon in the above month, that the carpenter who had been detained in the city, during the previous part of the day, chanced to return, either by accident or design, at an earlier period than he had given his apprentices reason to anticipate. He was about to cross the threshold of his workshop, when finding the customary sounds of manual labour were not audible from within, he gently raised the latch of the inner door, and cautiously entered the room, resolved to administer a summary castigation to a certain youth, if he found the suspicions he entertained of that youth's present idleness duly verified by his own observation.

The apartment, into which he had thus stealthily glided, had perhaps little to distinguish it from other workshops appropriated to the ancient craft of carpentering at that period. The usual variety of tools used in the trade was to be seen scattered about in disorder, and on the floor thickly covered with shavings and sawdust, were numerous indications that a repast consisting apparently of bread and cheese, had been just disposed of. Near the door were placed some planks awaiting their transformation into future chests and packing cases, and behind these the carpenter ensconced himself, ready to act as occurrences might decide. What he saw was certainly sufficient to confirm his worst suppositions. On a stool, placed upon the high bench that occupied the most prominent position in the workshop, was seen a stripling of about twelve years old, poising himself on tiptoe, whilst with a knife, instead of prosecuting his proper employment, he was diligently engaged in carving out his name upon the huge oaken beam that stretched away beneath the roof from one extremity of the room to the other. His dress consisted of thick plush breeches of a dark colour, and a capacious waistcoat of grey drugget, both of which articles of costume had evidently been at some period the property of a person considerably his senior.

As he turned round to observe whence proceeded the slight sound that Mr. Wood made on entering, his quick intelligent features were lit up with animation, and with an expression of mingled audacity and awe, he fixed his full hazel eyes on the place where his employer was secreted. A forehead of average width and deep black glossy eyebrows, would have made his countenance somewhat intellectual, had it not been for those unmistakeable indications of sensuality that lurk about the mouth, and which here evinced in their possessor a tendency not only to coarse indulgence, but also to a feeling of indifference as to how it was obtained. His hair was closely cropped in accordance with the boyish custom of the day, and this, with the prominent cheek-bones that rose conspicuously among the other features, imparted a peculiar effect to his physiognomy, that we can now only find in the heads of those Spanish vagabonds that formed the chief study in the works of the old masters.

Satisfied from his glance that he had, as he believed, no intrusion to fear, his strange employment was resumed with additional energy, and he now broke forth in a strain to lighten his labours that might possibly have suggested the achievement at which he aimed.

THE NEWGATE SCULPTOR.

When Claude du Val was in darbies caged,
He cut out his name on the stone for a pal;
"Ho! ho!" quoth the cove who saw him thus engaged,
"You have graven your tombstone Claude du Val.
With your writing so fine, tra la!

"I must manage this H a little better," cried the singer. "Whether its an X or an Izzard, hang me if I can tell now," and he altered the letter slightly as he spoke.

The next who came was Bill Simpson, he
Carved his name on the selfsame spot for a joke;
"Ha! Ha!" cried the cove "you'll astride soon be,
Of the wooden horse that was foaled by an oak,
With your writing so fine, tra la!

"Confound it!" exclaimed the apprentice in bewilderment, looking at the result of his labours, "I ought to have cut out John instead of Jack; no matter, I've been always called Jack as long as I can recollect I was called anything, so Jack let it be."

"Then Whitney, and Willis, and Jones, and Ball,
All chiselled their names on that stone, d'ye see;
"Aye! Aye!" cried the dubsman who witness'd it all,
"You'll each have a swing from the leafless tree."
With your writing so fine, tra la!

"I've a good mind to give the shop the slip, and crack a crib myself," added the carver, "Should'nt much fancy this beam turning out as fatal as the Newgate stone did though."

For a dozen brave cracksmen from first to last,
All wrote their names on that dungeon wall:
And every one in that dungeon cast,
Met the very same fate as Claude du Val.
With his writing so fine, tra la!

"There! that'll do I think!" remarked the apprentice, surveying his novel workmanship, "and I don't think Claude himself could have made a better job of it," and leaping from the bench as he spoke, he closed his knife and sprang to the very part where Wood was waiting.

"And a pretty job you *have* made of it," cried the carpenter behind him, boxing his ears, "I'll teach you, you young rascal, to deface my walls, and idle away your time in this manner;" and as each successive word was uttered, Wood administered an extra blow.

"I ain't agoing to be struck for nothing," returned the boy reddening with anger, as soon as he recovered breath, and overcame the surprise of this interruption.

"Ha! you rascal, you'll come to be hanged," said Wood—"and I have a good mind ——"

Jack, fired up at the prospect of another chastisement, with so much anger, and manifested such a determined spirit of resistance, that the carpenter deemed it advisable, for his own personal safety, to suspend his threat, and changed his tone from that of denunciation to remonstrance.

"Who taught you the song that I heard you singing, when I entered?" he inquired, in a less authoritative strain than that he had before assumed.

"I heard it at the Cock and Magpie, at the end of the street here," answered Jack, without hesitating.

"The most iniquitous den in the neighbourhood," ejaculated Wood, and I suppose that thief of a landlord, Tom Dillon, taught it you."

"No, it was a fellow who goes there, they call Blueskin," replied the apprentice—"It was that song that made me think of carving my name on the beam, but I didn't mean any harm by it."

"Blueskin!" rejoined the carpenter;" why he is one of the most nefarious scamps we have now upon town, and only escaped being hung last session, by turning king's evidence. Pretty companionship for an honest carpenter's apprentice, truly. If Jonathan Wild hadn't done him a friendly turn, and saved his neck from the gallows, he wouldn't have been drinking o' night in Drury Lane."

"I beg your pardon, master," exclaimed Jack, changing his demeanour, and assuming a more respectful tone, "but did you ever see this Jonathan Wild?"

"Once," answered the carpenter; "on the night of the great storm, about ten years ago, we met under somewhat peculiar circumstances, but I think I should know him again if I saw him."

"He is rather short, isn't he, sir,—with a foxy beard, and a look that seems to pierce you through!"

"Not a bad likeness of him, I must confess," replied the carpenter, "but what reason have you to put such a strange question?"

Jack Sheppard hesitated.

"Come!" cried Wood, "I'll not harm you, if the truth be told. What made you speak of this notorious man?"

"Because," added Jack, with a downcast gaze, "I think he must have been the one I saw with Blueskin the other night, drinking at the Magpie. He gave me this lump of wax, and promised me a guinea if I would press it against the locks of your strong box and bring him the impression."

"Why zounds," returned Wood, with some emotion, "did you mean to rob your old master, Jack?"

"I was so confused, sir, with the offer he made," stammered the boy in reply, "that I scarce knew what I did, but now I see my error, and wish to confess it, if you will forgive me."

"Well, you have been trembling on the verge of a dangerous precipice, Jack, and if this man had once got you in his clutches, I can see very well he would not have scrupled to bring you to the gallows, so that his own bad ends were answered. But it is a good horse that never stumbles, and as this is the first, as I hope it will be the last, error you will commit, I promise you not to say anything more about it. As for this thief-trapper, who would have led you into a sin, from which there is no escape, I will hereafter take occasion to repay him as he deserves, and in the meantime remember, Jack, that an "idle brain is the devil's workshop," for if you had been paying attention to the trade, that will be the means hereafter of getting you a livelihood, there would have been no time left for mixing in such bad company as this."

"You shall have no cause, master, to complain of me again," sobbed the apprentice, now beginning to see the full force of the carpenter's reproaches.

"Well, time will show," doubtfully returned Wood, "but there—throw that wax into the fire, give up going to the Magpie, and now tell me why you have not finished that packing-case for Lord Orford! It must go to his house to-night."

"I'll get it done in another hour," exclaimed Jack, seizing his tools and working away with alacrity—"I did not think you would come back so soon, or I should have got it done long ago."

"Ah! a good will makes work light," muttered the carpenter as he left the room,—"but keep your word this time, get it done, and I'll forgive you the idleness of the morning."

"Leave that to me, and there shall be no fault-finding now I promise ye," returned the apprentice joyfully, as he watched the retiring figure of his employer. And he applied himself to the execution of his task with a combination of energy and skill for which none would have given him credit who had contemplated his previous indolence.

Punctual to the time appointed, Jack finished his labours, and under the direction of the carpenter prepared to set out on his way to the mansion of Lord Orford, situated in what was then open country, the site of that nobleman's residence being the grounds at the back of the Broadway in Westminster.

Threading his way through the Strand and crossing the marshy tract that then extended from the Palace of Whitehall to the other side of Westminster Abbey, Jack proceeded with his burden on his shoulder, to the old Gate House that gave entrance into Tothill Street, and which not being demolished till 1777, was then an handsome structure used as a prison for state offenders, as well as for felons and debtors. The former were brought there through Thieving Lane and Union Street, to prevent the possibility of a culprit's escape by entering the hallowed liberties of the sanctuary.

At this time it must be remembered there were only a few detached villas and cottages between Buckingham House and the Thames. The market, called Westminster Market was a large open place in King Street, and had numerous stalls and shops, but all around it was the suburb, wherein most of the nobility of the period had taken up their abode. It was here that the sombre, dull-looking mansion of Lord Orford was built, and leaving our hero to deposit the packing case which he had brought, we must now return to the old house in Wych Street where events were in progress with which it is necessary for the reader to be acquainted.

CHAPTER II.

THE SUPPER AT MR. WOOD'S.

"Such a deal of wonder has broken out within this hour, that ballad-makers cannot be able to express it."—WINTER'S TALE.

WHEN the carpenter returned to the other portion of the house used for his private dwelling, he found the buxom partner of his joys in a state of unusual flurry and excitement consequent on the expected arrival of a certain Mr Kneebone, a woollen draper of considerable mercantile renown, and of unquestionable Jacobite principles. Mrs. Wood, who was a fine woman of the "fat, fair and forty," description of beauty, had set off her comely attractions with a dress on which more than ordinary attention had been bestowed. The ample proportions of her figure were displayed by a flowing range of drapery that together with a sparkling stomacher and a profusion of black patches, set, as was customary then, with considerable art on the less conspicuous part of her features to set off the remainder—formed a galaxy of attractions which, though the carpenter took pride in beholding, gave him serious uneasiness as to their effects. Nor indeed, if popular rumour was to be credited, was he without cause in thus suspecting their intention, for the gossips of the neighbourhood had long since attributed the frequent visits of the draper to the house, more to attractions belonging to the carpenter's wife, than to the carpenter himself. However, be this as it may, before the carpenter could expostulate with his superior moiety on the needless display of her present apparel, the gallant draper of the Angel, in St. Clements, made his appearance. He did not on this occasion, come, as was his wont, by himself, but begged to introduce two most particular friends of his—travellers, as he alleged, for a large wholesale house in the linen-trade—and whom he now severally ushered in as Mr. Jeremy Jenkins, and Mr. Timotheus Tomkins.

These remarkable personages were dressed exactly alike, and strange to say their natural defects seemed to have been similar also, for each wore a huge black patch over their left eye, and had a corresponding obliquity of mouth that would have answered admirably the purposes of disguise, had such been their object. Not at all abashed by the coolness of their reception, they at once proceeded to make themselves at home, in the most frank and careless manner imaginable, and when Mr. Wood offered refreshments to his guests, the proposal was accepted with a delight that strongly imbued his wife with a belief that her newly-acquired acquaintances were more characterised by want of refinement than want of appetite.

"Dear me," exclaimed Mrs. Wood, as she took advantage of the first opportunity to draw Mr. Kneebone on one side, "how could you bring these creatures with you, on such an occasion as this too."

"Couldn't help it, my life," whispered the woollen-draper in return, and ardently squeezing her hand, at the same time. "You little know who they are."

"Eh? you give me some uneasiness, Mr. Kneebone!" replied the fair intriguer.

"What if they are foreign nobleman in disguise, come to distribute funds for the good cause?"

"Lor!" ejaculated Mrs. Wood in astonishment; "and I have treated them so rudely too."

"I met them by chance this afternoon," pursued the draper, "and they told me they were only waiting the lucky moment to strike."

"I see! then the Chevalier is really determined at last to make a desperate effort to obtain his rights!"

"Unquestionably!" and we, like Jacobites staunch and true, Mrs. Wood, will then —"

The conversation was here interrupted by a hearty and prolonged peal of laughter from the two visitors who had been earnestly intent on Mr. Wood's recital of his adventures in the Mint, ten years ago. This, to confess the truth, was always the stock story with which he endeavoured to entertain every guest, and told with considerable embellishment of detail, was a theme on which it was his pride to dwell.

"Ha! ha! ha!" roared Jenkins, unable to restrain his mirth, "and so they actually found you in the Mint, eh?"

"Ho! ho! ho!" chimed in Tomkins, who imitated every accent as well as action of his companion, "What a very adventurous idea!"

"It is a fact, gentlemen, indeed!" rejoined the carpenter, "but excuse me if I say that whenever I have told the story before I have invariably had sympathy and not laughter."

This remonstrance only served to increase the hilarity that prevailed, and the supposed foreign noblemen in disguise, exchanged such significant glances with each other, that at last the carpenter was fairly compelled to cease frowning, and begin, for the sake of sociality, to show some symptoms of returning good humour.

Soon after, supper was announced, a very substantial, if not elegant repast, consisting chiefly of such extemporaneous dishes as Mrs. Wood's larder would afford, and with these the foreign nobleman in particular made sad havoc. Such annihilation of steaks and terrific onslaughts upon pies, were never witnessed before in the carpenter's domicile; and Mr. Tomkins, entered so freely into an appreciation of his host's good cheer, that dish and bottle no sooner came before him than they were returned empty, with a solicitation for more. Thus wore on the evening merrily, and when the fragrant weed of Virginia and Trinidado came upon the board, in juxta position with a reeking bowl of hot punch, prepared under the superintendence of the carpenter himself, the merriment became so uproarious, that had Messrs. Jenkins and Tomkins been travellers in the wholesale way for fun and facetiousness of every description, they could not have displayed their samples with greater readiness or more efficacy.

"Come!" cried Jenkins, "I will give you a toast: Here's to the health of our future monarch, King James III., and the deuce take his enemies."

"Flat treason and profanity, as I live," interrupted Wood, refusing to drain his tankard, "mine shall be on the contrary: Success to King George I. and the deuce take *his* enemies."

"Owen!" remonstrated his wife, "have you forgotten the respect due to your guests?"

"I own allegiance to but one king," cried the carpenter resolutely, "and to him alone will I pay it!"

"Well! I quarrel with no man's opinions," observed the draper, "but I confess myself to be an adherent of the good cause—an upholder of the real claimant to England's crown!"

"To be sure!" ejaculated Tomkins, "I like to see everybody stick up for their rights. But there—don't let's have any squabbling about it, we'll drink one king's health after the other, and that can give offence to nobody," and as the speaker gave vent to this very patriotic ebullition, the bumper placed before him disappeared at a draught, and the one he replenished immediately afterwards was disposed of with similar rapidity.

The laughter with which this proposal was received speedily restored the equanimity of all present, and the conversation took a general turn.

"You have an apprentice here, I believe," observed Jenkins, winking at the same time to his companion, to restrain his bibulous propensities—"one John Sheppard,—the son of a poor woman, who lived once in the Mint!"

"Aye!" returned the carpenter, "it was to her I was paying a friendly visit on the night of the great storm, when the adventures occurred, which I was relating to you before. He is a clever, sharp lad enough, but I wish I could say as much for his industry—."

"There is some mystery about his birth and parentage, I think," continued the other; "his mother, though now in very humble circumstances, was once the associate of those moving in a higher sphere."

"Ah!" sighed Wood, "she has seen some reverses of fortune, poor soul; her son I took into my employ for those reasons, and having a little cottage of mine to let, at Willesden, I have given her leave to reside there, until a tenant is found; which," added the good-natured artizan, "shall never be during her life-time, if I can avoid it."

"But her husband," pursued the questioner, "have you not gleaned any tidings of where he is, or what he was?"

"None!" returned Wood, "but I would give a trifle to possess the information."

"Well, then settle the terms in your own mind, and I will undertake to bring those here that can tell you both."

"You seem to be strangely acquainted with this history," replied the carpenter, looking on his guest with astonishment, "and excuse me, if I add, that your voice now appears to be familiar to me. I heard a similar voice in the Mint once, belonging to ——"

"Whom!" earnestly inquired the visitor.

"Jonathan Wild!"

The brow of the querist darkened, as he heard the name, and he endeavoured to laugh away the impression, but instead of being able to remove the carpenter's suspicions, his laugh only confirmed them.

"Stay, sir, this must be inquired into," cried Wood, with a determined tone—"the mystery you have thought proper to assume, must be cleared up before I can suffer you to depart."

"Ho! ho! then it is the hour," exclaimed Jenkins, arousing his companion, who had apparently been overcome by the spirit some time previously.

"For what!" mumbled the other, shaking himself into wakefulness.

"The capture," returned Jenkins, drawing a pistol from beneath his coat as he spoke.

"Ready," answered Tomkins, rising from his seat, and producing a similar weapon.

"In heaven's name! what is the meaning of all this, gentlemen?" cried Mr. Kneebone, alarmed by the disturbance, and suddenly breaking off an interesting conversation with Mrs. Wood, that he had been carrying on for some time, whilst the attention of the rest had been otherwise occupied.

"Aye, sir! what is all this to lead to?" inquired the host starting from his seat.

"Simply, sir, the apprehension of a rebel," sternly rejoined the supposed Jacobite; "Mr. Kneebone, if you please, we are waiting for your company."

"But really—a-hem—my good friends—" stammered the draper.

"No trifling, sirrah, now," thundered Jenkins, "you must away with us at once—here is a warrant from the Secretary of State, for your apprehension!"

"What, by one of our own party! one who has come here to join in aiding the cause of the Chevalier!"

"No! By one who has come here only

to trap you into a confession before a witness, of your being a traitor to the cause of your king, and an agent in the treason of the Pretender."

A general dismay pervaded the assembly.

"Confusion!" muttered the draper, "that I should have been fool enough to be entrapped by such a wretched plot."

"Who, then, are you?" cried Wood, seriously alarmed for the credit of his own house, at the turn that affairs had taken.

"Further disguise is needless," answered the other, throwing off wig and patch, "your suspicions are correct, I *am* Jonathan Wild!"

"I thought as much," groaned the carpenter.

"Come, on with the ruffles, if he won't go quietly, Blueskin," vociferated Wild to his companion, as he saw some preparations made for a resistance.

"Oh! my dear Mr. Kneebone, is this your foreign nobility?" reproached Mrs. Wood.

"Come, sir, are we to have bloodshed in this experiment or not?" resolutely demanded Wild, as he presented a pistol at the head of his prisoner.

"Stop!" interrupted the carpenter, urged thereto by the alternate threats and entreaties of his wife, "you have chosen to violate the laws of hospitality as well as of common justice by your appearance here under a false pretext, but I cannot suffer an invited guest of mine to be thus treated, without, at least, protesting against this spy system. As a constable of this parish," continued Wood, coolly taking down his official staff, and stepping before the door to prevent egress, "I arrest you Jonathan Wild, and your confederate Blueskin, alias Joseph Blake, on a charge of attempted felony."

"A very ingenious artifice," retorted Jonathan, "but one, that this time at least, will not answer the end you have in view. Besides, what proof have you to adduce of the truth of such a charge, in the event of it being brought before a magistrate?"

"The best!" answered Wood—"do you remember giving some wax to a certain person for a certain purpose, or shall I refresh your memories by entering into particulars."

Wild was both astounded and irresolute.

"Let your prisoner free," continued the carpenter, taking advantage of the impression he had made, "or I open the window and obtain assistance from without for your immediate caption."

"One moment if you please," said Jonathan, not caring to push matters to extremities, and advancing slowly to Wood as he spoke—"I possess the information you require respecting the birth of your apprentice, and can render both him and you essential service if I am allowed to pursue this affair unmolested. On the contrary, attempt to thwart and hinder me in this project, and I can whisper a hint of that boy's existence in a certain quarter which would make his life not worth a week's purchase."

"Come! why don't you arrest him," shrieked Mrs. Wood tenderly detaining Mr. Kneebone, from the rough grasp of Blueskin.

"You have your choice of terms," coolly observed Wild, as he saw the carpenter wavering in his determination.

"Enough!" I am decided!" returned the carpenter, after a moment's pause. "Release your prisoner!"

"Very well, sir!" slowly uttered Wild in measured accents; "very well, sir, you have heard my determination. Blueskin, let him go, and follow me. We shall have another opportunity never fear, before long; as for the boy," he continued in a low voice to Wood, as he passed, "*to-night will be his first peril.*"

And as the words were uttered, as impressively as the hoarse guttural voice of Jonathan could convey them, the speaker replaced the pistol in his vest, and strode out of the apartment.

"Vell," cried Blueskin, following the example of his leader, "I suppose Mister Jonathan knows the caper he is a vorking for, but I'm blest if I vould have let a chance like this slip so easy. Here you old fogey," he continued, addressing Wood, and tossing a bundle of papers to him, "read these, and then let that woolly-headed monkey there try the soft soap business vith your vife arterwards if you like!" and with this elegant observation Blueskin vanished.

"'Sdeath! the rascal must have stolen those letters from my pocket," cried Kneebone in confusion, to the lady; "What's to be done?"

"I must brazen it out, you scapegrace, that's all," returned Mrs. Wood, observing her husband earnestly perusing their contents, "how could you be so careless?"

"Why, Dolly, all these are in your handwriting," ejaculated the carpenter in astonishment, "and have a superscription to Mr. Kneebone? What *is* the meaning of all this? My mind misgives me."

"Forgeries! wicked forgeries all—of those designing men," returned his wife with impurtable assurance, and in her most tender accents. "Oh! Owen, how could you think for one moment they were otherwise. But I see how it is, I shall have to go into hysterics!"

And, as if determined to keep her word, Mrs. Wood, immediately fainted away, after having taken the precaution to summon her servant, and was removed to her own room, alternately shrieking and laughing violently.

In the confusion that now prevailed, the woollen-draper was glad to make his own escape good, and he departed accordingly, without venturing to add a word of explanation.

"Ah! fool, fool that I was!" ejaculated the carpenter, burying his face in his hands, and groaning audibly, at the treachery he had discovered in his own family. "Why, *why* did I marry for beauty! I should have remembered beauty like a scar is only skin deep, and makes many a heart ache."

CHAPTER III.

THE FIRST ESCAPE OF JACK SHEPPARD.

"'Upon my word, friend,' said I, 'You have almost made me long to try what sort of robber I should make!' 'There's great art in it if you did,' quoth he. 'Ah! but there's a great deal more in being hanged,' said I.'"—*Life of Gazman d'Alfarache, the celebrated Spanish Bandit.*

The rapidly increasing strength of the Jacobite party, gave rise at this period to the most wild and sanguine hopes of success among the Pretender's adherents in London, and of these, from the power and influence he enjoyed, Lord Orford was fairly entitled to rank as one of the principal. For some time past, also, great activity had prevailed among the government officials, under the direction of Mr. Walpole and his secret committee, in order to counteract this influence, and as spies were everywhere retained to forward information and collect intelligence of fresh conspiracies, Jonathan Wild, at at early part of the proceedings, was about the first to offer those services, which were accepted with alacrity.

Day after day did this zealous, but unscrupulous agent of the reigning powers, display fresh evidence of his qualifications for the task he had undertaken,—and the success with which his endeavours had been attended, was manifested in sundry weighty considerations that only served to increase his desire to obtain fresh victims. It was thus that he had endeavoured to entrap the plotting woollen-draper, Mr. Kneebone, into a confession of his guilt, and having failed in that quarter, from events occurring which he had not anticipated, he was now desirous of making up for one mischance by a more bold and energetic attempt to capture one of far greater importance to the state, and it was chiefly with a view to this project, that after leaving the carpenter's, he bent his footsteps in the same direction as the carpenter's apprentice had taken about two hours previously. Having thus taken up the thread of our narrative at that point where it is necessary for the reader to be acquainted with the events that had preceded the boy's arrival at the gate, we now return to the adventures of our young hero himself, who little dreamed that he had had a follower in his path.

It was now getting dusk, but by the faint twilight that lingered in the sky, Jack could see that the mansion was overshadowed with gigantic trees that increased the venerable aspect of the place. Ivy and innumerable creepers covered one side of the house, and long weeds cumbered the deserted road. On one side rose a square narrow turret surmounted by a gilt dome and quaint weathercock, and on the other side of the bow window a huge buttress projected its mass of shadow on the ground. Having in vain endeavoured to attract the notice of the domestics to the gate, Jack quietly undertook the office of porter for himself, and unfastening the latch, walked in; crossing the gravelled carriage way that swept in a curve round the lawn, he came at once under the turret tower, where from the sound of voices in earnest conversation, he judged the owner of the mansion and his guests were assembled. Depositing his burden on the ground, and being impelled thereto by a natural feeling of boyish curiosity, he determined to climb up the tree that grew against the building, and see what was proceeding in the interior. His agile body and nimble feet speedily placed him in a position to obtain his desired object. From the leafy concealment of one of the branches, he found that he could easily view the room in which the earnest converse was being carried on, and being himself sheltered by the increasing gloom of the evening, and having his view illumined by the introduction of lights from within, he was under no fear of his hiding place being discovered, whilst he could penetrate the most remote recesses of the apartment with ease.

When he first gazed into the room, the crowd of domestics was so great, as to prevent his at once recognizing the chief personages present, or the purpose for which they had assembled, but bringing his ear closer to the window, Jack heard a peremptorily order given to them to leave the room, and then saw that a lady, evidently an invalid, was reclining, in the last stage of debility, upon a couch, and that at her side was a personage evidently the proprietor of the mansion, and her relative, as appeared from the likeness between them. The latter was a tall, slim man of mature age and of dark gloomy features, that seemed to manifest the mingled feelings of sorrow and remorse. As he bent over the thin emaciated figure of the invalid, a transient gleam of sympathy appeared to soften the proud and revengeful expression of his visage, but it was immediately succeeded by a sterner and more savage glance as he addressed her.

"Well, Lady Stafford," he exclaimed, "now that the servants have quitted the room, in accordance with your decision, do I know your fixed determination?"

"You have heard my final answer, brother," feebly uttered the lady; "the funds you wished to possess, are yours, for the furtherance only of the cause in which we are embarked, but respecting the will I am still resolute, and refuse to alter it."

Lord Orford ground his teeth in anger at the firmness with which his requisition was rejected.

"In vain you attempt by threats to alter my fixed resolve," pursued the invalid; "my nephew, the child of that brother whom you have injured so deeply, if not destroyed so murderously—*he* shall inherit the whole of the remaining property that is at my disposal."

"How know you that he still lives? I told you that his father on the night of the great storm, perished on the Thames!"

"But his son—"

"Did not survive that night," answered the nobleman.

"Then Heaven pardon you the murder of both," ejaculated the dying woman, clasping her thin attenuated fingers together.

"Will you make a codicil in my favour *now?*" demanded Orford with a savage glance at his sister whom he had held violently by the hand during this last appeal. He waited vainly for an answer. The grasp became relaxed and the hand grew cold, and as he continued to look with blended rage and awe upon the fearful change that was going on, he found that the last chance had departed with the ebbing life of his sister.

Lady Stafford was dead. She had died of a broken heart. For a short time Lord Orford stood rooted to the spot as if transfixed, and from his pale cheek and quivering lip seemed to have been terrified into a repentance of his crime. Such short-lived regret, however, soon gave way to a consciousness of the necessity there was for immediate action, and summoning his domestics, he hastily and with some emotion, acquainted them with his sister's decease. The rapid entrance of a number of servants both prevented Jack from seeing or hearing anything further, but strangely interested in the scene he had witnessed, he felt unwilling to quit the spot until the body was removed under the direction of a medical attendant who had been waiting with the rest in an adjoining room during the interview that had thus sadly terminated.

The apprentice now fearful of detection from the increased bustle about the mansion, slowly descended the tree and regained the ground. He had scarcely done so before the quick tread of a messenger past him, compelled Jack to take refuge on a flight of steps at the back that seemingly led into the interior of the house. Afraid of his presence in that portion of the grounds being discovered, he hastily ascended these and found himself in a lobby of considerable length, the door leading to which had been left open by the person who had just crossed his path.

Forgetting almost the purpose that had brought him thither, in a train of thought engendered by the harrowing scene he had encountered, Jack Sheppard threaded the passage to its extremity, guided by a faint light that appeared at the end, and turning shortly off into a chamber with which it communicated proceeded through the folding doors into an apartment of considerably larger dimensions.

Here he paused to breathe awhile and reflect on the manner in which he should acquaint the servants with his mission.

Jack was now within the library, a large room about fifty feet in length, and proportionably wide. It was somewhat dark, for the light only came in from one large window, and the book-cases too were of dark oak, and whilst the gilding about them had been much discolored by time. The ceiling elaborately covered and carved with grotesque images, preserved its gothic character, and at each end of the room was a fireplace with a huge chimney-piece of oak, in one of which some half-burnt logs seemed to indicate the recent occupation of the apartment. By the faint light that gleamed from the smouldering embers, Jack saw on a long table that occupied the centre of the room, a miniature set in diamonds, that sparkled in the faint gloom with a radiance that immediately arrested his attention.

Impelled by an impulse for which he could scarcely account, to examine the portrait nearer, the apprentice removed it from the table, and was earnestly engaged in its examination by the light of the fire, when the sudden entrance of the servants into the room, startled him from the reverie into which he had unconsciously fallen.

"Help! here! thieves! robbers, "cried the foremost, lifting up the lamp he bore, in great trepidation, as he detected Jack standing bewildered with the miniature in his hand. The rest in amazement drew back for an instant, but seeing that the formidable depredator they had to contend with, was only a stripling of fourteen, they gathered courage and seized him by the shoulder, shaking him vigorously.

"I only came to deliver a packing-case here, from Mr. Wood of Wych Street," cried Jack, looking with surprize on the individual who had first brought such a charge against him.

"You must tell that story to his lordship" returned the other incredulously—"Away with him to the hall—we can have no explanations here, young housebreaker.—Away with him!"

And thus vociferating, Jack was borne away to another part of the mansion, without being able to do more than continue his remonstrances and repeat assurances of his innocence.

Whilst Jack had thus been involved in a charge which was likely to prove of serious consequences, a stranger had been announced to Lord Orford, who declared his busines to be such as did not admit of any delay.

Believing him to be a messenger from Scotland, with important tidings of the Pretender's movements the nobleman did not hesitate to give orders for his immediate admission, notwithstanding the family calamity that had just occurred within his walls, and the servant speedily returned with——Jonathan Wild.

"Your business?" inquired the nobleman sternly as he found he was deceived in the character of his visitor.

"To serve you if you will let me," returned the new-comer, "if not to serve myself."

"Those features are familiar to me," cried Orford, as he cast a penetrating glance towards the visitor—"We have surely met somewhere before, though how or when has escaped my recollection," and he mused thoughtfully as he spoke.

"You have a good memory, my lord," answered Jonathan. "We *have* met before —ten years ago in the Mint at Southwark."

"Ha!" exclaimed Orford, grasping his sword involuntarily, "Your name?"

"Concealment of it is not one of my present objects," rejoined the other with provoking calmness, "My name is Wild—Jonathan Wild!" and he chuckled triumphantly at the effect it produced.

"You are a bold man to venture hither," remarked Lord Orford, "a very bold man to come alone into the presence of one who is acquainted with the services you have rendered to government as a spy, and one for whom———"

"I have a secretary of state's warrant in my pocket," interrupted Jonathan with a grin. "But I am too expert a marksman to miss my aim in these matters. In the first place I am very well able to defend myself, and in the second if any harm be done me here I have lodged instructions with a certain party, who in the event of my not returning by a certain time, will make the title, head, and estates of Lord Orford, the immediate property of the crown. You see that I have not come unprepared."

"Hum!" hesitated the peer, revolving what he had just heard in his mind, and looking with rage and astonishment on the coolness with which Wild was assisting himself to a glass of wine from the table before him, whilst he awaited the issue of the pause that had ensued. "What then is your present object in coming to me?"

"Money and revenge," answered Jonathan "two things which I value more than all the world beside. I can assist you on certain terms in an affair as important to your life as to your estate. Grant me those terms and my services are yours."

"You speak in riddles, sir," returned Lord Orford haughtily. "I know of nothing so eventful as that to which you refer?"

"Indeed!" smiled Jonathan incredulously; "Well! perhaps you are right not to be too communicative at first, but there is no power you possess of disguising affairs from me, and no necessity for so doing if you could. In as few words as possible then, you have a nephew whom it would be to your interest to see put out of the way."

Lord Orford stung to the quick started from his seat.

"Nay, my lord, retain your composure, or "I cannot go on," pursued Jonathan quickly. "You give me one thousand pounds for the trouble, and I will not only bring you where he is, but also undertake to prevent his ever troubling you again."

"I cannot—dare not injure him," rejoined Orford, catching at a chair for support, "too much blood has already been shed in this matter." "Nay, then I must produce the warrant," laughed Jonathan scornfully.

"Hold, sir, I consent, but let me have assurance that I am fairly dealt with in this affair, urged the nobleman."

Wild was about to reply, when Harris the butler entered and whispered hastily to his master,

"Caught a boy secreted in the house for the purpose of robbing it!" exclaimed Lord Orford,—"this is better disposed of without my interference now, I am but ill-fitted to engage in business."

"He says, your Lordship," continued the butler aloud, "that he brought a packing-case here from Mr. Wood the carpenter in Wych Street."

Jonathan started at the fortunate coincidence that had thrown the boy in his power and was at first hardly able to conceal his delight and astonishment, but finding from the significant look given him by the peer that it was believed to be through his agency, he assured a triumphantly sagacious aspect and drawing Lord Orford on one side, exchanged a few words with him out of the butler's hearing.

"Enough!" said Jonathan, as he concluded the colloquy by retiring, "I am glad to find you have now faith in what I can do."

"Harris!" said Lord Orford to the domestic, "this gentleman is in my confidence, and I have deputed him to act for me in the examination of this precocious thief. You will receive his instructions as if they were my own."

The butler bowed in acquiescence with his master's orders.

"My house is in the Old Bailey, opposite Newgate, and next door to the Coopers' Arms," cried Wild, in an undertone, as he quitted the room with the butler; "short accounts form my way of doing business, my lord, so when the thousand is convenient—"

Orford bent his head in assent, and casting an expressive glance at the nobleman, Jonathan followed by the domestic strode out of the apartment.

"That man," ejaculated the Peer, as soon as he found himself freed from the presence of one he so much dreaded, "is as savage as an Italian bravo, for, sparing neither friends nor enemies, he exhibits neither fear nor remorse."

The immediate proceedings of Wild may be easily anticipated. The ceremony of a mock examination was gone through, for Jonathan would not listen to, or believe a word that Jack uttered in explanation, and having sternly refused all the boy's entreaties to acquaint Mr. Wood with the unexpected position in which he was placed, he gave him into the hands of his janisaries to be conveyed to St. Giles's round-house.

The building thus denominated was an old structure that stood in a corner of Kendrick Yard close to the outer railings of St. Giles's Church. In shape it was not dissimilar to a huge barrel set up on its end, and the likeness became more striking from the circumstance of the only mode of ingress or egress being a circular aperture like a capacious bunghole, which formed a conspicuous feature in its architectural arrangements. Being at some distance from the ground, as the prison was two stories high, it was essential to form a communication with the door by a flight of wooden steps and this imparted to the building a singularly strange and windmill-like appearance. At the summit, over a very strong iron roof, was an old-fashioned gilt vane shaped like one of those enormous keys occasionally brought on in pantomimes, and the windows which were of small dimensions and very strongly guarded, looked out on one side into Kendrick Yard and on the other into the burial ground of St. Giles's Church.

At the sight of this odd-looking prison, Jack, who with the elasticity of youth had ceased for some time to shed those copious floods of tears in which at first he had indulged could here hardly repress a scream of loud laughter, and conscious of the real injustice of his committal, determined to make the time within, pass as pleasantly as he could.

"Now then young pepperbox," cried Lockit the gaoler, who had the control of the prison, "I wish you'd move a little more nimble out of that coach."

"With all my heart," cried Jack, gaily, leaping out of the chariot in which he had been brought and running up the wooden steps of his own accord, "I've never seen the build of a box like this before, and I'm rather curious to know how they're made, in case I turn prison-builder to his Majesty."

"Ha! you're three feet and a half of iniquity, *you* are, I can see *that* with half an eye," observed Lockit, laying considerable emphasis on the pronouns, and ushering as he spoke, Bowyer and Abrahams, Wild's two janisaries, into the little room he occupied. "You are a nice article to teach his Gracious Majesty how to build prisons, I don't think!"

"But *I* do," cried Jack rather pleased than otherwise with the novelty of the adventure, and determined to show his spirits were not affected by the change. "I think I could give his Majesty a useful hint or two, for I know the prison isn't built yet that could hold *me*."

"We shall see that, young Brimstone," returned Lockit, "if yer can get out of the crib I'll stow yer in, I'll give yer a pension for life and teach yer old Parr's secret into the bargain."

"Lead the way then, St. Giles, and mind I don't come to claim it—that's all!" said Jack, assuming the utmost nonchalance; "I mean to take these very airy and most commodious apartments for a night or two, and as you neither ask for rent nor reference, I won't be very particular about the accommodation."

Thus bantering the jailor, Jack Sheppard was handcuffed and conducted into the inner cell or stronghold, apportioned to such prisoners in the roundhouse as were likely to prove refractory, and which, from its strength and the quantity of massive iron-work that supported the roof, was well calculated to justify its appellation. As Lockit passed the two attendants that Wild had in his pay, Jack took advantage of the rapid but earnest colloquy that ensued between them, to secrete a file that his quick eye detected on the ground, and this he thrust into his vest to be used as circumstances might require. The few words that were exchanged between them escaped Jack's ear, but the way in which they were uttered was sufficient to convince him that mischief was intended, though from what source he was rather puzzled to surmise. As Bowyer and Abrahams quitted the room, a glance of significant import bestowed upon the janitor confirmed his suspicions and he inwardly resolved to lose no opportunity of making his escape at once sure and speedy.

Lulling the unsuspicious Lockit into a belief that he neither wished nor cared to change his quarters, the door was trebly locked and bolted upon him, and Jack found himself by the feeble light of an oil lamp that streamed through the window from the opposite side of the way, in a confined but compact chamber, built of stone, and only admitting the necessary properties of light and air through a small aperture, which, defended by triple bars of iron served the purpose of a windowed grating.

He had not been there more than a few moments writhing under the pressure of the galling gyves that Lockit had placed round his wrists, than he began to look about him to see what prospect there was of gaining an outlet. The cell was narrow but exceedingly lofty, and chiefly strengthened by iron braces that were driven as supporters into the corners of the ceiling. The wall which formed the exterior of the roundhouse, was composed of stone and flint strongly cemented together, and contributed to increase its outward resemblance to one of those old Martello towers that watering-place visitors are familiar with as the defences of our southern coast. It was in this wall that the window was situated glazed with horn, for glass was at this period a luxury beyond the reach of prison accommodations, and as night had now far advanced, it was only by the flickering illumination of a street lamp beyond, that our hero was made aware of its existence. Well aware that the guardian of the roundhouse was in the adjoining apartment, he at once saw the necessity of drowning any attempt he might make to recover his freedom in such a burst of assumed hilarity as might impress the other with a belief that he was merely exerting his vocal powers without any reference to an object to be gained by the employment of them. Jack, therefore, had no sooner tested the width and strength of the window, with a view to ulterior proceedings, than he gave vent to a chaunt of such uproarious character that the first effect it produced was as Jack desired, to bring the jailor down to the door of his cell with a remonstrance.

"Come, young saucebox," exclaimed an angry voice from the outside, "I wish you would let your tongue rattle less and allow me to have a snooze."

"I'm only practising a song for the occasion," said Jack, continuing his vociferations more lustily than before, and which, though deadened by the thickness of the separating wall were not only sufficient to conceal any noise that he might make, but also calculated to render the gaoler's slumbers uneasy.

"I must try another stave," and he broke forth thus:—

"The clouds rob the sea and its moisture will drain,
And the earth robs the clouds of their booty in rain,
Whilst the plants rob the earth of its treasures again,
Sing Lillibulero, luddi,
Luddi, fuddi, heigho!"

"Ah! you'll sing on the other side your mouth to-morrow," interrupted Lockit through the keyhole.

"That's as may be," said Jack to himself, making earnest endeavours to slip his hands through the manacles, and working them against the file that he held tightly between his knees, as he continued—

"The moon robs the sun of its heat and its light,
The earth robs the moon which of course serves it right,
And mankind rob the earth such a prig to requite,
Sing Lillibulero, luddi,
Luddi, fuddi, heigho!"

"Only wait till Mr. Jonathan Wild arrives, and he'll put out your pipe, my fine fellow!" shouted the gaoler.

"He must catch me first," thought Jack, and he worked away still harder, singing all the time.

"Death robs us of life in a queer sort of way,
And the grave will rob life of its troubles they say,
But the worms in return rob the grave of its prey,
And sing Lillibulero, luddi,
Luddi, fuddi, heigho!"

"Nearly off, by gosh," cried Jack; "another effort and then—

'This I think is enough, angry feelings to smother.
Since here I have proved without any more bother,
That all through existence we rob one another.
With Lillibulero, luddi,
Luddi, fuddi, heigho!'"

The irons upon Jack's wrists were coupled together with two long and thick links, which gave him much use of his hands, although they greatly impeded the progress of his labours, and these, as we have said, were the first objects of his attack. Quickly he drew across the end of these links the keen file that he had possessed himself of, and pausing every now and then in his work to listen if the grating noise caused any attention within, he severed them, but not before the perspiration upon his brow began to trickle down in globes about his cheeks. As this last triumphant feat was achieved, he shouted out the burden of his song with increased energy, and, as with a throb of pleasure he saw them fall apart, he began with renewed energy to file asunder each of the thick-locked clasps from his fretted wrists.

It was a fortunate circumstance for him at this crisis, that the moon, which was now rising brilliantly and without a cloud to dim her lustre, flung a bright ray through the grating of the stronghold in which he was immured. This afforded sufficient light to enable him to keep cutting in the same spot, and though the keep file slipped occasionally with the weight and vigour of his nerved hand, and inflicted many a flesh wound in so doing, yet the experience taught him by the carpenter's craft came in good stead and he maintained his purpose steadily. At last he had the satisfaction of hearing one of the clasps fall clanking to the ground with a startling sound, and working afresh with the freed and unburdened hand, he had not many minutes to wait before the other snapped from his wrist.

Elated with his success, Jack roared out the chorus more lustily than before, and stretching out his arms as if to assure himself that he really was free from all restraint, took two or three strides with the air of a conqueror across the chamber.

Having regained his breath, which had been nearly exhausted in this last achievement of vocalism, he listened at the door to hear if his noisy operations had attracted any attention, and was gratified to find from the stillness which prevailed, that Lockit, unable to quell the disturbance raised by his prisoner, had retired to another part of the building, confident in his security and anxious only to escape from the din which he had inwardly resolved to punish on the arrival of Jonathan Wild.

"All right, I find!" said Jack, communing to himself and glancing thoughtfully at the grated window as if determining what course to take. "That I think is the only chance I have got, and yet the window is so confounded high, that for a stripling like me to attempt to reach the bars in order to cut them through, is but a wild scheme, enough!"

He eagerly felt round the walls of the cell to see if he could obtain the means of climbing to the grating some ten feet above his head, but there was nothing—not even the chance projection of a stone.

"If a could but jump high enough even to fix myself with the clutch of a little finger to a single bar, I would soon manage the rest," thought Jack, as he measured the intervening distance with his eye, but the first vigorous spring he took convinced him that all endeavours to gain the window would be ineffectual by those means, for it was even then several feet beyond his grasp. He was almost tempted to stay where he was and abandon the enterpraise in despair.

At last, as reflection came to his aid, he began to think of an expedient which might enable him to attain the desired height. "I have it," cried jack, "and I shall baffle them all yet." Thus resolved and reassured, he commenced digging the wall with the point of his file, some few feet from the floor and immediately under the window which he had before given up all hope of gaining. A few vigorous and well-directed thrusts, and though the stones were old and indurated by time, Jack soon felt by the indentation which his sense of touch discovered, that he was making a slow but certain progress. The sparks flew from the steel and clicked against the gray, age-worn flints as if in mockery at his efforts, but still Jack felt an internal consciousness of success. As he dealt every blow with a cautious hand, he turned a quick ear to listen if his proceedings were overheard, but finding no interruption, he persevered in his purpose with a manifestation of strength and energy which in a youth of his early years seemed almost incredible.

The reward of his exertions at last began to be made apparent. A hole, sufficiently capacious to admit a hand or the extremity of a foot, was dug out of the wall, and encouraged by this, Jack zealously set to work and formed another about two feet higher to the right. Thus progressing, and using each successive aperture as the step of a ladder for his ascent, Jack was enabled to get within reach of the grating, and grasping a bar firmly with his left hand, he swung in the air whilst he used the file in the right. There were three bars to be thus removed, and changing hands as often as one got strained and cramped, Jack found the iron, rusty and neglected, yield to his file sooner than he anticipated, and as the teeth of the instrument became buried in the last, the bar snapped in twain with his weight and he fell heavily to the ground with the wrenched iron in his hand.

What, however, were a few bruises to him? Liberty was within his reach, and without pausing a moment to examine the extent of the injuries he had received from the fall, Jack sprang eagerly up the wall and dashed his hand through the horn window. The cool fresh air of a spring morning—for his work had cost him a few hours to accomplish—flowed in upon his heated brow, and he worked his slender body through the aperture with a feeling of triumph fluttering about his heart that was not the last he was destined to experience from the like cause. A gentle fall into the blind thoroughfare of Kendrick yard, a sudden bound to his feet, and a determination to gain the longest distance in the shortest time, rapidly succeeded, and off he sprang like a deer from the hounds, in what direction he cared not, so that he could contrive to elude pursuit, and avoid all risk of detection.

"Where is your prisoner?" exclaimed a stern voice immediaiely after Jack had cleared the window—"where is the boy I committed to your custody, Mr. Lockit?"

The voice belonged to Jonathan Wild, and as the gaoler unfastened the door which led to the cell, he summoned his janizaries to the threshold.

The door slowly revolved on its hinges, the works of Jack's handicraft strewed the ground and with mingled rage and astonishment they found their prisoner had escaped.

Jonathan clenched his teeth in all the desperation of anger as he exclaimed—

"I shall hold you responsible to his Majesty's government for this escape, Mr. Lockit. Call out your men and track him instantly, he cannot be far from here. If no time be lost we shall have him yet, quick!"

And this was the first escape of Jack Sheppard.

CHAPTER V.

THE FUGITIVE.

"What thoughts are his, while all in vain
His eye for aid explores the plain;
What thoughts, while with a dizzy ear,
He hears their clamour rising near;
Still for concealment doth he burn
And still to shun his peril turn."

WALTER SCOTT.

In order to make future events intelligible to the reader, he must be reminded that at the period of which we write, the now busy thoroughfare of Tottenham-Court-Road was little better than a narrow green lane, dotted here and there with cottages, and that all beyond the range of buildings by Fitzroy-Square and the streets leading therefrom, was open country. A bridle way traversed the green fields at the back of Oxford Street, then known as the Tyburn Road, and from here to Hampstead, the prospect was uninterrupted, if we except the occasional appearance of some straggling wooden habitations, grouped together for companionship and security, and which were afterwards destined to become the nucleus of those interminable lines of splendid shops and mansions that are now erected around the spot where they stood.

Into this narrow lane and across the deeply rutted bridle-way, Jack almost unconsciously struck directly he left the boundaries of the roundhouse. It was scarcely daybreak and no early risers appeared yet abroad, likely to intercept his path. Creeping as much as possible under the edge, so that one gazing down the road could hardly detect him among the overhanging branches that skirted the path, Jack sped on and did not dare to turn his head or slacken pace until he had gained a distance of about half a mile from the prison, the extremity of the bridle-road, and saw only an undulating expanse of pasture-land before him, with the thin gauzy mists of morning curling up like a fragrant stream from the meadows.

At the corner of this lane—which the present metropolitan denizen will properly localize if we tell him that he may identify it with

that spot where Great Portland Street now forms a junction with the New Road—there stood a small hostel, then the favourite resort as a tea-garden for parties from London, and even now perpetuating its former notoriety by a sign that sets forth the celebrity of its eel-pies at a cost which would enable four of them to be purchased for a penny.

Jack, who had tasted nothing since the preceding noon, and whose appetite was now sharpened by the unwonted exercise he had taken, wistfully eyed the projecting sign-board which announced the excellence and variety of the entertainment to be obtained within, and saw with delight the stable-boy who came out to detach the door-shutters, appear from the out-houses in the rear. Requesting the transfer of a draught of milk and a substantial slice of bread which the other produced, Jack gave him the few copper coins that he had in his pocket, and these the future ostler of the inn slipped into his own pocket with a gratified alacrity that showed he considered the exchange to have been one that resulted considerably in his favour.

Whilst he was thus resting on the stile and eagerly consuming the repast with which he had been provided, the sun had fairly flung his rays through the last curtain that night had left upon the earth, and the gladsome burst of the sunbeams now awoke all nature unto life and energy. It was a bright, laughing, spring morn, and music came from every twig and bough. Butterflies and bees sipped and sucked the early fresh-born flowers of the field. The violet, blue as the sky above it, faintly tinged the gale with its odoriferous breath, the pale primrose timidly peered from the hedge side, and the sparkling stream sent forth its song of joy as it went rippling and bounding over the pebbly shallows. The soaring lark trilled high his ringing notes and then stooping from his dizzy height dropped like an arrow to his mate in her grassy nest. Everything seemed rejoicing in the returning warmth of the season, and as our hero playfully scattered a few crumbs to the birds that hopped round him, he felt that influence come bland and cheering to his heart.

Suddenly a loud shout arose from behind him, and as Jack turned, he saw a party of men rushing swiftly onward to the spot where he sat. A glance sufficed to show him that he was the object of pursuit, and to leap from his seat and bound over the low hawthorn hedge before him was the work of a moment.

On he went, with the voices sounding in his rear, and amongst these the tones of Lockit, Bowyer, and Abrahams, were distinctly audible, calling upon the stable-boy who stood aghast at these proceedings to join in the chase and bring assistance with him. Jack had however got a tolerable start of his pursuers and he showed by the rapid speed of his running, that if strength of limb and lungs held out, he had an excellent chance of increasing the distance between himself and them.

A thick hedge and broad ditch that interrupted his progress for a moment, were crashed through and cleared, and Jack saw the sloping eminence of Primrose Hill rise before him. A woody country he knew lay on the other side, and to reach this was his immediate object, trusting to the seclusion of the spot and the intricacy of the tangled underwood there for his safety. The men behind him raised a furious shout as they saw him leap the ditch which they hoped would prove an efficient barrier, and away went Jack with the speed of light to the place he aimed at. Some labourers were coming to their work in an adjoining field, through which he intended to pass, and as he saw them evidently disturbed by the shout and watching with wondering looks his hasty movement, he turned off short to the left, intending to gain the wood by a circuitous route.

"Stop him!" roared Lockit, observing Jack's bewilderment, "stop the boy—he has escaped," and never had the gaoler's lungs been exercised more vigorously.

The labourers still remained quiescent resting on their implements of husbandry and gazing with an enquiring look upon each other.

"Stop the boy, I tell 'ee, he has escaped from the roundhouse!" vociferated Lockit, more impatiently than before as he came nearly up with them out of breath.

The men still seemed ignorant of what was required of them.

"I'll give you a couple of guineas to the man who first catches him," cried the gaoler pausing to make his words understood, and to regain time for breathing. The offer had the desired effect.

"Zounds!" exclaimed the foremost labourer throwing down his spade, "I don't mind making one for the fun of the thing," and off he started with a loud "whoop" joined by his fellows to assist the gaoler in re-taking the fugitive.

This conference had enabled Jack to gain considerably ahead of his pursuers, but the increasing daylight, and the repeated shouts had the effect of doubling the number of those engaged in the chase. Others, too, who were just awaking to another day of toil, sought to gain a temporary respite by uniting in the hue and cry that was raised, and the whole district being alarmed, Jack found his retreat cut off in nearly every direction.

At one time there appeared free and unbounded scope to his speed, and then as the din decreased in his rear, others swarmed in the path before him, and parties thronged to the right and to the left, and at last the whole neighbourhood seemed intent upon the capture of the carpenter's apprentice, and on the crowd went, gaining in numbers every instant, and making their discordant outcries echo far and wide.

Jack doubled and turned like some hard-pressed hare, and with as little knowledge where to run from the danger that threatened him. Still weary, faint, and oppressed with the torments of thirst, he strained every nerve to elude the fate that he knew awaited him if he suffered himself to be caught, and crashing through brake and briar, skimming over rail, fence and ditch, dashing through stream and swamp, away went Jack over hill and dale, with a determination at least not to be retaken without his last pulse failed to throb in his starting veins.

He had been compelled from the way in which his road had been cut off at various times to strike out across the country by the most unfrequented paths, and necessity had therefore compelled him to diverge several times from the direct route he had at first chosen. In this way he had traversed the open space that then stretched between Acton and Ealing, and having now gained the high grounds of Hanger Hill he bent his steps onward in the direction of Harrow. As he paused awhile on the summit of the hill to survey the stragglers that still pressed on in his rear, he had the satisfaction of finding that during the last mile he had improved his prospects materially. Several had dropped off exhausted by the run as they found the expedition was likely to lead them farther than they anticipated from the scene of their employment, and with the thoughts of return came many a lagging foot and a changed mind. The two janizaries, one of the labourers, and Lockit, were all that remained, and it was evident from their unsteady gait and bated breath that they were now getting heartily tired of the chase.

Seeing this, Jack nerved his courage for another desperate effort which he trusted would be the means of final safety and diving down the hill at an increased speed he bounded along into the coppice beneath and was making head for its outlet on the other side, when a treacherous pitfall covered with the shattered boughs and faded leaves of the preceding autumn, received him, and he fell stumblingly into its depth.

As the crisp, crackling sound of the broken twiggs fell on his ear, it suggested that the accident might possibly prove the means of escape, and burrowing underneath the cavity, which was about six feet beneath the level surface of the ground, he remained perfectly still and motionless scarcely daring to breathe.

The rest having gained the hill and there lost all traces of the fugitive, concluded that he had taken refuge in the copse, and accordingly dispersed themselves about it and examined the landscape round. Lockit had even dropped his hat over the very hole where Jack was secreted; but so steadily did he hold his breath that not a sound or a rustle of a leaf met the ear of the gaoler as he stooped to regain it. Whether the certainty of his having taken that path and the ignominy that awaited their return on being compelled to make confession that they had been baffled by a boy, would not have caused them to recommence their search with greater scrutiny is a question which might have been easily turned against the probability cf Jack's escape. Fortunately, however, at this crisis, the labourer called out to his companions that he saw a lad running across the fields at some distance towards Harrow, and collecting their remaining strength the party set off at full speed to secure the supposed culprit.

Blithly did the tidings of this mistake fall upon the ears of Jack as he heard the exclamation that led to this movement, and never did sound come more musically to the heart than did the dying footfall of the last of his pursuers as it vibrated on the quick pulse of our hero. He gently thrust his friendly covering aside and moved onward through the trees until he came to a point of vantage which commanded a view of the country beyond. Across the plain he saw his late followers careering as fast as their jaded limbs would carry them, on an erroneous supposition that their unwonted endeavours would speedily be rewarded with the object of their pursuit, and shrewdly judging that on discovering their mistake they would procure vehicles and return to town rather than continue an uncertain chase, already so much protracted, Jack made his mind up not to return to his hiding-place but to stay where he was and watch the course of events as they were likely to arise.

It was now past noon, and Jack having regaled himself with such slender fare as the remainder of the bread he had thrust in his vest on starting, and a draught of water from a pool in the vicinity, began to consider his future proceedings.

"It's no use going back to old Wood's," muttered Jack, "he wouldn't believe the real truth of the affair if I told him and besides I am heartily tired of such a hum-drum life. I wish I could make my name famous somehow, for I know I could do something if I tried;" and Jack meditated on the success that had attended his escape from the Roundhouse.

And here also must we be permitted to meditate upon the result of this train of thought in which our hero indulged as he stretched himself thoughtfully on the green sward and let the warm beams of the sun glance down upon his exhausted frame. Jack Sheppard's ruling passion was vanity, a fault that though usually considered in the mere light of a petty foible, is in fact the most dangerous of vices, and one, which together with the force of circumstances, led him to the commission of atrocities afterwards at which his better nature would have revolted. Not only is vanity contemptible in itself and injurious to him whom it governs, but, as the terrible truth can never be too often enunciated that the commission of small crimes may lead men to greater, it is in weak and uneducated minds, too often the stepping-stone to iniquities of the most startling and criminal description. Narrowly should the growth of the first seeds of vanity be watched in the human heart. As the rest somewhat recruited his strength and spirits, Jack remembered that by the kindness of his master the carpenter, his mother had been allowed to tenant a cottage at Willesden, which he knew from a visit he had once paid to her there, was not a great way from the place where he then was. Taking advantage of the early twilight therefore, he set out once more upon the road, aand enquiring of a carrier he met, the path he should take, was not long in getting to the little village which he hoped to make his destination for the night. Lights were gleaming from a few of the cottage windows, and at the roaring, blazing forge stood the blacksmith, with his sleeves upturned and collar unbuttoned, reeking and steaming over his work. From him Jack learned the habitation of his mother, and pausing for an instant before a neat thatched cottage, which, with its little strip of garden in front gave evidence of the taste and attention of its owner, the carpenter's apprentice gently announced his presence at the threshold, and in another moment the door was opened, and mother and son stood clasped in each others arms.

CHAPTER V.

MOTHER AND SON.

" Labour is life ! 'tis the still water faileth,
Idleness ever despairing, bewaileth;
Keep the watch wound for the dark rust assaileth,
Plants droop and die in the stillness of noon;
Labour is glory! The flying cloud lightens,
Only the waving wing changes and brightens,
Idle hearts only the dark future frightens,
Play the sweet keys wouldst thou keep them in tune."
ANON.

HAVING obtained such needful sustenance as he required, Jack briefly related to Mrs.

Sheppard the events that had caused him to come thither in that plight, and urged his determination not to return to the carpenter's shop.

"I am sure, mother," said he, "Mr. Wood will doubt that I only took up the miniatnre at Lord Orford's to look at, and as I think he bears me no good-will already, I am quite sure he will punish me for remaining out all night. Besides, I have another motive for not returning to my labours in Wych Street," he continued, casting his eyes upon the ground.

"The love of idleness, I am afraid, Jack," sighed Mrs. Sheppard, penetrating his thoughts, "it has been the bane of many, and I fear will be the ruin of you."

"I am sure I work hard enough when I like," returned the apprentice, somewhat sulkily, "even Mr. Wood acknowledges that I am the best workman he has got."

"Ay! would that the will always seconded the way, Jack, but your master is a kind one, and will, I am convinced, at my intercession, forgive your first error. But you must strive not to offend again."

"Then would you have me submit to all the correction and indignities he may offer me?"

"And why not, Jack?"

"My spirit won't bear it."

"Your false pride, Jack, I am afraid."

As his own conscience told him that such a supposition might be, after all, the right one, Jack checked the answer that rose to his lips, and preserved a moody silence.

"But if you refuse to go back to the worthy man, your employer," observed Mrs. Sheppard, by way of changing the subject, "what prospect have you of earning your livelihood, Jack, by the knowledge of a trade?"

"The prospect of making myself famous," cried the boy, with startling energy, his eyes flashing fire with enthusiasm, and his whole countenance kindling into animation.

"Famous? How?" ejaculated the mother, in tones of unfeigned astonishment.

"Nay, mother, I know not, but I have wild thoughts ringing in my ears, and strange fancies fluttering in my heart, whenever I think of it. I feel that for good or evil I bear a charmed life."

Mrs. Sheppard thought of the terrible denunciation uttered ten years before by Jonathan Wild, and pressing her hands to her face, she turned her head aside, and wept bitterly.

Jack had scarcely heeded the change in his mother's features, for dreaming only of his future fate, he sat lost in reverie, picturing scenes of gallant exploits and daring adventures, out of the glowing embers that were clicking in the grate before him.

"If you would not break your mother's heart, Jack, let me intreat you to alter your present resolution," exclaimed Mrs. Sheppard, still averting her head to conceal her tears.

Jack still bent over the fire, but not without a struggle to conceal his emotions.

"Do you love me, Jack?"

The youth at once demolished the airy castles he had been erecting, sprung from his seat, flung his arms fondly around his mother's neck, and kissing her, blended his own tears with hers.

Oh! what a holy, deep, devoted passage is a mother's love! When once it has been created in a woman's breast, it lingers there for ever. Poverty and straightened circumstances are as naught—seclusion from society only draws such hearts into closer union—and the nearer they approximate the better are they known. They are the alchymists of their own happiness, of which their hearts are the crucible; like them, a mother finds in the love of her first-born the elixir of life, and that true philosopher's stone, whose touch or presence converts everything into a pure, bright, and golden vision of peace, happiness, and joy. In her waking and her dreaming hours, that love is still present with her. She would not resign it for worlds, nor her life, and she could not if she would, for without it her bosom would be a dreary void, and her existence a mere blank. Oh! ye who possess that inestimable treasure—a mother's trusting, doting love,—trifle not with the precious boon. Loves she you once, she loves eternally. Change as ye will, no change can alter her. It glitters like the pole-star, clear and constant in the firmament, shining steadily on through the darkest night of adversity, silvering with its holy lustre, the troubled waves of life'sstormy sea, and fixed as the luminary itself, that is without variableness or shadow of turning.

Jack felt all his angry feeling and vicious thoughts quelled and allayed by this sudden burst of affection, he would have done anything then—no matter what—to have spared his mother an extra pang. He even himself proposed the return to his master's house in Wych Street.

"You will give up, then, all these idle fancies, Jack," cried his mother, "and go no more to those dreadful places of resort for the vile and dissolute."

"*All!* all mother, I promise ye," cheerfully assented the youth.

"And above all," continued his mother," "shun as you would a serpent in your path, a man called Jonathan Wild. He hath vowed to lay snares for your destruction, and will not hesitate to adopt any means by which his vile projects can be executed. He is a fiend in human form, a man whose whole thoughts are centred in your ruin, and whose power is too great to be spoken of lightly. He is one, in short, who is,——

"*Here!*" cried a deep voice at the window,

and throwing it open, Jonathan Wild, with two of his adherents, sprung into the apartment. "I'm much obliged to you, Mrs. Sheppard," bluffly exclaimed the thief-taker, after the first alarm at his sudden appearance had somewhat subsided, and left Jack safely secured by the two constables who attended him,—"I'm very much obliged to you for the flattering picture you have drawn of me, for the especial behoof of my worthy friends here, and I am only sorry they cannot apreciate the likeness. We listened at the window to know whether you had company before we intruded and of course expected the old proverb to be fulfilled."

"Monster!" ejaculated Mrs. Shephard, "a time will come yet when your iniquity will be punished. You, who first tempted my son to quit the path of virtue should be the last to betray him!"

"I am innocent of *this* charge, mother, at least," cried Jack, observing that she leaned to the belief of the robbery at Lord Orford's.

"Fool!" answered Wild sternly," you have been known as the companion of thieves in Drury Lane; you have been marked; your manners, habits, place of resort and all. Who, think ye, would believe your story?"

"Oh, Jack!" sobbed Mrs. Sheppard, mournfully, "this it is to become the associate of men like these."

"Besides," continued Wild, more for the sake of establishing his position with the constables than from any desire to be the historian of the boy's marvellous achievements,—"he escaped last night from St. Giles's Roundhouse —a crime of itself, if none other was proved against him, which would place his neck in jeopardy—and baffled the pursuit of the most vigilant officers in my employ. Fortunately, hearing from them as they returned, the result of their expedition, I guessed the cover the hare would fly to, and you see my suspicions were correct. Away with him! we must lodge him in the cage here to-night, and to-morrow he shall appear before his Majesty's justices of the peace."

"Oh, spare him—spare my son!" urged his mother, in a paroxysm of anguish, falling upon her knees to the officials, for she knew it would be useless to address any remonstrance to Jonathan.

Jack stood calmly between them, fixing a stern, unshrinking eye upon the thieftaker.

"We are here bound to discharge our duty," responded the first constable in a more bland and considerate tone than might have been expected; "however much we may deplore the cause that has brought us here."

"Of course!" said Wild, striding towards the door and flinging it open. "We have already overstayed our time. Come, bring him to the cage."

The constables took the boy off between them, regardless of the intreaties of the distracted mother to share his imprisonment for the night.

"Fiend or man, whichever thou art," exclaimed Mrs. Sheppard, seizing the arm of Wild as he moved to follow them, "How many years wilt thon give my son before thy terrible threat is executed?"

"SEVEN!" thundered Jonathan with a triumphant grin, as he flung her on one side and crossed the threshold.

The poor woman fell senseless on the floor.

CHAPTER VI.

HOW JACK SHEPPARD MADE HIS SECOND ESCAPE, AND WHAT BECAME OF HIM AFTERWARDS.

"You are a rash young man, sir,
Strong-headed, and wrong-headed, and I fear
Not over delicate in that fine sense,
Which men of honour pride themselves upon."
THE HUNCHBACK, Act, II. sc. III.

WILLESDEN cage was—or we may adopt the present sense, and say *is*, for it still remains to gratify the pedestrian curious in such matters—a small but compact round structure, standing about eight feet high, and having a pointed tiled roof, on the sides of which were inscribed the titles of the then potent officials of the parish, interspersed with sundry useful and ornamental notices to vagrants who might be found lurking about the parochial precincts. A strong door, secured by massive chains, and a padlock, formed the only means of ingress and egress, whilst a grating above admitted light and air. It was to this place that Jack Sheppard was now brought in the custody of the two constables, and under the immediate direction of Jonathan Wild, who did not leave the spot until perfectly assured that every precaution had been taken to ensure the perfect safety of his young prisoner. Business of political importance then requiring his presence at the Home-office, he mounted his horse that had been left at the village inn adjacent, and rode back to town, not before leaving strict injunction, with the constables to keep vigilant guard over the boy, and adding, that he should return early in the morning to place him in other care.

Leaving the adroit thieftaker to pursue his journey back, and concert those measures with Lord Orford, which were intended to have for their object, the removal of Jack Sheppard from the country, we now return to our hero, who being tired out with the rapid events of the day was not sorry to find the place of his incarceration so quiet, and the floor being profusely littered with straw, he soon relapsed into a profound and dreamless slumber.

It was about the break of day when he was

aroused by several loud and rather peremptory knocks on the door of the cage, and these were followed by a hoarse and bluff enquiry from the outside, as to whether he meant to sleep there all day or not.

"Who's there?" cried Jack starting up and rubbing his eyes.

"Your breakfast my lad," answered the voice, "a gentleman who has come down this morning from Mr. Wild has been good enough to bring a loaf for you from the village." And as these words were uttered, a sliding panel in the door was displaced and a loaf and a pitcher of water were introduced into the cell.

Jack, who under any emergency preserved his appetite, received the proffered meal with thanks, and speedily began tearing the loaf asunder to render its demolishment more easy. Whilst thus engaged, a sharp instrument came into contact with his eager fingers, and examining further, he found a small chisel and a screw-driver secreted in the loaf. His astonishment increased, when a voice, that he immediately recognised as one familiar to him, uttered in quick short sentences—"Come, my kinchin—slammock the jib and crack the pannum—dubsman I've duffled but stash the bars or the beak 'll blab!"

This elegant oration through the key-hole was luckily more intelligible to the practised ears of Jack than it would have been to the reader, and he instantly interpreted it as a warning from some friendly scout to make speedy use of the implements he had transmitted in the bread, and escape from the cage or the constable who had been sent on a fictitious errand by the speaker would return before the escape could be effected and arouse the neighbourhood. Jack immediately returned a signal to his unknown deliverer to show that he fully understood what was required of him, and that he was ready to execute it, and now eagerly looked round the walls to see the place that afforded the best and quickest outlet. The door was too well secured, and the walls were too thick to make more than one glance necessary, but the lath and plaister ceiling—if he could reach that—he fancied there would be but little difficulty in forcing a way out. His success in breaking through a stronger barrier than that which now opposed him, left him little doubt of the result of his present endeavours, and springing up to the roof by availing himself of the projecting ironwork of the door, he began to dig away with his chisel into the ceiling. The plaster fell round him in a shower of dust, and he soon picked a hole out large enough to enable him to see the direction of the laths beyond. One by one these snapped, and fell at his feet, and having wrenched himself up by a cross-beam that swept across the roof, he next succeeded in chipping away the mortar around the tiles. One being dislodged, the rest was an easy task, and making a breach large enough to pass through, he worked his agile body up between the timbers, and the next moment was breathing the fresh morning air from the top.

"Qvite a Villum the Konkeror!" cried an admiring voice in ecstacies, as Jack leaped down into the road," it's a perfectly vonderful and mirack'lous affair, which vould have done honour to the werry best cracksman going!"

"What Blueskin! Is that you?" exclaimed the boy, as be gave a friendly greeting to the creole, "who the deuce could expect you to be such a reglar trump as this?"

"Vhy, I always told yer I took a likin' to yer from the first, master Sheppard," responded Blueskin, "and did'nt I christen you as my protegy, vhen yer was not higher than a couple of kwart pots—vhy in course I did—but come along—I've got a konweyance at the end of the lane and I'll tell yer all about it as ve cuts along."

Hastily running across the ploughed field opposite and reaching the bye-road, Blueskin thrust Jack into the covered cart that a man was holding in readiness for him, and telling the carter to drive as fast as he could through the cross-country lanes back to the Borough, away they soon sped at a rapid pace. Blueskin then explained how he had overheard Wild give instructions to the captain of a smuggling craft in his pay, to be in readiness to remove Jack on the following night; how, hearing by that means of his imprisonment he had come down purposely to effect his liberation, and owing Jonathan a grudge, how he had determined to thwart his projects and serve his pupil at the same time; how he had persuaded the master of the Mint to lend him a tilted cart for the expedition, and how, pretending to be sent from Jonathan Wild, he had sent the constable on duty to obtain the handcuffs prior to his prisoner's removal, and how he himself had volunteered to keep guard during his absence. All this, and much more did the creole relate to Jack's astonished ears, and with such flourishes and embellishments as his fancy prompted.

"What can possibly be the reason of Jonathan wishing to get me away," mused Jack, when, less fearful of discovery they were conversing at their ease, as the lumbering vehicle rumbled over the narrow streets of the city, towards the south side of the river,

"I'm blessed if I can diskiver," said his companion who had heard the remark, "he must be a deep cove who can tell vot he's arter. There's no circumwenting him nohow. Von has to git up unkimmunly early in the morning to be afore him, but I'll be quits vith him yet."

"Jonathan seems to be no favourite of your's, Blueskin," remarked Jack.

"*He*," sneered the other; "vhy he'd sell his best friend, as he's done me, if any von offered him price enough. You attend to me, Jack, valk in my vays, and listen to the fine sarmons about crib-cracking as I'll preach to yer, and then yer will be a honour to yer perfession and a 'spectable member o' society, but as for Jonathan Vild—psha!" and the speaker, not finding sufficient vent for his indignation in the emphatic snap of the fingers that followed his speech, squared at an imaginary opponent furiously, and concluded by thumping his hat indignantly over his eyes.

They had crossed London Bridge, and entered the precints of the Mint, when Blueskin, awaking from the sullen reverie in which he had indulged during the remainder of the way, suddenly called upon the driver to stop, and springing out of the vehicle led Jack down a narrow court to the threshold of a public-house with which the reader is already acquainted by name.

It was the "Fox-in-the-Mint" wherein the singular inauguration of Jack's christening had taken place some ten years previously.

"Ve'll in here and lush, my kinchin," cried Blueskin, in the customary flash language of his calling; "and I'll put yer in the road to live like a nobleman vithout vork! Come along my Villum the Konkeror!"

Jack paused on the threshold as he remembered his mother's earnest appeal and he beheld the scene of vice and debauchery in which he, so young, was about to be initiated, but it was but for an instant. The thoughts of living luxuriantly, without hard work, his ruling passion, vanity, and the fear of encountering the taunts and reproaches of his companion to whom he felt himself under an obligation, all united to overthrow his better resolutions, and the next minute he entered, with a resolve to participate in the orgies of the den to the utmost.

The scene that Jack's eye encountered on entering the large room that formed the parlour of the flash ken, to which he was thus introduced, was one indeed well calculated to interest a novice in iniquity from its novelty and variety. Grouped around various tables were men, some of them mere striplings like the new-comer, drinking and playing cards, the stakes for which, from the round oaths that escaped freely from the lips of the players, being more their object than any amusement to be derived from their pastime. At the back of these hopeful youths were seated a jew fence, or receiver of stolen goods, who intent only upon the closeness of his bargain with an experienced footpad who had brought a couple of watches to dispose of, left untouched the reeking bowl of punch that had just been brought in to relax the demands of the other. Women, steeped in vice and lost to all the attributes of their sex, sat drinking at the side of the rest, urging on the gamblers to stake more deeply and the drinkers to order fresh supplies of their favorite potations. Next came a party of housebreakers ranged by themselves and over the discussion of sundry glasses of hot fluids, laughing at the successful termination of some of their most recent exploits and arranging the preliminaries of fresh depredations; whilst at a side-table, deeply engaged in conversation, were seated three gentlemen in flowing perukes and long riding dresses evidently accoutred for the road, and fortifying themselves for the journey by formidable inroads upon the roast fowl and bottles of wine before them. Most conspicuous in the throng, dissimilar in appearance, but alike in habits and pursuits, were two females, known respectively to the rest by the appellations of Poll Maggott and Edgeworth Bess. The former was a powerful muscular woman of nearly six feet high and with breadth of figure in proportion. The latter presented a striking constrast to the masculine build of her companion. She was a girl of not more than seventeen though with all the premature maturity of twenty. Light, laughing blue eyes, auburn hair, a brilliant complexion and a pair of rich voluptuous lips that seemed pouting to be kissed, were the chief prominent characteristics of her fine intelligent oval features, whilst her figure displayed a form and grace that made up personal attractions of no inconsiderable kind. To see her, the belle of that miscellaneous assembly, occupied in the discussion of topics that formed no fit themes for ears polite, and wasting the spring of her life in a den that sheltered the very dregs of society, was a picture that would have roused the deepest pity and sympathy in the heart of a moralist. It was the symbol of a bright and beauteous flower rotting on a dunghill. The entrance of Blueskin and our young hero was the signal for one general tumult of applause and congratulation, for the creole had established himself amongst the riotous crew as an universal favorite. Proceeding to take the chair of honour that was simultaneously assigned him, Blueskin made his protegy sit at his side to share the numerous proffered glasses that were handed towards him from every source. Silence being in some measure restored, he began to eulogise in glowing colours the courage and prowess of the young aspirant to Tyburn honours, and related at some length the two escapes of Jack from the Roundhouse of St. Giles's and the cage at Willesden, till the chief actor in these adventures began to feel himself growing quite a hero not only in his own estimation but also in that of the company assembled. As nothing could possibly create such a favourable and welcome demonstration in his behalf as the knowledge that an offender so young had twice set at nought the bars and bolts of His Majesty's prisons; the enthusiasm at the boldness and skill of Blueskin's pupil rose to an amazing height, and the health and future prosperity of the "high-spiced Toby Kinchin" as they playfully designated him, were proposed and drank in overflowing bumpers ordered all round for the occasion. As for the two women above described, they were both in ecstacies, and the fair Edgeworth Bess was so far infatuated with the accounts of his bravery and exploits, as to fling her arms lovingly around Jack's neck and impress on his lips one of her most alluring and burning kisses.

From that time Jack's fate was sealed. A new world seemed opening to him; the vigour of a fresh existence awakened in his frame. Precocious as we have already hinted, for his age, he now felt for the first time his veins inflated with the transport of love. His heart thrilled with ecstasy unknown before; his cheeks burned and crimsoned, half with shame and half with delight, and he felt that he could achieve anything, endure anything, to be the possessor of the beautiful creature that bounded before him.

Whilst thus heated by the presence of his fair enslaver, who, passing his willing arm around her warm waist, contrived to inflame his passion, Blueskin plied him with strong beverages which he drank eagerly to quench the scorching fire within him. Surrounded by viciousness of every description, contaminated by the most depraved companionship, and stimulated to excesses by the frequency of his potations and the example set by those around him, it is no wonder that Jack found the few sparks of virtue that he had hitherto retained, now wholly extinguished, and he yielded himself up to the tempter almost without a struggle.

For three days did he thus resign himself to the saturnalia of the Mint, sleeping off his excesses one hour to resume them with encreased energy the next, and during the whole of this time, the two women and Blueskin were his constant companions. Lost in a dream of feverish excitement which he fancied pleasure, Jack was enraptured with the mode of life which he now followed, and with the uproarious hilarity of the minters with whom he had been made acquainted. The contrast between the unrestrained freedom he now enjoyed, and the curb and check placed upon his actions at the carpenter's, made him thoroughly averse to encountering the comparatively dull routine of his work as an apprentice, and he vowed never to return to his employment any more. On the third night of his initiation into these horrible mysteries, when these feelings were stronger than ever within him, and he had drank deeply in common with the rest around him, to drown all thought but that which had reference to the pleasures of the present, the attention of the company was suddenly diverted by the entrance of a female, who, attired in deep mourning and presenting in her features the most unequivocal manifestations of profound sorrow, evidently not unmingled with disgust; exhibited a marked contrast to the careless joviality of those amongst whom she had so strangely appeared.

Her eye rapidly wandered over that revolting and riotous assemblage until it settled upon one group more revolting and more riotous than the rest.

There was seated Jack Sheppard, manifestly bordering on the last stage of intoxication, his dress disordered, his hair clotted and matted over his fevered brow, a pipe between his lips, and a bowl of punch half-emptied before him. There he sat, receiving and reciprocating—or rather attempting to reciprocate, for he was scarcely master of his actions—the fulsome blandishments of Poll Maggot and Edgeworth Bess, one of whom was leaning over the back of his chair, seemingly whispering her fondness in his ear, whilst the other, as a more recognised favourite had passed her arm round his neck and now pressed her glowing cheek to his.

No sooner had this singularly matched trio caught the visitor's eye, than regardless of all save her son's debased condition, Mrs. Sheppard—for it was her—could not repress the scream of horror which rose to her lips, and the alarm startled the whole throng as well as the individual who had been its chief cause.

"Hollo!" cried Jack, gazing round the room and trying to fix his unsteady eye upon the source of the piercing ejaculation. "Who have we got amongst us now?"

"Your mother, Jack," replied Mrs. Sheppard in an earnest tone of appeal; "your mother,, who wishes you to return home with her!"

"How the deuce did you find me out here!" hiccuped Jack, describing several circles in the air with his pipe, as if to render his speech more imposing and authoritative.

"There is a pursuit now going on, the officers are seeking every where to discover your hiding place, and I—I was afraid I should find you here, Jack," sighed his parent convulsively.

"And you want to get me nabbed again," stammered the boy, turning to the amazon who had come from behind his chair at the commencement of the scene—"send her about her business, Poll."

"Ay! to be sure I will, Jack!" responded mistress Maggot, coming up to Mrs. Sheppard in a threatening attitude. "You'll be pleased, marm, to go, or I must make you!"

"Oh, Jack! leave these debased wretches, and come with me," implored the poor woman.

"Who do you call wretches?" retorted Poll Maggot, with a very unfeminine imprecation which we do not care to repeat. "I'm bless'd if I stand any more of this nonsense;" and considerable violence would have followed this indignant outbreak had not Blueskin fortunately interposed his brawny hand in time.

"Come, marm!" cried the creole, in as persuasive accents as he could assume; "I'm glad to see yer vonce more in the Mint, and if so be as how yer like to have a friendly glass vith us for old acquaintanceship, vhy there's my bottle ready for yer and velcome, but if so be as how yer von't, vhy ve'll thank yer to mizzle and not make a row about it."

Mrs. Sheppard looked at her son imploringly, as if wishing to try the effect of another appeal, but finding it useless, as he averted his head contemptuously, she yielded to the solicitations of Blueskin, and turned her steps sorrowfully homeward.

"And now, my lads," exclaimed Blueskin, as he saw he had succeeded in effectually silencing the interruption, "ve'll make Jack Sheppard a sworn pal of the Mint, and right good luck to him, for he's von of the right sort; so fill yer glasses all round and drink the toast I'm a-going to perpose. Here's Jack the prison-breaker, may he never vont a crib to crack, nor a pal to help him!"

And as this classical sentiment was received with enthusiastic demonstrations of approval, Jack was about to rise and return thanks for the honour that had been conferred upon him, when the effects of the night's previous debauch, became strongly perceptible, and he fell exhausted and inebriated beneath the table.

The rest, familiar with such results, merely thrust him on one side on a bench where he might sleep off his intoxication, and then proceeded to celebrate their festivities in a way which can be best described by drawing a curtain over the scene and leaving the details to be imagined from the silence we are compelled to observe concerning them.

CHAPTER VII.

HOW JACK ROBBED HIS FORMER BENEFACTOR.

"Tis woman that seduces all mankind,
By her we first were taught the wheedling arts,
Her very eyes can cheat, when most she's kind,
And robs us of our money with our hearts."

GAY.

A FEW days after the events narrated in the preceding chapter, Blueskin and Jack were seated in the upper room of a certain house in the Mint, engaged in conversation. They had removed from the tavern in order the more effectually to prevent the discovery of their haunt, and now before the inspiring presence of a huge wooden bowl of rum punch, compounded by mine host of the "Fox," they were thoughtfully bent upon the projection of some plan for the future, which might tend to augment their resources, now nearly at their last ebb, and satisfy the clamorous demands of the females whose extravagancies Jack had been compelled to maintain.

"I have half-a-mind to crack a crib and sack the plunder," at last exclaimed Jack meditatively, as he helped himself to another brimmer, this sort of life agrees with my constitution amazingly.

"Vhy vot else *vould* you do?" retorted Blueskin, "yer vould'nt be so green as to go vork for your living? No I thought not," he continued, as Jack's indignant toss of the head refuted such a supposition, "knowed as how my little vide-a-vake cove vos a trifle too game for that—raytherl!" and the speaker quaffed off his draught in the perfect assurance that he had not miscalculated the intentions of his pupil.

"The worst of it is, Blueskin," replied Jack, "I don't know where to begin first, I've been thinking about the affair for some time, knowing that I ought to return the money I have had of you, but I must own I am sadly puzzled to make a good start."

"I know von place that I have been a thinking of all along," returned his companion, cautiously approximating his chair nearer to the other, "a place I thought of when I helped you out of Villesden Cage, and which I should have done afore now myself, but I vanted your assistance;"

"Where's that?" inquired Jack.

"Yer old master's, Mr. Vood's the carpenter's, in Wych Street," answered the other.

The boy was not yet hardened enough in iniquity to listen to such a proposal without apprehension. His heart revolted at the contemplation of making the generous old man who had been his earliest benefactor, the first victim, and after the first surprise had abated, he temperately remonstrated with his instructor in theft.

"Vhy vhot are the odds?" returned Blueskin in astonishment at the rejection of his—what he considered very liberal offer. "If you don't do it, others who are not so particular *vill*, and so you may just as vell share the swag as shirk the cracking."

"Talk as you will," responded the youth, "I cannot, will not, rob my generous old employer of hard earned money. Let us find some other house for our schemes, but that where I have been myself so kindly sheltered."

"Vell!" growled Blueskin, in a tone half of disappointment and half of anger—"if yer von't yer von't, but the next time I find yer locked up in von of his blessed Majesty's limbo palaces, why yer may stop there for me, that's all."

"I have not forgotten your friendly aid, believe me, Blueskin," said Jack, stung by an allusion to his imagined ingratitude, "but you task my powers of resistance to the utmost, when you ask me to enter there."

"Vell! I vos only thinking vhot Edgeworth Bess would say, vhen she heard you could'nt buy her that handsome necklace she had set her heart upon. How she vill cry her pretty eyes out to be sure."

"True!" ejaculated the youth, "money I must have, come from what source it will."

"And then," continued Blueskin in his wiliest manner, not heeding the interruption, "how pretty Poll will stare and turn up her elegant nose when I tell her how her favorite fancy-man, Jackey Sheppard, was too great a coward to crack a crib, when it would let him pay his debts like a trump, and buy her that new dress he promised her."

"Coward!" vociferated Jack, fiercely, starting up from his seat, "say that again and I'll cram a dozen of your ugly teeth down your throat."

"Vhot my little protegy turning rusty at

his old schoolmaster?—vell that *is* a go!" exclaimed Blueskin, raising his hands and eyes up to the ceiling, as if calling upon the whitewash above him, to be a witness of the insubordination he had experienced,—"How Bess vould have stared and gone on, had she heard it,—but no! she couldn't have believed it, if she had—it would have been quite impossible for her to have dreamed of such a thing, even vhen she had put her pretty face into a nightcap and made up her mind to try—quite impossible—quite!" and thus lost in wonder at the bare thought of such a thing, Blueskin clasped his horny hands together in bewilderment, and finally concluded by draining to the dregs the punchbowl itself, as though some extra stimulus were needed to enable him to sustain such a prolonged contemplation.

Jack had been himself lost in a reverie during the protracted and inciting speech of his companion, and only thought of the pleasures and society of the two females, whom his denial of this burglary, would cause him to lose. He pictured to himself the realization of the picture drawn in such skilful and glowing colours by Blueskin, of the contempt with which his hesitation would be received, and the taunts and jeers that would be showered upon him from those lips, which had hitherto been employed only in his praise. He could resist this no longer, and by such miserable sophistry is the uneducated mind governed, that before the words of Blueskin had died away npon his ear, he had converted the deed about to be considered, from an act of culpable ingratitude, into an achievement of justifiable emergency.

"Say no more!" cried Jack, "I am ready and agree to assist you in this, but it must be on one condition only."

"What's that?"

"No violence must be used."

"Vell I am agreeable to anything," returned Blueskin, "so as we gets the blunt. There, give us your hand and now let us have another beaker in, to wash out the old score."

The additional supply was soon brought, and as the entrance of Edgeworth Bess diverted the current of the conversation to more gentle topics, the festivals of previous evenings were terminated in the same result.

Late on the following night, when the steady sober citizens of London were comfortably reposing in their beds, and tranquilly dreaming, or listening to the pattering of the rain against the windows, two figures might have been seen stealthily threading the labyrinth of narrow courts, that led down into the upper part of the Strand. From the cautious way in which they avoided the casual glare of an oil-lamp, and only slunk along the dark sides of the street through which they passed, it was not easy to identify in the two late stragglers of the night, Blueskin and Jack Sheppard.

As they neared their destination, Jack, who led the way, halted, and breaking the silence he had previously observed, addressed his companion in a low voice, with a hint to slacken pace, and ended with a caution to stand on one side in a doorway, until a watchman, whom he saw approaching from the end of the street, should have passed.

They immediately receded into the dark portico, afforded by the projection of a shop front, which, as at this period was common, overhung the pavement, and trusting to the heavy rain that still came perseveringly down, to afford an excuse for their position, should they be discovered, the two burglars sheltered themselves within the recess. The footfalls of the guardian of the night came nearer, as they scarcely breathed.

"Past twelve o'clock and a rainy night," called the watchman as he passed them and pursued his beat. They watched him until he had turned the corner of the street and thus got out of sight when knowing that, as far as this sleepy constable was concerned, they should be free from interruption for another hour at least—both emerged from their hiding-place in the consciousness of perfect security.

"I don't know how it is," observed Jack to his companion as they proceeded on their way, "but this job goes against the grain with me dreadfully. I told you before I couldn't cotton to it exactly, and now the affair is so near coming off, I like it worse than ever."

"Ah! you are sich a very rum chap!" returned the other—"there is no knowing vhere to have yer. Yer seem to be all pins and needles about this affair, like a voman's vorkbox!"

"It don't seem right, like," continued Jack, "it seems as if my conscience said—don't go!"

"I don't know vot yer conscience—as yer call it—may say, but I know vot Edgeworth Bess vould say, ven she saw us come back empty-handed," answered Blueskin.

"Why what would she say?" enquired Jack.

"That ve vere both afraid," retorted his companion in cold sarcastic accents, "but then never mind her. Vot is a beautiful voman like Bess to the ugly, stupid old vhot-ly'e-call-it that says yer mustn't do it."

"Aye! but I *do* mind her!" replied Jack, on whom the cunning suggestion of his companion had produced the desired effect—"I do mind her. We'll do it, come what may."

"That's right!" responded Blueskin approvingly, "I knowed as how yer vould'nt disappoint a petticoat!"

"Here then is the place," cried Jack, suddenly stopping short, and gasping his words quickly as though to drown reflection,—"it would be madness to attempt it the front way, we must go round to the back, and crossing the workshop enter the house in that direction. The money is kept in Mr. Wood's bed room."

"Vhot a blessed babby it is, for knowing all about it!" xclaimed Blueskin in a transport of admiration. "But how do ve get there, my champ..on of Kristendom?'

"This alley leads down, at the back of Lord Craven's mansion, to the court that runs at the back of the houses. Over the second wall and we come to the carpenter's workshop— it's an easy way. I've done it myself many a time when I have given the slop the slip to come over to the "MAGPIE" on the sly, and have a game at cards with you and the rest of the gang. nobody ever found me out."

"A perfect Harchbishop of Canterbury!" rejoined Blueskin, who had his own original notions of perfection to which he thought Jack was constantly approaching—"I votes for putting that remark into the next edition of the Proverbs, and giving———"

"Hush, Blueskin—not so loud," interrupted Jack, who was not so much averse to hearing his merits trumpeted forth as he was afraid that they might be overheard by some one who wouldn't appreciate them so heartily.

"It's so confoundedly dark, I can hardly see where the turning is," cried Jack, feeling his way along the sides of a narrow brick archway which led into the midst of a maze of buildings, afterwards cleared for the present dwellings and chambers in the new Inn. At last his right hand suddenly coming to an acute angle with the wall, he added,—"It's all right, Blueskin, follow me and keep to the left, when we get to the end here. The wall can be cleared at the first leap."

The injunctions given by Jack were rigidly adhered to by his associate. Muffling himself up to exclude the rain that now poured down in one uninterrupted stream, he clambered up the wall with Jack, and was preparing to descend, when the low growl of a dog on the other side warned him of a large kennel beneath, that had a vigilant Newfoundland spaniel within.

"It's Mr. Chatterley's dog, next door," whispered Sheppard, "it is impossible to get down here—he is as savage as a tiger, and they've turned him out here—I can see, to be prepared for some game of this sort."

"I'm blest if ve turns back agin after having come so far," cried Blueskin, fumbling about in his vest for a small packet which he afterwards produced;—"it's a lucky thing I brought my persuader with me, so here, old boy—here's something for supper which you will have plenty of time allowed you to digest." And tossing a piece of prepared meat into the yard they had soon the satisfaction to perceive the dog, who had begun to bark violently, leave the kennel and fix himself on the meat which he was devouring as eagerly as the most inveterate hater of the canine species could possibly desire.

"There's nothing like a bit of doctored liver to silence a cur," exclaimed Blueskin, watching the disappearance of the meat with interest. —"That vill soon make you glad to turn tail into your kennel again," and leaping down into the yard he beckoned Jack to follow his example.

Proceeding with stealthy tread over the intervening space, they cautiously scaled another wall beyond, and then silently dropping down into the back portion of Wood's premises, to which they had now arrived, Jack felt about for a particular window, and having discovered the object of his search, received from his companion the necessary implements with which to commence operations.

In a few minutes the outer shutter flew open—then the window—and creeping noiselessly up over the sill, the next minute Blueskin and Jack Sheppard were in the room. Carefully closing the shutters so as to exclude the light, Blueskin took out a muffled flint and steel, and ignited the oiled wick in his lanthorn. The room they were in was the workshop, where numerous indications of Jack's skill as a carpenter's apprentice, were still scattered around, and holding up the lanthorn Jack could not refrain from pointing out to his companion the name that he had carved on the beam. The side-door which communicated to the interior of Wood's dwelling was locked on the outside, but to Jack this was but a momentary impediment, for striking a chisel in between the door and its surrounding framework, he forced back the bolt with ease. With so much rapidity and so little noise was this operation conducted, that if even any body had been on the alert, and prepared for such an attempt, the sound would have passed undetected. Repeating his caution to Blueskin to use no violence, Jack cautiously opened the door and disclosed a carpeted flight of steps leading upward.

They then took off their shoes and ascending the stairs on tiptoe, so cautiously, that not a board creaked with the weight of a foot, Jack led his companion to a door at the extremity of the second landing, and pointed it out as the bed-chamber of Mr. Wood, where the plate chest and money-box were usually deposited. On trying the handle, Blueskin to his dismay found the door locked with the key left in it on the inside. Jack, however, was too expert a craftsman even at this early period of his history, to be much influenced by trifles like these, and taking out a centre-bit and knife, he speedily succeeded in cutting through a pannel, making an aperture sufficient to enable him to pass his hand through, reach the key, and unlock the door.

Assuming the crape mask, as was usual amongst the craft to escape being identified in the event of being seen, Blueskin and Jack entered the room, the former approaching with a bared knife to the bed of the sleepers and waving the light several times before their eyes. The slumbers, however, in which they were indulging, were too real and profound to be easily broken.

Jack now held in his breath and eagerly peered round the apartment to see where the little bureau was placed in which he knew that Wood kept his money. Finding it covered with a remnant of cloth upon the toilet-table he threw over it a piece of lined wash leather to deaden the blow and using a small crowbar for the purpose, speedily succeeded in breaking it open.

Whilst Jack was thus busily engaged in rifling the box of its contents, and filling his pockets with bright golden guineas, Blueskin had opened a store-closet in the chamber, at the head of the bed, and emulating the industry of his companion, was as intently occupied in filling a hugh canvas bag with the contents of the plate chest. Trays, tankards, and chocolate dishes, sugar tongs, waiters and candlesticks, were all stowed away with such skill and dexterity, that although thrust miscellaneously into the bag, they never jingled in the slightest degree. Jack was now prepared to depart, having appropriated as many articles of wearing apparel as he could carry to his own use, when, as he was decending the first step, a loud outcry from the carpenter's room alarmed him, and he immediately afterwards saw Blueskin, struggling desperately with Mrs. Wood, appear at the door.

With the quickness of thought Jack extinguished the light, and bounding down the stairs called upon his comrade to follow.

Mrs. Wood however, maintained such a tight hold of the canvas bag, that he found it impossible to comply with the injunction, at least, without leaving the chief part of the plunder for which he had risked everything behind him.

"Confusion!" muttered Blueskin in a towering passion at being thus baffled—"Leave go, I say, or I'll make you!"

"Give me my plate back again!" cried the carpenter's wife with energy,—"Help, thieves, murder, help, Mr. Wood."

"Will you loose your hold, woman," growled Blueskin from between his clenched teeth, dragging her out to the landing; "it will be worse for you if you do not." And he searched for his knife in the vest.

"Help! Owen—Owen! help—thieves!" screamed Mrs. Wood, pulling a bell violently at her side.

"Come along!" cried Jack, "let her go, the street is alarmed—come—quick—quick—to the door."

"Curse you then" exclaimed Blueskin, savagely drawing his knife and opening it with his teeth—"since you will have it then, take that!"

And dragging down her head by the luxuriant back hair that he had twisted firmly round his left hand, he with the other, brandished his knife before her eyes and drew it with a frightful, crunching force across her throat. A heavy fall upon the landing and a thick gushing sound that ensued, told the murderer, how fatal had been the blow.

Before Mr. Wood had become thoroughly awakened and conscious of the loss which he had suffered, Sheppard and Blueskin had sprang through the window of the workshop, and in an inconceivable short space of time, they had regained their old quarters in the Mint.

CHAPTER VIII.

THE COMPACT.

"Thus ill he lived, much evil saw,
With men to whom no better law,
Nor better life was known;
Deliberately and undeceived,
The bad man's vices he received,
And gave them back his own."
WORDSWORTH.

THE house which Jonathan Wild claimed as his residence, was a heavy, dismal-looking mansion in the Old Bailey, adjoining a tavern then known as the Coopers' Arms; and the site of which is now occupied by a railway van and waggon office. A square court-yard, paved with stone, and surrounded by an iron railing, separated it from the street, and even seen by the bright and cheerful light of day, the sombre massiveness of the brickwork imparted to it a dull and suspicious aspect. Every window was grated, every door barred, and the general appearance of the building was as much like that of a prison as possible. The interior was as formidable as the outside, for huge stone staircases and gloomy corridors, stretching away into the darkness beyond, gave the visitor the impression of traversing the Spanish dungeons appropriated to the officers of the inquisition, and produced a chilliness of the heart which made few enter it without fear, or leave it without satisfaction. The thousand and one tongues of popular rumour, gave credence and circulation to the most appalling and wonderful stories connected with its history. Coiners, note-forgers, and transmuters of stolen metals, were said to inhabit the upper portion of the house, whilst cellars and subterranean passages beneath were supposed to communicate with the dreary vaults and dungeons of Newgate opposite, or serve for the concealment of such criminals as the thief-taker desired to screen from justice. Fearful apparitions were alleged to appear at midnight in the court before the house, and proclaim the commission of fresh murders within; in short, there was no report too wild or improbable concerning its horrors to be told or believed, and the belated passenger would turn aside and shudder as he passed its precincts, with a timorous dread of even the very railings that looked like gaunt iron spectres in the darkness. Fortunately for the existence and credit of the house, those better informed knew or surmised that most of these dreadful legends emanated from the owner himself, who circulated them with a view to repress idle curiosity respecting the scenes daily enacted therein; and government knew too well the value and habits of the man they employed, on secret service, to listen to the appeals that were constantly being made to them to have the house examined and demolished. Thus, both Wild and his transactions were enveloped in a cloud of mystery which it was useless to attempt to penetrate.

On the morning after Mrs. Wood's murder, Jonathan was seated alone in one of the loftiest and largest apartments of this repulsive habitation when the announcement of a visitor below awakened him from his meditations.

"Did he give his name, Abrahams?" inquired Jonathan, of the Hebrew janitor who officiated as the announcer.

"Yesh! Mishter Vilds," responded the Jew; "Lord Orford."

"Admit him."

The Jew disappeared and the nobleman entered.

"Punctual to your time at least, my lord," said Jonathan, without rising from his seat, and bestowing on his visitor only a slight salutation by a short bow. "You have found me out, I see; I was afraid you might have mistaken the direction."

Instead of answering the remarks made by the other, Orford advanced to the table at which the thief-taker sat, and looking cautiously round to see that they were not overlooked, haughtily deposited on the green baize, a small roll of bank notes.

"There is the sum you require, I believe," cried the peer, coldly, "Count it."

Wild ran his fingers over the notes, and his eyes glistened as he summed up their value. Having terminated his scrutiny, he coolly opened a pocket-book that lay upon the table, placed the notes therein, and turning to the nobleman, acknowledged the accuracy of the amount.

Orford remained silent as if absorbed in thought.

"A thousand pounds seems a large sum, your lordship, for the mere riddance of a boy," remarked Jonathan, with a view to provoke conversation, "but when you remember that boy could not only dispossess you of your present estate, but attach eternal infamy and dishonour to your name, the price at which the silence is bought, will appear, I am sure, a trifle in comparison."

"I was not pondering, sir, on its cost," returned Orford, fixing his full dark eyes on the other; "At our first interview, I neither hesitated about the terms you proposed, nor wished now to depreciate their value. How you became so fully acquainted with the secrets of my family I know not, but chance or design, has certainly led you to guess my intentions aright. I *do* want that boy disposed of. I have now bought over your will—I would know the means."

"Your lordship forgets that there are secrets attached to every trade, which are not always proper to be revealed," answered Wild. "Suffice it for you to know that the means *are* in my power,—that I exerted them on your behalf, when I threw the boy into St. Giles's Roundhouse;—that I have never since lost sight of the boy, though he has twice—with a skill wonderful for his youth—eluded the vigilance of my officers;—and, even now, though he can little dream of such restraint, at this very moment, when he fancies himself most secure—he is more deeply tangled in my web than ever."

"Then why not terminate his life at once?" inquired Orford,—"deeply does his existence embitter mine."

"Because," rejoined his companion, with a triumphant glance, "it would not answer the end I have in view. Like a cat, I must play with my victim, before I destroy it. Double the sum you have given would not recompense me, had I not an object to gain myself, by furthering your's. The passion that has prompted you in this affair is avarice—mine is revenge!"

"And what then do you propose, sir?" cried Lord Orford, indignantly, resenting in his look the familiar tone, adopted by his companion. "Am I to be baffled in *my* scheme, because it interferes with *yours?*"

"Nay, my lord," responded Wild, "we may take different roads, but both result in the same point at last. You wish merely to see him out of the way, so that you may no longer dread a future claimant to the property. Let it be so. Consider, that such is firmly and definitely settled between us. You retire to your country seat, and the bargain on my part is fulfilled, if you hear no more of him."

"Whilst you——?"

"Steep him in wine and infamy to the lips—cause him to pursue a career of crime unparalelled in the criminal annals of the country, and finally conclude by consigning him to the gallows. You see our result is the same, though our motives are different."

"If I cannot applaud your intentions, I must at least admire your sincerity," rejoined Orford, "I am willing to leave him to your care."

"Our interview may then be considered over," returned Wild, rising from his seat as he spoke, "You must excuse my abrupt manner in appealing to your lordship's sense of business, but Sir Robert Walpole is not a man to brook waiting for others, and I have an appointment with him at noon, on urgent matters of state import."

"One word, sir, before I depart," pursued Orford, "You had a state warrant for my apprehension, as an adherent to the cause of the "Pretender," as the loyalists choose to call him. Am I to consider myself safe, from its not being put into operation."

"Hum," hesitated Wild, apparently considering for a moment.

"Your answer."

"Your lordship must excuse me from giving a decisive one, now," resumed the other, "What its ultimate destination may be, circumstances must decide hereafter. It will possibly be sufficient for you to learn that it is still in my possession, and will remain so, till—"

"When?" gasped the Jacobite, eagerly.

"*The heir to the Orford estate appears to claim his rights,*" was the response.

An exchange of significant glances followed.

The entrance of Abrahams, with a note, which he handed to his employer, interrupted further conversation. Lord Orford took his leave, and Wild was again alone.

"The thoughtless fool!" muttered Jonathan, as he watched from his window, the nobleman ride away, "he has forgotten that whilst the mother is living the boy might well be spared. That *she* still exists is a secret, however, I reserve for my own purposes—the ruin of her son will at least feed my revenge!"

The thief-taker curled his lip in triumph at the thought of yet over-reaching the peer, and so engaged had he become in the speculation of future greatness, that it was not until his quick eye glanced again upon the table, that he remembered the note which awaited his perusal.

Tearing open the missive, he instantly possessed himself of its contents, which appeared to have some cause of gratification in their nature, for his rigid cheeks relaxed into a smile, as he finished reading.

"So, so!" he cried, as he locked up the document in his bureau, "Edgworth Bess plays her part bravely. I was afraid she would get really fond of the lad, and thwart my measures for his entanglement. I'faith where mischief is concerned, there is nothing like a woman to make a plot ripen. This burglary at Wood's, and the murder of his wife, must, however, be looked to——. Within there! Bowyer, Abrahams."

The two Janizaries answered to the call.

"Take this, one of you, to the printer's, and tell him to have the placard, as soon as it is finished, posted in every thoroughfare, as usual," cried Jonathan, handing a hastily written paper to Abrahams, as he spoke. "And the other run to Mr. Purley, the ordinary of Newgate, and tell him that I have offered a reward of £50 for the murderer's apprehension, and will myself lose no time in putting the constables in the right track. Away at once—both of ye."

And the attendants quitted the room upon their errand.

"I must make some show of exertion in this affair," said Wild, meditatively to himself, as he arranged his papers, "or my power may begin to be doubted. It will frighten the rest into submission to my rules besides, and as for Jack's hiding-place in the Mint, why I can pounce upon him at any time. And now to Sir Robert Walpole."

Thus regulating in his mind the course afterwards to be pursued, Jonathan Wild resumed his hat and cane, and was speedily on his way to the residence of the wily politician, with fresh evidence of the Pretender's machinations in his possession.

Whilst these events were transpiring in the Old Bailey, a scene of a totally different character was being enacted in the Mint. Amidst the reckless revels, in which his companions indulged, from the proceeds of the previous night's plunder, Jack sat moodily apart, revolving in his mind the nature of the crime, of which, if he had not instigated, he had been, at least, the cause. Resisting the fascinating blandishments of Edgeworth Bess, and leaving to the less scrupulous of his associates the duty of absorbing the potations that were plentifully scattered on the board, the young housebreaker felt his soul at last stained with crime, his hands imbrued with the blood of one who had been the wife of his best and earliest benefactor. He had plunged into the fatal vortex of that seething whirlpool of vice, and now he felt that it would be too late to retrace his steps. Shame, horror, and regret, were visible by turns, as he traced the current of his emotions, and now, that the first gush of joy at being the possessor of so large a sum, had given way to a calmer feeling of reflection: he would have given worlds to have exchanged his ill-gotten riches for the restoration of the murdered woman's life.

"Come, Jack," exclaimed Blueskin, pouring out a bumper of gin, and staggering across the room to Sheppard, "what's the utility of being down in-the-mouth with this affair? Eh, my prince of cracksmen? It vos a haccident, you know, and if the old voman vould run her throat agin my knife, vhy how could I help it, so let's mop the max together and make it up."

"Leave me, answered Jack, resolutely, "if you and I are to work these rigs longer together, you will understand that whatever conditions I make in these affairs I must have attended to. I told you no violence must be used, and look at your conduct!"

"Vell, my noble kinchin, I tell yer, it shan't happen agin,"—remonstrated the creole, in his most winning tone; "here's buxom Bess, a veepin' like a villow on a vet day, and all because yer von't come and jine in as von o' the right sort. She says as how yer have seen somebody else, vith a face yer thinks prettier, and as how if you go on thinking about her so, she means to be jealous."

"Psha!" muttered Jack, gloomily.

"It's very true though, Jack," interrupted that frail damsel, winding her alabaster arms round Jack's neck, as he rejected her endearments, "I *am* beginning to get jealous of you, but I see how it is—you know I am too fond of you, and you take advantage of it?"

And as she bent her lovely face down before the eyes of our young hero, and her warm and fragrant breath fanned his cheek, is it to be wondered that his fortitude gave way? He pressed her pouting lips to his own—all, save the enjoyment of the present hour, was forgotten, and he yielded to the blandishments of his fair companion, with a reciprocated assurance to Blueskin, that he had cancelled the outrage he had committed for ever from his mind. So weak is humanity, when contested by the temptations of the erring daughters of Eve!

The night past, like all preceding ones, in a career of vice and debauchery, which it would be sickening to detail, and the next day, as Jack was reading the placards, concerning the robbery and murder, to Blueskin, who regularly accompanied him in his predatory expeditions, the conversation that he overheard, between two chance passengers, in Cheapside, arrested his attention immediately, whilst the other was attempting to puzzle out the reward offered for his apprehension.

"It's too true!" replied the citizen, in conversation with his friend, "I heard it this morning from Mr. Wood himself, who vows that he firmly believes one of these who entered his house the other night was his old apprentice, Jack Sheppard."

"Ah! I never did like the appearance of that lad," said the other, "I was sure no good would come of him. And so Mrs. Sheppard has gone mad, through the misconduct of her son? Poor woman!"

Jack felt the words scorch his brain like fire.

"Aye!" continued the first speaker, "she is mad sure enough. They have sent her to Bedlam, to see whether they can get her senses back again, but it is a hopeless case. Poor Wood, the carpenter, is so grieved, at the calamities that have fallen upon his house, that the unfortunate man is well nigh demented himself, and stands a tolerable chance of following her thither."

At this crisis the self-reproaches of Jack, became so acute, that he for a few minutes lost all consciousness of the busy scene around him, and when he turned his head once more to the direction whence the voices came, he found the speakers had passed out of hearing, and Blueskin waiting at his side, anxiously gazing on the countenance of his young companion, which had become suddenly pallid and ghastly.

"Vhy what has come over you Jack?" inquired Blueskin, as he took the arm of our hero, and led him down into a bye-street where they might be less observed. "Yer has'nt been a swallowin' whitewash surely?"

"I have heard that, within the last few minutes," answered Sheppard, "which might make any cheek pale if there was a drop of true blood in its veins at all. My mother has gone mad—she is in Bedlam and I must visit her."

"Vhy yer must be going that vay yourself to think of such a thing!" remonstrated Blueskin in alarm; "yer had better first take care of your mother's son. It's running

one's head into the lion's den at once, look at the risk!" "Risk or no risk, I shall venture it," replied Jack,

"Vell! yer von't go vithout me?"

"Yes, I must take the hazard of discovery alone," pursued Jack, "you wait my return at the Fox."

"Ah! I shall never see you again, Jack," urged Blueskin—"your blessed body vill be valked off with as sartin as fate."

"Well! we shall see," rejoined the other, "I must take my chance of the game, but should I not return, take this purse to Bess and tell her to make her mind easy about me, and that if they do take me, they shall have some trouble to keep me—that's all."

So bidding farewell to his associate, who vainly endeavoured to dissuade him from engaging in such an undertaking, Jack cut short his exhortations by a sudden bolt, and diverging through the back streets, speedily arrived without any impediment at the asylum for the insane, then standing in Moorfields.

No fears disturbed him during the dangerous progress, for his mind was entirely pre-occupied with the account he had heard of his mother's melancholy situation.

CHAPTER IX.

OLD BEDLAM—THE MANIAC.

"When the lamp is shattered,
The light in the dust lies dead,
When the cloud is scattered;
The rainbow's glory is shed.
When the lute is broken,
Sweet tones are remembered not,
When the lips have spoken,
Loved accents are soonest forgot."
SHELLEY.

OLD BEDLAM—or Bethlehem Hospital—every vestige of which has been since cleared away and its former site now occupied by a range of handsome structures—then stood upon the eastern side of Moorfields, bordering upon the remains of the ancient city wall. It was a vast and magnificent structure erected in 1675, at a cost of £16,000, and designed after a plan of the palace of the Tuileries in Paris. Louis Quartoze incensed at the architect making his palace a model for a hospital for lunatics, revenged himself by a very whimsical, though not a very decorous proceeding, and had some out-houses erected on the same plan as St. James's Palace, and ornamented in a similar manner. The two fine figures, one representing RAVING, and the other MELANCHOLY MADNESS, sculptured by the father of Colley Cibber, stood on the pedestals behind the gates which were fronted by a large garden. The interior of the building chiefly consisted of two large lobbies or galleries, ranged one above the other, and only separated in the middle by iron gratings, and so ill-conducted were the general arrangements of the place, that these lobbies which should have been most studiously kept free from intrusion, were left at all periods of the day open to loungers and casual visitors, who amused themselves by passing a few hours away in witnessing the frightful scenes enacted by its inmates. The severest censure was thus drawn down upon the governors, but it was not till 1812 that the progress of insanity in England, or rather perhaps the greater attention that was then paid to the subject, enforced the necessity of a larger and more commodious building being raised, and where the memorable "Dog and Duck," tavern, then stood, a suitable and advantageous site was found for it, in the—at that period—untenanted waste of St. George's Field's, Lambeth.

Passing through the exterior gate and entering upon the broad gravel walk that wound through the garden, Jack Sheppard ascended the steps, and was admitted, on giving a small fee to the porter, into the interior of the building.

As the porter led the way, along a succession of dark passages, to his mother's apartment, he was almost stunned by the deafening clamour that resounded on every side. From every cell he passed came sounds of despair. From one were emitted deep sighs, such as sanity, in even the extremity of suffering never gave vent to—from another, groans—from a third, a wild and melancholy song—and from others, shrieks and execrations, and the horrible clank of chains. In one he beheld a miserable creature, covered with rags—for he would permit nothing else to remain on his shivering limbs—stuck up, like a statue, rigid and motionless, in a corner of the dungeon. In another, he saw only a hideous face, which almost touched his, as he passed, and made him start back in dismay. Amidst all, however, came the idle sneer and laugh of several light-hearted groups, to whom the misery thus manifested was a mere amusement, and Jack was not sorry when he escaped from this heartless throng, to visit the cell of Mrs. Sheppard, to which a matron offered to conduct him.

Oh! there is no solitude more terrible than the maniac's cell; no sound more hideous than the wild and impassioned cry, which marks the dethronement of reason from its seat. It is scarcely possible to keep the blood from curdling to the very heart, while one stands between the four bare walls that enclose the miserable lunatic. The wretched pallet on which the emaciated form reposes; the chill sluggish atmosphere the maniac breathes; the perpetual gloom that pervades, if relieved only by the light that flashes from the sleepless eyes: these are sufficiently repulsive to scare even affection's self far away. How many of the world's denizens fancy, in their ignorance, that they nourish love stronger than death; that there are beings in existence, from whom, even this most terrible of all maladies cannot separate them; but how few, how very few, have stood the ordeal, and repaired on a visit of mercy to the den of despair. It is a test which even the strongest minds have impulsively shrunk from.

So thought and felt Jack Sheppard as he paused before the door to which the matron pointed.

"She is quieter to day than she has been for some time past," said the woman as she ushered him into the cell, "poor creature, it has all been caused through her son."

"Leave us alone, my good woman, for a few minutes," interrupted Jack, slipping a golden coin into her extended palm. "I am a relative of the unfortunate creatures, and would wish to speak with her.

"As you please, sir," rejoined the matron with a curtsey—"she is chained and cannot hurt you, and besides she is not very mischievous. However, there are plenty within call, if you want the keeper to come and quiet her."

And thus imparting her injunctions the matron left the lobby and Jack entered the cell.

Although he had been in some measure prepared for a violent shock to his feelings, he could hardly have anticipated so great a change in the appearance of his mind-smitten mother, who with her arms closely folded over her lacerated heart, sat huddled up amidst the straw in a corner of the dungeon with an iron belt round her waist which secured her with a chain to the wall. Her countenance was of a ghastly white, and the bones protruded to an extent that told a fearful tale of suffering and privation.

Muttering some incoherent words to herself at the entrance of Jack, the poor woman hastily twisted together a band of straw, and fixing it on her head for a crown drew herself up as stately as though she had been a monarch receiving titled visitors.

Jack attempted to speak but his sighs

choked him, and his words were drowned in tears.

"Do you not know that I am a queen in my own right?" cried Mrs. Sheppard in tones of dignified surprise. "I am kept here because they want to cheat me of my kingdom. This is no home for me. The grim horrible faces that inhabit it—the jabberings that pervade it through the day, and the shrieks that fill it in the night, are not the sounds that should soothe the ears of a titled and highborn lady. Take me hence to my throne."

Jack scarcely knew what to say or what to do.

"Ah! I see how it is," she exclaimed bitterly, "the wretched have no friends. When I was happy, how they all crowded round me, but now they are all buried, like my son, in the wide weltering sea."

"Mother! Dear Mother! do you not know me," gasped Jack eagerly.

"Hush! I'll tell you my dream last night," pursued the unfortunate being—"I thought my son had turned a thief, and they were going to hang him at Tyburn. Well, I went with others to see the sight, and then instead of Jack—my son Jack—they—ha! ha!—they hung Jonathan Wild."

"Mother, speak to me, I am he—I am your son, your miserable repentant son," sobbed the lad falling on his knees beside her.

"Hush! be silent! I hear Jack speaking to me—he comes and whispers in my ear at night—in the cold, dark night when all is quiet and the stars look down upon us, and he tells me things so strange that—but he has been dead, you know, dead these two months, and they buried him in the freezing earth at Willesden churchyard, and they tell me I went mad—mad over his grave."

"Oh! this is horrible!" cried Jack, pressing his hands before his face, as if to exclude the painful sight.

"And then they scourge me with burning whips, because I ask them to give me my son back again, and—but who are you—why do you come into this dreadful place?" enquired Mrs. Sheppard staring eagerly upon him.

"Because I am your son—Jack—he that you loved so much."

"Oh! my dear boy," cried his mother, on whom the temporary light of reason had shed a flickering flame—"I know you now"—and she strained him to her heart, whilst the erring boy gave vent to his emotions in a flood of hot, bitterly repentant tears.

"And you will never leave me again, Jack, will you?" sobbed the poor woman flinging her thin attenuated arms around him.

"Never, mother, never!" cried Jack with emotion, returning the pressure of her embrace.

"We shall see that," muttered a hoarse voice behind him, and turning round, Jack saw Wild with his two attendants, Abrahams and Bowyer, at his side.

"I expected to find you here, Jack," cried Jonathan, "you are my prisoner."

"You shall take my life first," exclaimed Jack, throwing himself into a posture of defence—"I will not be dragged from my poor mother whilst she is in this dreadful place."

"And who has brought her here?" rejoined Jonathan with a sneer. "Psha! your resistance is idle. Upon him, lads!"

And the two janizaries sprang upon him and secured his arms.

Mrs. Sheppard for a few minutes gazed wildly upon the new-comers and seemed unconscious of their purpose, but as the officers moved to bear Jack away, she uttered a loud and piercing shriek and bounding as far as the trammels of the chain would permit, besought him in touching accents to spare her son.

"Nay, mother," exclaimed Jack, "do not kneel to him. I do not care for myself I deserve this, and much more, but it was for you I struggled to obtain my liberty, and for you I will still struggle to regain it."

"Bolts and bars are not always to yield to *your* hand Jack," scornfully returned Wild—"*this* time you will be better looked after. But there is one condition on which I will even now set you free."

"Oh! whatever it is he will grant it, I am sure, "cried Mrs. Sheppard with an imploring glance at her son.

"It depends entirely on yourself," rejoined Wild.

"On me!" ejaculated the maniac looking round her and scarcely comprehending, even in that lucid interval, the duty that was required of her.

"Ay! on *you*," returned Jonathan fiercely. "Give me your hand in marriage and that moment your son is free to depart whithersoever he will."

"Heed not me mother," interposed Jack, with a sudden comprehension that some important event, what he hardly knew would result from this impulse of his enemy—"Heed not me, but by all the love you bear me, do not yield to his request."

"Come! your answer! quick!" said Jonathan, impatiently clinking the chain in his hand as he spoke—"I have no time for the fooleries of love-making now. You rejected my suit before, and I should not now renew it, in your present imbecile condition especially, did I not wish to make it mutually advantageous. Resist and your son will speedily have his doom determined."

"Oh! mother! I implore you, do not link yourself with this fiend, who must be contemplating some evil deeds in making the proposal," pursued Jack with energy.

"Your answer, woman!" demanded Wild, "I cannot stand here chaffering about this bargain all day."

"Oh! leave me and let me die,"—said Mrs. Sheppard, her reason forsaking her.

"Get married first, and die afterwards, as soon as you like, "remarked Wild brutally, "and the sooner the better, for my purpose at least."

It was fortunate for the speaker that the arms of Jack Sheppard were at that moment restrained by the powerful grasp of his two detainers, or the savage words would have been followed by a blow that would have incapacitated the utterer from repeating them.

"I agree to what he wishes,"—answered the poor woman in a faltering tone.

"You hear that Bowyer—and you Abrahams?" said Wild triumphantly appealing to his witnesses, "you hear—this woman consents to become my wife—she has willingly, and of her own accord, given her hand to me. Run one of you to the Fleet, and get me a parson quickly, I will soon finish this business off hand."

"No! thundered Jack, "I will not stand calmly by, and see this vile proposal carried into execution. My poor mother is a lunatic, and I know enough of law—to feel, as such she cannot be made responsible for her words, or her actions. Had she been in her right senses she never would have thought of thus selling herself."

And as if the spirited words of her son kindled some lingering spark of sanity, the maniac roused herself furiously up as Jonathan bent over her, and emplanting her fingers in his cravat strove to strangle the maker of such a proposal, but her strength failed her, and she sank in the contest.

"S'death you accursed jade," roared Wild, as he struck her furiously with his clenched fist, a violent blow in her side, "let that teach you to behave more civilly for the future."

The wretched woman staggered back, uttered a low moan and fell, exhausted and senseless, upon the straw.

"Monster!" exclaimed Jack, "that blow shall cost you dearly."

"There is no occasion it seems to bestow another in the same place," returned Wild with a malignant grin, as he turned the inanimate body over with his foot, "and now to the magistrates."

Leaving the precincts of Old Bedlam, but not before Jack had given hurried directions to the keeper, to pay every attention in his power to the unfortunate woman, if she survived the blow, a hurried examination ensued before the magistrate, and Sheppard was charged by Wild with having been the chief promoter of, and most active agent in most of the robberies and burglaries that had then excited and alarmed the town. Jack Sheppard, however, by way of reprisal, brought such serious accusations against his accuser, that it was deemed most likely to further the ends of justice, by giving him the opportunity to substantiate his statements, and he was therefore remanded to the New Prison in Clerkenwell, until enquiries could be made into their truth.

As Jack was conveyed away in the cart, and Wild was looking on at the removal with an expression of disappointment, and chagrin at the result, one of his assistants brought him intelligence that Edgeworth Bess had confessed to Blueskin how she had been engaged by the thieftaker, to serve as a spy upon their actions, and to entrap Jack into the commission of crime.

"Very well," answered Jonathan coolly, "you know where to find her—arrest her immediately for that old robbery at Mr. Lutestring's the mercer. Since she chooses to play into his hands she shall share his imprisonment. I will have them both locked up in the same cell."

The messenger departed on his mission.

"That's the worst of the women," growled Jonathan when left to himself, "you never can place any dependance upon them. Drop a little soft water upon them in the shape of tears, and like sugar they will melt at once. I'll never place trust in a petticoat again.

CHAPTER X.

HOW JACK SHEPPARD MADE HIS THIRD ESCAPE AND THE STRANGE EVENTS THAT FOLLOWED.

"Forth from the chains of steel he broke,
As soon as dawn the daylight woke;
Through wall and fence his path he made,
And safely gained the forest glade."

ROKEBY.

As the desperate character of Jack Sheppard had now become well known to the town, his incarceration in the New Prison at Clerkenwell, was attended with manifestations of greater care and more jealous watchfulness over his security than any former imprisonments. He was fettered with chains of an unusual size and ponderosity, and placed in a compartment of the prison, which from its greater strength and safety was endowed with the apt appellation of "The Newgate Ward," a title partly derived from it being the appointed dungeon for those who afterwards were to be committed to Newgate itself. This ward was about four yards in width, and six in length, and furnished with windows reaching nine feet from the floor, but instead of glass they were secured with thick iron bars and an oaken beam that secured the whole together.

Along the basement of the cell was stretched a huge iron bar welted into the sides of the wall, and to this Jack's chain was attached by a large ring, only giving him freedom sufficient to enable him to move from one side of the chamber to the other.

The only prisoner in the same cell with him was Edgeworth Bess, who was loud in her imprecations on the treachery of Wild, but her presence rather softened the pangs of Jack's vexation at his imprisonment, than, as Wild intended, increased them by the contrast afforded between his present position and the orgies in which they had indulged together in the Mint.

The excellent spirits of Jack which had now returned with all their former buoyancy, never deserted him for an instant.

By his fun and drollery he had so ingratiated himself with the turnkey, that every indulgence was afforded him compatible with his condition, and the news of his capture, to which his former escapes had imparted great interest, spread far and wide.

As Wild had lodged information against him of the robbery at Mr. Wood's, and more charges were daily expected to be made, the public excitement, which had not then the gratification of daily newspapers, rose to an alarming height, and the most exaggerated rumours were rife of the disclosures that Jack had promised to make in return against the thief-taker. As day after day flew by, the visitors flocked in increasing numbers to behold the stripling whose deeds had already created such a general sensation, and most of these, by bribes to the turnkey, who suddenly found his situation become one of great emolument, were admitted to see the precocious prison-breaker.

On the afternoon of the day prior to that on which his examination was to take place, an old man, attired like a venerable country squire, applied to the turnkey, and slipping a gunea into his hand, requested permission to see the juvenile prisoner, having a suspicion, as he said, that he was one of a gang who had broken into his country mansion some nights before, and one of whom he could identify by his having caught a glimpse of his features as he attempted to escape.

The turnkey influenced by the amount of the bribe, and having had orders to admit those who came with a view to recognize him, and establish his connections with a number of recent robberies, the perpetrators of which had never been discovered,—admitted the applicant at once, and made both Jack Sheppard and Edgeworth Bess pass in review before him.

The old squire shrewdly and narrowly scrutinised his features, viewing him in every light and from every angle, to obtain a conviction of his identity with the culprit of whom he was in search. Edgeworth Bess—for he resolutely persisted in asserting she was one of the burglar's assistants—was subjected to a similarly severe examination, and as he approached her to compare with his own height the attitude of the woman, to ascertain if it corresponded with that of the figure he saw, the old squire passed his arm round her waist with some alacrity. As this was considered by Jack to be an unnecessary gesture, and as the features of the young lady herself were illumined at the moment with an expressive smile which would scarcely be construed by the most imaginative person into a feeling of dislike to such a preceeding, the passion of jealousy became roused, and he glanced on his visitor with a furious scowl, which showed that if his limbs had been unshackled, the present position of the squire would have been more interesting than secure.

"Well, sir, are you satisfied that these are connected with the gang of housebreakers you mentioned?" inquired the turnkey.

"Hum!" hesitated the squire, "I am not so positive about the boy, but I still have no moral doubt that he is one of them, though I shouldn't like to swear to his identity. Of the female there, I think I can be positive, and I shall give instructions to my solicitor to-morrow to bring that charge against her at the trial."

"Very well, sir," assented the turnkey, taking a note of the proceedings,"—what name shall I set down sir."

"Jonathan Bolton," answered the squire, "of Bolton Hall, Lancashire."

"I will inform Mr. Wild, sir, of your intention," added the official, finishing his insertion of the address.

"Blueskin taken yet?" asked the visitor as he was being bowed out.

"Not he, sir. He is too wide awake to give us a chance of taking him, though here is a reward of £50 offered for his apprehension? But, betwixt you and me, sir," continued the jailor, placing his hand upon the inquirer's shoulder, "I think I know where to lay my fingers upon him at this very moment."

"Indeed?" exclaimed the other, starting back in dismay.

"Aye, sir, I have my suspicions," whispered the turnkey, mysteriously, in his ear, "I have my suspicions that——" and he looked cautiously round to see that no one was within hearing.

"Eh, well? Suspicions, why—what—where?" cried the squire, impatiently awaiting the reply.

"That he is concealed somewhere about the Mint."

"Psha!" muttered the other, "I thought the rascal really knew."

"What did you observe, sir?" said the turnkey, who had only caught the words imperfectly.

"I was saying he was the greatest rascal I ever knew," repeated the squire, as he crossed the threshold of the prison; "he is one who would take steps to get away from a turnkey himself."

"Ah, I should like to catch him at it," observed that individual, who thought the remark savoured much of a personal reflection.

"I dare say you would," pleasantly returned Mr. Jonathan Bolton, assuming his most jocose tones, "I dare say you would —I've no doubt you would—*but you won't*," and as these three last words came with a very different accent from his lips, it is probable that the squire might have left a very different impression behind him, but fortunately for his unimpeached character, the words were uttered out of the turnkey's hearing, and directly afterwards the squire took to his heels, and ran away with a most eccentric, and apparently uncalled for display of his pedestrian powers.

During this short colloquy between Mr. Titus Tibbins, the turnkey, and Mr. Jonathan Bolton, the squire, a very animated but angry discussion was going on in the cell they had just quitted: Jack vehemently challenged Bess with having favoured the advances of his visitor, and followed his denunciations up with such energy, that not a word by way of denial or explanation could be thrust in by the other. Indeed, as Bess answered every fresh outburst with a triumphant smile, and stood with folded arms as unabashed as though she really gloried in what she had done, Jack felt his indignation rise higher and higher, until his wrath—boiling over in a torrent of abuse—found vent at last in the concentration of every exasperating epithet in one of the most opprobrious terms which a woman can receive. He then sullenly relapsed into silence.

But still Bess looked on and laughed, if possible, more wickedly and roguishly than before.

"All over, Jack?" she asked, in one of the most provoking and tantalising ways it is possible to conceive.

"In the name of all that's mysterious, what is the meaning of all this, Bess?" cried Jack, as he saw his companion evidently neither annoyed by his reproaches nor stung by his allusion.

"Why, simply this," returned that young lady, playfully dangling a small bundle covered with a handkerchief before his eyes, "that you haven't half the sharp eye and quick ear that I gave you credit for—that you are a stupid noodle for thinking what you have said about me, and lastly, it means that you have been as regularly done to-day as ever you have been in your life."

"Explain, Bess, there's a good girl," cried Jack; "What's in that bundle, and from whom did you get it?"

"Why, from Blueskin to be sure," answered the girl, "I knew who it was directly, dressed up as the old squire, and his nonsense about Bolton Hall. How the turnkey was bamboozled!"

"What! Jonathan Bolton, Blueskin? "why, what a fool I have been, to be sure," laughed Jack.

"But who on earth, Bess, could have imagined he would have played his part so well," continued Jack, and as if struck afresh with the humour of the incident, bursting out into an uncontrollable fit of laughter, "besides, I never thought he could act the old country gentleman like that; at least, I never heard him talk like one before."

"Ah! you don't know him half so well as I do," returned the fair partner of his imprisonment, "why, bless you, he was a very respectable sort of cove once, before he took to the prigging line and came down to the Mint. Ever since then, he has pattered flash like the rest of 'em, and I suppose it comes more natural to him than his old lingo."

"By all that's lucky," cried our hero, "he deserves to have the place he gammoned old Tibbins into the belief he was the possessor of. He has come to our aid just in the nick of time, though I should have tried hard at something or other to-night. However, I forgive him everything for this, and now, Bess, for the bundle the old fellow has brought. Let us see what we have got inside of it."

The examination of the parcel proved its contents to be of a most useful and miscellaneous kind.

The tools thus conveyed by Blueskin, turned out to be selected with much skill and judgment, and were evidently, from their strength, chosen with a full knowledge of the arduous duties they would have to perform. Three gimblets, a piercer, crowbar, two files, and a chisel, were the articles which Blueskin had so dexterously conveyed, and which Edgeworth Bess had so adroitly concealed.

"I'faith," cried Jack, as his eyes glistened over the timely present thus displayed, "these are quite enough to show Jonathan Wild his boast is as worthless as himself. Egad, its almost worth while to be sent o prison for the purpose of escaping from it."

Ripping open with one of the tools a small portion of the flooring, they secreted the rest carefully beneath the boards, hiding the chisel with which this had been effected behind the cross-beam that guarded the window. It was a fortunate occurrence for Jack that this precaution had been taken, for scarcely had the plank been replaced, before the turnkey, with his attendant, entered the cell and commenced the usual nightly search of the prisoners. Whether he had any belief in Jack's public assertion, that he would make his way out of the prison to return to his mother, or whether he really entertained any suspicion of the old country gentleman, after his departure, is a matter involved in doubt, but certain it is that his examination of their persons, and the premises was more strict than ordinary. Finding nothing, however, to cherish such a supposition, he took his leave, tolerably satisfied with the state in which he had left everything, as he fancied, secure, and with a firm conviction in his own mind, that it was a matter of impossibility for Jack, this time at least, to increase his reputation as a prison-breaker. Being certain now that no farther interruption was likely to arise, Jack regained possession of his tools from their hiding-place, and commenced setting vigorously to work to free himself from his fetters. This, thanks to the rapid attrition of the file he employed, was a task completed in less than an hour.

Calling Bess to his aid, he next clambered up to the window, which, as mentioned above, was strengthened by bars of iron of enormous thickness, and crossed in the centre by a great oaken beam. A spirit less courageous than that which animated Jack would have been daunted by the sight of impediments so formidable, but the animosity he felt towards Jonathan Wild, and the energy with which he felt determined to brook no curb or chain in his career, made him laugh at those obstacles which would have deterred others.

To work then he resolutely went, and having, with wonderful industry, filed away two of the iron bars, he had succeeded in wrenching out a space sufficient for his body to pass through, when his trusty file snapped in twain, and had Blueskin not thoughtfully provided him with another, he would have been compelled to have abandoned the task in despair, for the huge beam of oak, and its stout iron braces still had to be encountered before an egress could be effected.

This then, though the only one, proved the most formidable obstacle to his flight. A moment's reflection determined him how to act. Boring with his gimblet a number of holes close together he succeeded, by driving his chisel in amongst them, in piercing through and cutting asunder the lower part of the bar. The same operation having been gone through with the upper portion, a very slight exertion was only necessary to wrench it away altogether, and great was Jack's triumph and his companion's delight when the beam thus fell away, and a gap quite large enough to answer his purpose was revealed.

Leaping down from the window he next persuaded Bess to partly disrobe, and tearing the gown and petticoat which she took off, into long shreds, he contrived to weave them into a kind of rope which he twisted round and round until it was strong and long enough to answer the end for which it was intended. Fastening this securely to the lower part of the window, he raised but not without difficulty Edgeworth Bess to its level. Then twisting a kind of slip-knot he passed the running noose round her body, and squeezing her through the bars, he took a firm hold of the line, and prepared to direct her descent. As Bess however, had no faith in the strength of her wardrobe and as in fact the experiment was exceedingly hazardous, she no sooner saw the appalling distance she would have to drop than clinging to the three remaining bars she earnestly implored Jack do desist from the attempt as one too perilous to encounter.

Her lover, though really anxious about her safety, had proceeded too far to retract, and he used all the eloquence of which he was capable, to convince her there was no danger, and that the darkness of the night deceived her in the estimate of the distance she had to drop. At last, partly induced by threats, and partly by Jack's urgent entreaties, she was prevailed upon to trust herself to the frail tenure of her own changed habiliments, and relying upon Jack's strong and steady guidance, she closed her eyes and threw herself off. It was an effort requiring all her fortitude and strength of nerve to support, but the eye and hand of Jack, were true to the task and she landed in safety.

Almost before she had gained a firm footing upon the earth, Jack's nimble fingers slid down the line, and he was at her side in an instant. All was however not yet accomplished, It is true they had escaped from the New Prison, but the wall of Clerkenwell Bridewell, by which that prison was formerly surrounded yet remained to be overcome. This almost impregnable enclosure of the jail was upwards of twenty feet high, and protected on the top by a formidable and bristling *chevaux de frieze*. Having surmounted however, former difficulties nearly as great, Jack was not likely to be baffled by this, and after a short consideration with the partner of his dangers, they finally hit upon an expedient. Jack once again ascended the line and climbed into the cell from which it had taken so long to escape. Here he regained possession of his tools and once more sliding down the attenuated garment which only gave way with this last demand upon its continuity, he showed Bess the gimblets with which he had returned and having tested their strength he now entered upon his last and most hazardous experiment.

The night was pitch dark, yet without a drop of rain or breath of wind. That kind of marbly black compact sky which seems to hold the labouring moisture above it enclosed as in a firm dark rock. Not a footfall was heard about the precincts of the jail, and stealthily venturing to the great gates Jack inserted his gimblets at intervals in the wood-work. These, serving as points on which he could rest his foot, formed a sort of ladder for his ascent, and up these fragile supporters Jack nimbly climbed. When he had gained the summit, he contrived by fixing his dress to the pointed spikes at the top to pull Bess up after him, and then, though not without considerable risk he managed to let her fall gradually over on the other side. Having thus duly seen his mistress safely down, he descended after her, leaving a considerable portion of his apparel impaled on the iron-work as a memorial of one of the most daring and difficult escapes that the criminal annals of his country had then ever afforded.

At this period the whole of what is now a densely populated district north of the House of Correction, was a mere tract of waste ground with open fields stretching away to the suburb of Islington. About a quarter of a mile off was a place of very questionable resort, known by the appellation of Merlin's Cave. This was occupied at that time by an old crone, who got her living by the double employment of telling fortunes, and receiving stolen goods, which she sold to the Hebrew transmuters of precious metals, who had thus early established a colony in Houndsditch. To this woman, who was familiarly called "Black Moll," Jack determined to confide his companion, who was now incapacitated from fear, and the excitement of the unwonted exercise she had undergone from proceeding further. Casting a last look at the upper windows of the prison and finding there was no prospect of immediate pursuit, they proceeded at a moderate pace through the deserted streets, and crossing several tea-gardens and bowling greens for the northern part of London at that time abounded in such amusements, at last reached the excavation wherein the cottage of the old sybil was situated.

Committing the almost fainting girl to her care, and promising a liberal reward if she looked after her health and safety, Jack left Edgeworth Bess asleep in the humble tenement of Black Moll, and having concealed his tattered dress by a smock frock which the old dame lent him, he struck across the fields by Canonbury, intending to lurk about the suburbs for a few days, until the excitement of his last escape had blown over.

And such was Jack's marvellous escape from the New Prison, which has been since admitted to have been the most daring feat ever executed within its walls.

CHAPTER XI.

HOW JACK ENTERED UPON ANOTHER STAGE OF HIS HISTORY.

"Night came, the dreary night
Which severed hearts can ne'er unite.
Go, dearest mother! and in calm repose
And sweetest slumber banish far thy woes;
Yet bless, oh! bless thy son,—then gently sleep.
Mother! this is no night for thee to weep.
Sleep! for if absence sink thee in such gloom,
How wilt thou bear death's everlasting doom?
That hour may come too soon; yet in that hour,
Glad solace! thou shalt feel the spirit's power!
Sleep! and ere the sun's first rays are shed,
Mother, thy son will kneel beside thy bed.
God pardon, then, what tears may flow:
More than one mother man can never know."

SUNSHINE AND SHADE.

We have said that Jack had crossed into the fields by Canonbury. His object in so doing was to elude, by seclusion, the hue and cry that he expected would be set afoot by Wild on the intelligence reaching him of his escape. For some time he had wandered on, fearful of returning to the Mint, to confer with Blueskin, yet anxious to borrow from him sufficient from the relics of the robbery at Wood's to supply his immediate necessities, and he now found his wayward progress had led him as far as Finchley, at

which place he paused awhile to arrange his future proceedings.

The sun was still shining brightly upon Finchley Downs as he traversed the narrow winding track that wound across the heathy common, until it was lost in the umbrageous solitudes of the old leafy forest beyond, and though it had nearly attained its extreme point in the west, its beams fell with soft and golden light on the greensward, and cast every dell and opposite slope into deep broad shadow. The scattered bushes and stunted hawthorn glades and the distant wood with its towering beeches alone caught the rays in their full splendour, and as Jack, meditating on his future prospects, sought to penetrate the recesses of the copse to which he was now half unconsciously wending his way, the slanting beams of the declining luminary revealed to him afar off a gang of gipsies, who with that love of nature, apparently inseparable from their tribe, had selected for their encampment the most inviting and picturesque position in the landscape. Actuated by a vague desire to make one of their number, and impelled besides by the dire necessity of applying somewhere for the sustenance of which he was by this time much in need, Jack determined to approach the group, and turning off across the meadow to the skirts of the woodland, he was enabled to come close upon them before his presence could be perceived, and consequently before any unpleasant intimation could be given of it not being desired. As he drew nearer he could see that a fire had been kindled, and as the sticks crackled and the blaze rose, the savoury odour from the pots which were now being removed, showed that some careful culinary operations were being proceeded with, and that the merriest meal of the day was about to be commenced. Around the fire were grouped some dozen forms, male and female, in the centre of whom appeared the chief reclining . pon the ground, with his elbow supported by a projection of the bank, and a young girl, evidently his daughter standing at his side. The whole party were amusing themselves with loud laughter and broad jokes, only chequered at intervals with the sounds of contention and affray, occasioned by an old pack of cards that were being dealt eagerly round to a select few that set apart from the others.

We may here remark that this singular race of vagrants then found in the many extensive wastes about England, the less perfect system of police, and the greater credulity of the lower, and even the middle classes of society, a much wider and clearer field for their vocation than the more stringent laws of the present period would admit.

As Jack approached, he caught in the last part of a song which one of the company had just volunteered, some indication of their reckless love of a life of liberty, so much after his own heart, and the concluding verses in which this admiration was conveyed, we give, in evidence, as they reached his ear.

SONG OF THE GIPSIES.

Be it peace or be it war,
Here at liberty we are;
Hang all constables we cry
We the justices defy.
Where's the nation lives so free
And so merrily as we?

We enjoy our ease and rest,
To the field we are not pressed;
And when taxes are increased,
We are not a penny cessed.
Where's the man who lives so free
And so merrily as we?

Nor will any go to law,
With a beggar for a straw:
All which happiness he brags,
Is mainly owing to his rags.
So the man who would be free,
Had much better come to me!

The tumultuous applause with which this most characteristic ditty was received, had scarcely subsided, when Jack, emboldened by his own wants, and encouraged by the good humour in which he found those who could relieve them, stepped deferentially before them, and solicited a small portion of that inviting cheer which was now being divided amongst the throng.

A few questions were put by the chief, to which Jack gave a ready answer, concerning his past mode of living, and the cause of his present application, and having satisfied themselves that he was not among them as a spy, a share in the steaming porridge was readily accorded.

After the cravings of his appetite were in some degree appeased, the chief of the gipsies whose name appeared to be Nestor—such at least was the appellation bestowed upon him by his fraternity—drew Jack on one side, and asked him whether he would like to join a tribe the members of which roved about so independently of the rest of the world.

As this agreed in some respect with our hero's views, he readily accepted the offer that was soon after made him, and at once staining his face with walnut juice so as to disguise his features, and assuming the garb of the gipsy tribe, he found by this timely meeting that he could now not only pursue his original intention of remaining concealed for a few days about the neighbourhood, but that he could also rely upon a constant supply of food during the time, without exposing himself to the hazardous risk of personally obtaining it.

With this roving band he remained four days, sharing the hospitalities of their table, and lending his aid, which from his experience in the craft was by no means valueless, for those predatory excursions which were undertaken at night to provide for the exigencies of the ensuing day.

At last, late in the afternoon of the fourth day of his sojourn amongst the friendly wanderers, Jack, unable to repress his anxiety about his parent and to say truth, being also somewhat anxious to meet with Blueskin and Edgeworth Bess—determined to make an effort to obtain an interview and watching the opportunity of the attention of the rest being diverted, he silently withdrew himself from their society, and proceeded without exchanging a word of parting, on his way to the retreat at Islington.

It had grown dusk by the time he had reached the northren environs of the Metropolis, and before he came to the district in which was situated the home of Black Moll, night had far advanced. Cautiously approaching the excavation, he looked eagerly around for some indication of its inhabitants, but though Merlin's Cave still marked the spot, all signs of occupancy had fled. There was neither a light as usual at the window, nor the customary signal of the red tape round the door-post to show that the reputed witch might be consulted on questions of futurity. All was still and deserted, and when Jack knocked at the door there was no reply to his summons, but the mewing of a spectral black cat within, that had apparently been forgotten by the other inmates. A circumstance so strange and unusual as the absence of the woman at this hour, excited the most intense curiosity of Jack, and animated by an earnest wish to sift the mystery to the bottom, he resolved to force open the door of the cottage and see if anything had been left behind, which would furnish a clue.

It required but little exercise of strength on the part of Jack, to force open the crazy old door off its hinges, and striding across the threshold, he called loudly out to those in the house—if any such there were—to come from their hiding place and show themselves. There was however no sound in answer to his inquiry but the echo of his own voice, and convinced now that neither Edgeworth Bess nor the woman to whose care he had intrusted her, were within its walls, he left the building with his mind a prey to the most agonising and torturing suspense.

At one time he conjectured that Wild had found out her lurking-place, and had by forcible measures consigned her once again to prison, but still the improbability of this was so great that almost as the idea occurred to him he dismissed it from his thoughts. Then he fancied that Bess had recovered and sought out another abode, and that she might possibly have found a mode of communicating with Blueskin, and entrusted him with the secret of her present habitation. At last wearied out with these and fifty other suppositions equally as uncertain and as unsatisfactory, he determined to make his way at all hazards to the Mint, and see if he could gain any tidings of either her or Blueskin.

On his way thither he had to cross what was then rural enough to be called the "Lover's Walk," but which now forms a portion of Goswell Street Road, and at the corner of this thoroughfare looking towards the City, stood a long white building, the latticed casements of which opening out upon the wooden galleries that ran round the walls of the house, low angular roof, and paved court yard, recalled to the observer, the plan and appearance of the carrier's inn of the days of Shakespere. This was the famous tavern known as the "Old Red Lion," and over the doorway was inserted a square slab of white marble carved with the arms and crest, now nearly effaced by time, of the family who formerly possessed the manor-house which stood once upon its site. Collected on the benches laid out in the trim garden plot before the inn, were groups of artizans and tradesmen discussing the amber home brewed ale, for which the house was famous, and the local news and topics of this day.

Thirsty with his walk and attracted by the cheerful appearance of the place, Jack walked into the enclosure, and occupying a vacant seat in the porch, prepared himself a draught of ale and a rest to encounter long walk that was in store for him.

He had not been seated long before to his great surprise, as well as gratification, he saw an individual enter whom he recognised in a glance, as the one who had done him such essential service in the new prison. Still attired as Jonathan Bolton, this personage appropriated a vacant seat opposite to Jack, and calling for a tankard of home brewed and a pipe, became speedily enshrouded in the copious clouds of tobacco smoke that he emitted at short intervals from his lips.

The first impulse of Jack was to attract his attention, and make his presence known, but immediately reflecting that such a mode of proceeding might unintentionally invite the notice of the rest of the company, and place the safety of both in jeopardy, he contented himself by keeping his eye watchfully upon him, and determined to await a more convenient opportunity. This was speedily afforded—the arrival of one of the north-country waggons, with the bustle of baiting the horses and removing the luggage and passengers, broke up the quiet assembly and amongst the rest Mr. Jonathan Bolton, having finished his roadside refreshment, laid down his pipe and retired also, followed immediately by Jack Sheppard.

Still keeping him in sight, Jack followed his former associate down the road, preserving a respectable distance till the thoroughfare became more free of passengers, when suddenly quickening his pace, he came up to his side and in a hollow but impressive voice ejaculated his name.

"Blueskin!"

The assumed country squire shortened the stick that he held in his hand, with a threatening movement of his elbow and started back at the sound, but immediately his apprehensions were removed by Jack, whose Gipsy disguise had proved most efficacious, and making himself known, his delight was most unbounded and he could hardly refrain from bursting out into a congratulatory "Huzza!" in the road.

"Vhot, my little crib-cracker!" exclaimed the creole, "here's a fortunate meeting—here's a lucky chance for a cove to pick up as he valks along—vhy, where have you been, and vhot have you been doing, and vhen——but stop a bit, it won't do to run out so with a chance of listener's being about, so as we have got werry near to my present crib, 'spose ve toddles silently in and lets out our knowledge boxes over a comfortable kvartern."

To the propriety of this proposal, Jack at once assented. It appeared that Blueskin, having been driven from his old quarters in the Mint, by the earnest pursuit of Wild and his emissaries, hadtaken up a temporary abode in a region of narrow tenements and unscrupulous tenants at the back of Smithfield, and here, letting himself into the room with his key, Blueskin speedily made Jack be seated on the only article of furniture his room afforded—a ricketty chair—and establishing a tub upside down for his own accomodation, he promptly kindled a fire, produced a bottle of potent spirits, and blending it with the contents of the kettle that he soon set boiling on the hob, the two sat themselves down to a long conversation, mingled with such a display of conviviality as would give a welcome zest to the entertainment.

Jack, in a few words, explained the particulars of his escape, and the result of the other's friendly mission. He alluded to his successful and secluded sojourn among the gipsies, and his unceremonious departure therefrom, and finally ended the history of his adventures with an enquiry after the fate of his companion, Edgworth Bess. But to this Blueskin could give no satisfactory reply. He had found, as he said, the old sanctuary, which was fast losing its immunities, becoming too much infested with officers and spies for his safety, and he relied upon the disguise which had hitherto proved impenetrable, to protect him in the present quarters he had chosen. Of the proceedings of the rest he had learned nothing, save that the escape of Jack had created much excitement everywhere, but Edgworth Bess he had never seen since he left her in the prison.

"And my unfortunate mother?" inquired Jack.

The countenance of Blueskin immediately fell, and his brow darkened.

"Has any new misfortune befallen her?" asked Jack, his voice trembling with emotion.

"Alas! She is dead."

"Dead!"

"That blow Jonathan Wild gave her was her death."

"Inhuman monster!" exclaimed Jack, with energy, "but I will yet repay him for it dearly."

"She only lived to breathe your name, I hear, and then immediately expired," continued Blueskin—"I heard it all told yesterday by one of the turnkeys who was in the neighborhood here."

"My poor Mother!" cried Jack, with an earnest display of feeling, "I am afraid that I have been the cause of all. When will she be buried?"

"On Sunday next, as I understand," returned Blueskin, unwilling to check by any flippant remark, the pathos in which his companion indulged, and having besides that innate respect for grief, like his, springing from the heart, which deterred him from striving to divert its course. "On Sunday next, poor woman she will be consigned to her last home!" a painful pause ensued.

"I will attend her funeral."

"Jack!"

"Nay," continued the youth with firmness, "do not attempt to dissuade me from my purpose. I have a sacred duty to perform and I must fulfil it."

"But consider the danger, Jack," interposed Blueskin.

"It is no matter. Go I must and will. If Jonathan himself were there, I would boldly stand beside her grave, and denounce him as her murderer."

Finding all remonstrance was useless, Blueskin persuaded Jack Sheppard to remain with him during the intervening days, and then all the previous arrangements having been made, Jack was permitted to set forth on his filial mission of attending the obsequies of his deceased parent.

CHAPTER XII.

HOW JACK SHEPPARD ATTENDED THE FUNERAL OF HIS MOTHER.

"How still the morning of this hallowed day!
Mute is the voice of rural labour hushed
The ploughboy's whistle and the milkmaid's song.
The scythe lies glittering in the dewy wreath
Of tedded grass, mingled with fading flowers
That yestermorn waved blooming in the breeze."
GRAHAM.

It was scarcely daybreak on the morning of the ensuing Sabbath, when Jack Sheppard, leaving the hospitable home of Blueskin, bent his steps sadly and sorrowfully in the direction of Willesden. Although he could not fail to accuse himself of being the chief cause of his mother's lamentable end, there was blended with this feeling, a strong hatred of his persecutor Jonathan Wild, whom he taxed, and not unjustly, with having been the principal agent in her death and his own downfall. Musing, as he went, on the steps by which he could best secure retribution, he was too much occupied in his own thoughts to heed the beauty of the scenery that was opening around him.

It was a bright summer morning; one of those glorious daybreaks in the month of July, which seem so intimately associated with the thoughts of life and enjoyment, rather than of death and the dark, cold grave. Jack had deemed it more prudent to preserve the disguise he had assumed whilst in company of the gipsies, and fearless of discovery, he now passed without shrinking from the few early stragglers that the brightness of the opening day had called from their slumbers. It was noon before he reached the hamlet that was to be his destination. The villagers were thronging to church, and the peaceful serenity of the scene around him contrasted strangely with the turbulent emotions that agitated his own breast. He hurriedly gave a passing glance at the cage which had witnessed his recent escape, and turning into an adjoining house, where though the landlord was the very constable who had received him in charge, he was not recognised. Jack ordered some breakfast to be prepared, and watched from the window those images which were so familiar to him, by way of passing the time in the interval.

There are few things which strike more painfully upon the heart than the immutability of physical objects, whilst the mind itself becomes so much changed. The river glides on murmuring to the air and glistening to the sun, whether we are sad or sorrowful; human frames shoot, ripen and decay,—human hearts bud, bloom and wither, —but nature and nature's works remain unchanged. They present the same aspect though all with us has been shattered, uprooted, and reversed. Everything with us is altered—everything with them is so painfully the same. So felt Jack as he gazed on the well-known cottage wherein his mother had resided, on the fields which he had so often traversed, and on the stream where in the early days of his apprenticeship he had so often come down to enjoy a summer bathe. All wore to his eye the same appearance as of yore. but how great the change that had befallen him! Then had he been pure and honest, his mind uncontaminated by vicious principles; now was he a convicted thief—a proscribed felon and an outcast.

Leaning upon a stile that led by a narrow winding pathway to the churchyard, Jack saw one of his former playfellows pensively watching the effect of the waving shadows as the sunbeams glanced through the foliage of a tree near which he stood. There he was with the seal of death already on his brow, the ravages of consumption visible in his hectic cheek, a fading relic of mortality, withering away amid the universal blush and bloom of reviving nature—its bright and beautiful creations, so soon to be seen dimly and indistinctly through the gathering mists of death—and yet at that moment, Jack conscious of the hardy strength and robust health he possessed, would have gladly exchanged conditions with his dying playmate. He felt, so great was his compunction, that to pass away from the earth with a soul unstained by crime was in itself a passport to happier regions. Better an early grave with integrity of principle, than a long life of viciousness and roguery.

Yes, such were the reflections—strange ones indeed for him—that now arose within him as he gazed in reverie on the calm prospect. Scarcely could he admit to himself the elevating nature of his thoughts, so different to those the associations of his nightly revels had given birth to. Hardly was he conscious of their assuming a form clear and palpable within his dizzied and distracted brain. It was as if he had entered upon a second life, as if he stood upon the threshold of a new and purer existence. It might have been the associates thronging around him, the peaceful aspect of the place itself, or the calm hopefulness that pervaded the Sabbath day. Any one of these influences might have struck upon the better chords of his heart and vibrated again those tones of loving exhortation and gentle instruction which he had listened to in his boyhood, but to Jack it seemed as if the spirit of his mother, freed from all earthly restraint and trammels, was hovering around him and whispering words of counsel in his ear. The sudden tolling of the bell startled him from his reverie and he now saw that divine service being over, the preparations for the funeral were about to commence.

Each stroke of the dismal peal went coldly to his heart as he left the private room he had engaged at the inn, and followed a party of loungers to the churchyard, as if like them he had been impelled thither merely by curiosity.

A few of the villagers who had assembled to pay the last tribute of respect to the deceased, were standing beside the new-made grave. The sexton had thrown aside his mattock and was now resting upon his spade, awaiting the remainder of the ceremony. The party pressed on from behind, and Jack leaning forward amongst the rest, beheld the grave that had been dug to receive the remains of the last relative he had.

There is a gratification, mournful indeed to the last degree, but not the less real, in lingering over the grave of one we love. Whilst sorrow in its first gush of wild intensity, weighs down the heart, immediate contact with its cause may be avoided; but when time has wrought its soothing work upon us, when despair has subsided into sorrow and sorrow again has softened into sadness, then indeed to mourn over the tomb of what we have loved on earth, is food for the heart, subduing the wildest passions of our nature, and pouring a tranquil flood of resignation on our soul.

The sudden shock at seeing the future resting-place of his parent, almost threw Jack off his guard. He had the utmost difficulty to keep his emotions under control, and he would doubtless have betrayed himself by giving vent to his acute feelings had not at that instant the remarks of a bystander drawn off the attention of the rest and announced the approach of the corpse to the churchyard.

From the conversation of the villagers near him Jack gained some intelligence respecting his mother's decease for which he had not been prepared. From this he learned that before Mrs. Sheppard had breathed her last, she had sent for Mr. Wood, and had had a long interview with him; that the carpenter had been made the confidant of some important information respecting the nature of which the speaker was in doubt, but surmised that it related to the disposal of some relics belonging to her husband, who had so singularly disappeared; that the poor woman had since the fatal blow given by Wild, recovered her reason, and that her last wish was to be buried in Willesden churchyard—a wish that Mr. Wood had made her a solemn promise to see fulfilled. This another added he had carried out at his sole expense, and with a feeling that did him honor.

The melancholy procession approached, Mr. Wood was leaning on the arm of a relation, and passing up the pathway entered next after the coffin into the church. He held his handkerchief to his face and the hood of his mourning cloak was drawn over his eyes, yet as it reminded him of a scene similar in its nature that had taken place not long before, the marble whiteness of his cheeks and the quivering of his muscles, showed too plainly what was passing in his mind within; a portion of the service was performed in the church, and this perhaps is the most mournful part of the whole. As the morning service had long since terminated, and the burial was not deemed of sufficient importance to attract a vast number of stragglers, the church was nearly empty, and the cold struck piercingly up to the very bones, from the effect of the stone pavement of the church and its vast uninhabited space.

The sinking the coffin into the grave, is the most impressive part of the ceremony of burial. It is then that the dead seem cut off from all comunication with the world; true that we lose sight of them for ever. The harsh grating sound of the first handful of earth that fell upon the coffin, fell truly like the knell of all his hopes upon the ear of Jack. He started, trembled, and overcome with anguish, would have thrown himself into the grave, had he not been forcibly held by a bystander, who attributed his excited behaviour to some intimate acquaintainship with the deceased.

As the earth was being again thrown into the grave, by the quick hand of the sexton, Jack heard on every side of him expressions of heart-sprung sympathy, felt for the deceased, and execrations liberally lavished on the conduct of her son. He knew how much both had been deserved, and keenly felt the justice of their blame. At this moment the penetrating gaze of one of the assemblage pierced through Jack's disguise, and as he was about leaving the precincts of the place, Jack felt a gentle hand with a detaining grasp placed upon his shoulder. He turned round prepared to encounter the rough grasp of his persecutor Jonathan, when his eyes rested upon the pensive countenance of his master.

Surprise and a feeling of self-reproach choked the exclamation that rose to his lips.

"I was convinced it was you Jack," said Mr. Wood in a clear tone of voice, and leading him out of the hearing of the rest—"I noticed your agitated demeanour, when the mortal remains of her whom you have assisted to destroy, were placed in their final earthly abode. That you *are* here gives me a better opinion of you, then I before entertained. It speaks to me of reformation for the future—of the beginning of a better course of life than that you have been latterly leading. Tell me, am I right?"

"I did not expect to meet *you* here, sir," returned Jack, evading the question.

"And you are afraid now you have encountered me that I shall render you up to justice, is it not so?"

Jack looked an affirmative, though no words were uttered in reply.

"Listen to me, Jack," pursued Mr. Wood in the same conciliatory manner that he had adopted before—"I have said that your thus attending the funeral of your lamented parent, convinces me that the last spark of virtue in your breast is not yet extinct. But you have much to answer for. You have behaved towards me ungratefully, in striving to reduce the produce of many years of hard labour, by a cruel and most heartless robbery; to this your comrade added the viler crime of murder, and thus besides the act of theft you have imbued your hands in blood."

"Oh, sir, spare your reproaches," interrupted Jack, "I have never since ceased to regret the unlucky deed, believe me."

"I do believe you," continued the worthy carpenter, "else I had not thus spoken camly of what has broken up my house, and left me a scantier pittance for my declining days than that to which I was entitled to look forward. But I believe you to have been led away from the paths of rectitude by bad advice, and vicious associates. Remember I once cautioned you against this before, but, alas! you heeded me not. I now again warn you of the dreadful end to which all this will lead. A word from me would in a few minutes consign you to the walls of a prison—From there the next step would be to the scaffold. But in the first place I would not wish to take a mean advantage of a visit your better feeling prompted you to pay, and in the second, I have still have some hope of your yet being a creditable member of society. You have energy and skill—go, seek some means of obtaining an honest livelihood, and if the ill-gotten gold of which your companion robbed me, is, as I suspect, all squandered away, in drunkenness and debauchery, I will supply you with the present contents of my scanty purse to enable you to apply it to a better purpose, so that you may not be driven into evil society again for lack of means to exist."

Jack's heart was too full to enable him to return the answer that he wished, and as Mr. Wood proferred the handful of coins for his acceptance, he could only stammer out a few inarticulate words in rejection of his considerate offer.

"You refuse my aid then," said Mr. Wood.

"I thank you, sir," returned Jack respectfully, after a pause "but I do not stand in need of it."

"Then remember that whilst you adhere to the good principles, that I trust the events of this day have awakened in your heart, you have in me a friend to whom you may hereafter apply If you still persist in your evil ways nothing will save you from a sad and shameful end, and the day may come when the words I now have uttered will ring with awful warning in your ear."

"I shall remember, sir," cried Jack, casting a rapid glance round him for fear this protracted interview might have excited suspicion.

Wood guessed his meaning and continued —"I hope you will profit, Jack, by what I have said, and now I must leave, for there are those about here, who are not so indulgent as perhaps on this occasion I may have foolishly been. If you had still attended to the honest craft I brought you up to, Jack, all had yet been well, but there is yet time to repent, and reform. You have another chance open to you—do not lose it —more, much more depends on your future mode of life, than you can now be made aware of. Your poor mother on her deathbed, confided to me certain papers of importance, which, when you come of age, I am to deliver to you—but not before. She made me promise, too, not to take any steps for your apprehension—you can best tell how I have kept my word But go—seek to live by the honest labour of your hands —let me hear that you are no discredit to the honest craft of carpentering, Jack, and my blessing on your endeavours. There—good bye"

Jack Sheppard, still under the influence of the melancholy scene, of which he had been a witness, wrung his benefactor's hand with fervor, and renewed his acknowledgements of gratitude, and confession of repentance.

"There that will do," returned his former employer, "you have now a career for good or evil before you—choose your path and let my hand be a fingerpost to the right one."

Mr. Wood then rejoined his friends that he had left waiting in the porch, and Jack returned meditatively homeward, musing on the strange and unexpected interview which had so great a tendency to change his future mode of life.

Fatigued and jaded with that long day's travel, it was night before he had arrived at Blueskin's lodging. Finding that his companion had not yet arrived, Jack threw himself down on the extra palliasse that had been provided for his accomodation and in a short time was buried in a profound slumber.

From this he did not awaken until late in the next day, and then he found Blueskin waiting at the side of his humble pallet, dressed to his surprise in a garb altogether new, consisting of a richly embroidered blne riding coat with silver broid and flowing ruffles, and his entire apparel such as was generally worn at that period by country gentlemen of independent property.

After rubbing his eyes to convince himself that he really was awake and not dreaming, Jack could not refrain from uttering an expression of astonishment at the metamorphosis he witnessed.

"Oh! I thought you would stare a bit when you came to see me in all this fine toggery," cried Blueskin, watching with satisfaction the admired gaze bestowed on it by his pupil, "I would'nt disturbe you before I was dressed, so that I might regularly come the out-and-outer over you all at once."

"Why, were the duece did you get such a rigging from," inquired Jack.

"Oh, I think its the tipey, is n't it?" was the reply—"but I have got just such another for you, so open your peepers as wide as you like, clap on your new suite, and listen to the scheme as I am agoing to propose to you."

As one of Jack's reigning follies, and one which hitherto he had not had the means of gratifying, was a love of dress, no very strong inductment was needed to persuade him to avail himself of the rich apparel that Blueskin had brought.

"And now, look here," said that indi_

vidual as soon as our hero had downed his garments accordingly, "I did'nt get to this blessed crib till it was too late, last night, to put you up to a fakement that I have had nursing in my noddle for some time past. I have been thinking, Jack, the best thing that was to be done, when all the money was gone, so what do you think I hit upon at last."

Jack confessed his utter inability to imagine.

"Why I went down to old Aaron's in the Minories yesterday after you left and laid out half of it in these togs."

"Well but what have these to do with this notable scheme you talk about?" inquired Jack, "What's the fakement you mean to be after now?"

"I'll tell you—that's the point I was coming to," responded the other. "This last affair of ours has put all the beaks fly to our old haunts—it's nix my dolly as far as London cracking goes—for some time at least—the topping coves are getting too wide a-wake for us hereabouts—and so—"

"Well," impatiently urged Sheppard, who though tolerably used to the long-winded harangues of his associate, was now somewhat anxious to ascertain what this protracted preamble would lead to—"what do you propose?"

"Having a quiet shy at the cribs in the neighbourhood, or if needs must, taking a morning's walk into the country for the benefit of the air, and the improvement of our present prospect," rejoined Blueskin, "in this sort of caper there's no one who would find us out, and as we shall be able to go amongst the nobs there's not much chance of our being suspected. I know a lot of places where the swag is easy to be got and the fakement can be managed without much chance of the trap."

"And so you mean to try this at once, and get me to join you in it, eh! Blueskin?" remarked Jack.

"Why you don't seem to fancy the spec—you arn't agoing to desert your old pal when it comes to a push like this?" cried Blueskin in surprise.

"Listen to me," answered Jack—"I am going to change my mode of living—I am going to turn honest."

"No!" exclaimed the other, whose amazement at what he had just heard curtailed a long speech he was about to have made, to a mere monosyllable.

"Yes, Blueskin—the sight of my mother's grave yesterday, and some other circumstances which occurred there, have set me thinking a bit, and I have now determined to work for my living!"

"Oh, things arn't quite so bad as all that I hope,"—rejoined his companion, to whom such an event seemed to be the most terrible misfortune that could befal a person. "You're joking, Jack!"

"Not I. I mean to turn a journeyman carpenter again."

"Ah! you are sich a wag!" pursued Blueskin.

"I assure you I was never more serious in my life." returned our hero solemnly.

"Well then—I see how it is!" pursued the other, in a doleful tone, as though a moral backsliding had to be lamented—"some unprincipled fellow has been a pisoning your mind."

"I have expressed my determination," answered Jack with apparently a fixed resolution to maintain it.

"Vell, I never thought you would turn shabby and shirk a respectable perfession like what I have taken such pains to eddicate you for," continued his comrade,—"vhot an extravagant sin it is, to be sure, to leave all this blessed money vhot is ready to jump into your pockets for a poor living to be got from a trumpery hammer and nail. To put on a miserable jerkin instead of cutting about in these here handsome clothes and be a mere sneaking vorkaday cove who hasn't the real spirit of a bluebottle about him."

"Blueskin," interrupted Jack, "remember it is not cowardice that influences me," and he felt his good intentions somewhat shaken.

"Ah, people call things by different names," continued the wily tempter, "but the article is just the same call it how yer vill. Here am I a vorking every day to think how I can serve yer, a going down ever so far to get ever so much, entirely on your account, and just as I hits upon the right sort of caper and reckons upon the aid of my old pal—vhot does yer do—? vhy yer goes and puts the extinguisher upon everything and leaves me to manage how I can."

"Well, for one more crib you shall have my assistance," at last exclaimed Jack, unable to resist any longer: he taunts and bantering of his associate—"but remember only *once* more."

"Vell, then if it must be so," rejoined Blueskin, somewhat softened—"only once more be it. There! take my hand and we vill vork this last—how the vord sticks in my throat—this last fakement together. Only vonce more! Vhy I shall have to go into mourning arterwards."

Once more! it is the fatal error of mankind—the power to stop when another false step is taken, is beyond the frail controul of erring mortals.

Alas, Jack's resolution failed him and he had not the moral courage to resist and

firmly return a negative when his lips most heeded it. Like the habitual drunkard who knows that the goblet he is about to drain is poison, yet he swallows it. Like him he knows, for the example of thousands have painted it to him in glaring colours, that it will deaden all his faculties, take the strength from his limbs, and the happiness from his heart—oppress him with a weary life, and hurry his prospects to a dishonourable grave, but still he drains it under a species of dreadful spell, akin to that by which the small creatures are said to approach and leap into the jaws of the loathsome serpent whose fiendish eyes have fascinated them. Once more! the final path is determined on, and too late will it be to retrace the false step. The guardian angel of Jack spread her wings and flew away in despair—unchecked and uncontrolled, he was left in the power of the fiend of evil, and he was now—once more—irrevocably lost beyond the chance of recovery. having the double effect of baffling his future

Once more the friendly exhortations of Wood were forgotten, and once more he plunged into the vortex of crime beyond the possibility of extrication.

CHAPTER XIII.

EDGEWORTH BESS.

" How vice and virtue in the soul contend,
How widely differ yet how nearly blend,
What various passions was on either part.
And now confirm, now meet the yielding heart."

CRABBE.

WHILST the preparations are making for the new foray of the two housebreakers, we must now follow the fortunes of another personage who figures in our history, and whose singular disappearance together with that of the old crone at Merlin's cave, had so much excited Jack's curiosity. The a imosity roused on the part of Jonathan Wild against Edgeworth Bess, must be already familiar to the reader, and this intentions, and disappointing him in a project nearest to his heart was not easy to be allayed. So complete were Jonathan Wild's machinations, that with a spy system as extensive as that of the Jesuits, it was a matter of uncertainty who were in his confidence or not. Thus in thwarting his views, the one who was daring enough to be his antagonist, had to contend with the complicated machinery that a word from him could set motion. There was no safety in anything but immediate flight, if indeed any distance was sufficiently great to be beyond the reach of Jonathan Wild, and thus a powerful control was always exerted over his adherents,

On the second day of the sojourn of Edgeworth Bess with the old dame before mentioned, an old customer of Black Moll's came and paid her a visit, taking with him in exchange, for some current coin, of his Majesty's Mint a packet of gold trinkets which had been the produce of a previous robbery consigned to the unscrupulous dame, who served as a fence or go-between in such transactions. During this interview, Bess, who had quite recovered from her temporary indisposition happened to be present, and the earnest glance which the new comer directed towards her on her entrance did not escape her penetrating eye. After his departure she communicated her suspicions to the old woman but she confidently insisted on his perfect honesty of purpose and freedom from Wild's control that her fears for her safety were speedily removed.

It so happened however that this very individual had been the one employed by Jonathan to track out the fugitives, and under his direction he had visited the various houses resorted to by escaped felons; as the thief-taker rightly conjectured it would be to one of these, that Jack, and his mistress, would fly for concealment after their escape from Clerkenwell.

Accordingly, towards dusk, a loud knocking at the door of the cavern warned the inmates of danger, and before any effectual steps for their security could be taken, the door had been violently broken open, and the janizaries of Wild strode into the apartment. Edgeworth Bess was instantly secured and having gagged and blindfolded her, Bowyer and Abrahams forced her into a vehicle that they had in readiness, and proceeded rapidly in the direction of the Old Bailey with their prize, Having been consigned to one of the numerous cells, with which, as before described the thieftaker's mansion abounded, the bandage was removed from her eyes and she found herself left in a narrow dungeon with a faint light streaming from a flickering oil-lamp at her side, and a scanty allowance of bread and water left for her immediate use. Edgeworth Bess was at no loss to attribute her abduction to the hand of Wild, and knowing how she had betrayed his interests in her love for Jack, was fully prepared to experience the old weight of his revenge now he had her in his power. But of the locality of the place to which she had been consigned, she had no knowledge whatever, and as there was no aperture for light or air, but a small grating over the barred door, all hope of escape was entirely precluded.

Wearied out with apprehensions of danger, from a quarter whence she knew no mercy was ever known to come, Bess fell off into a deep slumber, and on awaking a few hours afterwards, for night or day was in that subterranean cell, equally unmarked by other light than that of the lamp, she heard the heavy door turn on its hinges and Abrahams entered.

"Mishter Vilds, ma tear, vishes to speak a few vords to you," exclaimed that worthy with a sinister smile, as he entered.

"Then tell him to come and talk to me here if he wants" answered Bess, "If he has brought me to this cold place to sleep, I am sure its quite good enough for him to say what he wants with me in."

"Ah, Mishter Vilds knows best about that," muttered the janizary, "If yer don't come vith a good vill, I must carry yer—that's all."

"Well, then since I must go I suppose I had better let him have his way. My turn will come though sooner or later."

And following the few though long corridors of stone, and up apparantly interminable flights of stone stairs, Edgeworth Bess was at last ushered into the presence of the thief-taker, who surrounded by heaps of documents and papers was seated in the same room that had previously been the scene of his interview with Lord Orford.

"Ah! you're a clever girl, Bess," said Jonathan Wild as she entered, and they were left alone, "but you see I knew were to overreach you at last. I am sorry I couldn't grant you an interview last night, but however to day my time is less occupied, and I shall be happy to introduce you to his majesty's officers of Newgate for that old affair of yours,—pray be seated, I expect them here every moment."

"It's of no use attempting to come the polite over me Jonathan, "rejoined the lady, "I'm up to your gammoning tricks, and know the meaning of them. If you mean to send me off to quod, why here I am and they can take me as soon as they like, but if you don't why tell me what you do mean and be quick about it too as I want to be off somewhere or other."

"Well, that is frank enough, Bess," continued Wild, "I don't want to do you much harm for the sake of old acquaintance, but where is your dare-devil paramour Jack Sheppard, and what is he doing now, eh?"

"How should I know? Better find him and ask him that yourself," was the quick and abrupt reply.

"Cut you, Bess, for a fairer face and now wants to get rid of you, isn't that the case?" insinuated the artful thieftaker.

"Not he!" answered Bess, bridling up and somewhat nettled at the hint of such an occurrence—"he knows when he's well off, and that's more than other's do—or you would be content to have me here without bothering yourself about him."

"Well, then to come to the point at once. You have betrayed my confidence already, and so you cannot expect that I should place much reliance on your promises for the future, but I have it in my power to do you a service if you will immediately undertake to render me an essential one in return."

"It's not to deliver up, Jack, or injure him him in any way, is it? Because if it is I may as well tell you at once, flatly, I shan't do it."

"I'll attend to him," returned Jonathan, "What I want you to do has reference to another person. One Mr. Kneebone, a Woollen Draper in St. Clements."

"Ah, I've heard Jack speak of him often" rejoined Bess.

"His apprehension is of consequence to the state, and I am anxious to be the medium of his capture," resumed Wild,—"twice has he foiled me already, but this time I think I can make certain of my prey. Now look here, Bess, the case simply stands thus. I knew you wouldn't come to me willingly and so I employed force in conveying you hither. I could now send you to Newgate with no other trouble than giving a signal to the officers across the way, but that wouldn't answer my purpose. I wish to turn you to better account. I'll undertake to screen you from the fate that otherwise awaits you, if you will give me your assistance in this affair."

"But I really don't see at present what I have got to do," responded Bess.

"Listen. This woollen-draper is a vain, conceited coxcomb, always boasting of his influence over your sex. Wary as he is in every other point, this is one in which he may be easily attacked. You have only got to throw yourself in his way and exhibit that coyness and bashful reserve, which you so well know how to assume, and he will at once be smitten and make advances to you. Of these you must take advantage—worm yourself into his confidence, and ascertain where the list of adherents to the Pretender, which I know he has got among his pa pers is deposited. This with any other documen that you think is likely to be important you bring to me and you can take any little valuable away for yourself at the same time. But remember, woman," added Jonathan in a more impressive tone, "you will be narrowly watched, and if you attempt to play me false in this affair, I'll have you subjected to a torment from which you would thank death for releasing you."

"Oh, I don't mind having some fun with this Kneebone," answered Bess carelessly, "but if you turn rusty upon poor Jack, mind I don't answer for the consequences."

"Well, then you are now free to depart on your mission," said Wild, opening the door with a spring to admit her departure,—"you can make certain of your man?"

"I am no true woman if I don't," replied Bess, "Mr. Kneebone, St. Clements, I shall remember," and smiling at the singular and unexpected result of her conference with the thief-taker, at whose instigation she expected some measures of severity would have been taken against her, Edgeworth Bess took a farewell of the designing schemer, and proceeded on her way to the woollen-draper's.

"Plague on the wench," ejaculated Wild as soon as she had gone, "I would have rather managed the business without her help if I could, but all the rest are so confoundedly old and ugly, and as for Poll Maggott, why the very sight of her would have been sufficient to have frightened the gull from the snare. However she is now as securely in my clutches as though I kept her in the cell beneath, and for her own sake this time she must be true to me. As for her cully—the-prison-breaking-imp—whose daring becomes every day greater with his impunity of committing crime, I shall attend to him after I get this state business out of hand in a way he little expects."

"And thus reserving his future proceedings against Jack for a more convenient opportunity, Wild resumed his examination of the mass of documents before him, and was speedily absorbed in the contemplation of their contents.

As for Bess she was hardly satisfied in her own mind of the justice of the part she was called upon to play. Although she would not have scrupled to appropriate without any compunction, the most valuable of trinkets that happened to lie within her reach, she could yet hardly reconcile to herself the hypocrisy of a scheme that involved almost as one of its necessary conditions, a degree of faithlessness to her paramour, to whom she had really began to be warmly attached. Besides, with that instinctive purity of feeling which all her early associations and temptations had failed to wholly eradicate, she shrunk from the barter of herself for liberty which was the real nature of the bargain established between herself and Wild. There was, however, no alternative but to forward his deep designs, and as her instrumentality was necessary, she felt compelled to sink all scruples in its necessity.

Before she had quitted the vicinity of the Old Bailey, Wild had sent after her a present of three guineas to enable her to obtain the outfit that was necessary to make an appearance requisite to inveigle the woollen-draper's attention. This she was now anxious to dispose of to the best advantage, and remembering a place in the neighbourhood where the articles of dress she required might be obtained, she proceeded thither, and lost no time in arraying herself in the finest and most becoming costume that the limited second-hand wardrobe of the old woman who supplied her could afford.

This region of economical apparel was situated in the upper room of an old but extensive building, subdivided into numerous apartments, but tenanted chiefly by the poorer class of artisans who therein sought by the produce of their needle to gain a scanty subsistence by the sale of their day's labour to the mistress of the wardrobe's above them.

As Edgeworth Bess, exulting in the possession of her newly purchased finery, was descending the stairs with a joyous step, she heard a mournful sigh issuing from the half-opened door of one of those rooms, that checked the gladsome spirit in which she was then indulging. There was something so sad—so inexpressibly mournful—about the sound that prompted by a better feeling than that of curiosity, Bess suddenly stopped short upon the landing, and took advantage of the half-opened door to look into the room.

There was little in that narrow chamber to need describing; nothing but the absence of everything that contributes to make life easy and comfortable. The walls were of old wainscoting that had once been white, but now time-stained and time-dishonored, let in many a cold and piercing gust of wind. The ceiling, black with the murkiness of many a smoky chimney, had cracked itself into the semblance of a map of the world. The floor cold and worm-eaten reminded one of the grave.

And then the furniture—a tiny grate not set, and though too small to contain more than a handful of combustible matter, yet half-filled with pieces of red brick to prevent a too extravagant combustion of fuel; a tin fender, painted green, a bed made upon a sofa, but covered over with a scattering of work and a shawl to hide it, a little deal table and two odd chairs of different make, and date completed the garniture of the room. Within that ill-conditioned and comfortless chamber sat two young girls, both of them pale and emaciated with sunken eyes and colourless lips. Beauty still lingered over features from whence the light of life seemed departing.

The bonnet and shawl of the elder one showed that she had only just entered and a bundle was lying upon the table.

There had been the silence of a few minutes between them as Edgeworth Bess came to the door and the deep drawn sigh that she had heard was the first effort of the youngest girl to break its painful duration.

"Alas! Marian," said the eldest, "our last hope of procuring food for the day is gone—we must now sit calmly down and fast—for to-night at least. Perhaps to-morrow we may get more work to do.

"We will submit—we will make the best of it,"—rather asked, than said the younger one, with a fainting and sickening apprehension.

Together from the hour of their birth, cradled in the same misery, fed on the same bitterness, the character of the two girls was still distinct.

Sickness and suffering and want had only softened the younger into more submissive meekness. Sickness and suffering and want had made the elder one rouse herself to struggle by some means—no matter what—to free herself and sister from this impending evil. Had she been alone in her destitution she might have sunk under her burden, crushed but uncompla'ning, but as day by day the blight withered deeper and the canker spread deadlier, and the grave seemed to come nearer and nearer; and as day by day the weak and fragile girl whom she watched with lynx-eyed love, seemed drooping and dying, and the rich treasure of life, the life of youth, the life of her whom she loved best on earth, was floating and vanishing before her eyes, and all for the lack of the commonest sustenance, which all her daily toil, all her efforts could not win—rising up early, and so late taking rest—then it was that her heart swelled into rebellion, then she rose from her seat and whispered a horrible suggestion in the ear of her youngest sister.

But what was the reply?

"No Susan," said the girl trembling at the thought—we have withstood temptation so long, and we will not now sell ourselves for the bread of infamy. I would rather perish first."

And then it was that Edgeworth Bess felt how infinitely superior were those two destitute sisters conscious in the exaltation of their own virtue, to herself who had squandered away life in comparative affluence by the indulgence of a career of vice and depravity. She flung the few remaining coins that her purchase had left her, into the room, and springing down the stairs, rushed into the street to evade any opportunity of acknowledgement. She was still woman and though her veil was drawn more closely over her beauteous features than before, and she shunned the main thoroughfare for the bye-streets, it was only to conceal by those means from public observation, the hot tears that coursed down her burning cheeks, and made her heart throb as if it would have choked her.

CHAPTER XIV.

OF AN ADVENTURE THAT JACK SHEPPARD MET WITH IN ST. GEORGE'S FIELDS.

"The stream just ere it rushes o'er the cliff,
Runs swiftest; so men on the brink of ruin
Seem oft to run into destruction. Fate
Doth film their eyes and they pull dowu their death
On their own proper heads."

OLD PLAY.

THE arrangements of Blueskin and his apt pupil for their future predatory expeditions, having been completed, the creole informed our hero that there was a place in the suberb of Kennington, of which, from the information he had procured, he anticipated great things, and earnestly proposed this as the object of their immediate enterprise. Blueskin proceeded to explain how the mansion belonged to Sir Thomas Rivers, who with the family had left town for some time, and added that though it had been left in the care of only the butler, who was an infirm old man, the store of valuable pictures, jewellery and plate that it contained were sufficient of themselves, besides the chance of money, to render the projected burglary highly advantageous to their fortunes.

"I'll only ask you to be my pal to-night in this fakement," continued Blueskin, "and if all goes right, why we shall be able to live as honest and vartuous as a prince for ever arterwards."

The great amount of the expected plunder was not lost upon the active temperament of Jack, and whilst he resolved to secure it, he had also settled in his own mind how the produce should he appropriated. He therefore immediately yielded an affirmative to the proposal.

It was then settled that as it might be dangerous, notwithstanding their improved change of costume, to venture together through the streets even by twitlight, they should depart singly and meet about dusk somewhere in the neighbourhood, where they could then concert the measures to be afterwards taken. In accordance with this resolve Jack took with him a few of the lighter implements that would be required for the purpose, and leaving Blueskin to bring the rest, fixed the old milestone that then stood in the centre of Kennington Common to be the place of their rendezvous, and departed.

It was early in the afternoon, and as Jack had a few hours of daylight yet to dispose of, he resolved to pay a visit to his old friends in the mint, and try if he could learn anything of Edgeworth Bess. Relying on the unsuspicious character of his dress to shield him from discovery, he proceeded boldly through the most frequented thoroughfares and over old London Bridge without a single recognition, and arriving at the "Fox" he gave the old pass word of the minters and was admitted into the tavern without further questioning. The room, which was the same that had a short time before been the scene of Jack's initation into the career of crime, was now perfectly empty and the unusual order and regularity of the drinking vessels, that were suspended in polished rows over the bar, showed that the custom had fallen off materially since the period of Jack's last visit.

In answer to Jack's demand for a draught of Nantz, the landlord himself appeared with the desired liquour, and setting it down on the table with an extra degree of formality, in compliment to the external respectability of his guest, he was about to depart for change, with the goldon coin that had been offered, when a word from Jack brought about a recognition.

"What have I grown out of your knowledge too, Giles Shalders," exclaimed Jack with a laugh as he saw the host gazing with most speculative eyes on the silver-laced doublet he had assumed, "or art thou dumbfounded with my impudence in venturing here, when I know there's a prize upon my head, and that there are fifty within call who would be glad enough to earn it."

"That last is something more like it I must confess," returned Giles, but deuce a bit Mr. Sheppard would my tongue wag a word that would turn switch upon you. Honour amongst—

"Never mind whom," interrupted Jack with a smile, "I don't think the name of the profession sounds too agreeable. However, I was certain you would'nt betray an old customer."

"Not a bit of it; but lor, what wonderful escapes you have been making to be sure," continued the landlord, again lost in profound astonishment at the bare contemplation of them—"Why all London has been ringing with the history of your mighty achievements."

"Ah! it will ring louder yet," exclaimed Jack in reply, with a conscious feeling of his triumphs over the bars and bolts of prison discipline, "but somehow or other I have missed Edgeworth Bess and thinking she might have come down to the old quarters, I wanted you to give me any information about her that you could."

"Bless my heart, I haven't seen her," ejaculated Shalders with a mournful shake of the head; "But I'll wager now if any harm has befallen her, its all owing to that scoundrelly informer Jonathan Wild."

"If I thought so," exclaimed Jack, starting up at the suggestion, "I would—but no; it is impossible—he knew not her retreat!"

"Ah! Jonathan don't know what an impossible thing is," observed the host, "least ways so he is always saying, and as for finding things out, why he can draw a secret out of a cove as easily as our barber chirurgeon here could draw a hollow tooth."

"I'll make myself sure upon that point at least," said Jack, "but how is it that the old lot is gone. What's become of Sampson Kirby and the rest of 'em?"

"Ah! Jonathan Wild has done it all," responded the host, "business ain't with me what it was," and he sighed deeply at the retrospection.

"Them as paid him his reglars got off all right enough, but them as wouldn't or couldn't have all been in the stone-jug for some time. The respectable society of minters is well nigh broken up!"

"I heard as much," answered Jack—"That man is a complete vampire. He has sucked the blood out of the very men who assisted him to be what he is, but I have a long bill against him which he won't much like the settling of one of these days. I'll pay off the score of injuries he has done to me and mine with fearful interest."

"Ah! you really are a plucky cove," cried Giles admiringly, "I little thought vhen that human inkbottle, old Blueskin, brought you here on the night of the Great Storm to be christened, vhot a reglar out-and-outer you vould be! But stop—it don't do to talk of Wild in this way, for like another individual to whom he must be closely related, when you mention his name he appears sure enough. Besides I've seen some of his men lurking about here for a day or two, and I won't swear it isn't you they want."

As if to confirm his supposition an impatient knock at the outer door announced the presence of some one without, who began clamouring loudly for admission.

"I was afraid of it, Jack," cried the cautious publican speaking in a low tone "it's one of Jonathan's crew. "I'll be bound, and one who has seen you enter. But there"—he added, disclosing a sliding panel behind the bar, which formed the entrance to a secret passage—"there is the lobby through which you can make your retreat good, and it runs direct into the lane at the back. This place did'nt have the name of the "Fox" without deserving it."

Jack hastily expressed his thanks and proceeded to avail himself of the aperture

"Stop, here is the change for your guinea," cried Shalders, as he saw Jack making rapid progress along the windings of the recess—"nineteen shillings for you."

"Never mind it now," returned Jack Sheppard still keeping on his course—"if I ever get nabbed Giles and thrown into Newgate I'll give you a call and get the change, *the very day on which I make my escape from the stone-jug*. Adieu, Giles," —and Jack disappeared in the gloom.

"That will never be I am afraid, then," observed Shalders, rather to himself than to our hero, who had got out of sight as well as hearing—"for no one ever came out of Newgate yet that the law didn't give permission to, and I am sure there isn't much chance for a slim slip of the gibbet like you! Howsumever there's the cash sure enough for him vhen he chooses to call for it, but if he vaits for giving Newgate the go-bye, I think he vill have to vait a longer time for it than he'll like, that's all. And now to put on a sanctimonious face and ask the old griffin outside vhot he vants."

That many a true word has been spoken in jest, the experience of all ages past and present will testify, as well as the proverb. Jack had merely uttered the words as a careless brag, but the hour came when he fulfilled them; *How*—the progress of our story will reveal.

Leaving the trusty landlord of the "Fox" to satisfy the unwelcome applicant at his door, that he must have laboured under a mistake concerning Jack's identity, we follow the footsteps of our hero, who was rapidly making his way soon after, from the narrow lane, to which the lobby formed an outlet, into the broader paths of St. George's Fields.

This locality, afterwards so memorable as the scene of the Gordon Riots in 1780, was then a mere piece of waste ground with its wide expanse of grass-land only clotted here and there by a low hut tenanted by laundresses, carpet-beaters and other followers of humble occupation. On the site where Bethlehem Hospital now stands rose a place of entertainment called the "*Dog and Duck*," that then was in its infancy a Tavern and Tea gardens where mineral waters were drank, but which in its declining days became a rendezvous for the most lawless and desperate characters, and where bull-baiting, badger-drawing, cock-fighting, and other knavish sports drew together the foolish and brutal of all classes, titled and untitled, about London.

Passing this Spa and its pleasantly laid out grounds, which were very open and picturesque, and developed then to great advantage the sloping uplands of the Surrey hills, Jack went on, intending to regale himself at a little ale-house that had been built on the rising ground beyond, when he became aware from the manner in which a single straggler had isolated himself from the group by the tavern, and pursued the irregular course that he himself had purposely chosen, that there was a follower in his track.

Fearful of showing his irresolution by turning back to confront his pertinacious companion, and judging besides that by such a mode of proceeding he should only be courting the chance of a recognition which might now be the mere effect of a mistake, he continued his progress in the same direction, and not apprehending any danger from a single assailant, stopped as he at first designed by the roadside public-house, and there resolved to wait till the increasing twilight brought on the hour at which he had proposed to meet Blueskin.

This delay gave his pursuer—for such he now evidently was—an opportunity of coming up with him, and as Jack had not been able to previously survey his appearance from the distance that had been between them he could now hardly refrain from laughing at the object he saw, or smiling at his own fears, when a closer interview gave him the power of making a more minute inspection.

The new comer was a tall old man apparently near seventy years of age, with a complexion bilious and yellow like one in the last stage of the jaundice. He stooped very much and as he limped along supported his steps by a short crutch stick. His low crowned and broad-brimmed hat flapped over his forehead, and from under his wig, which was of a dingy white colour, and full-bottomed, came a large black patch, worn directly across his right eye. His body, which age appeared to have bent nearly double, was enveloped in a thick camlet great coat, the larger cape of which was so placed as to hide the lower part of his face, and his legs were carefully wrapped up in flannel, hanging over the instep of his shoes, only so far as not to conceal the little narrow silver buckles that fastened them. Such was the odd appearance of the tottering valetudinarian of whom Jack had been in such dread and who now took up his station at the very table at which our young hero was seated.

The self-invited guest soon gave ample proof that whatever the indisposition might have been that led him to try the remedial virtues of the Spa, neither his appetite nor his diet, were in the slightest degree restricted. During his prolonged and hearty meal Jack noticed that several furtive glances were thrown in the direction where he sat and this contributed to make him in some respect uneasy, as to the probable result of this encounter, but as the aged invalid finished his third tankard of ale, and a roguish spark of satisfaction and good humour kindled in his sinister eye, possibly with a double brilliancy from the other not being exposed. Jack felt all his suspicions vanish and he called for his reckoning with a mind perfectly at ease that no settlement of a pugilistic, instead of a pecuniary nature, would have to be made before he departed.

It was now approaching the hour when Jack had to meet his associate in the robbery that had been planned, and leaving the old gentlemen, who had caused him so much disquiet, to smoke the pipe that he had already assumed, in the solitude of the Inn parlour, our hero emerged from the porch of the Tavern and quickened his steps towards the place of meeting.

Blueskin was waiting at the miles-stone as Jack came up, and after a brief examination of their implements to see that all had been brought and in good condition, the two set off from the common on their nefarious expedition in company.

Behind them rose the crazy turrets of old Kennington Church in all their ivy-hung irregularity—for then a humble village church of ancient date and small dimensions was sufficient for the few inhabitants of the olden manor—and afar off, to their right, appeared a cluster of red lights which marked the locality of the great city, and served to give a faint idea of the accuracy of the direction in which they were going. Beyond mingled with the ruddy tops of chimnies and the dark yellow surfaces of thatched roofs rose a thickly wooded grove of trees, which stood out in bold relief against the horizon, and continued to form one uninterrupted line across the country in a south-westerly direction for some miles. Such was the Kennington Road and its vicinity at this period—a thoroughfare that is now adorned with some of the most stately edifices in the neighborhood of the metropolis besides being itself the centre of a busy traffic.

Guided by the faint light of the crescent moon, which shone out at intervals through the clouded sky, they pursued their way across a marshy and uneven track, skirted on both sides by open fields and at last coming to a high brick wall, Blueskin announced this to be their destination and the boundary of the mansion belonging to Sir Thomas Rivers.

It was a portion of Blueskin's plan to climb over this wall and remain concealed about the grounds for an hour or so, until the night became more advanced, but judging from the unprotected appearance of the place and its lonely situation that there would be no risk in making an immediate attack, the mode of operation was so far changed and they both clambered over the enclosure and dropped silently into the garden on the other side, intent upon the immediate execution of their scheme.

It was an old-fashioned spacious garden in which they now found themselves, neglected from the absence of its owner, but looking in the half-veiled light of the rising moon almost as beautiful as if it had been kept in trim order. Although the gravel walks were green with moss and grass and the fruit-trees trained against the wall had shot out a pleutuous over-growth of wild branches, which were hung unprofitably over the borders, the luxuriance of nature was of itself nearly a substitute for the adornments of art. Amidst the rank crops of thistles, groundsel and blindweed, which choked the beds, arose the slimy trace of slugs and snails, gleeming in the transent moonlight, and the groups of elms that clustered round the lawn, seemed to point with their broad massive shadows, to the building as to the cause of the neglect that was to apparent beyond.

The aspect of the old place was of one deserted and desolate, nor did the appearance of the mansion itself, which Blueskin and Jack Sheppard were now approaching by the chesnut avenue, tend to dissipate by its architectral beauty the solmn gloom that pervaded the surrounding scene. A huge square red brick house rose before them, with rooms and windows of large size and fair proportions but utterly destitute of any external interest. There were no pointed roofs, no fantastic gables, no grotesque projections, no pleasant porches, in the angles of which the woodbine and the clematis could ascend on the sombre ivy cling, nor any of those picturesque clusters of spiral chimnies like those which surmounted the truly English turrets of the Elizabethan era—all partook of the heavy gloom and dulness of the time of James the Second, to which epoch the period of its constitution might been referred.

A moving light that fitfully glimmered in the eastern wing warned Blueskin that the Butler, who according to the information he had received, was the sole inmate of the mansion, had not retired to rest. There was little however to fear from the resistance of an aged man, and therefore the knowledge did not deter them from at once commencing operations. Assuming the crape masks which were then always adopted to conceal the features, Blueskin made such skilful use of the crowbar, whilst Jack was as busily employed in forcing back the lock, than in less than ten minutes the portal yielded to their exertions, and the two burglars entered the passage, without difficulty and almost without noise. They had not, however, gone far before their progress met with an impediment in the shape of an inner door, stronger than the first, and one which baffled all attempts to wrench it off its hinges.

Jack's centre-bit was after a little consultation then brought into action, and cutting out a panel, Jack worked his nimble body so adroitly through the aperture, that in a few minutes the impeding bars were quietly removed, the bolts drawn back, the door opened, and the last obstacle to their entrance overcome.

With a pistol in one hand and a strong cord grasped in the other to secure the butler in the event of any resistance being offered, the creole ascended the broad stone staircase, followed by Jack, who relied on the massive crowbar which he carried as a sufficient means of defence. No sound as yet had been heard in the building to alarm the stealthy tread of the two burglars, and emboldened by this, as well as not caring to resort to violence, except in a case of urgent necessity, Jack threw open the first door they came to, which led into the drawing, or dining room. By the light of the lanthorn which Blueskin unmasked, they found the place into which they had forced their way, was an apartment of spacious dimensions with panels of richly grained oak, and in a recess stood a massive article of furniture which Jack at once surmised was the plate chest of which they were in search.

They had scarcely inserted a lever between the lid and the under rim to reduce the supposition to a certainty, when the rapid trampling of horses up the carriageway in front of the house, startled them from their work and with an inquiring look towards each other Jack and Blueskin mutually suspended their operations. At the same instant the butler, who had himself been aroused by the sound, seeing a stream of light issue from the door which they had forgotten to close, at once surmised the reason of their presence, and with a movement quicker than they could avert, shut

[The "Dog and Duck," St. Georges' Fields.]

the door, turned the key, and thus succeeded in making them prisoners.

Rage and disappointment were visible in the features of each as they saw the nature of the artifice by which they had been betrayed. The first impulse of Blueskin was to rush to the bow window and break away a sufficient portion of the frame to enable them to make their escape through it, but as the first pane was removed and Jack had thrust his head through to reconnoitre the premises below, it was evident to them that an outlet by that means was impracticable, for, through the gloom, two figures were clearly discernible, who had taken up their station on the grass plot beneath.

"This ain't accident, Jack," at last cried Blueskin in despair, "somebody's been and sold us, that's certain though how they could have known vhot you and I have been a thinking of, puzzles my comprehension to diskiver."

Jack reflections immediately turned towards the old man that he encountered on his way, but not exactly seeing the nature of any connexion that he could have had with the present affair, he refrained from making further allusion to the circumstance, and merely urged his companion to force back the lock of the door, so that they might endeavour to get clear off from another part of the building.

No sooner was the suggestion made than it was immediately put into practice, but in the meantime the tumult of the horsemen without had become louder, and from the commotion that prevailed below it was evident that a large party of men were ascending the stairs, leading to the very room from which the two adventurers were now earnestly endeavouring to force their passage. At last the door yielded to their efforts, Jack and Blueskin burst through, and at the same instant found themselves surrounded by a group of about twenty personages in military costume, through whose ranks it would have been madness to have attempted dashing. Expecting to be the victims of a contest that would immediately ensue, Jack and his amazed associate stood on the defensive, but scarcely hoped to make a successful resistance to the overpowering number of their adversaries.

To their inexpressible astonishment they were however, received with a derisive shout of welcome, and amongst a few at the further end arose a hearty peal of laughter, at the warlike characteristics of the combatants, who had as yet with bated breath watched, by the glare of the torches carried by the soldiers, for the commencement of the fray, whilst Blueskin, with an inquiring glance towards Jack, was puzzling himself mightily to fathom the cause of this strange demonstration, a tall and stately personage, evidently of more importance than the rest, stepped from amidst the crowd, and bidding the rest wait for his return, beckoned the two burglars to follow him into the room they had just quitted.

Sullenly assenting, for as yet the whole affair seemed wrapped up in mystery, Blueskin and our hero obeyed the invitation, and followed by the butler who was in attendance, the door was again closed and Jack with his associate remained in anxious expectation of what would be the result of this extraordinary interview.

They had not to remain long in suspense. The silence was soon broken.

You see I was right, Sir Thomas, in my information," observed the Butler, " notwithstanding the doubts you yourself entertained. The report about your honour leaving town was not circulated you see without effect, and these two vagrants here were the first to take advantage of your honor's absence. I was certain when I saw the daring stripling yonder at the alehouse in St. George's Fields, that to night was the time they intended to put their plan into execution."

A gleam of light became simultaneously thrown upon the meditations of both Jack and Blueskin. The latter now saw that he had been egregiously misled in the report of the house and its contents being so carelessly guarded, and the former that his previous apprehension had not been without cause and that the tottering old invalid who had tracked him from the Spa and the butler, who now addressed his master as Sir Thomas Rivers, were one and the same person. Still the unusual and somewhat ceremonious manner in which they were treated perplexed them exceedingly, Blueskin, with an indomitable assurance that never forsook him, was about to urge in his defence that their presence there was altogether the result of a mistake, when a gesture from the baronet, who had been conferring in the interim with his domestic, caused him to relapse into silence, and from the character of a speaker, he found himself compelled to assume that of a listener.

"You have no occasion to deny, either of you, the purpose for which you came," cried Sir Thomas, "in fact, it was partly through my agency that the attempt at robbery was made. I mention this first to show you that you need be under no apprehension concerning my views of your intention, and its mode of punishment. The guard of honor that awaited you on the landing-place will convince you that I have not been remiss in making preparations for your reception."

Jack felt himself more bewildered than before.

"Your honor's joking with us," responded Blueskin, hardly knowing what to say.

"Not I," continued the Baronet, "I am anxious to secure your services. In short, to speak plainly, for there is no need of concealment between ourselves, I wanted you."

"Wanted us!" echoed the burglars together in a reciprocated tone of amazement, as if the possibility of such a thing alarmed them even more than an order for their incarceration would have done.

"Ay! to be frank with you, I require your aid in two most important undertakings, and the reward shall be commensurate with the risk of both. I may rely upon your secrecy?"

Both volunteered an assurance that what confidence was reposed in them should not be abused, particularly when paid for accordingly.

"Then to explain my wishes in as few words as possible. Even in your lawless profession there is a certain kind of reputation to be obtained, and this—one of you named Jack Sheppard—has earned by his exploits in breaking out of some of the strongest prisons in the metropolis."

Blueskin pointed to Jack who stood almost dumbfoundered at this complimentary prelude.

The Baronet continued;—"What my reasons are for giving out a report of this mansion being uninhabited, there is no occasion now to communicate further than that a desire to attract you here has lately formed one of them. You are aware probably that there is at present a strong party in London of those adherents to the only true monarch, King James the Third, that our enemies choose to call the Pretender."

Jack, who remembered the Jacobite scene at his master, the carpenter's—related in a preceding part of this history—at once assented, and Blueskin though he had never before given a thought about the matter, warmly asserted his staunch adherence to the same cause.

"Well then, to come to the point, an intimate friend of mine, Colonel Keightley, and one who is of the very greatest importance to the cause, is now imprisoned in the Savoy for his avowal of the principles he has the nobleness to confess. If suffered to remain there three days longer his execution will follow as a certainty. Every effort yet made to save him has been thwarted by vigliance of the authorities, and for obvious reasons you see I cannot appear myself in this matter. Will you Jack Sheppard—yourself an experienced defier of restraint—undertake to liberate him for one hundred guineas?"

"With pleasure, Sir Thomas," cried Jack, delighted at the importance of his position and feeling the consciousness of its increase with every moment, "I shall only claim the fee when I secure the freedom."

"Nay, succeed in your undertaking and you shall not complain of our liberality, but here is a purse for present uses—share the contents between you; it will be a more profitable guerdon to you than any plunder you would have had to-night from the mansion, for in faith there is little enough of value in it," and as Sir Thomas Rivers concluded his speech, a somewhat weighty purse, which was handed to Jack attested that the proposal was one made in earnest.

"When would you like his honor the Colonel to be liberated, Sir Thomas?" inquired Jack.

"To-morrow night at the latest," was the reply.

"It shall be done, Sir Thomas, as you wish," rejoined Jack confidentially; "Col. Keightley shall be with you by eleven."

"You see I have faith in your wonderful powers, Jack," said the baronet, smiling at the strange course of events that had rendered the assistance of a housebreaker necessary for the support of the cause.

"You may place every reliance in them," cried our hero in return," with me the will and the way mean the same thing."

"Your honor was saying that there was another little affair you fancied we could execute," remarked Blueskin, inquiringly, after brushing his hand over his hat, to assist his eloquence, and desirous of not suffering his companion to monopolise all the attention.

"It is a daring and dangerous theft," mused Sir Thomas Rivers, "but if it could be done—"

"Could be done," echoed the creole, "it shall be done or my name's not Blueskin! "It's quite in our line."

"Well, on second thoughts, I will arrange that business with you at our next meeting. I have a troop of gallant soldiers below for King James, who I must send off to Scotland at midnight, and I have a few gentlemen amongst them, whose appetites will hardly brook waiting long for the supper I have provided. You see that the mansion is not likely to be so quiet as you appeared to anticipate."

"In course if we had known that yer honor vas agoing for to come home to supper, ve vould never have made our appearance here without being invited," apologised Blueskin, with a comical attempt at politeness.

"Well thought of," cried the Baronet as they were about to leave, and turning to the butler—"Davis, take these gentlemen—ahem!—of the road, down to your buttery and see that they want for nothing," and whispering aside in the ear of the domestic, he suggested a caution to remove out of their reach such articles of plate as might be likely to attract their notice.

"Much obliged to yer, Sir Thomas," acknowledged Blueskin, and after a reiterated assurance from Jack that the Baronet might depend upon their fidelity and prompt execution of the proposed scheme, the two knights of the post, whose own plans had become so singularly changed during the evening, descended to the basement with the butler, whilst in the upper apartments resounded one of those frequent demonstrations of reckless mirth and jollity that formed a principal feature in the haunts of the Jacobite conspirators at this period.

That in the gastrionomic art our hero and his companion were by no means deficient, the larder of the "Fox," had long ago proved, and inspirited by the important mission they were about to undertake, which had all that dash of adventure about it so fascinating to his eager mind, Jack manifested a display of his bibulous powers which put the butler's former prowess in the afternoon, into the shade completely. In fact, the festivites that were proceeding upstairs, whilst they emulated with great success, the contents of the bottles decreased so rapidly, and the objects around them multiplied so fast, there ere the midnight hour arrived, both had attained a state of blissful ignornnce, which would have scarcely needed a philosopher to recommend as a position in which it were a folly to be wise.

CHAPTER XV.

THE SAVOY.

————"The night is moody
And the wind frets and moans in fitful gusts,
Hurrying the clouds as to some rendezvous
Of Storm, like squadrons ere the battle join,
'Twill be a threatening gloom, but all the better
So that its rage stoop not directly here."

THE WANDERER.

BEFORE alluding to the result of Jack's preparations for the escape of the Jacobite prisoner, it will be necessary for us to explain the nature and locality of the place as it then stood, in which he was confined. The celebrated Hospital of the Savoy was at this period converted from its previous uses as a receptacle for the poor and needy, into a prison for those disaffected persons to the government who had not yet undergone their trial on a charge of High Treason, and who were consequently awaiting their sentence either of decapitation or imprisonment in the Tower. The front contained several angular projections, and two rows of angular mullioned windows. Northward of this was the *Friary*, a court formed by the walls of the body of the hospital which in its ground plan was of the shape of a cross. This was more ornamented than the south front, and had large pointed windows and embattled parapets lozenged with flints.

At the west end of the Savoy Hospital was the guard-house, a strong and noble building used as the place of imprisonment for spies and such as had deserted from the army. It was secured by a massive buttress, and had a gateway embellished with Henry the Seventh's arms, and the badges of the rose and portcullis: above which were two windows, grated with iron. The descent from the Strand was by two flights of stone steps nearly to the depth of three stories, and a dwelling-house. Its aspect now is widely different. The demolition of the surrounding buildings for the erection of Waterloo Bridge has quite destroyed the chance of any of the above localities being recognized. The wide opening called Savoy Street occupies the site of the Old Savoy Gate and though the German Lutheran church, once part of the Hospital still remains, that church is of brick and of modern construction.

The approach to the bridge from the Strand formed by Wellington Street and its Western continuation Lancaster Place, covers the entire site of the old Duchy Lane and the outbuildings of the Savoy, and nothing now remains of the old Palace and Hospital, which had once an annual revenue of twenty-two thousand pounds, but the church with its small mean tower, a few fragments of walls and the triple flight of steps, still called Savoy steps.

Adjoining the Savoy, and at the corner of Duchy Lane, then stood a shop, where woollen goods, and ready-made apparel were arranged to catch the attention of the passer-by. To this shop seeing an announcement in the window, that a room upstairs was to be let, Jack accordingly went early on the following day, and secured the vacant apartment.

Passing himself off to the owner of the house as a personage of note, who having just arrived from the country was desirous of making a long sojourn in the metropolis, our hero was enabled to evade the slightest suspicion of his intentions, and having with the aid of Blueskin, who disguised himself as a ticket-porter for the occasion, conveyed thither in a trunk those implements for which he had especial use, he patiently awaited the approach of night to put that plan into execution which he had already framed for the prisoner's escape.

The day had been remarkably hot, and as evening came on, though the sky was unusually clear, and the stars twinkled with a sharp and piercing brilliance, not a breath of air was stirring. Jack threw open the window, which was above the old Savoy gate, to admit a cooler current of the atmosphere, and then discerned, hovering above the horizon, a pile of dense black clouds which combined with the stifling stillness of the air, he knew threatened the speedy outburst of a violent thunderstorm.

Determined to take advantage of the tempest, for the progress of his labours, Jack lost no time in strengthening the ropes he had brought with him, by an additional line, and this he twisted firmly round to a strong iron which he had previously bent into the form of a hook. He next attached a saw, file and chisel to the folds of his belt and thus prepared, clambered from the open casement, on to the upper leads of the house. Here he had a distinct view opposite to him of the window belonging to the Guard-house which grated with stout iron bars, he had laid previously pointed out to him as the scene of Colonel Keightley's captivity.

In the meantime the darkness increased and the presages of the coming storm, became more and more apparent. The firmament was overspread with clouds; dark lurid masses of vapour, and these having, as it were, taken up their station, stood still as though awaiting some command to pour forth their dreadful artillery. The slight electrical gust which had previously been felt by Jack from his elevation was now hushed, and from the streets, where every passenger he had watched, hurrying eagerly homeward to obtain the shelter of a roof, had now disappeared, not a sound proceeded. The thoroughfares were all silent and desolate, and the earth seemed mute with terror.

The deep sonorous chimes of the clock at the old Savoy church now sounded the hour of ten, and on the solemn stillness of the night came a loud and reverberating peal of thunder, as if in answer to its summons. Early as it was, Jack saw that no one would risk exposure to the contending elements, and not dreaming of a rescue from the quarter where Jack had taken up his position, the warder had merely gone his nightly round by the portals that were effectually guarded from intrusion by troops of soldiers, and having performed his customary task of seeing that each prisoner was secure in his respective cell, he locked up the double doors of the several lobbies to prevent the possibility of egress, and betook himself, confident of security, to his own apartment. This Jack saw and understood from the glancing lights of the Guard-house, as they gleamed in various parts of the building successively, and satisfied now that no further interruption would have to be feared from that source, he prepared himself for action.

The upper part of the Savoy was at this period surmounted by a slanting roof, protected along the summit by a barrier of short iron spikes, and immediately beneath this was the grated window of the room where the Colonel was imprisoned. Jack's intention therefore was to throw his rope across to the roof and entangle it in the spikes by the aid of the bent iron attached to it. That done he hoped, by swinging himself across the opening by the gate, to reach the opposite side, and lower himself down to the window which he had then to open by forcing away the grating. The width from the point where he stood to that which he endeavoured to reach, was nearly twenty feet across, and an erring aim or a slip of the rope or spike would precipitate him with fearful force to the pavement, some forty feet below. The danger was therefore one that had to meet with a strong heart and steady hand.

Suddenly the sombre gloom that had enveloped the sky, was torn aside by a flash of forked lightning and in the momentary brilliancy that lit up the locality, Jack threw the coil of rope in the direction of the spikes and in the midst of a startling peal of thunder which made the house quiver from base to roof, he uttered an exclamation of triumph, as he found by the tightened end of the rope he held in his hand, that he had succeeded in his attempt.

The turbulence of the elements now increased fearfully. No longer was the lightning serpentine and darting, but revealed itself in large sheets of fire, the constant flashes of which made the succeeding darkness more black and dismal, wrapping in flame the spires and turrets of the surrounding buildings. In a little time the wind, started from its trance, arose, and swelled into a hurricane, driving with mighty force against the solid masonry, which as if in defiance tossed it back towards the quarter whence it came. Returning to the contest the mad gusts raved onwards, bringing with them a torrent of fierce hail, which smote the windows beneath with such violence that every pane of glass was shivered by the assault into innumerable fragments.

The position of Jack now became one of imminent peril. Tightening the rope to make sure of the end he had thrown across being securely attached, he fastened a portion of the other end round his body, and then clinging with his hands to the frail tenure of the line, swirled off from the roof into the dark chasm before him. He had, however, measured his distance so well that after the first violent jerk was over, he found he had brought himself within a few feet of the very place he desired. Swinging by the rope, and warding off from his face by projecting his body forward, the dense masses of hail that came sweeping through the air, he contrived to make his way up to the window, and having gained a temporary resting place by winding his left arm round one iron bar on the outside, he set himself vigorously to work to clear away the rest with his tools.

The rasping noise of the file, though from the violence of the storm inaudible to the ears of others, soon reached those of the Colonel within, who at once understood them as auguring well for his chance of escape. The expert hand of Jack speedily wrenched three from their fastenings, and by the other two he was now clinging on to the sill of the casement. Colonel Keightley had watched the proceedings with breathless interest, but when Jack employed his saw and cutting away the woodwork forced his way into the cell, the Colonel's joy and amazement rose to their height, and particularly was he astonished at finding in his deliverer one so young.

There was however no time for other than a few brief words of explanation. The Jacobite prisoner was soon persuaded to entrust himself with the rope and Jack cutting away the upper portion, left it dangling on the spikes above, and made another and a more secure attachment to the remaining bars of the grating. Down this in the midst of one of the most tremendous thunderstorms by which the metropolis had been for some time visited, the Colonel swung himself under the experienced guidance of Jack and soon after alighted in safety.

Jack then followed and climbing over the low walls of the Friary, an outlet was thus gained into the open street, from which even the watchful "guardians of the night," had fled in terror at the first effects of the furious elemental warfare.

The deserted appearance of the metropolis so far favoured their designs, that there was but little chance of a re-capture, and as they came to Holborn, where Keightley proposed to stop till the morning under the roof of a relative, Jack suggested that as the storm appeared then likely to abate, he would leave the Colonel and go to his own lodgings in Clerkenwell.

"You have not only done myself and the good cause an important service, my intrepid deliverer," exclaimed Keightley, as they shook hands at parting, "but you have earned for yourself some tribute of gratitude besides; name the sum you require and I will send it in the morning to any place you may appoint."

"I have already obtained the recompense I undertook the affair for," returned Jack, "but as a guerdon of your satisfaction you can give me the ring which now glistens on your finger."

"It may lead to my detection or endanger your own safety perchance," observed the Colonel.

"I am willing at least to run all hazards of that," responded our hero,

"There then—and take my best wishes with it," said the other, transfering the jewel from his own hand to that of his deliverer," and now tell me, to whom am I indebted for this bold achievement on my behalf?

"*To Jack Sheppard*," exclaimed the youth with an air of triumph, and waving his hand to the Jacobite, he waited not for the utterance of that expression of surprise that trembled on the lips of the Colonel, but crossing to the back of Gray's Inn, he quickened his pace and was speedily out of sight.

The next day the extraordinary escape of a prisoner, confined on a charge of high treason, in the—what had previously been deemed the impregnable—prison of the Savoy, created the greatest amazement and formed the chief topic of conversation throughout the coffee-houses. The affair underwent a judicial investigation but nothing was elicited that left any clue to the identity of the party by whose assistance Keightley had escaped. The draper, fearful of consequent loss of time and character, should he be called upon as a witness, and being besides, to confess the truth, not indisposed to favour the pretenstions of the Jacobite party from whom, in the way of business he had received several large orders, kept a close tongue on the subject of having let his room to a tenant who only stayed one night, though he entertained his own views of the matter, and thus the whole affair was enveloped in mystery. The rope that Jack had left entangled in the spikes, perplexed the authorities mightily for they could scarcely imagine that one would be found daring enough to hazard a flight of twenty feet over a deep opening, even though they were assisted by the rope, and this the warder, who was deemed a competent judge in such matters, declared positively not to be of sufficient strength to warrant a man of ordinary weight trusting himself to its support. Pending further information, therefore every one was compelled to draw their own conclusions on the matter, and whilst the majority inclined to an opinion that bribery had been resorted to with the officials there was not wanting a select few who traced in the bold conception of such an achievement another demonstration of the wonderful powers and capabilites of Jack Sheppard.

The chief originator of these surmises and conjectures heard, with triumphant pride, the exploit of the preceding night, made the universal theme of conversation through the day, wherever he went.

Accompanied by Blueskin he again sought out the mansion of Sir Thomas Rivers in Kennington-lane, and accordingly reached that sequestered habitation late in afternoon to receive the remainder of the sum that had been promised in the event of the adventure turning out so successfully as we have seen it had. The Baronet had been expecting their arrival, and had given orders for their immediate admission, there was therefore no occasion to resort to such a professional mode of gaining an entrance as that they had adopted on their former visit. Ushered into the drawing-room, the knight opened the conference in what Blueskin whispered to Jack was the most satisfactory and polite manner imaginable, for he instantly gave orders to the butler to pay the remainder of the sum that had been agreed upon to the two fellows of the craft of housebreaking that had rendered him such an essential service.

"You vos a sayin', Sir Thomas," cried Blueskin, after this agreeable ceremony had been gone through, "that there vos another little job in our line?"

"I was indeed thinking of some such thing," responded the Baronet, "and the very expert manner in which you have contrived the escape of my friend induces me to believe I may trust you."

"Oh, honor bright!" exclaimed Blueskin eagerly, and he was about to confirm his attestation of the confidence that might be reposed in him, by one of his frequent round oaths, when Jack silenced him by a gesture, and Sir Thomas Rivers continued.

"The enterprise for which I would engage your services is one of considerable risk, and in fact not only involves all the consequences of the commission of High Treason, but if caught in the very neighbourhood of the place where you make the attempt, instant punishment would follow. If you succeed however, I promise you a thousand pounds for your booty."

Jack listened with eager expectancy of what was to follow, and drank in the sound of the reward with delighted ears, but so intent was he upon hearing the nature of the proposal that not a word did he utter in reply. Blueskin, on the contrary, could not restrain the exhibition of extravagant joy; he shrugged up his shoulders, made sundry grimaces, which were intended as symbolical of profound gratification, and finally concluded by sending forth a loud and prolonged whistle.

"I twig!" exclaimed that individual in

the jargon of his calling—"it's a reglar bang-up swell crib that yer vant us to crack for yer. An out-an-out robbery!"

"Hem! It may be regarded by some as a robbery, certainly," returned Sir Thomas, "though I am more inclined to look upon it as a rightful act of restitution. However let it be called what it may, the end justifies the means."

"You may call it what you like so that you'll tell us what it is," bluffly remarked Blueskin, "we arn't particklar to a shade or two, so that there's a summut to be got by it."

"Do you think you could, either together or separately, get access to the King's Chamber?" inquired the Knight.

"Ve vould have a good try for it at least," answered the creole, who during Jack's reverie took upon himself the office of spokesman—"But vhot is it that yer vant us to prig?"

"*The Crown of the King of England!*"

Jack's eyes glistened at the proposition. This indeed was an object worthy to be aimed at and secured. In the wildest flights of his ambition he had never dared to contemplate such a theft, and the proposal enraptured him from the very difficulties which he foresaw there would be to encounter. He seized the opportunity of his companion remaining mute with amazement at the disclosure, to certify his readiness to undertake the affair, and make the attempt at least.

"I believe if it is possible to do it at all," said Sir Thomas, dwelling with interest on the animated countenance of the bold stripling, "that the power lies in your dexterous hands, Jack Sheppard, but be wary in your task."

"You may rely on my energy and secrecy to the utmost," answered Jack—"it is a dangerous game to play, I know, but I do not despair of its being accomplished nevertheless."

"Oh, my pal's the topping cove in the cracking lay. I eddicated him, sir, and his mauleys will fix the swag afore yer could douse the glim," cried Blueskin, with enthusiasm,—"I've seen him do it many a time!"

As the Baronet was, however, scarcely learned enough in the vernacular of the Mint to thoroughly comprehend the eulogium upon Jack's abilities, that had been passed, he proceeded without noticing the interruption;—

"There is a superstition in the north, that until the Stuart places the Crown upon his head that the King of England has worn, he will not be restored to his rightful heritage and possessions, and when once this bauble is in the hands of our party, we can therefore rely upon a general rising in our favour. You now understand my object in employing your aid, and the importance of the charge committed to your care."

"I will be true to the last," responded Jack, proud of the confidence placed in his zeal and fidelity "and there shall be no longer time than is necessary lost in securing the prize."

"I need scarcely say you will find it to your own interests to preserve silence respecting the parties who instigated you to make the attempt."

"You may depend on our word of honour," returned Sheppard," a bond is as binding to a highwayman as to a Knight of the Shire."

"Mute as milestones; you may reckon on our not blabbing," echoed Blueskin.

"I must then leave you to consult together on the means by which you propose to effect your object," said Sir Thomas, rising from his seat and preparing to depart—"you of course know were to find me, or my agent when required."

And the baronet then left the apartment, followed by our hero and his associate, whom Jack had the utmost difficulty in restraining from appropriating to his own use several articles that were in the lobby, of a portable nature.

Once freely out in the open air, however, the raptures of Blueskin at the possession of so much money, and the expectation of so much more, knew no bounds. He danced and sung, and leaped upon the road in the full exercise of his exuberant animal spirits, and it was only when Jack recalled to his mind the danger to which he was exposing them, that he could be prevailed upon to relapse into a more sober mode of progression. Jack's thoughts were all engrossed by the startling suggestion that had been made to him, and he looked forward with eagerness to the achievement of a deed which would throw all the previous exploits of his brethren of the road completely into the shade. As further labours in their vocation were now not immediately necessary, and, in fact, as Blueskin's outrageous hilarity had put them altogether out of the question it was arranged between them that being in the neighbourhood they should spend the remainder of the evening at the "*Dog and Duck,*" no less fashionable tavern being considered by the creole as worthy of brewing them a bowl of punch for the occasion, and to this place they now accordingly went. And here, leaving them a moment to pursue their devious steps, we would engage the attention of the reader a moment, whilst we discourse of matters appertaining thereto.

Recent historical research has proved that the incident and the compact above related, have no right to be considered of mere fabular origin. It is stated on the unimpeachable authority of contemporary historians, and corroborated by sundry letters and other valuable documents that have been recently brought to light, that among the wild and daring schemes resorted to by the Jacobites, to support the Pretender's claims was that which involved the engagement of the notorious culprit who figures so conspicuously in our pages, to abstract from the Royal Chamber, the regalia used by King George the First at his coronation, and which had not been then returned to the Tower. So far had the plan been carried out, and so confidently was the Earl of Mar, and others, of its success, that a box had been made and a vessel engaged for its transmission to the shores of France, where the Pretender was then waiting for the funds that the French king had offered him for the prosecution of his claims. The superstition alluded to by Sir Thomas Rivers, who afterwards suffered the penalty of his treasonable practices by decapitation upon Tower Hill, was then chiefly prevalent among the Highlanders who formed a prominent portion of the army which the Stuart had got in the north ready for the field. How the attempt, so boldly conceived and so confidently relied upon, came at last to be frustrated in the moment of expected success, will hereafter appear, but as all the other biographers of JackSheppard have most unaccountably omitted all mention of this important epoch in their hero's career, it has been considered advisable to append this brief explanation of its origin and its results as forming an interesting elucidation of one of the characteristic points in one of the most critical period of modern English History.

CHAPTER XVI.

THE "DOG AND DUCK."

"Love bears within its breast the very germ
Of change; and how should it be otherwise?
That violent things more quickly find a term,
Is shown through Nature's whole analogies;
And how should the most fierce of all be firm,
Would you have endless lightning in the skies?"

BYRON.

"False! false to me! Oh, Torture!"

OTHELLO.

ON the evening which they had chosen for their visit, the grounds of this fashionable Spa and Tavern were crowded with an assemblage of the chief leaders of rank and fashion in the metropolis. As this famous place of resort then occupied the position afterwards filled by the Marylebone Gardens, Ranelagh, and Vauxhall, amusements of the most attractive kind were constantly put forward to bring within its charmed circle the votaries of pleasure, and music, and rope-dancing formed prominent features in the entertainment provided.

An extra programme, comprising an additional concert both vocal and instrumental, had been the means of bringing on this occasion a very numerous company within its precincts. The public walks were thronged with promenaders, the leafy glade known as the "Thrushe's Grove," was one blaze of illumination, and the alcoves, wherein tables were placed for the refreshment of the guests, were filled by groups of laughing revellers, who over a game of brag or picquet, for public gambling was then universally allowed, were scattering the contents of their well-lined purses with wonderous nonchalance and good-temper.

In one of these recesses, bending over the steaming fragrance of a bowl of arrack punch, were seated Jack Sheppard and Blueskin. They had already had their ample china vessel replenished thrice with a supply of the potent potation, and as their fancies warmed, and their senses became more confused under its influence, they boldly conversed at random with the passers-by, and offered to engage in a contest at brag, with any who would stake five guineas on the main.

A challenge such as this was not likely to be long made publicly, before it found several who were inclined to test their skill in the encounter, and these were the more impelled to accept it from the belief they entertained of Jack and his companion being innocent of collusion, and being really what they stated themselves to be, young sparks from the country who were only anxious to acquaint themselves with the fashionable pastimes of the bloods in town.

They had thus formed an agreeable card-party, consisting of about half-a-dozen persons, besides those who merely officiated in the capacity of lookers on, when Jack, who during the pauses in the game, had been watching the sumptuous dresses and personal loveliness of the ladies who with arched neck and stately gait sailed by him, now found himself attracted by one in particular, who leaning lovingly on the arm of her gallant, was being escorted up the Sycamore avenue.

The female who had thus so irresistably engaged his observation was moderately tall but neither thin nor angular, her figure being

marked by the full and rounded proportions so happily characteristic of the female form. Her bust was the swelling throne of love, her tresses black as jet reposed with enviable luxury on her white throat and shoulders; and though above her forehead the hair was drawn upwards from its roots to a formal and preposterous elevation, still so captivating was her loveliness that even this absurd fashion of the day was with her perfectly becoming. Her pouting lips, partly open as she conversed, disclosed two rows of teeth which would in whiteness have outvied the cloven filbert, or shamed the purest ivory; while from her eyes, those natural indexes to the heart, emitted sparkling lustre, Jack watched the happy pair some time, until they took a turn down an avenue, which went under the appellation of the LOVER'S WALK, when his curiosity being further aroused, he followed after, and listened to their conversation, and what was his consternation, on hearing the voice of Edgeworth Bess, and in company with Kneebone.

"Oh, can it be she that speaks," whispered Jack, "give me but a hope that it is not so, and I shall be a happy man."

At that instant, the merry laugh of Bess caught his ear, which at once removed the spell that he appeared bound in, and in another moment, Kneebone measured his length on his mother earth.

This instantaneous act, caused Bess to utter such a shriek that brought the visitors in a throng to her assistance—she would have spoke, but at the sight of Jack her tongue appeared to cling to the roof of her mouth, and refused to give utterance to the words she would fain have said. Jack taxed her with having been guilty of infidelity and ingratitude, swore that she had played him false in leaving him who had rescued her, to sell herself to the wealthier possession of Kneebone, and accompanied each asserveration with a volley of furious oaths, and even blows.

The surprise and vexation of Bess at seeing the interloper was her old lover Jack, was great and poignant in the extreme. She attempted to assuage his anger and explain the causes that had brought her there, but so infuriated had he become that no remonstrance was effectual or even heeded by him.

The previous cries of Bess and the continued noise of the altercation that had ensued, speedily brought a concourse of people to the spot, who, however, would have regarded the tumult as one in which they would have been scarcely called upon to interfere, had not at that moment, Kneebone, who had been merely stunned for a moment by the blow, raised himself from the ground with the assistance of a bystander, and identified in the person of his assaulter the features of Jack Sheppard.

The excitement that ensued baffles description. All stood appalled at the temerity with which Jack—whose name had been placarded all over London, with a reward attached for his apprehensions—had forced himself into the midst of a company acquainted with the history of his atrocities, and assembled in one of the most frequented public resorts. The effrontery with which he surveyed the throng around him, now increasing every moment; the air of defiance which he assumed in contemplating the threatening looks of Kneebone; the anguish of Edgeworth Bess, who saw in the multitude she had attracted by her shrieks the cause that would lead to her lover's apprehension, and whose loud sobs of grief alone broke the stillness of the pause; all formed the component parts of a picture, which would have furnished a rare subject for the artist's pencil.

Suddenly the uncertain issue of the encounter was decided by the hurried entrance of two consequential personages, who elbowing their way through the crowd, speedily changed the scene from one of breathless suspense, to one of action. The hoarse injunctions of the first bidding the bystanders secure the person of Jack, at once proclaimed him to be the thief-taker, Jonathan Wild, and the apparel of the other showed him to be Jefferies, a noted constable of the day, whose services were then secured by the proprietor of the tavern, to quell with his official authority any riot or drunken brawl that might occur within its precints.

"Sieze him, I tell you, he is Jack Sheppard, the notorious young housebreaker," vociferated Jonathan from behind, attempting to force his way through the dense masses of persons that had gathered round Kneebone and his assailant, "Seize him I say, in the name of the King."

A couple of more forward gallants in the throng thus impelled, advanced to assist in the capture.

"Stand back," cried Sheppard, drawing a pistol from his side-pocket and retreating a few paces, "I resist the authority. This pistol is loaded to the muzzle. The shot can reach but one, it is true, but which of ye will choose to receive it?"

"Oh, fly from here, dear Jack," urged Bess through her tears as she saw the determined progress of Jonathan through the crowd.

"Cowards, why do ye not hold him?' roared Wild, as he advanced nearer and a lane was made down the startled line of spectators to afford him a free passage. "Knock his pistol aside, Jefferies, with your staff," suggested Jonathan.

Wild and the constable were now close upon him, and Jack levelling his pistol, which had kept all the others in abeyance, fired direct at the head of his foremost adversary. Owing however, to the unsteadiness of his aim flew harmlessly over the head of Jonathan, and the next instant a cord was thrown over his arms by Jefferies.

"'I've got him, Mister Wild," cried the constable in triumph, tightening the rope round his prisoner's arms;—"but it's so plaguy dark here, one can hardly find the way to make a slip-knot. Can't somebody show a light?" Wild threw himself forward, eager to secure his prize, but at the same moment the torch, that was being passed from hand to hand along the crowd, was suddenly extinguished, Wild was pulled forcibly back, the constable received a severe blow across his face, and then rose a loud cry that Jack Sheppard had escaped.

The back of the gardens, where Jack had been standing, was fenced in by a high quickset hedge, studded with trees, and whilst Jack, turning his head to watch the chance of a delivery from his peril, had received the coil of rope round his arms so dexterously conveyed by the constable, a friendly voice whispered in his ear the emphatic syllable of "Run!" He had scarcely time to recognise the tones of Blueskin, when he felt the cord cut by a knife, the ligature freed from his limbs, the sound of a heavy blow dealt across the head of the constable, and urged by an impulse which then flashed within him, he crashed through the thick boundary of the hedge, and was the next minute speeding through the fields beyond.

"Confound the fellow," muttered Jeffries, as well as the severe bruise he had received from the blow on the cheek would let him—"the rascal's as slippery as an eel. But there are more of the gang about the grounds, Mr. Wild, I'm sure."

"S'death," returned Wild, "why are there no lights here. He cannot have got far. We may have him yet! Send messengers out over St. George's Fields, here in every direction."

The cumbrous bucket lamps used for illuminating the gardens, were now brought forward on every side, and the general excitement that prevailed, was increased at this moment, by a report that the troops of Lord Cathcart, having quartered in the neighbourhood, prior to their being sent to Scotland, to suppress the rebellion, had been now despatched to secure some influential members of the Pretender's party, and that the missing culprit, was charged with having abetted them in their treasonable plottings.

"I see that black scamp Blueskin, about,"—whispered Jonathan to the constable—"you must have him if you can."

"Then here he is, sure enough;" exclaimed that functionary, as a dark shadow flitted across the trees—and he darted in the direction indicated—but before he could grapple with his fleeting antagonist the weight of a heavy hand unseen fell upon his head, and crushing his hat over his eyes, there was so mnch time occupied in removing the incumbrance, that in the meantime, the person of whom he was in search had escaped.

The prostrated condition of Kneebone now engaged the sympathy and attention of the concourse of visitors, but great was their surprise, when as the woollen-draper was moving slowly off to take a vehicle for his return home, the harsh mandate of Jonathan was heard, commanding him to await his pleasure before he stirred, and apprehending him as one dangerous to the government, and in the pay of the Pretender.

"The charge is monstrous, and without foundation," stammered Kneebone, appealing to the crowd, "you have no proofs of what you alledge against me."

"Only documents sufficient to ensure you a twelvemonth's imprisonment in the Tower, at least," sneered Wild. "Your mistress there has been kind enough to make such good use of her time, that all the names of your fellow conspirators, are now in my possession."

"Cockatrice!" ejaculated the amazed draper vindictively, darting a furious glance at Edgeworth Bess, who since the beginning of the fray had remained passively contemplating the course of events.

"It's of no use wasting such words on me," retorted Bess, "I told you from the first I never liked you, and now you know it."

"Never mind him, Bess," pursued Wild, "I will take care of his future morality. You can call at my office in the Old Bailey any time to-morrow, and receive your reward."

"I will take care, too, to represent the circumstances of the case to Mr. Walpole," muttered Kneebone; "It is not the first time, remember you have attempted to betray me by your infamous spy system. I will ascertain if the members of the government will countenance such proceedings, and see if they authorize you thus to entrap honest tradesmen like me by a robbery of their private papers."

"They *do* authorise it," replied Jonathan, "so make your mind perfectly easy upon that score. But this is not the place to banter idle words of why and wherefore. Away with him to my cage for the night, and to-morrow he shall have as much answering to as much questioning as he likes, before the secret Committee. You Jeffries can take horse and overtake that slippery imp of Satan, Jack Sheppard, before he gets beyond your reach."

Abrahams and the others Janizaries who had by this time squeezed their way to the place where their Master stood, now obeyed his last injunction by removing the helpless Kneebone, who repeated assurances of appealing against his capture to the last, and was vehement in his denunciations of the treachery that had been practised upon him, through Wild's instrumentality. Jefferies proceeded round to the stables to engage a horse for the pursuit, and the rest of the assembly who found that this unexpected episode, in the evening's entertainment was now over, began to disperse, making as they went, comments on the astounding hardihood of Jack, and some not over complimentary allusions to the conduct of Jonathan, which did not fail to reach his ears as he followed at no very remote distance behind.

The night, despite the absence of the moon, which was all the better for Jack's purposes of concealment, was fine and clear. The wind was perfectly still, and the sound of a footfall along the road could be distinctly heard. The quick intelligence of Jack, speedily convinced him therefore, that it would be hazardous to pursue the windings of the highway, and having been completely sobered by the excitement of the peril in which he had been placed, he knew that keeping to the grassy surface of the roadside, he could best ensure his safety. It was this expedient that baffled the constable, for on emerging from the Tavern, his first eager inquiries had been to ascertain the direction in which Jack had gone, and as those about the fields had heard no rapid tread of any one as in flight, they were compelled to give their answers at random. The arrival of a packman who stated that he had passed a figure, answering as far as the darkness of the night would permit him to judge, the description given of the fugitive, put Jefferies however, on the right scent, and clapping spurs to his steed, the officer of justice went off at a rapid rate in the direction of Croydon, which was the road the packman had indicated.

A chase at night with a bright warm sky above, and a fine open level road beneath, is a pleasant and exhilirating exercise enough, but to make it agreeable to the pursuer, there must be at least some chance of his making sure of the prize at which he aims. So thought and felt the worthy official, for after about an hour's hard riding without seeing or hearing anything of the fugitive, he considered it the wiser plan to turn back and await the next opportunity that offered for putting his duties of constable into efficient operation. Thus left unmolested from the long start he had got of his pursuer, Jack slackened not his pace until the break of day, found himself traversing one of those delightful parts of Surrey, which from its winding green lanes. with the trees, meeting over head like a cradle, its winding roads between coppices, with wide turfy margins on either side, as if left on purpose for the frequent gipsy encampment, and its extensive tracks of woodland, suggested to him that a sojourn of a few days in the vicinity, would best afford him an opportunity of returning safely back to the Metropolis.

Descending a steep hill he accordingly came in view of a sequestered village, which with its scattered cottages separated from each other, by long strips of garden ground, the little country Inn and two or three old fashioned tenements of somewhat higher pretensions, gave promise of a favorable locality. The old houses with their moss-grown orchards seemed to be completely shut out from the bustling world, and environed by their sloping meadows so deeply green, and the overhanging woods so rich in their various tinting, sent forth from the grey clustered chimneys, slender wreaths of smoke into the freshening morning air. So profound was the tranquility, that the narrow streamlet which gushed along the valley, and glittered in the rising sunlight like a thread of silver, seemed to Jack the only trace of life and motion in the picture.

"Here," thought he, "will I wait for a few days till the last adventure of mine is somewhat forgotten," aad here accordingly leaving him to recruit his health and spirits for fresh exploits, turn we to the fortunes of another personage in this history, whom we have of late last sight of.

CHAPTER XVII.

THE WELL-HOLE.

BARON. Now then unfold
  Why with such mystic preparation
  At this dark hour and unfrequented spot
  We are alone together.
FITZHARDING. Can you doubt?
  Your crime was murder; and it has been said
  Blood will have blood. Such a deed
  Cries for no common penance; whining prayers
  Self-castigation; wasting abstinence,
  A galling pilgrimage twice round the world;
  Your wealth, whilst living all consumed in alms:
  Or left when dead to raise up hospitals,
  These things will not absolve you from an act
  Which has but one atonement.
BARON. Name it.
FITZHARDING. *Death.*

OLD PLAY.

It was nearly on the stroke of midnight, when Wild returned to his house in the old Bailey, revolving in his mind the successful issue of those schemes upon which he had calculated in his visit to the "Dog and Duck." His myrmidons had before proceeded thither with the disconsolate draper, who had proved so refractory in the journey, as to render it necessary to bind his arms before consigning him to the stone cell for the night. The meeting with his victim, Jack Sheppard, was an event that he had never contemplated, and though he had dispatched Jefferies the constable in search of him, it was done more with a view to save appearances than from any hope or eager desire of his apprehension.

Retiring to his chamber which, in its sombre aspect at that hour, wore an increased appearance of gloomy discomfort, Jonathan ignited his lamp, drew his implements of writing before him and began drawing up a detailed account of the process by which he had secured the leading members of the Jacobite conspiracy. The having of Kneebone's papers furnished him with a complete list of all those engaged in the cause and amongst the names were those of Sir Thomas Rivers and his associates whose daring attempt to abstract the King of England's crown through the agency of our hero was thus frustrated by their unexpected apprehension. The length of this important document, which was intended for presentation to the Secret Committee on the following day, had considerably prolonged his labours and it was nearly dawn when the rapid tramp of a horseman at full speed aroused him from his task and the audible sound of voices engaged in altercation below, made him aware that his visitor—whoever it was at so unusual an hour—had dismounted from his horse and was now applying at the door for admission.

"Some government messenger I suppose, or that zealous fellow Jefferies returned," mused Wild, as he put aside the work on which he had been engaged and strode towards the window to decypher from the horse the quality of its rider—"I fear, Jack is too nimble in his motions and too expert a craftsman to be caught by the bird-limed fingers of a city-constable."

The entrance of Abrahams who had huddled on a few garments hastily to make an appearance in answer to the summons of the claimant for admission, interrupted his conjectures and resolved his doubts.

"Misther Vilds, Misther Vilds," cried the Jew at the door with an evident tremor in his voice.

"How now, knave," exclaimed Jonathan "What cause is there for this trembling. Who is at the door?"

"Oh Misther Vilds, Lord Orford ish vaiting down stairs, and vants to see you immediately."

"Lord Orford," echoed Wild starting up in astonishment from his seat—"Why I did not expect him till to-morrow evening at least."

"So I told him, Misther Vilds, but he vont take no denial."

"His coming here at this hour, alone and unwatched may be all the better for my purposes," continued Wild, thoughtfully pacing the apartment, "Where is he now?"

"Vaiting in the lobby, till I return to let him know you have consented to see him." answered the janizary.

Wild paused a moment as if busied in deep reflection. Apparently arriving at a fixed determination on the subject of his thoughts he threw himself into his seat and continued, "Enough, Abrahams, I have made up my mind I will see him. Tell Bowyer to take his horse round to the mews and be yourself in readiness at the black gallery during our interview. I may want your assistance."

"Very well, Misther Vilds," responded Abrahams obediently, and he retired to act according to his instructions.

"Orford so ready to renew my acquaintance"—meditated Jonathan—"there is more in this than I reckoned upon. However I have two ways of silencing his objections to my claims. One by putting the State warrant into force, and then if that should fail, I have readier and securer means at hand."

The approach of the individual who had given rise to the soliloquy, suspended further reflections, and Jonathan stiffly bending his head as a recognition, proffered a chair to the nobleman.

The appearance of Lord Orford was greatly changed since his former visit to that room, either from the effects of his recent long journey or from the inroads of habitual dissipation on his constitution—to which he had lately given way in order to drown the thoughts of remorse that rose within him—his features were now pale and haggard in the extreme and few would have recognized in that attenuated and emaciated figure the once gallant brother of Sir Hugh Trevanion.

The sordid and malignant disposition of the thief-taker was however one not likely to be affected by the contemplation of a change of this kind. On the contrary it seemed to afford him satisfaction, for as he gazed on his guest a sarcastic smile played upon his features for a moment, and then as if struggling to conceal it, he relapsed into his former chilling and repulsive demeanour.

"I was unprepared for so speedy a reply to my letter, "observed Wild, turning towards the peer, "and still less prepared for one in person from yourself. This however looks like business upon your part, and I am flattered by your haste in showing it."

"Do not deceive yourself, sir," returned Orford in measured accents, "I have come hither not to satisfy your exorbitant demands, so much as to make peace with my own conscience. You remember our last interview."

"Distinctly, you have a right to inquire into the appropriation of the thousand pounds I received from you, and shall have a due explanation."

"I require it not," returned Orford scornfully, "I have come to make restitution of my estate, to those whose title to it, is stronger than mine. I feel that my earthly career is nearly over, and would do justice ere I die, to those I have so deeply wronged, before the opportunity for so doing passes beyond my power."

"Your priestly confessor has been with you my lord, I perceive recently," sneered Wild.

"My resolution is not to be shaken by your profane sarcasms, Sir, I have certainly received the advice of a holy man upon the matter, and I have to thank him for fanning the slumbering embers of my conscience into a warming flame; but I have had no peace, night nor day, since I have been awakened to a sense of my guilt, nor shall I till I make that retribution due to justice."

"This is language more for the ear of a

penitent-making priest than mine," answered Wild," I am at a loss to preceive the drift of this conversation, or why a communication of this kind, should have needed such urgent haste for you must have ridden night and day here to make it."

"Before I proceed further I must have some proof of the knowledge you possess of my family, beyond the few hints you have at sundry times thrown ont."

"Hump!" smiled Jonathan—"you doubt I see, the extent of my power. Well, I shall not have to trespass long upon your attention, if I do unfold the chief secrets of your biography.—You are the son of Sir Reginald Trevanion, of Yorkshire, and Sir Hugh Trevanion was your elder and your *only* brother."

"Go on, Sir," exclaimed the nobleman, wincing under the emphasis laid upon the word.

"Your envy led you to plot the possession of those lands to which he succeeded at the death of your father, and your insatiable ambition fed itself on the hope of his living on unwedded; in this respect he baffled you, for he allied himself to one Constantia Sheppard, a girl of lowly but virtuous parentage, and of this marriage one child was the issue."

A cloud passed over the brow of the nobleman, at the reminiscence, but Wild heeded it not, and pursued his explanations.

"When your brother was on the road to Caversham, to make public his marriage, and to proclaim as you fancied, the blot on your family escutcheon, you bribed Sampson Kirby and the other lawless depredators of the Mint to entrap and waylay him, and by your orders he was imprisoned in the Mouse Tower, where you hoped only to effect his release on advantageous terms to yourself. But again fate thwarted your intentions, for he escaped and hired a boat on the night of the Great Storm in that year, to pass to the Middlesex side of the River. You followed—shot him—and fancied in the turbulence of that fearful night, your crime of murder would be for ever a secret confined to your own breast."

"Nay—cease your remembrances, I have heard enought" interrupted Orford, writhing under the tortures of memory.

"The biography is not yet concluded, my Lord, your violence caused the death of Lady Stafford, your sister, in whose name you took possession of the estate and title you now hold—your exertions to influence her in the disposal of her property are well known to me, and in default of obtaining that by fair means, you have had recourse to fraud. You forge a will in your own favor—nay, start not, I might have not been more scrupulous myself under the same circumstances—and since then the rightful heir to the Orford estate, has by *our* instrumentality become a proclaimed felon and an outcast."

"But whatever my motives were, Sir, and whether you are right or wrong in these lengthy conjectures, with which you have favored me, I shall not now dispute, there is no palliation of your own agency, which has made the boy become the associate of thieves, and so crippled his resources and distorted his better judgment, as to make him one himself. You at least have had no hope of gain in the affair beyond that I proffered at your suggestion."

"My motive was revenge," growled Wild, with a ferocious look;—"In my youth, I had loved his mother and she jilted me, I swore to be revenged, and the present position of her son is a proof how I have kept my oath."

Orford started with surprise and terror, with surprise for he had never before heard hinted a suspicion of the circumstance; with terror from the mode of its announcement. Mingled love aud scorn, the struggles of pride and passion—the strife of his whole existence seemed re-acted in that one moment.

"Yes, jilted me!" he repeated after a moment's pause. "I was not discarded because she loved another for she knew not that other then. Your brother came—wooed and won her. She is now gathered to her last home, but still my rage is neither abated nor extinct."

"I can now appreciate Mr. Wild the share you have so actively taken in my nephew's disgrace—but excuse me if I add, that I must have some ocular proof of the acquaintance you have had with my deceased brother, whom you charge me with murdering."

"You may recognise your brother's ring, posibly, which he gave me on the night of his murder." said Jonathan, exhibiting the glittering guerdon to the Peer, —"is it necessary for me to bring forward other evidences of your guilt?"

"Jonathan Wild," cried Orford, starting up from his seat—"your almost superhuman knowledge of my actions, has I need scarcely say astounded, if not satisfied me. I have not been prepared for this full disclosure. You estimate the price of your secrecy at——"

"——At six thousand pounds," interrupted Jonathan. "But I must now have besides the title-deeds of the Orford Estates."

"Never. They are reserved for those who have the right of justice to them—to those who must hold them for the future in reparation for the past.

"Give me the money then," demanded Jonathan with a smile of sarcastic import.

Lord Orford opened his pocket-book, and handed over to the thief-taker the amount of notes required.

"I must now, my lord, become acquainted with your future intentions," remarked Wild—"I am still anxious to learn the reason of your hurried visit to this my unworthy abode." Lord Orford suppressed the indignant reply that rose to his lips, and he continued in a milder tone, "though I do not admit, Jonathan Wild, your right to subject me to a catechism of this kind, I do not hesitate to acquaint you with my fixed determination to leave England this day for ever. At twelve o'clock a boat starts from the Tower, to convey me to the coast of France, and in one hour from this time, the documents sufficient to establish the title of my nephew to the lands of which I have wronged him, will be in the possession of a solicitor in the Temple, to appropriate them for that purpose. You now perceive the urgency of my visit."

"Indeed!" meditated Jonathan, drawing his desk before him—"I must know the place of your continental sojourn."

"Rue Rivoli, Hotel Colbert, Paris,"—answered the Peer—"all letters directed to me there, will reach me."

Wild wrote a few words upon a slip of paper—rang the bell—delivered the note to Abrahams, who entered—and after a glance of deep meaning, had been interchanged between them, unobserved by Orford—Abrahams left, and Jonathan resumed the conversation.

"I have been merely taking down the direction," observed Wild, finding that his visitor regarded the proceeding with suspicion, "these are memorandums that I generally entrust to the care of my janizaries, who know how to dispose of them."

"I have no doubt of it," sighed Orford.

"But come, my lord," cried Wild with a very lugubrious effort at hilarity. You have a long journey before you, and a glass of wine will enable you to recruit your strength, for excuse me if I say you are much altered since we last met."

"Yes, in all things; I am not what I was; but I trust a humbler and better man. I have been ill, since we made our last compact, and suffering brings thought. The shadow of death was over me—I learned to pray, as I had never prayed before. Pride was subdued by pain, and I saw myself, as I really was, a stern and sinful man, harsh and vindictive to my brethren, and rebellious to Him, who had so mercifully given me time for repentance and grace, to see my guilt, and turn to him. I had no peace by day—no sleep by night—and now I can only look forward with penitence to the few remaining days of my life, and hope that my repentance for the future, will be an atonement for the past."

"The arrangements you have made, will not compromise me, I hope, my lord,"—rejoined Jonathan.

"While I am living, you are safe from all charges upon my part, but after my decease, I can answer of course for your security, no longer," returned Orford. But I have already overstayed the time I allotted to this interview. I must depart, and for the better satisfaction of both parties in this matter, I would thank you to give me an acknowledgment of the monies you have received from me."

"It is hardly necessary, my lord, but if you desire it—of course you shall receive the acquittance you desire—perchance more fully than you anticipate,"—added Wild, proceeding as though for the purpose of obtaining a receipt for him there—"you will first allow me though to ring the bell, that my attendant may bring you some refreshment for your *long journey.*"

Wild touched the bell, and before it had ceased ringing, Abrahams, who had been waiting some time behind the door, in eager expectation of the signal, darted quickly, and silently behind Lord Orford, and throwing a cloth over his head, held it tightly in his grasp, whilst Jonathan, who had moved towards the recess previously, seized a thick bludgeon, that had been secreted in the corner, and swung it with all the force of his two hands into the face of the unhappy nobleman, dealing a blow with such fearful violence, that the blood spirted through the cloth, and stained the walls opposite.

"Help, murder, mercy!"—gasped Lord Orford, as the white cloth became dyed with crimson.

"Open the door of the Black Gallery—quick," cried Wild repeating his blows with eager fury, and sending the bludgeon with such force into the face of his victim, that at every blow a frightful crunching sound proclaimed the gradual dismemberment of every bone; Abrahams left his position a moment to throw open the door of the chamber that led to the gallery alluded to, and the desperate struggles of Orford enabling him to succeed in pulling off the cloth, there was disclosed a visage so appaling in its disfigurement, and so revolting it its mangled mutilation, down which the gory streams of blood trickled in sickening succession, that hardened and unflinching as these murderers were, even they stood for the moment aghast at so hideous a spectacle.

Orford felt for his sword, but Abrahams had taken care to remove it from the scabbard at the beginning of the fray. The wretched man then striving to clear his eyes from the thick tangled clots of blood that blinded them, sought some opening for his escape, and seeing the door that the janizary had just left ajar, dashed through it in hopes of effecting an egress into the street.

"All the better," cried Jonathan—"let him run to the end—follow him close up to the well-hole and we have him now without a word. Quick bring the torch with you."

Following rapidly upon the footsteps of the maimed unfortunate, Wild and Abrahams darted down the passage with the light.

At the end of this lobby was a narrow bridge, that crossed a dark circular vault extending beneath into a considerable well, which gave to this part of the building the name of the "Well-hole."—Few could tell what it had originally been constructed for. The sides were lined with a green slimy fungus, and at the bottom ran the dark waters of the Fleet river, winding on in its serpentine course to the Thames. The bridge was fenced in at the sides with a low wooden railing, and at the opposite end was a door to which the bridge thrown across this fearful abyss and its inky waters, formed the only means of communication.

On this apology for a bridge, Lord Orford had now got, and having dashed himself against the door opposite, in a vain attempt to make his way through, despair gave him courage, and he turned round to confront his assailants. A struggle of fearful intensity now ensued; Abrahams bearing a light was prevented from taking any part in the affray, and Jonathan being the first in the encounter, swung his bludgeon heavily round, falling on the ballustrade and splitting it. Orford, however, darted aside, and Jonathan had not time to recover himself, ere he fled past him, and would have regained the outer chamber, had not the Jew caught him by the throat, and hurled him back again. Rushing on Orford with the spring of a tiger on his prey, Wild passed his arms under the other's waist, and grasping the ballustrade against which he had driven him, pressed him with all the strength he could throw into his ponderous frame, between his body and the rails. In vain Orford, bleeding and weak with the copious effusion of his life's current, writhed in his powerful grasp. The blood purpled in his mashed face, his mouth opened, his blackened tongue, and his glaring eyeballs appeared to burst from their sockets as his respiration became stifled by the hug of his antagonist, whilst a crimson froth oozed from his lips and nostrils.

Thus rendering him incapable of further resistance, Wild caught him up in his arms and attempted to throw him over into the dark gulph beneath, but the dying man, with all the tenacity of despair, clung to the railings, and would not relax his hold.

"Oh, spare me—spare me," he groaned, looking upward upon the savage countenance of Jonathan.

Wild made no reply; but raising the sturdy weapon he had so frequently availed himself of before,—he prepared himself for a vigorous effort, and crashing the uplifted bludgeon down through the air, he struck such a desperate blow on the head of his victim, that Orford's skull was crushed in like an egg-shell.

A deep groan followed; but still the hands of the murdered man became more rigidly fixed round the rails, and even now the writhing contortions of his body, for the features of the head were utterly obliterated, showed that life was not yet extinct.

Wild felt hastily in his girdle for an implement to sever the wrist, and bringing forth a sharp clasp-knife, he began sawing away the fingers of the left hand: in so doing the writhings of his victim caused him to let it slip into the well-hole, and again he had recourse to his bludgeon. Smashing each finger successively the hands at last fell away unclasped, and with a hollow reverberating plunge, Lord Orford dropped into the black waters below.

Abrahams bent over the balustrade with his torch, and Jonathan, looking down into the murky abyss, saw that their deed of murder had reached its termination.

Not a sound came from the damp vault; and, breathless with their exertions, the murderer and his asssociate now glared upon each other with silent ferocity.

EPOCH THE THIRD.

1724.

CHAPTER I.

THE LAST LINK OF THE CHAIN.

PLAYER. But honest friend I hope you don't intend that your hero shall be really executed?

BEGGAR. Most assuredly, sir—to make it perfect, I am for doing strict poetical justice. My hero shall be hanged, and as for the other personages of the drama the audience must suppose they were all either hanged or transported."

GAY'S BEGGAR'S OPERA.—1745.

TEN years more had passed over the heads of all the personages who figure in this

history, and had wrought but little change in their several manners, habits, and pursuits, Jack, who with Blueskin had contrived to elude the vigilance of Wild, and his emissaries, had now grown up into a tall, and tolerably handsome person, whose conquests over the fairer sex, had been characterised by numerous *liasons* of too extensive and varied a character to bear recapitulation. His name also had become the terror of every magistrate, and the fear of every neighbourhood, for emboldened by the impunity with which he had practised his avocations, the glare of noonday, as well as the gloom of midnight witnessed their daring burglaries, and no bar was too strong —no house two well defended—to resist the enterprise of him, who had now become the notorious Jack Sheppard.

It would be but an idle and fruitless task, to enumerate all the various robberies in which during the above period, our hero had been so actively engaged. Each day brought with it some new iniquity to add to the mass of those that had preceded it, and not content as before with performing his exploits nearly single handed, Jack organized a band, which from its orderly irregularity, if terms o opposite may be used to convey our meaning, so awed the civil powers of the government, that whilst they felt themselves unable to repress the growing evil, they found it necessary to issue the most stringent regulations for the suppression of gambling in public houses, as being the places where they most did congregate, and in addition set forth a proclamation offering a reward of one hundred pounds for the apprehension of this renowned housebreaker.

The ravages committed by this gang were almost incredible, and extended over the whole of Middlesex, Essex, Kent, Surrey, and Berkshire. Scarcely a house of sufficient importance to tempt their skill escaped the vigilant eye and hand of Jack, who was now styled "Captain Sheppard," and his equally unscrupulous associate, who was also invested with the self important dignity of Lieutenant Blueskin.

Under these circumstances it is not to be wondered at, that the whole metropolis was kept in a state of continual ferment by Jack's atrocities, and the government took every step within their power to repress the outrages that had now become so frequent; and as Jack was the avowed captain of the gang, to him were all the attempts at seizure chiefly directed.

In Chandos-street—then an obscure thoroughfare leading from the Strand to the King's Mews—there existed at this time a famous hostel, where cash and liquor flowed freely and kept up a perpetual interchange of owners. This Tavern was known to the lower grades of the Londoners, by the sign of the "Golden Key" and owned for its proprietress a certain Mistress Maberly, who was, or else report belied her—the quondam flame of a personage of rank and title about the court, who had contrived upon his own marriage, to place her in the possession of Hostess.

This good dame though somewhat passed the grand climacterie that resolves the young unmarried woman into the title of "Old Maid," had, if her own assertion was of any value, spent the whole of her previous existence in a state of either single blessedness, or blessed singleness, as the reader according to his own notions of matrimonial peculiarities may choose to interpret the phrase.

In order to accelerate the desired consummation of matrimony, it had been currently reported that the onerous duties of a landlady, had been undertaken for that reason, and that she had been observed to frequently regard with loving eyes the elder frequenters of her tavern; but rumour, that hundred-tongued disposer of the fate and character of individuals, had provided the immaculate Mistress Maberly with a daughter, who passed under the more reputable appellation of her neice, and to whom as the minor arrangements of the bar were confided, the "Golden Key" was popularly supposed to be indebted for its attraction.

Janet, the "neice" in question, was a young girl just in the bud of womanhood, and of such an attractive beauty that few hearts was found capable of resisting its influence that came within the circle of its fascination. But Janet's chief fault—and it was one not uncommon among ladies placed in a similar position—arose from her coquetry, which caused her smiles, like the sunbeams they were so often compared to, to be almost universally diffused. On two indeed among the circle of her admirers she had seemed to bestow more attention than on any of the rest, and though many a gallant had cause to leave the house with an aching heart, on account of the fickleness of Janet, her love here appeared to be so equally divided, that neither could claim for himself a greater share of her attentions than she bestowed on the other. These two were a certain Edmund Walsingham, an officer on duty at the Savoy, and Captain Sheppard the hero of our narrative. Jack who since he had first seen her, had with his usual susceptibility to beauty, meditated the accomplishment of his designs, had been most constant in the expressions of his adoration. Night after night had he visited the house in disguise, and Janet, to do her justice, had not failed on her part to encourage his attentions.

Among the many presents which Jack had bestowed upon the fair barmaid, had been a valuable diamond-necklace which had fallen into his hands with some other things of a similar nature, in the way of business, having been part of the produce of an extensive burglary, in which Jack, together with his expert Lieutenant, had been recently engaged.

That necklace enchaining the alabaster neck of the fair Janet in its glistening folds, became but a few days afterwards the means of providing the neck of Jack with a less costly and attractive ornament. Such are the slender threads on which our destinies hang!

Walsingham conscious that he had a rival spared neither time nor trouble in ascertaining who that rival was. Accident discovered to him what otherwise might have taken years perchance to bring to light. The owner of the house, in which the burglary above alluded to had been committed, had privately circulated a description of the property stolen, and having been on terms of intimacy with him, the document had fallen under the notice of Walsingham, and whilst a reward had been offered for the apprehension of the robbers, to him had been entrusted an active share in the endeavours made for the recovery of the booty.

Now, as Fate willed it, one night when Janet had been with an ardour, warmer than ordinary, encouraging the addresses of her military lover—the eye of Edmund rested upon this necklace, and it needed but a few interrogations to convince him that the diamonds were the very same as those of which he had received so excellent a description in the account of the purloined property. In another moment he had learned to whom she had been indebted for the present, and judging from the circumstances that the giver could not have become possessed of the trinkets without being aware of the source whence it had come, he hurried off to Bow-street—then as now the focus of the constabulary force—to adopt such measures as would ensure the apprehension of one at least who could possibly afford some clue to the originators of the burglary. It is needless to say the appeal was promptly responded to, and by ten o'clock that night the "Golden Key" had become, unknown to all but Walsingham and the official detachment, surrounded by those who were anxiously awaiting the moment when they could secure the supposed thieves.

At his usual hour in the evening, Jack Sheppard, in his assumed character of Capt. Darville, entered the little parlour of the hostel which had been the scene of so many previous visits. As if anxious to make a still greater impression on the heart of the susceptible barmaid, he had bestowed on this occasion a more than ordinary care upon his toilette, and to do him justice the symmetry of his figure, which had now shot into the matured proportions of manhood, set off with considerable advantage to his person the sumptuous apparel in which it had been so recklessly clothed.

Beneath a full-dress coat, composed of the most expensive chocolate coloured velvet, prodigally adorned with flowered ornaments, and interlaced with silver embroidery, appeared a white satin waistcoat, also trimmed with similar costly appendages. A cravat of fine muslin, with ruffles of the same rare material; red-heeled shoes, set with dazzling diamond buckles; silk stockings with clocks to them, emblazoned in gold, and a jewelled hanger at his side from which depended a silver-hilted sword, completed the embellishments of one, who, merely judged by the dress might have been taken for a personage of the very highest distinction. Indeed such was Jack's excessive passion for finery, that the entire portion of his own share of the night's plunder was frequently devoted to the adornment of his figure alone, and as we have intimated in an early chapter, Jack's ruling foible being vanity, he lost no opportunity which the ill-gotten gold of each day afforded him, to gratify that seductive weakness to its fullest and most infatuating extent.

On the night in question, Jack had been more than usually fortunate, and he was accordingly in high spirits. The adventures of the day had been crowned with the most complete success, and whilst silently drinking the same fortune to his next exploit, glass after glass followed each other in rapid sequence. According to his former practice when engaged in the prosecution of this new amour, he had escaped from all his companions to pursue the tenor of his way alone, and thus unprepared and unprotected, everything seemed to conspire to render him an easy prey to the dangers by which he was surrounded.

As a part of Walsingham's scheme, the fair magnet of Jack's attraction had been withdrawn during the earlier portion of the evening by a supposed summons from a relation whose indifferent health was alleged to be the cause of the request, and hus Jack in the hope of her momentary return, had been delayed until the period of the arrival of the constabulary.

The few frequenters of the room that remained until so late an hour, were busily engaged in a discussion of the reigning political topics of the day, and Walsingham —who was unacquainted with the person of our hero, and knew the rival of his affections only as a certain Captain Darville, of whose entrance he sat in eager expectation, little dreaming he was already at his side,—had, to beguile the lagging moments, entered into conversation with Jack, who equally impatient for the arrival of another party, had been previously busily engaged in the consumption of those potent wines for which the cellar of the "Golden Key," had become somewhat celebrated. A pause had ensued in the conversation.

"Come, lad, you don't drink! the wine flags in your glass, and the bottle stays with you. Here s a toast which you cannot refuse to quaff if the last spark of sluggish gallantry lies not dormant in your breast.—Here's Janet Maberly!"

And Jack filled his glass as he spoke, his eyes radiant with enthusiasm, and his face flushed with the potations he had already so copiously imbibed.

"With all my heart, sir stranger, whoever you may be," responded Walsingham. "I pledge you in that toast with all my heart.

"Here's Janet Maberly, and may her virtue protect her from the designs of a libertine,"—and the speaker emptied his tankard, unconscious of the deep wound he had inflicted on the conscience of the other.

Jack Sheppard at once appropriating the epithet to himself, dashed the contents of the glass he was raising in his hand to the floor.

"How now, sir?" demanded he; "By what right do you annex a remark so personally offensive to a toast that I myself proposed?"

"If thy tender skin be pricked by the arrow I shot at random," pursued Walsingham, at once surmising that the hasty stranger was the Captain Darville of whom he was in search, "no wonder thy smitten conscience should recoil at the accusation," and he darted a scrutinising glance at the impetuous youth.

"Nay, sir," cried Jack, rising suddenly from his seat, and unable to withstand the penetrating gaze of his antagonist,—"this is an insult which neither my pride nor my honour will suffer me to pass unchecked. Draw thy sword, coxcomb, if the sheath at thy side be not a mere empty pretence at bravery. Draw I say."

"You are the worst for the glasses you have taken—your words betray it—and your hand is unsteady. It would be unfair to take you at such a disadvantage. I would cope with you at a time when our positions were more equal, for I have—if you are the person I presume you to be good cause for such an encounter." But continued Walsingham, coolly surveying the athletic proportions of the figure that stood before him,—"you need not fear I shall be ready to dispute your pretensions, even though enhanced by certain presents which———"

"Coward!" interrupted Jack, administering a contemptuous blow with his glove on the burning cheek of Walsingham, "let this challenge then explain the cause of your sneaking hesitation!"

Walsingham, starting up at this humiliating infliction, crimsoned with rage, and unsheathing his weapon, bade Jack look to his own safety, and threw himself into a posture of defence. A short but decisive conflict followed. Jack exchanged several passes with his antagonist, who warded them off with but little difficulty. But the former infuriated by disappointment and intoxication, made at last a violent hinge at Walsingham, who dexterously slipping on one side, avoided the blow, whilst Jack losing his equilibrium, fell against the opposite panelling, and from the force of his aim, the slouched hat which he wore for disguise was jerked off from his head, and the sleek black crop and striking features of our hero was revealed.

"Hold Walsingham!" vociferated one who had just entered, "Know you with whom you are engaged? That is the celebrated housebreaker Jack Sheppard, I knew him from a boy at Wood's the carpenter's."

At this a general consternation and alarm seized the whole assembly. Walsingham recovering from the momentary stupor of amazement, into which such an announcement had thrown him, gave at once the preconcerted signal for the officers of justice to enter.

Jack, on the other hand, overcome by the potent liquors he had taken had only sufficient strength and self-possession remaining, to make a faint attempt at defence but being speedily overpowered by numbers, his resistance was week and futile, and he fell a ready victim to what had been the bane of his career as well as that of others, wine and a woman.

"I am sorry I have not the power of letting you remain at liberty any longer Captain Sheppard," exclaimed a well-known voice at his elbow, as he was being led-off, "Your life has been a short but a merry one, *the lease of twenty-one years has expired however to-night.*"

The speaker was Jonathan Wild.

Heavily ironed and handcuffed, followed too by a crowd of people all anxious to obtain a view of the notorious criminal who had so long kept the metropolis in awe by his atrocities, the once well-intentioned, high-spirited and gallant Jack Sheppard was conducted to Newgate.

During his progress thither mingled exultations and lamentations rent the air. Here and there Jack, notwithstanding the darkness of the night, and his own imbecility, discerned the familiar features of some of his gang peering from the crowd, and exchanging with him a token of recognition The news of his capture, despite the lateness of the hour, had spread like wildfire, and multitudes at every thorougfare were pouring forth to witness his journey to the stronghold. Once, indeed, there was reason to believe that an attempt at rescue would be made, and a number of the old minters congregated near the Fleet Ditch, seemed to favour the supposition, but whether such a design had never been premeditated, or that the military force accompanying Jack was too great to render the chance of such a bold effort being successfully made, certain it is that at last Jack Sheppard was safely secured in one of the strongest cells in Newgate without the slightest symptoms of any turbulence being observed.

The rapid interchange of words between two of the spectators of his ignominious journey must not pass unrecorded. Half-hidden by the projecting wall of St. Sepulchre's and half-concealed by the pressure of the mob at that point, two figures were shrouded entirely from observation, conversing upon the event that had just transpired.

"Alas, poor Jack!" cried the elder one, "he has got his stone-jug allowance served out to him at last. I told him when he had once got into limbo, that he would never come to the bar of the "Fox," in the Mint again, as he promised he would."

"Did he promise you that?" inquired the other.

"Ay! that did he," responded the first speaker. "I'll come to you, says he, for the change of that guinea after I make my escape from Newgate!"

"Did the blessed babby say that?" exclaimed his companion with enthusiasm—"then take my word for it Giles Shalders, that Jackey Sheppard will keep his word, or my name's not Blueskin."

CHAPTER II.

JACK SHEPPARD EXECUTES A PROJECT WHICH HANDS DOWN HIS NAME TO POSTERITY.

" In truth he had been lofty from a child,
And e'en his boyish pastimes relished still,
Of a bold front and honourable pride,
I well remember in our infancy
When each would have a favourite plant or flower
He loved the wall-flower most because it roots
Itself the highest, and can brave the blast,
And climb the dizzy rock, or time worn tower
And he would praise the holly for it smiled
Despite the frown of winter, as the bold
Can live and flourish in adversity."

OLD PLAY.

The celebrity of Jack's exploits drew greater crowds to see this notorious malefactor in Newgate, than had ever before requested admission within its sombre walls. In not one single instance however, were the applications for leave to hold converse with him granted, as it was suspected and it is believed not without good cause, that the sympathy he had excited by his bravery and effrontery was so great, that many had come prepared with implements, which were intended to aid in effecting his escape. As some doubts existed in the mind of the Governor of Newgate whether the warrant then out against the prisoner was sufficient for the purposes of his detention and subsequent punishment, he started expressly off to Windsor, to consult with the higher legal authorities respecting the debated point, and in the meantime his trust was delegated to Jonathan Wild, who had risen to high repute, and who did not allow so favourable an opportunity to escape him, for adopting the harshest measures towards the criminals under his temporary jurisdiction and towards Jack Sheppard in particular. His elegant wardrobe was of course confiscated to the Crown, but not content with denuding him of the sumptuous apparel he had worn at the time of his apprehension, he was subjected to the grossest indignities, compelled to wear the coarsest and most filthy garments, and removed to the most repulsive portion of the prison denominated the strong hold. The hitherto indomitable spirit of Jack sunk under this accumulation of miseries, and as it was decided that his identity with the person named in the warrant must be distinctly and legally proved, the postponement of his trial to the autumnal sessions left considerable doubts on the mind of the turnkey, as to whether he would languish out the time until his sentence was pronounced.

As any other than a violent death was not what Jonathan desired, he gave orders to have him removed to a more commodious and salubrious cell, as soon as the intelligence reached his ears of the delay, and that Jack's health was seriously endangered, by his imprisonment in the noisome dungeon where he had been at first confined. He was therefore removed to another ward, called by the topographers of Newgate "the Castle" from its apparently strong and impregnable position. The place thus singularly denominated was on the western side of the gaol, and over the western gateway, and was remarkable for the numerous fortifications which had contributed to its supposed security. The cell, in which Jack had been deposited, was about fourteen feet high, ten long and as many wide, and was defended by three doors, each guarded by massive iron gratings and being trebly thick as well as numerous, were well calculated to resist invasion from without. The small loop-holes of windows were doubly barred and grated, the light being admitted with the air without the intervention of glass. The fire-place was without a grate and fenced in at the top with stout iron railings, which while it allowed free egress for the smoke, seemed effectually to prevent any substance more tangible passing beyond its boundaries. When to this it is added that the walls were of unusual thickness and that Jack prior to his incarceration had been carefully examined, to preclude the possibility of any file or other instrument being secreted about his person, it may be be conceded that never was a place better calculated to hold a prisoner in secure thrall, In the floor were four ring bolts and to these were attached his fetters made of wrought iron and secured round his leg by a padlock of complicated construction and of which Wild alone kept the key. These precautions it must be admitted have sufficient of themselves to prevent any possibility of Jack thinking that his previous exploits of prison breaking, could be there rivalled or realised yet, through obstables such as these it was his triumph to break and his early boast of no prison being built sufficiently strong to restrain him within its limits, was by his own daring hardihood and ingenuity brought within the scope of prophecies fulfilled.

Yet still day after day, did the importunities of the high and titled dignitaries of the land, to behold one so notorious as the prisoner increase. The Sheriff was constrained to order a general prohibition to the effect that no one for the future save the relations of the prisoner under sentence, would be permitted to enter into conversation with the criminals as it was found to be not only subversive of the arrangements of the gaol, and tending to the great unsetlement of the inmates of the place but also was the cause of many crowds and inconveniences assembling round the walls of the prison.

The sentence was at last pronounced.

It was DEATH.

The day drew near when Jack's existence itself was to be brought to a close. The hour approached which was to witness his execution; and as the fatal bell of Old St. Sepulchre's boomed each morning the hour of matins, the heart of Jack sank within him, as he reflected that the time was not far distant, when he should hear that hour tolled no more.

Disguise his own feelings as he would, Jack could not but feel that his situation at that moment had become a most painful and anxious one. He had buoyed himself up all along with the hope of a reprieve, and at last the utter unsubstantiality of the reed he had depended on, betrayed itself, and he sank bereft of hope into the most gloomy feelings of despair.

Bitterly indeed did he repent in such moments of his numerous misdeeds. The mother, whose fond warm heart he had broken,--the kind master he had wronged; the individuals he had injured; the homes he had plundered; the days he had wasted in vice and debauchery; all rushed back upon his mind with horrible distinctness; lighting up each dark cleft in his soul's deformity and exhibiting in fearful vividness the depravity of his heart. But what worked upon his feelings more than all, was the idea of dying an ignominious death upon the scaffold in the morning of his life, in the dawn of his bright manhood. Was it for this he thought that his life had been spared, that his plans had been successful; that his most sanguine wishes, his most greedy hopes of gain, had been accomplished? He could not contemplate the fate for which he had been reserved, with feelings of other than the most intense horror. To be the gaze of a crowd; the jest of the multitude; the hangman's toy; the ballad singer's theme; the human beacon pointed out by moralists to save others from the Scylla of vice, and the charybdis of temptation; these, these were things at which Jack shuddered as he imagined them.

And then at night when he sought on his humble pallet seclusion, from the dreadful thoughts that haunted him by day, he would dream---such dreams of fearful intensity and horror, that to him repose was but a renewal of the previous reflections that had tormented him, clothed in the semblance of reality, and vivified into the appearance of events that were really occurring round him. Shadows of hideous fantasies starting into substance a thousand times more hideous than his waking thoughts embodied.

Then would he fancy, in one of these appalling visions of the night, that the first faint beams of the last bright morning sun, which was ever to cast its refulgent rays on him, peered like a grey and aged monitor through the iron grating of his cell.

It was a cold winter's morning in January, and the dawn came on heavily and slow, leaving a long streak of darkness looming along the horizon for an hour after the sun had risen. The grey lights that streamed over the pointed roofs of the old clustered houses, the clinking of the fetters being got ready for his security on the road to Tyburn, the many eager faces peering from the different windows around the Old Bailey—and chiefly conspicuous amongst them, the triumphant gaze of Jonathan Wild—all united to increase the horrors of the scene. And then the hangman—the gibbet, and the——, but then with huge beads of perspiration on his brow, and a half-suffocated sensation about his throat—then it would be that Jack would awake, choking with a convulsive scream, to undergo anew the mental agonies of the preceding day.

A repetition of these constant tortures of mind and body could not be long borne, even by Jack's athletic frame, and then it was—like a drowning man catching at a straw, that he clings to in hope of being saved—that Jack set himself resolutely to work to devise some means of escape. The best portion of a long morning had been exhausted in the consideration of what plan would be best for him to adopt, and when Ireland the turnkey came in the afternoon to provide Jack with the necessary means of subsistence till the following day, he informed him that the Sheriff had appointed Thursday next for the day of his last sojourn upon earth, at the instigation of Jonathan Wild, who had his own reasons for hastening the ceremony and at the same time the janitor after making his customary examination of the prisoner's handcuffs and fetters, to see they had not been tampered with, announced that this would be his last visit for the night, as his presence was required in another department of the gaol.

The satisfaction with which our hero received the latter part of this intelligence, he could only conceal with difficulty from the keen eye of the turnkey, and from the tenor of the former part he saw, whatever was to be done must be attempted without any delay. The moment therefore the door had been closed and bolted, and Jack was again alone, he started to his feet and prepared himself for the achievement of an exploit compared with all which his previous out-breaks from thraldom dwindled into comparative insignificance.

As the handcuffs formed the first impediment to the free use of his limbs, his first efforts were as usual directed to the emancipation of his wrists from their restraint and in this he was speedily successful by biting asunder the leathern fastenings of the chain that connected them, and drawing the gyves over his hands by reducing his fingers into the smallest compass possible.

Then he applied his most vigorous strength to snap the fetters on his legs in twain, and this he likewise accomplished by a sudden jerk, after having twisted them round and round to weaken the links. Removing his stockings, he next fastened the remnant of the rings and chains which he found he could not sever, round his limbs to prevent their jingling, and arousing the attention of the gaolers. Tearing a long strip of calico off his shirt, he next slung them by those means from his waist, and thus also prevented them from impeding his movements.

The chimney, as has been already mentioned, was guarded by stout iron bars, and to get rid of these formed Jack's first difficulty. It was evident that the only mode by which their removal could be effected would be by making a wide breach in the wall, and as he was totally divested of every implement by which that operation could be attempted, a less resolute heart and a less experienced hand, would have been tempted at the onset to surrender the enterprise in despair. With Jack, however, the old adage of a will finding out a way was not long in having an exemplification, and availing himself of the broken links of his fetters, he contrived, by sharpening the end of one to a point by vigorous attrition of its surface against the other, to pick a hole in the plaster, just above the chimney-piece.

This was a very tedious and difficult task but its tediousness seemed only to increase his energy, and its difficulty to cause him to redouble his exertions. The wall, as he had imagined on his first test of its thickness, had been most solidly constructed of brick and stone, and the durable nature of the materials opposed to the slender implement with which he worked, caused nearly two hours to elapse before he could make a successful inroad upon its compact surface. At last Jack managed to dislodge a single brick, and aware now the rubicon of his exploit had been past, he became so elated with this trifling indication of his probable triumph, that as he flung down the brick to the ground, he burst into an exclamation of delight, and went with redoubled ardour to the prosecution of his fatiguing labour.

The purchase he thus gained for the use of his twisted chain which served him for a lever as well as a crow-bar, enabled him to proceed with wonderful rapidity, and a pile of bricks, and stones, mingled with the crumbling mortar, soon rose upon the floor. By the force of unrelaxing exertions, he speedily succeeded in making a hole in the chimney, sufficiently large to enable him to work away at it in an upright position, and he came soon after within reach of the first bar, which wrenching with both hands from its position, supplied him with an implement by which he was quickly enabled to dislodge, and break away the remainder. The clouds of dust that followed this achievement, almost choked him with the arid particles that floated in a vapour of lime through the air, but mindful only of the liberty to which he was devoting his exertions, neither thirst nor fatigue were heeded.

Whilst resting, for a few minutes from his tremendous task, a slight noise at the door of his cell, made him fancy that the turnkey was about to enter, and dismayed at the prospect of being discovered, when he had so far progressed with his work, a cold shudder crept through his frame, and he seized the iron bar with a fierce determination to srike down the first individual who should make his appearance. Listening with bated breath, and with his ear applied to the door, he speedily became assured that his apprehensions were without foundation, and indescribably relieved from this agonizing suspense, he resumed his occupation with tenfold energy. The aid of his new implement was found to be so serviceable that less exertion was required to break through the remaining obstacles than he contemplated, and having now effected a clearance which would enable him to pass with ease up the chimney, he returned to his cell, and whilst partaking of the frugal prison fare of bread and water, began to reflect on the succeeding steps which it would be necessary for him to take, before he could fully consider himself out of danger.

The various compartments of the gaol had been well noted as to their locality on previous occasions, and thus versed in what may be called, the topography of the building, Jack was well aware that the roof only would afford him the opportunity of escaping unobserved. To reach this was however the primary difficulty, and though *possible*, the numerous barriers that intervened, formed a strong argument against its probability. To abandon an enterprise of this nature on account of untried obstacles, however formidable, was not in our hero's nature, and he therefore, with an emphatic resolve, to be remembered, if only as a robber, at least as a bold one, clambered over the fallen rubbish that now formed a huge pile on the ground of his cell, and prepared himself for the ascent.

Having found by the projection of the chimney inwards, that he had gained an altitude sufficient for the purpose, he commenced making another hole in the wall with the iron bar, and forcing his way through the aperture, thus cleared, he found himself according to his conjectures entering the *Red Room*, a cell so denominated from that colour having been adopted in the painting of its walls: not having been made use of for nearly ten years, when the more turbulent adherents of the Pretender were here incarcerated, the apartment had a musty and disagreeable odour, which caused Jack to open the little window at the side, and let in a purifying gush of the fresher atmosphere without.

Having availed himself of the small opening to reconnoitre the exterior of the building, and assure himself that he was not proceeding in an erroneous direction, he was withdrawing his hand from the casement, when a sharp point punctured the flesh of his wrist and turning to examine the cause he found that the wound had been inflicted by an old and large rusty nail, which had been left projecting from the wood-work of the window.

"I'faith ? this will be the very thing for my purpose" remarked Jack, regardless of the pain, and withdrawing the nail from the wood, "I may have occasion to make good use of this rusty intruder," and so saying thrust it into his pocket, and proceeded towards the massive door which to his annoyance, though not to his amazement, he found doubly locked, and bolted from without.

With the nail he had just so fortunately acquired he attempted to pick the lock, but failing in this he had again recourse to his trusty bar, and at one well-directed blow he smashed in the plate, and with his dexterious fingers contrived to push back the bolts. Opening the door, he next entered a long narrow lobby, which he was aware from the survey of the building he had made, by craning his neck out of the window of the Red Room, led to the eastern entrance side of the chapel. To the left of him were two doors, each communicating with the debtors side of the prison, and directly leading to the Stone-ward, and the King's bench ward, whence came the stiffled sound of voices as a warning for him not to attempt egress through either of those portals.

As the passage had no other light admitted into it but what came from the opened door of the room, Jack was uncertain in the darkness, which direction he should take, but trusting to fortune for his adoption of the right one, he hurried onwards until he found that his further progress was stayed by a thick and evidently strong door which extended from one side of the passage to the other. Rapidly running his fingers over the surface he found to his inexpressible dismay that the lock was on the other side, and all endeavours to break open the door having been baffled by the heavy sheating of iron in which it was encased, he determined as a final recourse to break away a portion of the wall nearest the lock. This feat was of a more dangerous and hazardous nature than he at first anticipated. The wall unlike former objects of Jack's ardent blows, was composed wholly of stone, cemented with a hard mortar made of powdered flints, and this for a long time resisted Jack's most strenuous efforts. The noise too which he was compelled to make with the bar would be, he was afraid, the means of attracting the attention of the debtor's ward to his proceedings. Still, feeling that life or death depended upon the success with which he prosecuted his task, he struck away at the flinty interstices, until the sparks flew in a shower of coruscations round his head, and each reverberating blow, that was guided by that transcient light to its aim, enabled him to finally dislodge a huge fragment of stone.

Removing this, and thrusting his arm through the opening round to the other side of the door, he pushed back with some difficulty a heavy bolt, and then to his great delight, found that the door, turning slowly round upon its ponderous hinges, yielded to his hand.

Once more with the cheering influence of daylight to animate him, he hurried onward, and traversing the corridor in which were several niches containing fetters long disused and grown rusty from neglect, he found at the extremity a small oaken wicket, pushing through which, he entered the chapel, a large building at the upper part of the south eastern angle of the prison. The setting sun was flinging warm red rays through the barred and grated windows, seeming in its genial refulgence to mock the disconsolate and lonely aspect of the place, and as Jack passed the condemned pew—whence he had lately been sitting—and glanced at the associations which the remembrance of the sermon he had there heard, called up within his breast, he felt that one so unfit to die had yet to make a struggle for repentance as well as liberty. All the scenes of his past life—his early apprenticeship, his virtuous resolves, and

his mother's grave, were revolved before his eyes like the dim and fading phantasms of the dissolving views, and ere the sun had set he registered a vow, that he would strain every muscle to be free as the golden clouds that sailed slowly past above him.

As the large grated window that occupied the northern end of the chapel, looked out upon the interior of the gaol and was besides difficult of access, Jack considered is more prudent to adhere to his original determination and he went on to the southern side where there was a small iron gate strongly barricaded and crowned with spikes. Breaking asunder one of these and vaulting over the top of the gate, which he saw there was no occasion to force, he plunged down a short flight of stone steps into a long gloomy passage, where again he was stopped by another door, making the fourth he had encountered since his entry into the Red-room. The spike that he had brought away with him from the chapel, here rendered him essential service for picking the lock by its aid, he thurst the iron bar in between the wall and the door and succeeded in wrenching it open. The fifth door was dislodged in a similar manner, but, after proceeding about fifty yards further he found his progress impeded by a sixth, which from the accumulation of bars and bolts that he detected by passing his hand over the surface, appeared to present a final and insurmountable obstacle. It was as if every precaution had been here taken that the most suspicious architect and the most ingenious artizan could devise, and every obstacle that he had hitherto overcome with so much difficulty, appeared to be here increased and accumulated for the express purpose of consolidating all the separate defences of the gaol at its most critical but most invulnerable point.

Astounded, but not dismayed by this unparalleled demand upon his patience and energy, Jack set to work, using each of his implements in turn, but making little or no impression on the great lock to remove which, his first anxious efforts were devoted, with a harsh grating sound, though it seemed like pleasant music to the delighted ears of Jack, the ponderous lock at last fell away, after an hour of unremitting exertion. But still little had been done in freeing the portal from its impediments. A stout iron fillet screwed tightly into the wall, and one which it was impossible to unscrew from the door, without the instruments by which it had been secured, formed the chief, and indeed the apparently insurmountable obstacle. Resorting to his bar he again applied its leverage to the furtherance of his designs, and was nearly congratulating himself on the triumphant termination of his labours, when to his utter horror, the bar snapped in twain, and the divided fragments were rendered perfectly useless.

There was now but one alternative; he must either abandon altogether the attempt as impracticable, or return to his own cell for another of the iron bars that still remained in the chimney. Notwithstanding the imminent peril that attended his return, Jack chose the latter without a moment's hesitation. Retracing his steps, he darted down the passage, hurried through the Chapel, again threaded the stone corridor, regained the Red Room, and descended the chimney leading to his own cell; passing, with a feeling of conscious pride, over the litter of bricks and mortar rubbish, that he allowed to remain as a monument of his prowess.

After securing a second bar which he thought was sufficiently strong to answer his purpose, he finished the contents of his water-jug, which the thirst resulting from his wearying exertions, rendered a most welcome draught, and fastening the blanket which he took from his bed, round his shoulders, to serve in case of need, for the means of descent from the outer walls,—he cut with the point of the spike, the following inscription on the wall of his cell, where it remained for many years afterwards, a record of one of the most peculiar and daring achievements connected with our criminal annals, and a perpetual source of gratification to the curious.

The inscription ran literally thus;—

"I JACK SHEPPARD
MADE MY ESCAPE FROM NEWGATE
TUESDAY THE 14TH DAY OF OCTOBER
1724."

"There!" cried our hero, putting the finishing stroke to the date—"I wonder what old Ireland will say to that when he sees it in the morning. They won't forget the damage I have done to the walls in a hurry, I'll be bound. And now to the last scene of my triumph."

His second progress to the chapel formed a striking and pleasureable contrast to the first. There were no barriers to break through—no obstacles to be overcome—no impediments to be removed. All was attained—everything accomplished, save the resistance of the last door to which he now eagerly retraced his path. Plying the new weapon, which he had gone in search, the door yielded to his industry and perseverance, and he ascended a short flight of stairs on to the leads, only interrupted for a moment by a wooden door which being bolted on the inside he speedily opened. The place to which he had now got was the flat level surface of the summit of the prison, called "the Lower Leads," guarded on every side by walls about fifteen feet high. Northward of the door by which Jack had entered were the castellated battlements of the Gate Tower. A few wooden stairs led to the portal, opening on, by a winding staircase, to the upper leads or summit of the prison, and climbing over the spiked crest by which this extra door was defended, Jack adopted an easy mode of surmounting it, by placing his hands upon the ledge of the wall, and drawing himself up.

It was now nine o'clock, as the loud sonorous tones of the clock of St. Pauls, communicated the time, and Jack had thus been engaged seven hours in the accomplishment of his arduous achievement. Under shelter of the darkness, Jack proceeded along the battlements, and made his way with an elated heart to the summit of that part of the prison which fronts Giltspur-street. Beneath him was the flat roof of a house about twenty feet below, and not caring to hazard a fall so great, Jack untwisted the blanket from his body, and making it fast to the iron fence that surmounted the stone coping, he slid gently down and dropped behind the projecting buttress of the chimney belonging to the Turner's House, next door to Newgate.

CHAPTER III.

ADVENTURES AND MISADVENTURES.

"Housed is the steed within his stall,
The hound lies sleeping in the hall;
Hushed are the minstrels' warlike lays,
That told of other times and days;
The harp upon the wall is hung,
To whose soft strains he oft had sung,
E'en now it breathes a lonely lay,
When o'er its strings the soft winds play;
As if the spirit of some lord,
Still lingered there and struck the chord,
Returned a moment but to dwell
Among those scenes he loved so well."

OLD BORDER POEM.

CAREFULLY examining the spot where he stood, and satisfied that he had not been observed, Jack crossed the roof of the Turner's house, and finding the window of the garret below was open, he slided down over the wall by means of the leaden spout, and crept along the gutter until he came on a level with the raised casement. He had hardly entered the room and ascertained with his hands the position of the few articles of furniture disposed about it, so that he might avoid making any noise by stumbling over them, when footsteps were heard upon the stairs and immediately afterwards a servant-girl bearing a lighted candle in her hand entered the apartment. Jack adroitly slipped behind the door as she opened it, and watching his opportunity blew out the light, and hurried down the stairs. At the end of the second flight he ran against somebody who was ascending the stairs, doubtless attracted by the girl's scream, and rushing onward to the street door, which by good fortune he found open, Jack Sheppard once more felt himself breathing the free air of liberty.

Without pausing to assure himself that the inmates of the house he had just quitted were ignorant of his departure, the adventurous fugitive turned down the narrow unfrequented alleys, that then clustered round St. Pauls, and making his way by a circuitous route to Thames-street, began to ascend the acclivity which led to old London Bridge. At the foot of the Bridge were two persons conversing as Jack approached, and making an appointment, as it appeared from the part of the conversation our hero caught as he passed them, to meet at Tyburn on the following morning.

"It will be a rare sight, I warrant," cried the first—"Jack has given many a darby the slip but Newgate ain't so easily got out of, so there won't be much chance of a disappointment."

And a brutal laugh, echoed by the other, followed the speaker's remark.

Though burning to avenge the coarse allusion to his expected execution on the morrow, Jack more prudently quickened his pace and passed on. As he entered Southwark an itinerant hawker was retailing a penny edition of what his stentorian lungs proclaimed to be—"a full true and particklar account of the life, exploits and adventures of that notorious housebreaker, Jack Sheppard, with a history of his numerous escapes, and a pitiful ballad on his execution, together with his last dying speech and confession, as delivered this afternoon to Mr. Purly the ordinary of Newgate."

Jack could hardly help smiling, notwithstanding the solemnity of the event to which it referred, at the circumstantial manner in which these gross fabrications were detailed, and the avidity with which the hawkers' wares were bought up, was a manifestation more personally gratifying of the general interest and sympathy which his commital had excited.

A passenger had just made a purchase.

"Sold again and got the money," cried the fellow,—rattling a pocket full of coins and reiterating his invitation.

"Here, let me have a couple of those, please Mishter," interrupted a girl crossing the road to the hawker—"Missus has sent me over for one and I want to have another for myself."

"Ay, you are always my best customers, bless your little hearts," responded the itinerant with the licence accorded to his profession—"one penny each; thank you, my dear, twopence! Sold again and got the money."

"Ah, Jack was always a favourite with the soft sex," observed a bystander, with a cynical sneer at his companion. "Its the way with 'em all; the wickeder they is, the more they run after 'em They look upon men of spirit, as we look at spirited horses—take the vice out of 'em and they become good for nothing.'

Fearful of attracting attention by his disordered attire, Jack now continued his progress. Diverging through the back streets he soon after reached the place where he had anxiously directed his footsteps—"The Fox-in-the-Mint." As the strong glare of lights in the front parlour warned him that others might be in the public-room whose presence might be dangerous to his safety, he determined to go round to the back, whence he had before proceeded, and there effect an entrance.

His knowledge of the secret spring enabled him to do this without difficulty, and drawing back the inner bolt of the door in the winding passage, he issued out into the small room where the Landlord and himself had had there previous conference.

He had not long to wait, Giles Shalders, who kept therein his choice stock of such spirituous compounds as he only treated his special friends to the knowledge of, now entered the store-room on an errand of this nature, and when Jack made himself visible and reminded the other of his old promise to claim the change for his last guinea after his escape from Newgate, the amazement of the host grew beyond description.

"And now having told you how I came here," said Jack terminating a rapid recital of his adventures, "may I rely upon your aid and secrecy?"

"Ay, that may you," returned Shalders, "you shall never be taken again if I can help it, though the reward for your capture was ten times the amount. But there—go to my room. You will find some water, and a change of clothes; both of which I should think, judging from your present appearance will not come amiss to you."

Jack Sheppard, who begrimed with dust and mortar, felt that he stood much in need of such ablution, accepted the friendly offer with many grateful expressions of acknowledgment, and soon after rejoined Shalders with a considerably improved aspect, derived from the landlord's garments which he had assumed. Shalders, who had awaited his return below, had busied himself in the meantime with preparing a hot supper, flanked by some cheering potations of the host's best brewage, and Jack, who from his long abstinence and unwonted exertions, felt himself really in need of such refreshment, sat down to the welcome repast with eagerness, and did considerable justice to the savoury viands provided.

"And now," inquired Shalders, when he saw that our hero had concluded, "What are your future intentions, Jack, for it won't be long before the bloodhounds will be on your track? What do you propose doing to give Jonathan and his crew the slip?"

"Seeking honest service as a ship's carpenter, and making my way over to Holland by the first ship that leaves in the morning," was the response.

"I am tired of this life of chance and change, and would fain try to earn an honest living. I think I have enough knowledge left of the craft to gain all I want."

"I shall have the good luck to assist your views then, Jack," continued Shalders.

"A Dutch Skipper who uses my house occasionally, and from whom I have my stock of spirits without the bother of an exciseman to look after them, told me this morning he should want an extra hand, and you will be the very one for him. He won't start from the Tower stairs though, till to-morrow night."

"Hum!" meditated Jack — "I am somewhat puzzled to know where to stow myself in the meantime, for this will be the first place they will search."

"I have it"—cried Shalders, after a pause. "There is a brother of mine living in the Isle of Dogs, on whose honour we may confidently rely, for we do a little in the smuggling line together. You shall get down to Greenwich to-night—cross the water, and I will tip the office to old Von Hakslyt the Skipper, to take you up in a boat from there as he passes the point."

"Capital!" exclaimed Jack delightedly —"I will set off at once—but who is in the next room? I fancied I heard somebody listening at the door?"

"Only some of the right sort, Jack," was the reply. "There's Edgeworth Bess, and a few of the old boys of the Mint having a quiet booze together. By the way have you ever made up your old quarrel with the girl," continued Shalders fixing an inquisitive gaze upon our hero.

"Not I," answered Sheppard—"I have had too many new flames since then to attend to the worn out attractions of an old one. I believe I wronged her in thinking she really did like Kneebone better than myself, but I was tired of her faded charms, and flung her off—not sorry either to get rid of her so easily. But why do you ask?"

"Because," said Shalders in reply, "I have my suspicions about that girl's intentions, and should not much like you to come athwart her now. She has publicly sworn to be revenged upon you for her desertion, and it was only last night that I heard her say, she was glad you were safely locked up in Newgate, as it served you right in forsaking her for a certain Janet Maberly you were said to have had a sneaking partiality for. Rely upon it Jack, that Edgeworth Bess means you no good."

"Pshaw, Giles," returned Jack carelessly, "I am not afraid of the malice she can show. But tell me; have you heard or seen aught of Blueskin?"

"The lieutenant was in the neighbourhood about three hours since, trying to get a carpenter, who works at Mr. Birt's the turner's, next door to Newgate, to convey a few fakements to your cell, by which he hoped you would be able to make your escape. You, however, have managed matters in a wonderful way without his aid at all. Oous! how overjoyed he'll be when he hears you have given the dubsman the go-bye, and got safely off to Dutchland. My word for a thousand, Jack, the faithful fellow will find you out there, and you'll crack many a crib together yet."

"I am firm in my determination to give up the life of a housebreaker," said Jack resolutely—"but I should like to see him there nevertheless. You need not tell him where I have taken refuge, though I suppose my escape will be bruited all over the town to-morrow."

"Ay, that will it," responded Shalders, "but hark! they are getting impatient for my return. If I stay longer, my absence will excite suspicion."

"But I am as yet uncertain as to the place you hinted at just now, where I could pass the time till the Dutch lugger took me up on its outward passage."

"True!" ejaculated Shalders, tracing a few words hastily on a slip of paper—"here is the direction, and with it the passport to your friendly reception there. I have not said who you are, for fear of a mischance, but he is too used to the shelter of those who are pressed by the excise hounds to care much about cross-questioning."

"Eustace Shalders, Maltster, Isle of Dogs," repeated Jack, perusing the inscription he had given him on the paper—"I may find a time my worthy host when I may return the obligation and become less your debtor."

"Whisht! not a word about that—I like your spirit. But you have no time to lose, it is now ten o'clock. An hour's brisk walking will bring you to Greenwich, and by the waterside you will find plenty of ready scullers with a quick oar in their hand, and a silent tongue in their head to ferry you over."

A sharp rustling sound at the door here startled the acute ears of both.

"Some one has been listening to our conversation," cried Sheppard in alarm, turning to the landlord—"I hear footsteps now lightly retreating from the door."

"Mere fancy, Jack," replied Shalders after a pause, during which he failed in hearing a repetition of the sound, "you have been so dizzied with your cracking doors, and pounding walls to mortar, that you fancy every breath of air is one of Wild's Janizaries in pursuit. But there—I will detain you no longer. You will find my brother's crib is a ruined mill on the north side of the creek. He will give you a hearty welcome I promise you!"

"You have indeed proved yourself to be a true friend," exclaimed Jack, "and I scarce know how to thank you as I ought."

"Stop—you have perhaps no money about you—here is the guinea you gave me when you were last here. No words, but take it. I shall keep those broken links you have hammered off here from your Newgate fetters, as a security for its repayment some day, and a memorial of your wonderful escape from the stone-jug! There—not a word—but away at once."

Shaking hands with the warm-hearted landlord, who insisted upon pressing the proffered coin upon him, Jack bade adieu to the "Fox," but not before he had been persuaded to quaff off a bumper of Nantz brandy from the choicest corner of its cellarage, and once again availing himself of the secret passage, he plunged into the close, narrow street beyond. A few minutes more, and he was rapidly traversing the Old Kent Road and its continuation, which beyond the little hostel, even then recognized as "The Bricklayer's Arms," was a mere tract of waste land with a wide road through it, only dotted here and there by a few humble tenements, inhabited chiefly by market gardeners and their labourers. Lonely and unfrequented as the road was, and only lit by the intermittent beams of the waning moon, the fugitive's fear of discovery caused him to be continually on the alert, and once in the faint light of the moon's rays he fancied he saw in the distant gloom the shadow of one who was tracking his path. Still it might have been the mere delusion of his over-wrought imagination, and cherishing this belief, he resumed with increased speed his journey onward. Arrived at the river-side, by the old Hospital of Greenwich, he had not long to wait before he had concluded a bargain with an able sculler who was smoking a short pipe meditatively over the side of the boat, to convey him to the Isle of Dogs opposite. Besides the subdued refulgence of the nocturnal luminary, the stars shone like beacons in the clear blue vault above them, and gave sufficient light to ensure a knowledge of the locality. Their transit therefore was of short duration, and satisfying the claims of the waterman, Jack, bent his steps to the north creek where the grey, solitary habitation of the accommodating smuggler soon rose upon his sight. The isolated and deserted appearance of the building, however, as our hero approached nearer, suggested melancholy notions of the coldness and discomfort that prevailed within.

Corn was no longer to be found in its granary. The mill-pond was choked up with mud and gravel, and its surface was covered with aquatic plants and patches of that green crust, by which the stagnant pool is usually mantled. Nor did the mill itself exhibit symptoms of greater care, for the wheels were decayed, black and overgrown with thick dark moss, and the water which still dribbled through the rotten trough, came splashing down through rents in its side, while in the place of a mealy floor, portly-looking flour-sacks, and the cheerful tic-tac of the mill, there was a snake's nest in the bin, the croaking of frogs from the standing pond, and the rolling forth of a party of spotted toads from under the mill-stone.

But though such was the uninviting external appearance of the ruined building Jack found that the interior was by no means of such a forbidding description. His summons at the door for admission was promptly responded to, and the inspection of the recommendatory document was held to be so highly satisfactory, that he was ushered at once into the *sanctum* of the supposed malster, who as Jack judged from the evidence of sundry half-unfinished bottles on the table before him, had been disturbed in the midst of a quiet revel, where he had monopolized the potations as well as the conversation of his guests.

Eustace Shalders was a short thickset man of about forty. His eyes were deep and sunken, his nose prominent, his skin brown as the very doublet into which he had crept, and his general aspect that of one who having imbibed in early life the habits of a rough sailor, had not been entirely able to get rid of them, when adapting the peculiarities of a more amphibious pursuit. Believing Jack to be, from what his brother had written, one who was in danger of being punished for his reception, and concealment of contraband goods, he treated him with considerable hospitality, and after insisting upon his sharing the viands and liquids of unexceptionable excellence that were placed before them, for supper, a couch was provided for his nights rest, and on this, completely worn out with his arduous exertions of the day, Jack was not long deposited before he fell into a deep though not a dreamless slumber. The long-forgotten form of Edgeworth Bess was constantly before him, and at her side he fancied was Jonathan Wild inciting her to avenge the neglect with which he had treated her. So haunted was he indeed by these nocturnal chimeras that it was with gladdened emotions he saw the grey dawn stealing through the latticed casement, and heard the hoarse voice of Eustace calling upon him to arouse from his sleep, and keep watch for the Dutch lugger, that was expected to pass in the course of the morning.

In the meantime strange events were proceeding in town. About midnight a female closely veiled and impenetrably shrouded from observation, was pacing eagerly up and down before Jonathan's door.

Hour passed after hour, but still there she remained casting anxious and repeated glances in the direction of the various thoroughfares, from which the person of whose arrival she seemed to be in such impatient expectation, might be expected to come. It was daybreak before Jonathan Wild returned, and then a coach attended by his janizaries rattled up over the causeway, and the thief-taker was about to re-enter his mansion when the woman now cold and pale with the excitement of watching so long for his approach, rushed to the carriage and throwing back her veil peremptorily ordered Jonathan to stop.

"What Bess," exclaimed Wild in amazement, as he recognised the features of the applicant, "what mad freak is this? Have you come to give me another pigeon to pop at, after having plucked all his feathers yourself, or are you like the rest of the gang going to plague me with more prayers for ack Sheppard's release? If you come on this last errand, you may as well be off at once, for I am determined to hear nothing in his favour, and no intercession that you can make will have any weight with me.

"Stop! Jonathan Wild," said Edgeworth Bess sternly for it was indeed her, "Do not think that I can come here—I whom he has so deeply injured—with any whining supplications on his behalf. No, no, I loved him once, but it is the fiercest love that turns to the fiercest hate and now I would have my triumph as he has had his"

"What mean you then, Bess," inquired Jonathan in alarm at the wild looks and incoherent speech of the woman who accosted him—"If you have aught of importance to tell me concerning Jack Sheppard, say it at once and be quick about it too, for I have only just returned from Manchester, whither I had gone to take possession of my estate, and I much to execute before I can get by noon to Tyburn.

"Had you returned six hours ago I should still have been ready for you, and we might both have better ensured the fulfillment of our wishes," cried the woman, "JackSheppherd is no longer your prisoner—he escaped last night from Newgate!"

"Impossible!" ejaculated Wild in amazement and terror-stricken at the thought of Jack being once more at liberty, which would materially have interfered with his own views—; "impossible—the turnkeys are all in my pay, for their own sakes they would be faithful to their trusts and without their aid his efforts would be impracticable and futile. You must have been mistaken or imposed upon by one who thinks I shall relax my vigilance."

"Think what you like—attribute it to any cause you will"—responded Bess, "but rely upon it the fact is as I have stated it. Jack Sheppard last night got out of Newgate. At nine o'clock he was with Giles Shalders, the landlord of the old Fox-in-the-Mint, and there it was I saw and heard him speak. I know now where he has taken refuge, and I have tracked his footsteps for some distance on the road. But if you would re-capture him you have not much time to lose, for to-night he embarks for Holland, and you will lose sight of him for ever."

"What you have told me Bess is so strange and yet at the same time so like truth, that I hardly know whether I should place more faith in your being deceived, and in some object you may have in deceiving me, or whether I should lose my faith altogether in the hitherto impregnable doors, and walls of the prison. However you have started a suspicion," pursued Wild, on which I may make myself satisfied, and if he has escaped and you lead us to his retreat, I promise you I will double the reward that has been offered for his apprehension."

"It was my wounded pride, my wish for revenge," answered the woman, "that tempted me to overhear his words and betray his secret hiding-place, not the beggarly amount of gold that you can reward me with. But there is the direction at which you will find him," she added, giving Jonathan a slip of paper as she spoke "and now go over to the gaol and see whether my words are those of truth or not!"

Still half incredulous of what had been told him, and yet anxious to ascertain if there was any foundation for the report, Jonathan Wild immediately crossed the road to the portal of the prison and ringing the great bell startled the inmates so effectually from their morning's repast, that he had not a minute to wait before the door was opened by Ireland the turnkey in person.

A glance at the complacent smile which illumened the features of the jailor, assured him that the prisoners escape was not at least known to his turnkey, and thus somewhat re-assured, he entered the precincts of the outer yard.

"You are rather earlier with us than usual," remarked Ireland, gulphing down a piece of toast, with which he had emerged in his mouth, unaware of the quality of his matin visitor—"something new sir, I suppose?"

"I have only come to inquire after Jack Sheppard," responded Wild sternly.

"Oh you are too good to trouble yourself about him," returned Ireland with such confidence as to completely disarm Jonathan's suspicions, "he is safe enough, sir, I promise ye."

"I have a desire to be satisfied upon that point," resumed Wild doggedly, and I will thank you to come with me to the Castle immediately."

"Instantly, sir, but I hope you dont imagine any thing amiss has happened during your absence," rejoined Ireland—"here, Martyn, Spurling, look to the door, and now then, Mr. Wild, I am at your service.

Following the jailor, without uttering another word about what had led him to make such an enquiry, Wild proceeded to that cell in the castle, wherein Jack Sheppard had been confined, and as soon as the door was opened, a scene presented itself which made them both absolutely recoil in amazement. The vestiges of Jack's handicraft, so plentifully scattered over the floor, at once confirmed Wild's suspicions, and the statement ef Edgeworth Bess, but he had been far from prepared to behold such a spectacle as this. As for the turnkey, he was for some moments dumb-founded, but regaining his self-possession, he remarked, that Jack might still be secreted in the room above, and squeezing his way up the chimney into the red room, Wild following after stopped to peruse the inscription which Sheppard had left on the wall, and pausing to admire the audacity which had instigated so permanent a record of his extraordinary achievement.

As they continued their search, guided by the huge masses of bricks and mortar that the prisoner had left behind him, their surprise increased, for the doors through which Jack had brokeu his way, were held, and with justice, to be the strongest in the prison. Occasionally stopping to pick up a broken lock, or examine the ponderous pieces of stone that had been rifted from their supporters, Wild entered the chapel—then came to the three strong barriers that had so toughly resisted Jack's energies, and finally approaching the upper leads, an unquestionable evidence of Jack's escape was produced in the blanket-strip that still fluttered from the railings in the morning's breeze.

"This is a most marvellous affair, sir," cried the turnkey, after their examination had been concluded, "in future I shall place no faith in the strength or safety of the prison's defences. He must have been aided by some supernatural power, for it is impossible he could have done all this single-handed, with merely that nail and bar of iron that we have found on the lower leads."

"More likely aided by some lower power within the walls," sneered Wild in reply, "but I will take care that the governor has this matter sifted to the bottom, and whoever has been found to render him any assistance, shall be hung to a certainty."

With this comfortable reflection Jonathan retraced his steps, gave orders for the repairs to be instantly made, which it was estimated an outlay of two hundred pounds would scarcely defray, and taking his janizaries with him, Jonathan next proceeded on horseback with the utmost speed, to the place indicated by Edgeworth Bess as the refuge of Jack Sheppard.

Consternation and dismay pervaded the minds of all classes in the metropolis when the news of Jack's escape became known, and was the all absorbing topic of conversation with all classes of society, and was more particularly canvassed in all its most minute bearings by the frequenters of the "Fox," in the Mint.

CHAPTER IV.

THE BETRAYER AND THE BETRAYED.

" I know not; if they speak but truth of her
These hand shall tear her, If they wrong her
honour,
The proudest of them shall well hear of it.
Time had not so dried up this blood of mine,
Nor age so eat up my invention,
Nor my bad life 'reft me so much of means,
But they shall find awakened in such a kind,
Both strength of limb and policy of mind,
Ability in means and choice of friends,
To quit me of them thoroughly."

SHAKSPEARE.

THAT the "love of woman" is, as Byron describes it to be, "a lovely and a dreadful thing" how many lips could confirm by dearly bought experience in its truth! In sooth it is a dangerous toy to trifle with the earnest emotions of the hearts. Love cannot be dealt out in fragments? it must be given wholly or not at all. Disappointment of Edgeworth Bess—sunk and depraved but still a true woman in the strength of her impulses—when she first awoke from that delusive dream in which her warm and credulous fancy had lulled her, and found a cold and icy heart, instead of the warm and glowing burst of passionate feeling. When in the eyes where she fondly deemed love had taken up an eternal residence, she saw only a fitful and transcient brightness lavished upon all alike and indifferently, when the lips that she imagined would only breathe her name, could, like an instrument, be played upon by all, and utter the same endearing sounds to every one that touched them.—A growing desire to be revenged upon him—how she knew—cared not so that she was avenged—had taken possession of her like a spell. To the execution of this she had wrought up all her hopes and energies, and she had at last succeeded in her wish. He was betrayed—betrayed too by her hand, and at the time when he counted upon his own safety with confidence. The bold stakes for which she had so long played for were in her possession---- the game was her own; she had deeply revenged the insult her love had received but still was her sense of justice gatified? No! By one of those strange contradictions of human nature, no sooner had she made the disclosures to Wild, than she repented of her treachery. Directly had she left Jonathan in the possesion of Jack's secret, to retrace her way to her own miserable apartment, the consequences of her conduct burst upon her in all their fearful intensity, and the bitterest revulsion of feeling ensued. Then it was that with repentance came a desire for reparation, and then it was that she framed the sudden resolution to anticipate Jonathan's arrival by going to Sheppord's hiding-place herself and counteracting the effect of the communication by placing him on his guard

Tired of tracing the manifold forms and destinations of the numerous vessels that had sailed slowly past him, Jack now walked impatiently round by the old mill pond, scrutinising with a practised eye the appearance of the firmament above, where cold ragged clouds were drifting rapidly along, now revealing, and then again obscuring the bright starry specks that had begun to gem the azure arch of heaven. The wind sweeping in fitful autumnal gusts over the marsh, whirled about the fallen leaves, in sere and yellow groups, and moaned dismally among the walls of the dilapidated mill. There was something inexpressibly cheerless and dreary in the whole scene, and Jack felt an involuntary dread creep over him—a presentiment as of approaching evil, when he gazed around and witnessed the still, death-like silence that seemed to envelope the whole of nature.

Suddenly something like a footfall smote upon his ear. He paused to listen. The water unintermittently splashed through the broken wheels, and fell with a melancholy sound in the black trough below, where even by day the eye was unable to discern the bottom, but mingling with this murmur, his acute ear was enabled to distinguish the sound of approaching footsteps coming too nearer and nearer the place where he stood.

He hardly knew whether to remain or retreat, but before he had fully determined on either, Edgeworth Bess, pale and trembling, appeared before him.

"Jack, dear Jack," she commenced as soon as the words were enabled to escape her lips, "I have come to save you. Fly, fly for your life, there is not a moment to be lost. Within another half-hour, Jonathan Wild and his janizaries will be here, to secure you in a dungeon from which there will be no hope of escape. Stay not to question but seize the opportunity I have given you, and away at once."

"How!" exclaimed Sheppard, almost speechless with surprise—"You here, Bess, and counselling me to flight! what is the meaning of all this? why are you here, and how came you to learn the secret of my retreat?"

"You shall know all, Jack; I have been wrong---very wrong, but your neglect goaded me to it; your slights and inconstancy cut me to the heart—I sought out Jonathan—informed him of your escape and

present refuge, which I overheard Shalders give you at the Fox—and—"

"May thy tongue be blistered for thy treachery," interrupted Jack, his rage choking his utterance, "but say on."

"And he has but stopped to ascertain the truth of your escape from Newgate, before he came to re-capture you here. Oh, Jack! Woman's pride and revenge prompted me to betray you, but the love I did, and still bear for you, impelled me, though I was the cause of all, to come hither and endeavour to save your life. Believe me, Jack. I am repentant for having done you this injury; but, by heaven I meant it not to end fatally. I did that in the paroxysm of a moment's frantic passion at which my cooler nature revolts. My heart now only throbs for your safety—for your welfare." And as the affrighted woman uttered these words, she sank oppressed with remorse at the feet of the man she had betrayed.

Jack Sheppard, maddened by the reflections which this confession aroused, cast a furious look upon the woman, and as she rose to repeat her assurances of contrition, he lost all control over himself, and caught her tightly by the throat. His victim gasped a few inarticulate words with her departing breath, and as she became suffocated by the pressure, her face, blackened, her aspirations grew less frequent, and her eyes, glazed in death, were fixed rigidly on his. Involuntarily relaxing his hold, Jack was about to remonstrate with her, when she suddenly heaved a convulsive sigh, and fell back at his feet a corpse.

A perfect and death-like silence followed this action—a silence rendered more thrilling from the rapid breathing of Sheppard. After listening for a few minutes, he fell down upon one knee beside the inanimate body of Edgworth Bess. A gurgling sound broke in upon his ears—it was the blood bubbling from her mouth.

Dizzy, sick at heart, with a tumultuous throbbing at his heart, and a wild humming in his ears, the wretched man staggered back in horror. The rapid tread of horsemen approached. He started to his feet. A glance through the gloomy vista of the old mill ruins sufficed to reveal to him the proximity of Wild and his janizaries. In an instant he had made up his mind for flight—he would seize the last chance of escape that opened to him. Casting one more lingering look on the lifeless body of her by whom he had first been led into crime, he covered the face over with a handkerchief, which he untwisted from his neck, sprang to the waterside, and seeing a boat by the bank, disengaged it from its moorings, and allowed it to drift into the centre of the stream.

His pulse still throbbed with a hope of baffling his pursuers, for he had scarcely proceeded fifty yards with the tide, which was running strongly up towards London, when the rounded clumsy build of the Dutch coaster was seen veering the point.

"At last," cried Jack with exultation, "I may elude the cunning malice of Wild, and yet be free!" He watched with impatience the lugger's approach. Wrenching forcibly off the seat from the centre of the boat, he used it as an oar to guide him to the vessel's side. A light glimmered as a beacon on the bow—it was to him a beacon of hope. A rope-ladder was visible depending from the stern; he was evidently expected. He hailed the ship—it was returned. Again was he safe. A few moments more and he should be far beyond the reach of capture. With a quick hand he swirled the boat round under the prow. With a light heart he sprang up the chain of ropes that had been thrown out for him. The next instant he stood upon deck. A few sailors were grouped curiously around him. A stout burly Dutchman was awaiting his arrival by the foremast.

"Now," ejaculated our hero with triumph, "I am safe, and can defy the machinations of Jonathan."

"Stop a bit, Captain Sheppard, you are not quite out of our reach yet." said a well-known voice behind him, and before he could turn round, a rope had been slipped adroitly round his body, and he was handcuffed and secured by a party of the sailors, who had clustered round him to prevent his flinging himself overboard.

"There you are Mr. John Sheppard, as scientifically grabbed as one would well wish to see," cried Ireland, for he was the speaker; "we have got you all right this time, so now ware ship and back to Newgate," and the flapping of the sails and creaking of the cordage, showed that the order had been put into immediate execution. Jack's rage and annoyance at finding himself thus taken, was unbounded.

"This is another act of base treachery," he exclaimed, "Shalders has employed you to entrap me here for the sake of the blood-money he will get by it."

"Not a bit of it," rejoined the turnkey, "Mr. Wild was too wide awake to trust to taking you in the Isle of Dogs, after what your old mistress, Edgeworth Bess had told him, so in case you should give him the slip, and swim to the lugger, as it came up the river, what did we do but change the crews, and make sure of you that way. The thief of a Dutchman, Von Haksluyt is safe enough in limbo for smuggling by this time, and if you give us the chance of letting you go a second time, why you must be Satan himself, that's all.

Despite these taunts, and many more in a similar strain, Jack, finding that his last reliance had failed, preserved a fixed and dogged silence during the remainder of the passage. As the name of Edgeworth Bess was thus carelessly uttered, a cold shudder passed through his frame, but soon recovering his self-possession, he suffered himself to be led, rather than conducted, silently back to the prison which on the previous night had been the scene of his startling and wonderful escape.

Jonathan Wild, finding that Jack had according to his anticipations, taken to the boat, had preceded their return, chuckling over his successful precautions, and the intelligence of his re-capture soon became generally known. The lodge was crowded; and loaded by the heaviest manacles that could be found in Newgate, and chained besides to the wall of the cell in the middle stone ward, where he was constantly guarded by four of the gaoler's assistants, who neither quitted him for a moment, nor suffered any visitor to approach him, Sheppard found with the most acute feelings of regret, that all practicability of escape was denied him. Thus he gradually grew calmer, and more resigned.

He now held serious discourses with the ordinary, who seemed convinced of his sincere repentance, and finding that the day of execution was permanently fixed for the following Monday, he only expressed a desire to see, before he met the fate which he admitted he had justly merited, the punishment of Jonathan Wild, by whom he had first been instigated to the commission of crime, and who had never since ceased to follow and persecute him.

It was not long before a portion of this retribution, which Jack Sheppard so earnestly desired, was dealt out to the thief-taker.

The following night, when Blueskin and Shalders had heard the news of Jack's second imprisonment confirmed, a strong body of men from the neighbourhood of the Mint crossed London Bridge, and, gathering force and numbers as they proceeded, came at last into the very heart of the Old Bailey, and drew up in a formidable array before the lodge of Newgate. Here they waited half-an-hour, as if in expectation of others to join them; and the authorities, apprehending an attack upon the gaol, and an attempt to rescue their prisoner by force, made immediate preparations for defence, by barricading the doors, gates, windows, and other vulnerable parts of the building. After a pause of anxious suspense to the jailers, who were all ordered to be under arms, a bustling conference ensued among the ringleaders, and as it appeared that the strong exterior of the gaol was likely to baffle their views, or that some other scheme had been suddenly mooted and relied upon, the whole party, amounting to a mob of about one thousand persons, moved to the opposite side of the road, and directed their fury upon the mansion of Jonathan Wild.

The thief-taker was quickly writing in the room where we have before seen him resolving upon the murder of Lord Orford, and, undisturbed by the noise, had not noticed the alarming approach of the riotous mass until they were close upon his gates. The flaring torches that were borne wildly about among the insurgents revealed to him, conspicuous among the foremost group by his dark complexion and athletic figure, the chief ringleader of the throng—Blueskin. Without doubting for a moment that he was the object of their violence, and not hesitating as to the course he should pursue, Jonathan called to his janizaries to secure the doors, and loading a blunderbuss that he always had suspended in his chamber, he opened a window, and through the aperture thus made discharged his weapon with a deliberate aim at the creole, who, however, escaped unhurt.

This active demonstration of resistance exasperated the mob into immediate action. They tore up the iron railings before the door, and converted them into implements of assault and destructiou. Yells and curses rent the air, and the most terrific imprecations were vented upon Wild by the crowd, who thundered fiercely at the doors until they yielded to their strenuous efforts.

Abrahams and Bowyer, who with drawn cutlasses in their hands attempted to oppose their entrance, were immediately put to flight, and they then sallied impatiently into the various compartments of the building to wreak their vengeance upon Jonathan, who was, however, nowhere to be found, as immediately upon seeing how the fray was likely to terminate he had evaded their pursuit by egress through a secret vaulted passage, and fled over to Newgate, where he claimed and procured the shelter of its walls. In the meanwhile every valuable was abstracted by the concourse who had burst into, and taken possession of the house. Boxes were broken open, hoards of money distributed among the throng, and stores of wealth and jewels discovered which had been wrung from the people, and which were now recklessly appropriated by their representatives. Everything having been plundered, and every room ransacked by the insatiate populace, it was now arranged, at the suggestion of Blueskin, that they should set fire to the premises, and applying their torches to various portions of the building at once it was speedily enveloped in flames.

The ruddy glow of the flaming rafters flung a bright light on the windows of the gaol opposite, where Wild, with incensed feelings, was watching the progress of his own house being destroyed. By means of a powerful bribe to a messenger in the prison, he prevailed upon him to venture forth and obtain from the Savoy a detachment of the military to disperse the crowd and arrest the conflagration, which now threatened the adjoining buildings with destruction, and placed even Newgate in imminent danger.

Meanwhile the fury of the fire became greater, and a vast sheet of flame shot up into the air, which illumined the sky for miles round. The lead from the roof melted and ran down, as if it had been snow before the morning sun, and great beams and massive stones hissed and crashed through the burning rafters, with a constant crackling on the pavement that almost deadened the injunctions of Blueskin, who was striving to make himself heard, and endeavouring to excite the rage of the mob, now ripe for mischief of any kind, by pointing out Jonathan to them, as he stood revealed by the red glare of the fire, at one of the upper windows of Newgate, knitting his brows into an impotent attempt at careless defiance.

To Newgate, then, did the crowd now furiously rush. Ladders were procured by which they began to scale the walls; and the great wooden gate on the north side of the prison had already been set on fire, and was rapidly consuming. Everything seemed to augur well for their exploit, and, emboldened by this partial success, others were coming from all quarters of town to their aid, when the opportune arrival of the soldiers, who, several hundred in number, appeared with guns and bayonets, stopped the havoc that was going on.

It was not until the soldiers had fired repeatedly on the rioters that they desisted from their work of destruction. Several were killed, and upwards of a hundred of the most turbulent taken prisoners, but the ringleaders escaped. Engines were brought to play upon the still burning premises of Wild; but, though the adjoining houses were saved, of the thief-taker's once almost regal mansion nothing remained on the following day but a black and smouldering mass of ruins.

By a preconcerted arrangements Blueskin and Shalders, instead of returning to the "Fox," hurried on through Clerkenwell to another of their resorts in Golden Lane, which with its vicinity has been for more than a century a resort for all that is vulgar and degraded. The population of that region was then almost as dense as at present, and as amongst the many inhabitants that crowded its numerous courts and blind alleys, there were many who gained a livelihood in ways not peculiarly conformable to the strict dictates of morality, or the usages of polite society, this place was then, as it has been since, one of the most notorious rendezvous for thieves of any in London.

The two adventurers still keeping together after the dispersion of their associates hither directed their steps, nor paused until they came in sight of an old, peaked, antiquated building, which, with its pointed gables and wide diamond-paned windows, held out in the sign of the "Angel" a most uninviting aspect and savouring of anything but angelic purity in its appearance. Within the parlor of this convenient hostel did they however obtain the refuge and the refreshment they desired, and here, leaving them to concert fresh measures and organize another and more formidable band, for the rescue of Jack Sheppard on his road to Tyburn, we turn to the hero of our history once more whose last days upon earth were now rapidly drawing to an eventful close.

Immured thus in his cell, constantly watched and guarded, without the slightest probability of escape being opened to him, the reflections of Jack Sheppard were naturally diverted to that eternity, which he was so soon about to enter, and this wholesome and beneficial state of mind, the exhortations of the ordinary, who had daily visited him, tended considerably to maintain. Before the hopeful encouragement that reverend personage had afforded him, Jack had felt himself as one suspended over the abyss of eternal perdition, only by the fragile thread of life, which would soon part by its own weakness, and which division the wing of every minute was hastening. But now taught at the brink of his existence, a purer and nobler creed, he reviewed with sorrow and repentance the criminal transgressions of his past life, and nerved himself with hope to encounter the future.

It was whilst he was thus occupied in seeking consolation, that, on the evening prior to the day of his execution, a stranger was announced to him as one who by his earnest entreaties and liberal donations, had overcome the objections of the prison authorities. Fearful even now, however of Jack being left alone, lest the new comer should convey to him implements by which he might compass his escape, the gaolers were ordered to remain in the room, and the interview took place in their presence.

The door opened, and an old man, grey-headed, and with a feeble tottering gait, entered the cell. Jack languidly turned his eyes towards the visitor, and for a few moments failed to recognize him. A second glance then showed him to be his former benefactor and employer, Mr. Wood.

"My kind friend," cried Jack starting up and embracing his early protector, "this is indeed kind of you to pay me a visit in my last emergency. Had I abided by your generous advice, and followed the noble example you have so repeatedly placed before me, I should not now have been reduced to this miserable extremity."

"Alas! my poor apprentice," returned Wood, sympathising with the unfeigned grief of the repentant housebreaker, "I little thought when I snatched you up twenty years ago in the old Mint, that thy life, so full of promise, would have so sad a termination."

"I deserve it all—all," ejaculated Sheppard, mastering his emotion, "for my first step in crime was to wrong you of the savings of a most industrious and honest calling, but bitterly has the penalty been paid. My life has been all along a severe struggle with destiny, in the shape of——"

"Jonathan Wild," interrupted Wood, "I know it."

"'Twas he, sir," answered Jack," who first threw me into the paths of temptation, and afterwards betrayed me."

"Well, I came not to reproach you, Jack," pursued his aged visitor; "my mission here is one of mercy, not of malice. Your poor mother entrusted me with some papers on her death-bed, which I would have delivered to you sooner had the opportunity occurred, and which now I have come to deliver into your hands. They contain a secret of your birth, which, perchance, had you known sooner, might have deterred you from a career of infamy that has led to a result so fatal to all our hopes."

Jack Sheppard, with the sanction of the gaolers, who maintained a vigilant watch upon him and his actions during the entire interview, took the packet that Wood handed to him, and breaking the seal, commenced a hasty perusal of the documents it contained.

"Ha! what wondrous intelligence is

this!" he exclaimed, as his eye glanced upon one that appeared to rivet his attention more than the rest, "here is a will—bequeathing broad lands to the heir of the Orford estate. Is it possible that I am the son of Sir Hugh Trevanion!"

"The same," responded Wood, "and the nephew of that Lord Orford, who is supposed to have been so treacherously murdered by Jonathan Wild. The mystery of your parentage was well known to him, and there is too much reason to believe that he has converted the knowledge of it to his own guilty purposes. Your mother was in ignorance of your father's rank and station, until accident revealed both to her a few days before her decease. She had not then the means of communicating with you. Lord Orford is traced to have left Manchester, and to have come up to the house of Jonathan, where he doubtless intended to make provisions for your succession to the rank and title. From that moment, we lose all clue to his fate, and what I have hinted at, is generally allowed to approach the truth the nearest. You have had therefore the possession awarded to you of a handsome revenue, which, now in consequence of your violating the laws of your country, must, with the estate itself, be confiscated to the crown."

Jack, dazzled by the bright prospect which had so strangely been opened to his vision, only to be snatched from him at the moment it had been placed within his grasp, remained for a few minutes lost in reverie. At last he appeared determined on a new project.

"I am well aware," resumed Jack "that the fortunes of a condemned criminal go to increase the revenues of the country whose laws have been by him set at nought and broken. It is right that it should be so. It is the only recompense that he can make. But still it does not alienate from him the right of setting afoot an enquiry as to how those funds have been hitherto used and appropriated. I will myself draw up a petition to the Secretary of State, wherein I will advance reasons for bringing that monster of iniquity, Jonathan Wild, to justice; and Government shall then see how much those powers have been abused with which they have so long and so confidently entrusted him."

"I forbid all further communication with the prisoner," interrupted a voice from behind, the tones of which grated familiarly upon the ears of both Wood and our hero; "I must request you, sir, to depart without any occasion for force to be resorted to for your expulsion. Had I been present when you applied at the gate we might all have been spared some trouble; for most assuredly you would not have been admitted."

Wood had no need to alter his position to recognize the speaker. The import of the words themselves, and the tone in which they were delivered, proclaimed the new comer to be Jonathan Wild.

Knowing that resistance would be useless, he took a hasty and affectionate farewell of his former apprentice, and casting a look of horror and contempt upon the thief-taker, Mr. Wood signified to the janizaries who had accompanied Wild that he was ready to depart, and thus suffered himself to be conducted down stairs without remonstrance.

"Murderer," cried Jack furiously, as he saw his old master thus ejected, and glancing at Wild with mingled feelings of scorn and defiance implied in his animated features, "retribution shall yet be obtained. I am now made well aware of my high lineage, and the justice of those claims which you have so long with held from me, the time has come when, though I cannot enjoy, I will proclaim them to the world."

"Fool," sneered Wild, as he approached the manacles of the condemned, and hissed the words through his teeth, "I have not built a palace for myself, to be blown at the last minute to the winds by thee. *I* hold the title-deeds of the Orford estate—the rank, land, titles, all—all are mine—to you descends alone the heritage of the gallows! Ha, ha!

"Inhuman monster," retorted Sheppard with bitterness, "I will yet find a way to thwart thy plafis. The time has yet to come,"

"Well, we shall see; I can afford to wait for it," carelessly remarked Jonathan, relapsing into his former nonchalance and ease of delivery—"you will remember," he added, turning to the jailors, "I have peremptorily forbidden Captain Shepherd the use of pen and ink; and see that no writing materials are within his reach. No one must have access to his cell except those on watch-duty under any pretence whatever."

"Your orders shall be strictly obeyed, Mr. Wild," answered the elder keeper of the ward; "it was not our fault, but that of Ireland the turnkey below, that the old man came here to see the prisoner, and we thought it was perhaps with your sanction."

"You had better think a little more to the purpose next time," sternly pursued Wild, "Ireland will lose his place for this carelessness and neglect, and let his fate prove a caution to you. Remember you answer for the prisoner's safety with your own."

As Jonathan triumphantly completed these arrangements in the hearing of Jack, he gave a lingering look towards his victim, expecting, now that he was made aware of the impossibility of communicating with Government, to see his spirits broken and his heart bowed down by anguish and disappointment. Such, however, had been the effect of the examination of those papers Wood had brought that now the contrary was manifested. Jack, far from quailing beneath the dark, ferret-like eye of the thief-taker, returned his sneer with a calm and imposing dignity of demeanour that seemed as if it bade defiance to the precautions adopted by his persecutor, who, though maliciously chuckling as he went out over the success that had attended his schemes, now felt the measure of his triumph would not be filled to the brim until he had fully made Sheppard feel the poison that had barbed the arrow of his revenge.

How to debase Jack to the lowest state of degradation was now the next object of his ambition.

"Once this troublesome stripling is out of my way," mused Jonathan as he crossed the threshold, "and there is then not even a shadow between myself and the dignities to which I aspire. They may fire my house in their impotent fury, but they cannot kindle one spark of fear or compassion in my heart. I defy destiny, fate, chance, or providence—call it what you will or may—to thwart those schemes on which I have fully resolved. At this moment, curious to the believer in omens, Jonathan stumbled over a small pebble on the footway, which, rolling under his foot, prostrated him by the curb-stone which was then the place where the fetters of the criminal were struck off on their road to execution.

CHAPTER V.

ST. GILES'S BOWL.

"Ask what is human life? The Sage replies,
With disappointment in his lowering eyes,—
A painful passage o'er a restless flood,
A vain pursuit of fugitive, false good,
A scene of fancied bliss and heart-felt care,
Closing at last in darkness and despair!"

THE CRIMINAL.

QUICKLY and sadly to the eyes of him who had watched the first struggling beam of light through the nocturnal darkness of his prison, and slowly and murkily to the spectators, who had thus early gathered around its walls, dawned the morning of Monday, the 16th of November, 1724.

By the advice of Jonathan, who had been urged not to attend the ceremony for fear of personal violence, but who was not so easily dissuaded from being present at this, the crowning scene of his triumphs, a detachment of the military from the Savoy had been ordered for a sufficient escort, and as it had now become extensively bruited about, that an attempt at rescue would be made, as many precautions were previously adopted under his guidance, as though a state criminal had been the object of their care. Thus, with the earliest indication of daybreak, the tramp of horses' feet was heard around the precincts of the gaol, and presently to the surprise of the crowd, who had already assembled on Holborn-hill, a troop of about five hundred grenadier guards rode rapidly past, and took up their station within the court-yard of Newgate, a few only remaining without the walls, to keep the thoroughfare clear of impediments. An hour after their arrival, came up a regiment of foot soldiers from the Tower, and then in constant succession appeared the constables of Westminster, the Sheriffs, followed by their officers, and the civic authorities, who at that period were required to legalize the departure of every condemned criminal from Newgate.

As the solemn peal of the bell of St. Sepulchre's boomed upon the ear, the streets began to get thronged, and every window exhibited signs of the public interest and curiosity. Nor was the excitement that prevailed among the multitude at all confined to the mob. Numbers of respectably dressed persons were seen hurrying down the various passages leading to the one great thoroughfare, and most of the passengers were laden with that infinite relief to plebeian patience, the well-filled provision basket. Before eleven o'clock every place from which a view could be obtained, was occupied. The lower portions of the houses along the line of route were all closed, but the upper parts looked as gay and animated by clusters of anxious spectators as though the object of their interest had been a royal procession, rather than the progress of a criminal to execution. From the ascent of Snow-hill to the very extremity of the Oxford Road, the street was lined on each side with eager gazers, who by the presence of a strong force of the constabulary, were made to preserve a regular line. Such was the effect produced by the numerous escapes of Jack Sheppard which had so long engrossed so large a share of the public attention.

In the meanwhile the great hall of Newgate had become in its turn the focus of the chief officers, amongst whom a more subdued excitement appeared to prevail. By the side of a great stone block, with a chisel in one hand and a hammer in the other, stood Austin the under-porter, ready to strike the fetters off, as the condemned passed through the vestibule. Wild, from the tumult of the populace without, or from the impression left on his mind after the accident narrated at the close of the last chapter, having pronounced it dangerous to perform that ceremony in the usual place on the exterior of the prison.

The great door at the northern end was now slowly swung open, and preceded by the ordinary with the sacred volume in his hand, Jack Sheppard appeared. He was now deathly pale; but, beyond this, his demeanour expressed no other sign of agitation. Occasionally the slight quivering of a muscle as he saw the preparations made for his reception, or recognised some familiar face among the bystanders, betrayed him into a temporary manifestation of emotion; but the entrance of Jonathan Wild who now stalked grimly in with his old companion, the bludgeon swung under his arm, caused him to re-collect his energies, and he fixed such a glance of unsubdued pride upon the thief-taker, that even Jonathan was unable to return it.

Jack having placed his feet alternately upon the stone, and the dexterous blows of the hammer and chisel having done their work, Wild gave orders for the commencement of the journey, and led on each side by two of the turnkeys, Sheppard descended with a firm step to the outer quadrangle.

The precautions taken for Jack's security, were here shown in all their magnitude, and judging from the immense concourse of people, who burst out into a roar of applause as Jack came forth, and a deafening yell of hisses as Jonathan Wild followed, they had not been adopted without some cause for their strength. Before him, for several hundred yards, were troops of prancing horsemen, and at the extremity of the line thus formed, was the cart which was to bear him to Tyburn, with a powerful black horse harnessed to it, and a coffin, the symbol of his fate, placed as was then the repulsive custom, at the head of the vehicle. At various points of the street were regiments of soldiers stationed to keep off the mob, and horsemen were riding to and fro at the most unguarded points, to preserve the line of the procession clear and unbroken.

The Sheriff in accordance with legal custom, now asked him if he had any further confession, or any bequest to make before he proceeded.

For a brief moment Jack's eyes glistened, as a reply rose to his lips; but seeing a stern and vindictive glance directed towards him, he hesitated for an instant, and then answered — "*None*;" save that he hoped posterity would do him the justice to believe that his seeking after vicious courses had resulted not so much from inclination as from accident and from the temptations by which he had been assailed. Impelled by circumstances into a mode of life which every moment rendered more and more precarious, with the gates of society closed against him, and his name branded as one tarnished with infamy, he had no other source than that of seeking by stealth what the world denied him by industry; and if he had been on the one hand guilty of crimes which the law of the land deemed inexpiable, he hoped on the other that the circumstance of their being unaccompanied by violence would plead for him in a Higher Court than that before which he had just been brought, and that the sincern repentance of all his former follies might in some measure tend to atone for their commission.

"There is one thing more I have to say," added Jack, turning to the Sheriff—having chiefly addressed his previous harangue to the crowd immediately beneath him—"you have asked me, sir, if I have any bequest to make. I must conscientiously answer that I have. Of property to which I am by all the decrees of law and equity entitled, I haxe been, by a deep-laid scheme, foully and villanously wronged. The aggressor is now present—he stands before us in this present assembly; and I dare him to refute the charge I bring against him.

"Who is he, Jack?" "Name him!" "Name him!" cried several voices of the foremost in the crowd at once—"Who is he? that we may wreak our vengeance ugon him."

"His name," responded Sheppard in emphatic and measured accents, "is ——."

"Drive on, Martyn," exclaimed Jonathan Wild with impatience, and as the cart slowly proceeded, the name, if it was uttered, was drowned amid the execrations that were lavished upon the cause of the interruption.

The crowd, which now increased with every moment, threatened here for a short space of time to break through the barriers that restrained the people within certain boundaries. Every available nook, corner or projection had its occupants. Windows were filled, and the roofs of houses were covered with spectators, and the guards, who had now commenced their cavalcade, had the greatest difficulty possible in keeping the roadway clear.

Jack Sheppard heard, on every side, words of sympathy and encouragement addressed to him, and as he looked around there was many a friendly glance responding to his own. A succession of shouts, each more enthusiastic than the one preceding, greeted him all the way down Holborn, until he had arrived at St. Giles's; and a stranger would have thought with justice that the object of these huzzas, had been rather marching in triumph than proceeding to a loathsome and shameful death. Among the occupants of each window were some of the fairest of female forms and faces, and amongst the number were many that Jack recognized, and that struck the chords of memory with no slight distinctness. Under such circumstances the recognition was as painful to the recognizer as the recognized; and to the profusion of white handkerchiefs that were being prodigally waved at every window Jack could only respond by a broken gesture of the hand, and an inclination visible on the other side to conceal a few tears that would bedew the cheeks in spite of the most vigorous efforts at their repression.

Thus proceeding, they reached the corner of Drury Lane, where a considerable delay occurred from the turbulence manifested by the mob, who, having hastily thrown up a barrier, composed of broken wheels, tubs, and planks, had to be dislodged before a free passage could be gained. Whilst the way was thus being cleared, a desperate resistance was offered to the soldiery by a powerful reinforcement that issued forth from Lewknor's Lane and the sequestered regions thereanent; and with these a furious struggle ensued. Armed with cutlasses and knives, several cut their way through the troops that opposed their progress, and would have forced their way up to the cart had not Jonathan, with his bludgeon, which he wielded most vigorously, dispersed a few of the more troublesome ringleaders, and given orders to the cavalry to fire upon the rest. By this means quiet was again restored, and the rest of the insurgents were intimidated, but not before many had been killed and more wounded in the fray. Exasperated at being thus baffled, the multitude gave vent to their animosity not only by curses both loud and deep, but huge missiles were flung by unseen hands; and from one of these Wild received a severe wound in the face. On every side Jack was cheered and encouraged, and Jonathan hooted and execrated.

The train at length reached St. Giles's Roundhouse, where Jack glanced at the grey, crumbling fabric, which had been the scene of one of his earliest exploits, and here the cavalcade halted, that the criminal might stop at a tavern, called the "Crown," and drink from St. Giles's bowl the contents which were proffered as the last refreshment that the criminal under sentence of death, was to taste on earth. As usage decreed this was always to be presented by the clergyman of the diocese accompanied by a salutary admonition and benediction, but directly Jack received it from the hands of one, who appeared thus to officiate—being dressed according to another old custom, in a long white robe, and with the surplice drawn over his face, so as to conceal any manifestations of the reverend gentleman's feelings —Jack recognized immediately in the conventional words of the usual address, the voice of his old companion in their career of irregular appropriation—*Blueskin.*

Astonishment for a moment almost stifled the power of utterance, but as soon as the bowl was proffered, and before our hero could find words to express his amazement, Blueskin anticipated his exclamation.

"Hush, Jack, for your life, man, betray no surprise, or I am like to accompany thee on thy last excursion—sorry am I to say it. But I could not refrain from attempting once again to grasp the hand of my old friend and protegy. The scurvy rogues denied me access to you in prison disguise myself, how I would, so I was constrained you see, to get the real parson out of the way by stratagem, and appear myself in his stead."

"Still the same clever trickster as ever!" remarked Jack.

"Ay, and still thy warm-hearted friend, too, Jack," answered the faithful creole, "but, come — drink, man, drink, or the gaol-birds else will trap us."

Sheppard looked around. Wherever he gazed human heads streamed upon his view. Even the character of the sacred edifice before which they had stopped, could not save it from being the chosen "coigne of 'vantage" for hundreds of spectators, who, perched on every possible projection, from tombstone to pinnacle, made the old church of St. Giles's more akin to the appearance of the grand stand at Epsom on the Derby day.

The scene that accompanied Jack's colloquy with his disguised lieutenant, was eminently characteristic of the occasion, and the brutal character of the times in which it took place. Taking advantage of the proximity of the hostel, and allowed to indulge in such ill-timed pleasantries, by the usage of the day, the soldiers and others, who had accompanied the procession, gave way to a reckless indulgence in the spirits that were ordered in copious quantities, from the burly host of the "Crown," and a few, more dissipated than the rest, gave mouth to sundry coarse and obscene bacchanalian songs that were trolled forth with an energy more adapted for an evening's convivial meeting, than a procession so solemn and mournful in its nature.

At the door of the tavern there was one group that particularly arrested his attention. The chief personages who composed

it were Kneebone, Giles Shalders, Sampson Kirby, and a few of the old minters, who attired in long shabby cloaks, seemed from their bulk, to have some cogent reasons of concealment in adopting so convenient an article of apparel.

"Drink, Jack," repeated Blueskin quickly, as he detected symptoms of impatience on the part of Jonathan Wild and the Sheriffs, who were seated next him.

"I am here, you see, Jack," cried Shalders with a significant smile.

"So I perceive!" answered Sheppard, "and I heartily wish I was not," a sally that drew approving bursts of laughter from the crowd. Such was the effect, even then felt of demoralizing of public executions, and such was the brutality of the age.

"Come, Jack, drain a bumper to our next merry meeting," whispered Blueskin adding quickly and quietly—"make to the left as you leap off from Tyburn—there will be enough true and trusty lads there to carry you off safe yet."

Jack Sheppard, though not quite unprepared for the disclosure from what he had witnessed on his way, yet could hardly refrain from starting at the words so meaningly uttered by Blueskin, and animated by the hopes to which they gave rise. He turned round to conceal his agitation, and encountered the basilisk gaze of Jonathan Wild, as he was raising the bowl to his lips.

"Come, drink," brutally urged the thief-taker, as he saw that he hesitated in his draught, "the hangman will make you thirsty enough presently, I warrant."

"Not I!" cried Jack Sheppard, resuming his former dignity of demeanour, you may stand in need of this yourself ere long, and I therefore leave its contents to be quaffed by you." And he set it down untasted.

"So have said others I have brought to the gallows, but you see it has tarried patiently for you," returned Wild.

"You will call here for the bowl before another winter has come, Jonathan Wild," prophetically answered his victim; "your own parched lips may then be quenched by the draught."

And Jack Sheppard was in the right, though a contemptuous sneer was then the despised reception of his augury.

The procession now moved on at a more rapid pace into the Tyburn Road, or as the thoroughfare is now more agreably nomenclatured, Oxford Street. Directly it was out of sight, Blueskin flung off his robes, and seeing that the soldiers and constables had gone forward with the rest to the place of execution, and were hastening thither to guard against a rescue, he felt confident of his own security, and revealed himself without hesitation. Mounting the horse-trough that stood before the door of the hostel, he gathered a body of his own band immediately round him, and displaying a purse containing twenty guineas said that Captain Sheppard had left them that as a legacy, and that they might now have whatever refreshment they desired.

The tributary shouts at the announcement of this fictitious bequest, showed that Blueskin fully understood the effect it would have in opening the hearts of the multitude, and preparing them for the proposal which he was about to make to them. After a plentiful supply of liquor had been rapidly handed round and imbibed, the orator addressed them in a long speech, of which the import was to the following effect. "In the very heart of this great city, this day under the cheering daylight, a man is to be strangled to death;—a man whose strength has just come to its fullest power—whose blood leaps with the strong pulse of high health and mature manhood through his veins. This morning he rose, perhaps one of the strongest among one hundred thousand—ere that sun has set again, he is to be in his coffin: They have led him out from his dark cell into the pleasant sunshine, he will look for a moment, and for the last time—on the little spot of earth and grass at his feet, and upward at the blue sky above him, and then they will hang him up between heaven and earth—a dead man. And the hum of the busy city and the tread of the thousands of the hurrying feet of this Christian people will be the requiem for the departing soul. Is this humane? Is this justice? Are we to stand tamely by and see this murder done?"

"No—no!" indignantly responded a myriad voices.

"*Then to Tyburn and save him,*" cried Blueskin suddenly, and with this burst of energetic eloquence he himself hurried on among the foremost of those whose passions he had inflamed.

Away they sped—a human stream of stalwart, sinewy men—armed with cudgels, staves, bars of iron, and other weapons that they gathered on their route, pressing furiously onward to the scene of action.

Away over hedge and ditch—trampling down the green, glistening grass with the pressure of a myriad feet—away with the murmurous roar of many voices, sounding like the thunderous chafing of the billows on a stormy night at sea—away onward, o'erleaping and overcoming every obstacle on their path, went the reckless mob, under the guidance of Blueskin and Shalders, rendered careless and desperate by the drams they had taken, and prepared to engage in any contest, however deadly, by which their purpose could be gained. Beyond the Duke of Monmouth's mansion in Soho Square, all was then open country, and the fields that extended on each side of the Tyburn Road, thus afforded the opportunity for the rioters to get to the gate before the procession, which now was slowly dragging its length along by the Old Edgeware Road.

The quick eye of Jonathan immediately enabled him to perceive the mob, and to divine their object. Conferring hastily with the Sheriff, Wild offered if a sufficient body of the soldiery were allowed him for escort, to ride forward, and keep the ground clear for their arrival. The policy of this expedient was immediately seen and acted upon, and accompanied by a hundred grenadier guards, the thief-taker rode forward, and took up a position on the ground.

The train in the meantime had passed onward, until arriving opposite a neat cottage on the right of the road, the cart remained stationary for a few minutes at Jack's request, and from the door there then emerged, leaning on his stick from the infirmity of age, the old carpenter of Wych Street—Mr. Wood.

Making his way through the crowd, Wood pressed forward, and coming up to the cart, stopped and extended his trembling hand to the prisoner.

"For the last time Jack, farewell," cried the old man in weak and tremulous accents, whilst tears streamed impetuously down his cheeks—"Farewell!"

For a moment Jack was unmanned by the interview, and he was hardly able to return the salutation. At last nerving himself for the task, he reciprocated the affectionate pressure of his old employer's hand, and exclaiming with a valedictory ejaculation—"Adieu, my kind master, in a short time all will be over." The Sheriff gave orders for the vehicle to proceed, and each turning aside to conceal the violence of their emotions became thus separated for ever. The procession was thus again in motion, and Jack now began to pay serious and earnest attention to the pious exhortations of the Ordinary.

CHAPTER VI.

THE RESCUE.

"Ay! but to die and go we know not where,
To lie in cold obstruction, and to rot;
This sensible warm motion to become
A kneaded clod; and the delighted spirit
To bathe in fiery floods, or to reside
In thrilling regions of thick ribbed ice—
* * * * * * * 'Tis too horrible
The weariest and most loathed wordly life
That age, ache, penury and imprisonment,
Can lay on nature, is a paradise
To what we fear of death."

MEASURE FOR MEASURE.

THE last sands which numbered the minutes of Jack's sojourn upon earth were now falling rapidly into eternity.

The eventful goal of Tyburn was now close at hand, and over the heads of the concourse that had gathered round the fatal tree, Jack saw a black and dismal object rise. It was the gallows. He pressed his hands over his eyes, but his agony and repentant grief were too acute for the flow of tears; his eyeballs seemed hot and bursting, and there was not moisture to relieve the aching pain. When he therefore screened the hideous object from his vision it was less to shut that from his gaze, by which he knew he must so soon suffer, than it was to subdue the smarting which the intense working of his brain occasioned.

As the cart approached Jonathan Wild rode back to state that all the preparations were now made, and in a side speech he cried to Spurling the hangman—"get your job over quickly and a twenty-pound note extra shall be yours."

"You may leave all that business to me," answered the executioner, "I'll do it to your satisfaction, Mr. Wild, you may depend upon it."

"Is all ready?" inquired the Sheriff, in a deep voice.

"All," was the response which seemed like an echo of the former.

The soldiers, infantry and cavalry formed a circle round the fatal beam, and a fearful ominous calm-like that which heralds the approach of a thunderstorm pervaded the entire assemblage.

It was a critical and awful moment.

Not a breath was drawn.

At this crisis, Jack by a powerful effort regained and preserved his composure. As the black cap was being drawn over his face a faint smile was visible on his features.

"My poor mother!" he exclaim ed, "I shall soon be with thee!"

The rope was then adjusted round his neck.

"*Now*," cried the Sheriff, giving the preconcerted signal.

The next minute the bolt was withdrawn, and Jack Sheppard was hanging lifeless in the air.

Scarcely had the executioner turned his head to see that his task was completed, than with a loud shout a man of swarthy complexion was seen to leap into the cart with an open clasp-knife in his hand, and before the people round the gibbet could resist him, he had cut down the body and handed it to those who pressed on from behind. His interposition however, came too late. A blow from Wild's bludgeon felled him to the earth, and a volley from the muskets of the guards completely ended the eventful career of Blueskin.

The fearful example thus set of their leader, had no effect in intimidating the intrepid fellows he had brought with him; the body of Jack was passed from hand to hand over the heads of the multitude, and despite the constant firing of the soldiers in that direction where the fleeting figure of Jack was visible, it was at last lodged far away from Tyburn tree into the hands of Giles Shalders, who received it in a van at the end of Bayswater, where he had stationed himself for the purpose. A surgeon who was there ready, made a hasty examination of the body as the vehicle was driven off, but it was found that the shots of the soldiers had thwarted their well-concerted plans of resuscitation, for no less than three musket balls had pierced his heart.

Thus miserably perished Jack Sheppard.

Whilst Shalders with his burden was hastily proceeding towards Willesden, the mob had turned their fury and rage upon Jonathan Wild, who had the greatest difficulty in defending himself from the violence of their attack.

The exertions of the military saved Wild or that time from being killed, but he was only saved to perish a few months afterwards at the very same spot, and in a more ignoble manner, where Jack Sheppard had been himself executed by his base devices.

Through the bye-lanes and the most unfrequented thoroughfares, Shalders drove on with his load. The early gloom of a November evening had already closed in, and the descent of a drizzling rain made the roads heavy and marshy. But no obstacles that he had to encounter caused the driver to slacken pace. Willesden was reached.

A few stragglers had already stationed themselves in the cold, wet churchyard, and foremost in the group was one whose aged form and grey hair proclaimed to be the early benefactor of the criminal. Close to the grave of Mrs. Sheppard the mortal remains of our unfortunate hero were consigned. The clergyman who had been called from the parsonage, hastily read the burial service over the body, which passed for that of a deceased relative of Mr. Wood, and thus in congenial darkness was he buried. The thick misty rain, the impressive solitude that reigned around, unbroken by the lowing of cattle or the insects hum, the desolation of the wintry prospect, all forming a fit association of the obsequies bestowed on one who had come to such an untimely end.

A few years afterwards Wood himself was gathered to his forefathers, and borne to the same place for interment. And then some who remembered in the village the history of each, supplied an inscription for their graves. Over the worthy carpenter's was a full and deserved eulogy upon his worth—on the other, in a rude and simple framework of wood, merely were carved the following words;—

Here lies Jack Sheppard.

And now—a homily to our history—let us before parting with the reader, endeavour to force upon his attention the instructive lesson taught by the vicissitudes of our hero's career. Let it be from this remembered, that the wide world contains nothing of what is valuable, great or endearing, which is not comprised in virtue. That the whole universe with its lofty orders of intelligences, its monuments and trophies of intellectual power, its sciences, its riches, and its splendours, forms but the case of which this is the treasure, the storehouse of which this is the key, the machine of which this is the moving spring, the clay and changing body of which this is the undying and indestructable soul. It is virtue that affords comfort in sorrow, and light in darkness. It is virtue that can alone clothe youth in all the freshness and beauty of Spring and enrich old age with the luxuriant fruits of Autumn. It is this that alone confers true immortality, that raises a monument which the lapse of ages shall not impair,—that rears a temple of worship, of beauty, and of glory as prominent, and as enduring as the sun. It is this that casts a charm over the otherwise most unimportant and trivial of human accidents and actions, that has often irradiated the cell, and darkened the throne, transformed a palace into a hovel, and a hovel into a palace. In the present fallen world it is like the fair and fragrant rose amid noxious and odious weeds and thorns; or like the lowly and lovely violet which is ever discoverable by its reviving fragrance, rather than by its gaudy display, and in the Hereafter it shall shine as the sun for ever.

We may appropriately conclude—in reference to the moral taught by the career of our criminal—with the emphatic words of Dr. Johnson.

"Happy are they, my son, who shall learn from thy example not to despair, but shall remember that though the day is past and their strength is wasted, there yet remains one effort to be made; that reformation is never hopeless, nor sincere endeavours ever unassisted; that the wanderer may at length return after all his errors: and that he who implores strength and courage from above shall find danger and difficulty give way before him."

FINIS.

www.ingramcontent.com/pod-product-compliance
Lightning Source LLC
LaVergne TN
LVHW061250100826
845148LV00008B/1076

* 9 7 8 1 5 3 5 8 0 6 0 6 0 *